BETWEEN

THE

TWO RIVERS

JOHN MELTON

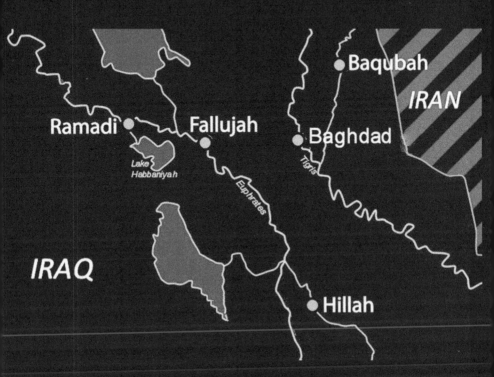

BETWEEN
THE
TWO RIVERS

A WAR NOVEL

BETWEEN
THE
TWO RIVERS
A WAR NOVEL

JOHN MELTON

ZIMBELL HOUSE
PUBLISHING
UNION LAKE, MICHIGAN

For permission requests, write to the publisher
"Attention: Permissions Coordinator"
Zimbell House Publishing
PO Box 1172
Union Lake, Michigan 48387
mail to: info@zimbellhousepublishing.com

© 2020 John Melton

Published in the United States by Zimbell House Publishing
http://www.ZimbellHousePublishing.com
All Rights Reserved

Hardcover ISBN: 978-1-64390-154-1
Trade Paper ISBN: 978-1-64390-155-8
.mobi ISBN: 978-1-64390-157-2
ePub ISBN: 978-1-64390-158-9
Large Print ISBN:978-1-64390-156-5
Library of Congress Control Number: 2020905136

First Edition: June/2020
10 9 8 7 6 5 4 3 2 1

ZIMBELL HOUSE PUBLISHING
UNION LAKE

To my family, and all our veterans. We owe them so much.

PROLOGUE

Darfur, Sudan 1993

Jamal shot up off the pallet that was his bed. Confusion lingered as he reached for the sheet he'd tossed onto the dirt floor. He rubbed the graininess out of his eyes. It was dark, just before the first light of dawn, he guessed. Relief settled in as the dream state faded, but the image of the unknown elder's face remained.

So did the command he'd barked. "Wake up now, boy!"

Other than his mother's heavy breathing a few feet away, all he heard was the rumble of thunder out on the plain. Jamal smiled. Rain meant extra sleep instead of an early morning tending the chickens. He balled up the sweaty sheet, tossed it toward the foot of his bedding, and reached for a clean one he kept folded neatly nearby. One always resided there because of his embarrassing problem of wetting the bed. It had been months now since the last time, but he was prepared nonetheless. He unfurled and straightened it to get a sense of the order he now adhered to after the chaos that marked the first decade of his life. Still sleepy, he lay down again under the dry sheet.

Storms were frequent during the two rainy seasons in southern Sudan since he'd moved from Iraq at the age of ten. Never had the thunder been so consistent, though. He reasoned it must be a deluge on the way and closed his heavy eyelids again. A second later, they were wide open as adrenaline coursed through him like an electric shock, stiffening the hairs on his neck.

They're coming!

The same ingrained fear that had swept through numerous Christian villages like his made him leap to his feet. He bolted for the only door in his mud-brick hut. Once outside, he realized it was later than he'd thought. The sky was already pale enough for him to discern the cloud of dust coming from the north. It wasn't thunder he'd heard.

Horses.

Janjaweed raiders—Muslim militia backed by the Sudanese government—were about to overrun his village. He ran back inside and jarred his mother from her dreams. She was moving an instant later without a word, grabbing a prepared bag near the door as they burst through it. Jamal was right on her heels but returned to take the machete he'd sharpened the previous day. The thought of using it for anything other than cutting brush around her garden frightened him.

"Hurry, Jamal!" she said in Arabic. "We must reach the forest."

The screams at the far end of the village filled his ears. Raiders threw their torches onto a dense grouping of huts, the early morning shadows on their walls replaced by a flickering orange glow. Automatic gunfire erupted, and Jamal turned to see a mounted horseman fire an assault rifle into a group of men. Their bodies flailed as they fell. Jamal felt an overwhelming sense of terror.

Villagers ran in all directions. Four howling raiders in turbans dragged a female friend of Jamal's into a hut, each man clutching an appendage. The young girl's screams elicited another jolt of fear, and he almost lost sight of his mother while the smoke swirled around him, flooding his nostrils. Emerging from the haze, he saw an elderly man stagger, maimed by a raider's machete—a notorious tactic, reserved only for the weak. Jamal knew if he and his mother didn't escape, a different fate awaited them. She would be taken away as a slave, and he would be made to fight for the horsemen.

Fear caused him to run so close behind her that she tripped, and they both tumbled to the ground. Before he knew it, they were up again. She led them into the warren of makeshift pens that housed pigs and chickens at one end of the village. The two of them ducked down behind a corrugated metal wall and gasped to catch their breath as chickens cackled on the other side in a panic of their own.

His mother turned to him. "If they circle the village before we get out, we will be separated from one another forever."

The report of machine guns echoed off the walls around him, making it sound like it had come from all directions. Pungent smoke made him cough, and he couldn't focus on his mother's face to heed her words, so she pulled him close. He trembled in her bosom, and she whispered in the calm voice he knew.

"Jamal. Look at me," she said, pushing his head away from her. "This is not the end. God has a plan for you. I promise. But you must pass His test first, so He knows you are worthy."

"Is the test hard?"

"It is so hard, my little man."

"What will I have to do?"

The calmness in her voice belied a sadness he saw deep in her eyes as she gave her answer.

"Survive, Jamal. Survive no matter what they make you do, and know that the Lord Jesus is with you all the way. You can pretend to follow Allah until you are free. But keep the deepest part of your heart pure and survive, son. God will use you for His purposes when the time is right."

"Yes, mother."

He didn't know what scared him more, the gravity of her words or the gunfire and smoke around him. But he also felt a wave of growing anger toward the raiders who would impose fundamental Islam upon Christians like himself, or gun them down if they refused. It didn't seem like they were even giving villagers a choice at the moment. He gripped the handle of the machete and wondered if God's plan for him would include standing up to them. He didn't take the thought any further because his mother grabbed him by the arm, and they were up again.

"Run, Jamal! We have just one chance."

They ran past a pen of squealing piglets, and within seconds, were in the tall grass outside the village. The edge of the forest was less than fifty yards away. If they made it there, they could wait out the attack under the cover of the trees.

Anxiety propelled him past his mother toward the safety of the dense foliage until the thudding sound of his footsteps appeared to have multiplied. He turned around and saw a mounted raider gaining on them, the flames in the village behind him setting the horseman's rippling robes and turban in silhouette. Once closer, the horseman yanked on the reins, which caused the animal to buck in protest. He quickly fired a burst into the air from his assault rifle, which stopped Jamal's mother in her tracks.

"Keep going, Jamal!" she cried before she turned to face the armed raider.

But Jamal's legs would only carry him toward her, while she pleaded with the Arab to spare her from capture. The raider's horse snorted and continued to kick up its front legs. Jamal sensed an opportunity when the horse raised again, this time spinning in its buck until the raider's back was exposed momentarily. Jamal covered the space between them in several loping strides before swinging the blade as hard as he could across the raider's torso. The wounded man howled and hunched over in the saddle but managed to kick the horse's flanks and it surged away. Jamal felt the fear again when the raider recovered to an upright posture, wheeled, and charged toward them. This time the weapon was aimed at Jamal.

"Allahu Akbar!"

With one hand on the reins, the screaming raider fired off a scattered burst that ripped into the ground around Jamal, who assumed a defensive position in front of his mother, machete in hand. Unexpectedly, the raider's weapon jammed in mid-burst, and Jamal's mother ran ahead. She waved her arms and shouted at the charging horse until it skidded to a stop. The wild-eyed beast reared up with an angry neigh, towering above her. The horse threw all of its weight down upon her and continued to trample her broken body.

"No!" screamed Jamal as he attacked again, swinging the machete wildly at both the raider and his mount.

The baying of the stricken horse and Jamal's howls of rage drowned out the sounds of chaos in the village, and he lost himself in the moment. After one two-handed swing, Jamal heard bone break and felt the blade stick in the shoulder of the groaning raider, whose body went limp and fell off the horse. The wounded animal trotted away with an uneven stride.

Jamal dropped to his mother's side and saw she was still alive by the blood she coughed up. He cupped her head in his hand and wiped the flow from her mouth.

"Jamal … You must go. Before more come. Go now, please."

"No. No, I won't. A doctor will come—"

"Too far gone," she said under labored and gurgling breath. "God is …"

She was still. Jamal sobbed while he held her until the sounds of fighting in the village quieted. Two more horsemen appeared with ropes to bind Jamal. In a state of shock, he was non-reactive to their rough treatment as he was dragged back to the village. The raiders tied the surviving adolescent boys together in a single file and marched them out of the village. Jamal came out of his daze long enough to take one last look at his burnt, shot up home. The sight of the dead bodies strewn about seared into his memory. He listened to all the younger boys' crying but remained stone-faced as he remembered what his mother had told him. He prayed for her soul and his survival.

So begins the test.

PART ONE

CHAPTER 1

For all those reasons, an American agent will never get close to stopping an attack like 9/11.

Major Winters mulled over the statement as he strolled past the Iwo Jima Memorial. A muggy haze hovered around the massive testament to sacrifice, the early morning humidity typical of September in Washington, D.C. He followed a gravel path to the burial sites at Arlington National Cemetery, alone but for a runner in Army gray shorts and tee shirt, who passed him going the opposite direction. When the rhythmic padding of loping strides faded, all the major heard was the broken record in his head and the morning calls of the birds that gave life to this somber place.

Never get close.

The words haunted him.

While mesmerized by the non-stop news coverage in the days following 9/11, he'd wondered how the nation's spy agencies could have been that far out of the game. Wanting answers, he'd reached out to colleagues in the Central Intelligence Agency and the Pentagon.

Once it became clear the perpetrators were members of *al Qaeda*, he'd asked the question, "Why didn't we have someone inside who could have warned us?" The answer was the same everywhere or a variant of it.

"If we do get an agent inside and they learn of a real operation— even a small one—they can't be complicit in its success to solidify their cover. They've got to provide enough intel to thwart attacks that could

take any American life. But then they're pulled. Their cover is shot. You don't get more than one bite at that apple before the al Qaeda types are on to you. Problem is, the current group think calls stopping any old attack a success. For all those reasons ..."

A week later, during a cryptic conversation with his mentor—a man with stars on his shoulder, and a leader of America's special operations warriors—the major was asked to represent the two of them this morning. The nature of the meeting was not revealed, but the major assumed it was initiated in response to the attacks that had just taken place.

It damned well better be.

He still wrenched over the cowardly assault on home soil. The idea that a bunch of hijackers with nothing more than box-cutters could pull off such a coordinated attack made the hairs on the back of his neck stand up.

What's next? Crippling the power grid, or worse, attacking a nuclear plant. Any one of a dozen types of a biological attack? Maybe the dirty bomb everyone has dreaded. Or even the big one. Doesn't matter. We're not ready for any of them.

He knew drastic measures would need to be taken out of desperation, desperation he felt grow each time he thought about it. Yet the counter to that mindset was a willingness on his part to make his contribution, even if it meant personal sacrifice.

At least when he left this place, he'd have some answers, and hopefully, reasons to feel more optimistic. Approaching the meeting area, he pushed the heavy thoughts away and walked down a slope toward the burial fields. Soon he was among thousands of graves of those who'd perished in service for their country. It was always a humbling experience to come here, and he wondered if this setting had been chosen deliberately for the clandestine meeting.

A reminder that sacrifice is needed for security to exist.

He took another path toward a smaller field of burial plots for recent conflicts. A gray-haired man in a dark suit knelt there alone by the grave of a Jewish American, as indicated by the star carved into the white marble headstone.

As the major approached, the man stood and turned away from the grave. In the few seconds before they spoke, the major glanced at the inscription—a Marine who had died on October 23, 1983. The date marked the infamous attack on American-occupied barracks in Beirut, Lebanon, where a truck bomb detonated by jihadists killed over two hundred service members.

"Major Winters, I presume," said the man.

The two shook hands, but the man did not offer his name. The major decided it was for the best. This might be the only time they met in person. And for meetings like this, not knowing names was always safer for him.

The major's gaze returned to the headstone. "I lost a few friends that day too."

"I lost my son."

So much for plausible deniability.

The man's jaw line tightened, and the major was moved to offer belated condolences, which the man accepted before broaching the topic of the meeting.

"Our mutual friend has told me you are well suited for running special projects."

"If by that you mean off the books, then I have some experience to offer," said the major. "I must tell you that he would only give me the vaguest of previews on what to expect."

"I'll be clear," said the man. "The attacks on our homeland last week have changed certain minds on how we should protect this country in the future."

So many things changed for so many people. Hell. The world changed that day.

The man continued, glancing toward the grave of his son. "Our enemies have been at war with us for years now, but most Americans don't even believe there is a war going on at all. In light of that disparity, we must at least know how they are planning to destroy us because it *is* their goal."

Despite the secluded setting, the man's voice lowered an octave when he said, "Bottom line is we need better intelligence and fewer restrictions on how to gain it. I represent a collection of influential individuals willing to look beyond the taboos that constrain our nation's intelligence services. The gloves came off with this brazen assault by *al Qaeda*, Major. We must stop at nothing to place sufficient intelligence assets within the ranks of radical Islamists, to stop the next 9/11—or worse—from happening."

"Meaning?"

"We'd like you to create a handful of special agents who could transcend those constraints in the field … Americans trained to reach the highest levels of terrorist leadership."

"Sleepers," said the major, raising an eyebrow. "You're talking about long term missions."

"Yes, and they would need to advance on the merits of their distasteful actions, I'm afraid. At least in the eyes of those they are meant to infiltrate."

"That would certainly qualify as a new approach."

Optimism welled inside the major, even though his instincts reigned in any outward show of it. At its face value, this was a chance to right the current wrong in the intelligence community to which he'd become keen. For that reason alone, he would hear this man out. He wondered how much the general knew, and looked with great anticipation toward their next conversation. But they'd been in this business long enough to know there were practical concerns to address before proceeding. The major looked off to draw the desired response. He was glad when the man took the bait. He had things to do.

"You would need protection."

"That's right," said the major. "I need to know there is real authority behind this program. And I can't speak for the general, but I'm gone if there's even a chance of me being hung out to dry on something this far into the black."

"Okay," said the man. "Let me see what I can do to alleviate your concerns. Give me a week. I can assure you will be satisfied."

"If you can make that happen, I think we'd be in business. I'm curious, where would the training occur? This isn't the type of thing that could be done in the open."

"The general says he can guarantee secrecy at Fort Bragg for the advanced soldier training, including special living quarters on the base. For the more questionable portions we have in mind, I have made arrangements with some Native Americans for the use of their land, which, as you know, has little or no government oversight."

"Out of sight, out of mind. Nice," said the major. "Can they be trusted?"

"For what we'll be paying them, they better hope so."

"On that note."

The major had barely said the words when the man handed him a folded piece of paper. The major opened it and saw the name of an offshore bank and an account number written below it.

"We need to discuss the timeline now," said the man. "I'm sure you are aware the call to action is ramping up quickly here in Washington. We will never be officially linked to strategic moves the Bush Administration will make, but we must use them to our advantage. That means being prepared when the levers start moving toward war. How much time would you need?"

"For everything?" There was a planned tad of doubt in the major's voice, a hedge on his part. He figured the man would not like any answer candor would provide.

"Yes. What will it take to make them into the kind of men capable of doing what we have conceived?"

"At least a year once they are fully in the fold. If we can get a decent group to begin with. And that's a conservative estimate. We'd have them flying all over the place. Minimal cadre for secrecy. Maintaining several training sites. It would be difficult."

"Yes. I know," said the man.

The major could sense some internal hand wringing over the news.

"Okay, then. A year it is, if not more. This program has long-term goals. Let's hope they can make a difference in time."

Jamal Muhammad closed his left eye and pulled the butt stock of the rifle snug against his right shoulder. The iron sight on the barrel found the target at center mass.

Breath in. Exhale. In. Out. Hold.

CRACK.

"Hit!" shouted the spotter.

CRACK. CRACK.

"Hit. Bull's-eye."

Jamal fired two more rounds. Each of them punched holes in the center of the upright target eight hundred meters away.

"You're done, Muhammad," said a drill sergeant over Jamal's shoulder. "Clear your weapon and move off the firing line."

"Roger, Sergeant," said Jamal in heavily accented English. He put the weapon on safe, removed the magazine, and cleared the remaining live round from the chamber. The smell of spent gunpowder left him once off the line, replaced by the odor of his sweat-soaked uniform. He walked over by the range tower and waited for instructions. He was the first basic trainee to qualify on the M16.

Another drill sergeant exited the base of the tower.

"What the hell you doin' back here, Muhammad?" he said with narrow eyes under the traditional wide-brimmed Campaign cap.

Jamal had received suspicious looks from the drill sergeants as well as his fellow enlistees since the moment he arrived at Fort Benning—Home of the Infantry. The isolation had led to loneliness, of course, intensified by the hostility he felt from some of the more prejudiced basic trainees. It was nothing new to Jamal. He'd grown up constantly aware—and continuously reminded— that he was some kind of "other." To the Arabs in Iraq because he was black. To the Muslims in Sudan when he converted to Christianity. To the Western aid workers in Kenya when he was a refugee. How much more "other" can one be when upon your welcome to America, you are labeled a "lost boy" from Sudan?

After emerging from the culture shock of his arrival in America less than a month ago—right before 9/11, to him a shocking event itself—he'd been less inclined to react impulsively to off-hand remarks or unequal treatment. He didn't like their instinctual need to racially profile him during this time but assumed he would do the same thing if he were in their position. After all, he was the mysterious African who had come from a terrorist breeding ground. And today he'd just checked off another box for the U.S. Army by qualifying on his weapon; that much closer to getting out there in the world where the enemy existed.

My enemy, Jamal thought.

He'd come to realize that being something other than a typical American might help him advance while knowing it would require a submissive attitude until he won them over. So instead of taking offense at the drill sergeant's skepticism that would otherwise bristle his combative personality, he offered his magazine and smiled.

"Finished, Sergeant. First to qualify."

The drill sergeant snatched it out of Jamal's outreached hand and indiscreetly glanced at the open receiver of the M16 to see if a round still hid in the chamber. Two more privates—both white kids—walked up with rifles and proud faces. The drill sergeant didn't seem so interested in securing their ammunition.

"Well, y'all are just hot shit, aren't ya?" he said to the three of them. "Guess what? Y'all should've taken your time 'cause the first truck headin' back is dropping maggots off at the chow hall for K.P. Duty."

All the enlistees were called maggots, or pukes, or knuckleheads, or just Joe.

Jamal and the others groaned. The drill sergeant kept his eye on Jamal, no doubt waiting for a stronger objection, which had been a common occurrence until Jamal's change of heart. So had the up and down motion of him doing push-ups. But no reaction was there to instigate punishment, the three of them were told to head for the truck.

He thought about his mother on the way, as he had every day since the day she was killed, the day the inextinguishable rage inside him was born. Since learning how to pray, he'd asked for ways to fulfill her promise that God would use him someday for a higher purpose. This path to becoming an American soldier had seemingly been laid out before him. He'd taken it as an open door to join America's newly proclaimed War on Terror, to fight a familiar foe.

They are the Lord's enemy too.

Suddenly, the prospect of cleaning pots and pans for a while didn't bother him, assuming that's what he'd get assigned to, after overhearing another black soldier grumble about getting stuck with the greasiest, sweatiest job in the chow hall. The rote task would afford some time alone in prayer, rejuvenation. Another black private joined Jamal and the two white privates in the back of the five-ton truck. The driver pulled onto the road that led to the barracks and shifted gears several times as the heavy vehicle accelerated. The wind that generated inside the canvas-covered bed provided relief on the otherwise stuffy day, and Jamal thought his sweaty fatigues might even dry out by the time they got to the chow hall. He sat alone on the wooden bench along one side. Across from him were the two white privates.

Further down their bench, the black one pulled out a pack of cigarettes and lit one up. The two white privates whispered back and forth, with frequent glances toward Jamal. One of them, a pimply-faced kid, prodded his reluctant buddy to initiate a conversation. The black private just shook his head.

"Why don't you just come out and ask him. 'Stead of acting all junior-high and shit."

The comment must have broken the ice for the nervous private. "So, Muhammad, is it true you killed a bunch of people in Africa?"

Jamal stared at him for a good five seconds without a word or change in expression. He shifted his gaze to Pimples, the instigator, who turned beet red and looked out the open back of the truck.

The black private snickered and bobbed his head a few times. "That's a cold hard look you got there, brother. I'd say that's the answer to your question, homeys."

In his heavy accent and steady cadence, Jamal said, "I did what was needed to survive."

The private who'd asked the question nodded, and said, "Okay. Why'd you join?"

"Same as you," said Jamal with a shrug of the shoulders. "Kill terrorists, right?"

- 9 -

The private gave an awkward look, maybe sensing Jamal was messing with him, which he was, sort of.

"Amen, brother," said the black private with the cigarette dangling from his lips. He reached across and offered knuckles to Jamal. Jamal returned the gesture, a new one of late for him.

"You think we'll get to see any action?" asked Pimples to the group in general. Jamal sensed his bravado was false by his wide-eyed look. "I mean the war just started. They say the Taliban might be toast in a few months."

"It's true that this war in Afghanistan just started," said Jamal. "But *al Qaeda* has been at war with America for a much longer time. Nothing was done to stop them, and now it's got to be done the hard way. And it will take some time." He looked at Pimples and said, "You're going to get your action, I guarantee it. And so will a lot more Americans. It's time to push back, hard—or get run over."

"Amen, brother," said the black private, much more subdued now. He didn't offer knuckles this time.

The back of the truck became quiet, other than the rumble of the engine and creaking of the chassis. Jamal leaned his head back against the canvas, pulled his helmet down over his eyes like a visor, and slumped his shoulders. It was at least a twenty-minute ride back to the barracks.

"*That* is why I joined."

CHAPTER 2

The major stood alone, umbrella held overhead, off to the side of the bleachers. They were filled with proud family members who huddled under a multitude of colored ponchos and rain jackets while waiting for their loved ones to arrive. To the major's left, a company of basic trainee graduates marched toward them in a box formation. A cold January drizzle fell upon Fort Benning's parade ground. It was an appropriate setting for a fresh batch of infantrymen to be introduced, thought the major.

You grunts might as well get accustomed to misery.

He shook an ever-present box of Altoids in his hip pocket, at first resisting the temptation because he could still taste the last one a little. Nonetheless, he opened the lid and popped one in his mouth without another thought. He scanned the leading platoon of graduates for the individual he would introduce himself to later in the day. Jamal Muhammad was in the group moving past him, broad-shouldered and a head above most of his peers.

Wow! Kid looks like he could play tight end in the NFL.

An imposing presence was a quality for which the major looked. He was glad to check something off his wish list already. The major studied Jamal closer. His face was elongated, with taut ebony skin stretched from high cheekbones down to a prominent chin. As he marched, he appeared to beam with pride, an expression that highlighted the contrast between his stark white teeth and jet-black complexion.

The graduates halted in front of the bleachers and executed a quarter-turn in unison, facing a raised platform where the assembled dignitaries sat, including his mentor, the only general among them. A podium stood in the center for the general, who'd been coaxed into a speech once certain people learned he was on hand for the day. The request hadn't come from the major, but he was the reason the general had swooped into Fort Benning on "personal business." The situation would no doubt cost the major a bottle of good Scotch, which they'd probably drink together anyway.

A few awards were handed out. The training unit's commander spoke. He introduced the general, who, in his address to the young graduates, challenged them to consider special operations. The major appreciated that and hoped Jamal was listening. After the general's speech, a small military band played nearby inside a covered pavilion, signifying the event was coming to an end. The emcee made his final announcements. Families stepped down the drippy bleachers and met their sons with warm embraces. The major noticed no one was there for Jamal, who strode off toward the barracks alone, but with his head held high.

When people dispersed in search of dry clothing and warmer confines, the two career soldiers moved toward each other. They exchanged salutes and stood at arm's length while the major raised the umbrella between them.

The general asked, "How have you been, Steve?"

"Good, sir. Sorry about the short notice. I wanted you to eyeball two prospective agents who are here on post. Did you know there was one in this group? Name's Muhammad. Jamal Muhammad."

The general shook his head in the negative. "And I thought you came by just to hear my speech."

The major's grin acknowledged the sarcasm until the general owned up. "Of course I saw him. Big black kid, third row in."

"There's another one over at the Airborne school—an Afghan. We can see him later today. He'll finish up next week, and then I'll introduce myself to him."

"How many do we have in the fold so far?"

"Just a handful who enlisted on their own. And two officers. I've also recruited a few from outside the military. They will start basic training soon."

"And we're covering our bases with the demographics, right?"

"We're looking at natives from several *al Qaeda* hot spots in Asia, sir, plus Iraq and Iran. Chechnya would be included if I can land the Russian on my list. Hopefully, the Afghan pans out. We'll need someone in there for the long haul."

"Good. Tell me about Muhammad."

The major uploaded Jamal's digital dossier on his Blackberry and handed it to the general, who followed along while the major summarized.

"Just turned twenty. The story is similar to the others. Rough start out there in the world, but recently immigrated to the States and enlisted. Speaks several dialects of Arabic. A little unique in that he's of mixed race. Father was an Iraqi Arab and a total no-show in the kid's life from what I can tell. Mother was from the south of Sudan, of pure African heritage. She and the boy spent the first ten years of his life among Arab Muslims in Iraq before resettling in Sudan. The Christians who live in the South of that country converted both. Ever heard of the Lost Boys?"

"What, the movie?"

The major smirked, not sure if the general was kidding this time or not.

"No. Young boys who survived the Sudanese Civil War in the nineties, orphaned when Muslim raiders attacked their villages in Darfur. After the men were killed, and most of the females hauled off as sex slaves, boys in their teens and even younger ones were forced to fight for the Janjaweed militia in Darfur. Muhammad was among them. He watched his mother die during the raid on their village. Apparently, she was trying to protect him when it happened."

"So, he's no stranger to death?"

"Or sacrifice. But he's a survivor. You'll note he ended up escaping the militia and linked up with some displaced boys from his village. Led them across the Ethiopian desert and ended up at some refugee camp in Kenya for several years."

The general took his eyes off the Blackberry. "Then the U.N. saved his ass."

"Yeah. They set up the Lost Boy program. He and a few thousand others were allowed to immigrate to the U.S. They're scattered all over the country. He's luckier than you think, though. Check out the date he was naturalized."

The general scrolled down the Blackberry screen. "I'll be damned … 9/11."

"His was one of the final flights out of Kenya last fall before they shut the program down for security reasons. Kid got his green card about ten minutes before the first plane hit in New York. Best part is, he was in line at the recruiter's office by lunchtime."

"Outstanding."

The general's gaze returned to the small screen to learn more about the young man they hoped to forge into a double agent like none America had ever sent into the field. He finished reading and handed the device back to the major.

The protégé recognized the distant stare of his mentor and knew he was having second thoughts about the program. "Still hedging on this thing, huh?" asked the major.

"You could say that. There's a lot I'm willing to do for God and country, but this could blow up in our face."

"You can keep your God, sir. Where was He on 9/11? Now the country is in deep shit. Your mysterious friend in D.C. thinks it's the only way to prevent more attacks like 9/11. I tend to agree. We got caught with our pants down that day for a reason."

"I know the talking points," said the general as he pulled out an enormous cigar. He didn't offer one to the major because he knew the major didn't smoke. "Too reliant on satellite and drone surveillance. Only willing to fire off cruise missiles from ships. I get it. We strayed from the means of infiltration that helped you do such good work against the Soviets."

It was the major's turn to look off as the general clipped and lit the stogie, his stare settling on another company of marching graduates across the drizzly parade ground. The bark of a drill sergeant echoed through the mist.

"Sir, we go wading into countries like Iraq or Iran—our troops will be fish in a barrel. If these agents can break into the highest levels of terror leadership, we'll have a nice card to play in a pinch. If we'd had a card like that to play at Tora Bora a couple of months ago, we could have snagged bin Laden right there and closed the books on Afghanistan by Christmas."

The general dragged slowly on the cigar, seemingly to consider the statement a little longer. He said, "When these wars begin, the most committed jihadists on the planet will flock to any American presence like flies on shit. There's no better situation for infiltration to take place than when those assholes are taking applications. And I have to admit, I like this idea of no handlers on board. No outside contacts with the agents during the mission. Less chance of sloppy field support making mistakes."

The major nodded in agreement, recalling the long lists of Cold War spies murdered because of betrayal, the by-product of too many people in the know. He was glad to see the general coming around.

"Still," said the general, couching optimism yet again with his shrug of the shoulders. "From what I was told, the training will be unlike anything we've done with Americans. We'll have to get inside their heads to make this work. They'll never be the same afterward. You think it's asking too much?" The general only let him consider the words for a second. "Then again, none of them are Americans, are they?"

The canned manner in which the general had spoken told the major he was supposed to read between the lines. The slow nod he offered indicated he understood. Expendability is on the table.

Train 'em up and use 'em up.

The general noticed two field grade officers and their wives approaching, no doubt to kiss his ass. He would rather stand here in the drizzle, smoke his cigar, and talk more about the program that he and the major were on the verge of initiating, maybe let his protégé use his persuasive skills some more. But there were appearances to keep up, so he and the major arranged a time to talk about the other potential recruit on base. The junior officer snapped off a crisp salute and took his leave.

As the major walked away, the general wondered if he'd understood the vague directive correctly, *but then again, none of them are truly Americans, are they?*

The major could have construed that statement in two ways, he now realized. Considering the major's level of patriotism, he probably thought it meant putting the foreign agents in harm's way or messing with their psyche would be easier for us to take because none of them are real Americans. In truth, the general had meant the agents' foreign status might translate to less hand wringing on *their* part over hurting Americans than it would for some kid who grew up playing ball on American soil. In other words, it would make it easier for them to get the job done.

The general's motivations were centered around the promotions that were in store for him if the agents proved valuable during the nation's time of war. Negative exposure of his involvement in the program, however, would certainly take the wind out of those sails.

I'll be damned if I let this thing ruin me.

That coin kept flipping in his head, though, and now he saw the upside of the program, a deep-cover sleeper agent who went the distance and who sat among the top tier of terror leadership until the time was right. The major was correct. It would be a smart card to play in a pinch. Maybe it would save the nation someday. The accolades for something like that would be off the chart. But the general had learned how to temper expectations in regard to any long-term planning. There were too many contingencies out there waiting.

Just be ready to napalm the whole lot of them if this shit goes south.

Jamal entered the battalion headquarters. After the summons he'd received in the barracks, he assumed he was in some trouble again. So, he'd taken his own sweet time.

Why ruin a great day by hurrying off to an ass-chewing.

He reached the third floor and followed the room numbers to the correct office. Through the glass panel in the top half of the door, he saw an officer sitting behind a military issue desk. He knocked and was waved in by the man. After entering, Jamal closed the door behind him and snapped off a salute.

"Private Muhammad reporting, sir!"

"At ease, soldier!" retorted the officer as he rose from his seat and walked around the desk. "You're late."

Jamal noted the gold oak leaf clusters on his shoulders, which indicated he was a major. He wore a heavily starched camouflage uniform, and it was hard not to stare at the spit-shined boots that reflected the overhead light as if they were mirrors.

"Sir. I was-"

"Take a seat, Private," said the major as he leaned on the edge of the desk. "My name is Major Winters. I'm with a military intelligence unit stationed over at Fort Bragg. You know anything about Fort Bragg, Muhammad?"

Jamal's broad shoulders and muscular back were rigid in the seat before the desk. His hands were placed palms down on his thick quadriceps in the military sitting position of attention.

"Negative, sir!"

"Damned right, you don't! You know why?" He didn't wait for Jamal's answer. "Bragg is where our most elite soldiers go to get trained. And we're not in the business of God damned show and tell."

Jamal was still suspicious but curious. It seemed his presumed reasons for this summons had been off.

"What is your business then ... Sir?"

The major's face produced a sneer. "You think you're special, Muhammad?"

"For what purpose, sir?"

"I'm talking about working with the most elite troops in the U.S. military. Your fluency in Arabic makes you a hot commodity these days."

Jamal was let down and cringed his mouth to make it visible.

"Sir, I joined to fight terrorists, not eavesdrop on them if you are talking about being some interpreter."

The major sat back in his chair and studied Jamal before asking in a mocking tone, "So you're ready to kill 'em all, huh, hero?"

Jamal played along to test the major, threw in a shrug of the shoulders for good measure. "And let God sort 'em out."

"You ready to die for your new country, kid? Cause that's what we need from our infantrymen."

"Hooah, sir!"

The major didn't appear to be fooled by Jamal's false bravado and shook off his response.

"There's more than that out there for you. This country needs you for another reason." The major crossed his arms upon his chest. In a much more relaxed tone, he said, "But before we get into that, tell me about your time in Iraq."

Jamal was suddenly taken aback. The only way the major could know he'd lived in Iraq was by getting his hands on U.N. documents. Jamal was under the impression that these were sealed after his naturalization. Iraq was a place he wanted to forget; he and his mother had endured meager living conditions for ten long years there, and the Arabs had treated them as outcasts due to their African heritage. Deep down, the memory of being tormented by Arab children daily still stung. So if the major wanted to know about Iraq, he'd have to show his hand for the information.

"Never been there, sir. I grew up in Sudan."

The major's head tilted slightly, the international sign of puzzlement.

Is this kid serious? Comes in here with an attitude, then tells a bald-faced lie to a superior officer and looks good doing it.

The major almost couldn't hide his satisfaction. Jamal was just what he was looking for—confident, with a presence about him, and possessing natural leadership skills according to all reports. The major was also surprised at how well this foreigner's English had progressed in the short time he'd been among Americans. Jamal's deep voice spoke in an even cadence that belied real fluency, but there was a minimal accent. The major took it as a sign of raw intelligence.

Check.

Jamal was one of those enlistees who enter the service for some ideological reason. They come pre-motivated, and after some convincing, typically overlook the negatives of any training to achieve the sought-after status as an agent. There was another type whom his shadowy D.C. contact sought, the type with a checkered past, or someone prone to violence. They are tougher to bring along and certainly possess less discipline. They can be as ruthless as needed when it matters, though. The major had found some of them as well. All of the potential agents were between the ages of eighteen and twenty-two, malleable like fresh potter's clay, yet already exposed to the horrible knowledge learned in war. The one before him certainly had been.

But never been to Iraq, my ass. Let's see what he does with this.

Jamal watched the major reach into the lapel of his uniform and produce a photograph, which he tossed onto the table like a tiny Frisbee. It slid to the middle and spun until motionless. Jamal bent over and picked it up. He didn't allow his surprise to show but was now aware the major had done more digging than just at the U.N. The photograph had been removed from his personal belongings, which he'd put in storage just like all the other enlistees before basic training started. It was one of a handful he possessed of his early years in Iraq and showed his tall African mother with a shortly cropped afro standing next to a large Arab in military uniform. Jamal had only kept the photo because it was a good one of her. The man he could've just as easily cut out with a pair of scissors.

A memory flashed of the man in the photo pressing up against his mother in their humble home. Jamal had watched from behind a piece of furniture as the big man's groping hands moved up and down her backside. While it was clear she'd been disgusted by his advances, Jamal's mind's eye told him her efforts at resistance were only half-hearted. He'd always guessed the big man had something on her, maybe even forcing sex from her. Of course, she never talked about it. He was a presence in their life for a while, then he was gone. Looking at the photo, Jamal recalled the wide jaw and thick mustache, and the intense gaze upon the man's face.

Those eyes.

Suddenly another memory flashed before him, but one he'd never recalled before now. It was of this man walking with him alone. Ramadi's Great Mosque loomed in the distance. That was all he saw.

"Do you know who this man is?" asked the major.

Jamal knew the major had seen him waver. He wasn't even sure if he could play out the string of denial now anyway. There was something about this new memory that stirred him and allowed more curiosity for the major's gambit. Apparently, according to this new memory, Jamal had spent time with this man away from his mother. He dialed down the skepticism yet another notch to learn more about the major's interest in a long-forgotten photo.

"No, sir." It was true. Vague memories couldn't fill in that blank.

"Are you sure?"

Jamal had stopped looking at his old photos years ago when living in the refugee camp because they only produced a longing for his mother. For the first time in a long while, he scrutinized this one, hoping to shake something else loose from the recesses of his mind. The way his mother appeared, Jamal guessed he would have been around four or five. He couldn't tell exactly where, but they'd lived in Ramadi, Iraq when he was four. He knew that. In the photo, his mother and the man did not appear to be intimate; instead, they stood abreast of one another, arms folded across their waists while gazing placidly into the camera.

"She couldn't have been romantically involved with him," said Jamal, essentially ending the pretense between him and the major, while not revealing what he knew. "Not an African and a full-blooded Iraqi Arab of his stature. It would be *haram*."

"Forbidden as a couple, yes. But could they have had business together?"

"I do not see how. We were poor as dirt. Who is he?"

"This is Hassan Barzan," said the major. "In the photo, he's a captain. Now he's a general in Saddam Hussein's Republican Guard. What memories do you have of him?"

"Very little," said Jamal. "Why would he be important anyway?"

"In about a week, the President is going to give his State of the Union address. In it, he's going to announce that America is now facing an Axis of Evil."

"How do you know this?"

"Doesn't matter. What matters is that Iraq is one of three countries in this ridiculously unrealistic alliance."

"Who are the other two?"

"Watch the speech, kid, if you want to brush up on current events," said the major. "They're irrelevant for our discussion today. The thing is, there are plans to invade Iraq already on the table in the White House. It's just a matter of time."

"What does invading Iraq have to do with me?"

"The plans I've seen are woefully inadequate when it comes to post-invasion security. It'll be chaos over there within weeks of us taking the capital. When that happens, men like Barzan will ignite an insurgency that will be a slow bleeder for the occupying forces. He will fight under a Baathist banner because he is loyal to Saddam and the Revolutionary Guard. But as a Sunni Muslim, and for added strength, I predict he will align himself with the Sunni jihadists in the country."

"The *al Qaeda* types," confirmed Jamal.

"Yes. Infiltrating *al Qaeda* has become a primary goal after the attacks on New York and Washington. We had no one out there who could provide actionable intelligence on their operations, so we got blindsided, Jamal. Pardon the pun, but we're starting at ground zero, and we can't let another 9/11 happen."

"Are all your 'we's' referring to the nation?"

"We as in you, me, and a handful of others, on behalf of the nation. Give me a year, and I'll turn you into the ultimate sleeper agent. You see, it's one thing to have a bunch of special-ops guys running around hunting terrorists. It's a good play in the media. And they'll get some big names. It's quite another to have someone on the inside who could do exponentially more damage. With your unique history, your language skills, and let's face it, your motivations for being here in the first place, you're a perfect fit for this program."

"What do you think are my motivations?"

"I'll bet my next paycheck you didn't sign up solely to protect this country."

Jamal exhaled slowly while holding the major's gaze. "A sleeper agent," he said. "That seems to imply someone who is in the organization for a long time, someone who has advanced in skill and stature. To do that ..."

The major nodded. "You'll have to get your hands very dirty."

"Very bloody, you mean." Jamal didn't have to work at displaying uneasiness. It was there on its own.

"This program has long term goals. Those of us who believe in it know that sacrifice is needed for security to exist—or scores to be settled."

Jamal wondered if this opportunity could be what his mother had meant when she told him God had a plan for him. Could this be the stand he was to take?

As if on cue, the major asked, "How much of your enlisting had to do with your religious beliefs?"

"I'll say that I believe God chooses the people He wants to fight His enemies. But God distinguishes between justified killing and murder. Killing innocents is murder. I'm not sure my soul is worth your security."

"I understand," said the major. "The idea of hurting innocents to advance in a group like *al Qaeda* is hard to get past. But our enemies have no limitations. The line between killing and murder is blurry now that we face total war with them. They will stop at nothing to see us burn."

Jamal's hesitancy remained. He offered the major nothing in the form of a response, so the major tried again.

"Consider this. How do you think a general makes the decisions he does in war? If he knows an attack on his enemy's defensive front will cost him five thousand, or even ten thousand good men, how does he justify ordering an attack with that high of a butcher's bill?"

"He looks at the bigger picture."

"Right. The bigger picture is the destruction of the enemy, so everyone can go home and live a peaceful life. If a general knows his offensive will be a strategic blow to the enemy, he accepts the tactical losses and continues to pursue victory."

"Let me guess. Now you're going to tell me that generals are somehow able to sleep at night."

The major just grinned.

Jamal was getting the sense his brashness had backfired on him. Maybe he should have acted like some backcountry simpleton. The major wouldn't need him and Jamal could stick with the more manageable plan of becoming a soldier and having people tell him where to go and whom to shoot. Suddenly, that didn't seem like a way to make an impact.

No. He's got me pegged, knows I came here to kill as many of them as I can. Now he's talking about putting me out ahead of the front lines. But what will that do to me? Will it kill me? What about my soul, Lord?

Jamal would need to sleep on something like this, but first, he needed more particulars. "So why the need to get in with Hassan Barzan first? He's not al Qaeda."

"In a post 9/11 world, an outsider can't just show up and join the *al Qaeda* ranks, or even one of their splinter groups. They are expecting us to attempt it now. In a place like Iraq—especially during a war that will brew up about when you'd finish the training we have in mind—you could work your way in by association with someone like Barzan first. It's a good method of infiltration because if you impress him, you'll have a resume and references from an established enemy of America when you approach the Islamists. In essence, you'll use him to get to bigger fish. In America, we call this a foot in the door."

CHAPTER 3

In clinical fashion, the Urdu speaking man's serrated combat knife plunged into the side of the neck, blade facing forward. The captured Russian soldier's eyes bulged, and blood spurted—so much blood. Jamal's muscles tensed as the sawing motion commenced, but the man's voice never wavered as he gave the instructions. Once the blade was free of flesh, he flipped it over. Working it back through the dying soldier's cervical spine seemed to require a little more effort. The man held the severed head aloft, using both hands because the soldier's buzz cut was too short to grasp. Jamal's addled mind was forced to wonder how much it would weigh when the man's fingers flexed as if picking up a bowling ball.

Jamal's head faced forward. He was strapped to an oversized, straight-backed chair like a death row inmate before electrocution while a looped video of despicable acts of violence played before him. Up next was the acid drip and the spine-tingling screams of the young girl. He really hated that one.

His eyes were wide open, literally and figuratively. After accepting the major's offer last winter, he'd undergone six months of advanced soldier training at Fort Bragg with the other nine recruits. Now he was sweating his balls off on the Qualla Boundary Cherokee Reservation, at the tail end of a sweltering North Carolina summer. All of it had taxed his strength, spirit, and emotions to the utmost. He suspected the purpose of this room was to desensitize the recruits before their missions.

His clothes were in tatters. He reeked of filth and days-old sweat, less so from the shoulders up, but only because of all the water boarding. During those sessions, he'd hovered over the precipice between breathing and repeatedly drowning, each time inducing a heart-pounding panic he'd never known. Even now, the bitter taste of the rusty well water infused his throat. There was no palate cleanser waiting for him, either. Not that he was looking forward to his next meal. The food they ate—when they were allowed to eat—usually came in the form of rotten meat or moldy bread. Or, rice with maggots that looked like rice. But every single one of the agents-to-be wolfed it down at each offer.

Loud pulsating music blared, a hindrance to sleep, despite his utter exhaustion. If he closed his eyes for more than a minute anyway, one of the major's cadre magically appeared and rapped his abdomen with a two-foot bamboo cane. Consequently, a deep bruise darkened by the hour across his midriff.

His immediate concern was the vermin that scurried about the dirt floor of the room. Frequently they approached his bare, grubby feet, causing acute anxiety. His calves were strapped to the legs of the chair, but loose enough that he could raise and lower his feet in a stamping motion when the rats nipped at them, sending them away. But after tasting flesh, they always came back.

Under the music, he could hear shouting in Arabic coming from adjacent rooms, and the tortured cries of his cohorts. Sobs of pain and disillusionment from grown men were hard to tolerate, and only increased Jamal's anxiety about his next session with the interrogators. He'd spent plenty of time in those rooms already, enduring brutal interrogations that went on for days. Prior to insertion into the camp, they'd each been given a nugget of fabricated intelligence to keep secret. Jamal hadn't yet revealed his, but he knew others had. Beneath the pain, hunger, and stress, he told himself this was just training, but everything seemed so real, so malevolent.

If I get mind-fucked one more time, they'll be able to drive a truck through my head.

He stamped down hard on a rat and must have crushed its tiny skull because a rush of activity ensued around his feet, the rodents clamoring over themselves to get a piece of their dead sibling. The extreme discomfort of the situation caused him to yell and twist in his restraints until they went away. A tidal wave of adrenaline surged, eliciting a hot flash that only subsided after prayers for mercy.

They hadn't seen the major at all since arrival at the camp. Just his wicked cadre. This added to the uncertainty. At night the ten recruits were thrown into a small room and harassed until dawn. They were never allowed to use a proper latrine, so the place always smelled of fresh feces and urine. When alone in the room together, Jamal and the others relied on their collective strength, the bond strong among them. Over the last couple of days, though, it had become about survival while the men looked inward for the will to make it through.

Surely it will end soon, right?

They'd been told anyone of them could quit at any time, but when the Pakistani, Choudary, had done so, he was made to watch the others take beatings from the vicious cadre until he recanted his withdrawal. And he really wanted to quit.

The video reverted to the beginning. As Jamal watched the first of many gory scenes—the maiming of an elderly villager (not unlike what he'd seen already as a boy)—the light went on in the room, and a high-pitched whistle chased the rats into a hole at the base of the cinder block wall. The video and music ceased, and the door swung open. One of the cadre entered and removed him from the chair. Jamal guessed the Middle Eastern man with the uncaring eyes was some sort of sociopath by his callous infliction of pain, like some warped kid who doesn't flinch as he tortures his neighbor's dog to death. True to form, he lassoed Jamal's neck with a leather strap and roughly handled him out into the hall where several other trainees were being led back to the room.

The major glanced at the screen as the Algerian jerked Jamal out of the chair. The large bank of monitors before him showed all ten recruits in their various states of distress throughout the camp. He rubbed his eyes and leaned back in the swivel seat, wondered how surprised Jamal would be if he saw what was on the other side of the hole in the wall, a homemade Habitrail that led the rats to clean, well-attended cages. One of the monitors showed a veterinarian's assistant in a lab coat, standing by to prevent infighting among the healthy, albeit hungry rodents the major had purchased from a breeder.

He'd just reviewed two days' worth of interrogations and was exhausted, experiencing a level of deviance he'd never known. The cadre the major had assembled for his simulated prison camp were mostly former guards from notorious detention centers across the Middle East or ex-members of the Algerian secret police. A foul-mouthed Ukrainian named Igor was in charge, a real asshole by anyone's standards. All of them had been paid a hefty stipend by the major for their services and their silence.

At least I'm getting my money's worth.

Earlier in his career, the major had attended the Air Force's Survival, Evasion, Resistance, and Escape school, known as SERE. The official Department of Defense guidelines dictated that none of the instructors inside those mock prison camps break skin or bones, but could use just about any other means of coercion to get their subjects to talk.

Those guys have nothing on this crew.

He remembered hearing about a platoon of SEALS who'd all gone through SERE training together. They bought into the rough treatment so much that they overtook their instructors and wouldn't release them until the platoon's real-world commander stood before them and verified that it was all just training. The major wondered if his guys were thinking the same way. He wouldn't blame them.

I almost wish they would. Igor seems to really enjoy this shit.

It was starting to seem like overkill, yet he knew a real *al Qaeda* hellhole or an interrogation facility used by the likes of Iran's *Qud's* Force would be worse if the agents were exposed.

Real sewer rats. Real beheadings. Real acid drips all day long.

They would also need to manage themselves while under as much physical duress as possible. As such, they'd only been given enough water to survive over their time in the camp. They barely had any food, and when they did, a virus to slow them down further tainted it.

He reached into his briefcase for the notes he'd started on the climax of the training; what he and his cadre had begun to refer to as the boulder test. He'd conceived of the idea after remembering the difficulties of his Ranger training years ago. At Ranger School, the U.S. Army's premier combat leadership course, candidates were placed in squad-sized groups of around a dozen men. The group had to complete successive phases of training together in woodland, mountain, desert, and swamp environments. At the end of each phase, the candidates were made to "peer out" one of their own.

Individuals privately ranked their fellow squad members according to how well he thought they each had performed throughout the phase. When the results were tallied, the candidate receiving the lowest ranking was forced to repeat the entire phase with another squad in the class behind them. They were peered out officially. The candidates called it getting recycled. The major remembered the process being akin to a litter of wild animals eating the runt to survive. He planned to use a similar, albeit warped peering process to weed out the least of his agents-to-be, and at the same time, get some blood on the hands of those who were the most committed.

Farouk al-Hakim, a fellow recruit of Bedouin heritage, broke the silence and whispered in Arabic, "Jamal, are you awake?"

Jamal lifted his weary head from the dirt floor of the crowded, smelly room. "What, brother?"

"Will you tell me where your heart is spiritually?"

The question was not what Jamal would expect from his usually quiet, newfound friend. He fidgeted as he thought about an answer. It was the middle of the night, and the recruits had been left alone for a few hours in the room, allowing most of the men to drift off. A few coughed in their sleep with unhealthy sounding wetness that Jamal was starting to experience himself, the chill of fever creeping into his bones despite the muggy summer conditions.

"I don't know. Sometimes I feel torn between the two religions I've been exposed to in my life. I lived under the banner of Islam for much of my childhood, but after a time learned about Jesus. I will use what I know of both faiths to execute my mission."

"You will have to choose someday, Jamal. Just know that. A servant can serve only one master."

Jamal considered the statement. "Do you ever wonder if they are two paths to the same place?"

"I have," said Farouk. He appeared to ponder the question while recruit Khalid al-Douri, a Shiite Iraqi, rasped at them to shut up and get some rest. "... Along with many others who have wondered whether all three Abrahamic religions are like spokes leading to the center of the same wheel. It would make things easier if we knew, would it not? To each his own here on Earth, and we'll all gather together in the afterlife."

"But if Jews, Christians, and Muslims are all God's children, he's sure got a rotten pack of squabbling, disrespectful siblings on his hands," said Jamal. "Why is that?"

Both men hushed at the sound of footfalls outside the door so that only the buzz of flies could be heard inside the room. They'd learned not to draw the interest of the guards.

Farouk scratched at the dirt floor with his broken, filthy fingernails until the guard had passed. He spoke softly. "I suppose it has something to do with being born into our beliefs. Like all the other habits, we learn from those who came before us."

Jamal tilted his head once, signaling disagreement. "We are not really born into a religion, Farouk. I just saw past the veil of Islam."

"I respect you for looking," said Farouk as he rolled over to steal some precious sleep. "It speaks to your intelligence and an open mind."

"And the grace of God."

Jamal crested the ridge at a jog. Sweat burned his eyes as he knelt by a fallen tree trunk to catch his breath. He was starting to get his legs back under him after the sickness he and the recruits had shared over the last couple of weeks in the mock prison camp. While reaching for the last of his water in the canteen, he took in the sounds of the forest, listening for signs of his hunters. There was no gentle autumn breeze up here on the high ground to cool him off as he'd hoped, but the stillness allowed him to hear the gurgling of the stream he sought in the valley below. It was welcome confirmation that he was in the right place after covering nearly three kilometers on a line generated by his compass.

He pulled a folded map from his hip pocket, oriented himself using a pen light with a discreet red lens. It was just after nine o'clock at night. He'd already found eight of the ten widely dispersed stations on the land navigation course. So far, he'd managed to avoid the teams of cadre and their hounds who patrolled the densely vegetated, undulating terrain, a box-shaped area in the foothills of the Smoky Mountains that covered ten square kilometers. Recruits who found their markers and avoided capture tonight were to be granted a two-day pass, the first of the entire summer. Those caught would be taken back to the awful camp for more interrogation resistance training.

No thanks. Find these last two and get on with the weekend they promised. If it's actually real. Better be. God, I need this.

He located the dot on his map, which represented the ninth station, and set off in that direction down the ridge, each step a little closer to his precious weekend respite. When the sloping flank of the ridge transitioned to the grassy valley floor, he crept along the bank of the stream. Soon he should see the simple post with a red marker atop it. But he wouldn't put it past the cadre to lay a trap near one of the markers, even though they said they wouldn't. There wasn't enough equity in trust and respect for Jamal to take them at their word, especially the one called Igor. Jamal guessed he was a former Spetznaz commando in the Russian Army before joining the major's payroll. The idea of him crouching in the trees caused Jamal to slow his gait further. A run-in now with the oversized bully would no doubt hurt his chances of checking into a hotel in downtown Asheville and ordering room service all weekend.

He saw the post in a small clearing illuminated by the half-moon. From the cover of a large willow next to the stream, he scanned the area. No one appeared to lurk in the bushes. Jamal filled his canteen with clear mountain water, dropped an iodine tablet inside, and approached. At the post, he wrote down the four-digit marker number and then decided the nearby foliage would offer better concealment while he derived the direction and distance to the final station. He'd barely taken two steps away from the post when he heard someone crash into the water upstream, about fifty meters from where he stood. He quickly found a spot behind the greenery nearest to the water's edge and waited.

The lone figure sloshed toward him. Since he heard no barking, Jamal assumed it was another recruit drawing attention to himself—and anyone unlucky enough to be around him. A few seconds later, he saw it was Choudary, the smallish Pakistani who seemed the most unlikely of the recruits and who had created hardship for the others. When he was closer, Jamal could tell he was a mess. His clothes were torn, and he was covered in mud. The man was clearly distressed. The reason became apparent as the sound of dogs now echoed in the direction from which he'd come.

Immersed in the shadows, Jamal shook his head, muttering, "Choudary …" As always, the emotional response was split. The competitive individualism inside was uncaring. It was the side that kept him silent as Choudary drew closer.

Maybe he'll find the marker and go away on the other side of the stream before the dogs track him down here.

There was, however, the side of him that gave a damn. That side of him knew the dogs would eventually catch up, and Igor would beat Choudary nearly to death in the camp tonight. Jamal suspected the major's plans for Choudary had little to do with fighting once he assumed his undercover role. His weapon against radical Islamists would be the Socratic method, his battlefield the mosques and universities of Pakistan, a burgeoning hotbed of anti-Western resentment.

Nonetheless, he was a soldier and needed to prove his commitment, just like everyone else. Every group of trainees has a low man. For that reason, Jamal and a few of the others had helped

Choudary whenever they could during all the specialty training last winter, especially in the true soldier skills such as weapons, demolitions, and hand fighting. But it had irked them when he showed little gratefulness for their efforts. Now it looked like land navigation was another weakness for the highly intellectual Pakistani.

As Jamal completed the thought, Choudary tripped on a rock and fell headlong into the stream, letting out a gasp of shock from the mountain's cold product. Jamal shook his head one more time and stepped out from behind the vegetation. Between the two of them, they spoke six different languages, but Jamal spoke in Arabic to move things along quickly.

"Are you hurt?"

Choudary stood in the stream and looked up at Jamal on the embankment with more exhaustion and fear than surprise. "If they catch me I am quitting," he said, also in Arabic. "I am done. It isn't worth it, and I CANNOT go back to that place."

"You are not quitting again. You're a few hours away from a reprieve we all need. You get a clean slate afterward. How many stations have you found?"

Choudary staggered on the uneven rocks and nearly fell, but managed to right himself and produced a soggy map with only a few smeared markings. He held it up, and Jamal felt that same emotional tug-of-war. He also could tell the dogs had crested the opposite ridge by the heightened volume of their eager pursuit.

Jamal finally gave in while Choudary clutched his map in the stream, shivering like a dog shitting razor blades. "Stay there in the water. Hand me your damned map and one piece of your clothing that has been up against your skin. Is that blood on your t-shirt?"

"Yes. I fell into some thorns, and they ripped into me on the way out."

"Give it to me."

Choudary's intellect no doubt prevented the need to question Jamal's intent, which was good because Jamal didn't feel like explaining it to him. Choudary wrapped the map inside the clothing and tossed them toward the embankment.

"What will I tell them when I finish without a shirt?"

"The truth. You tore it in some thorns and parted ways with it in the forest."

"That sounds silly."

"It sounds like something you would say."

Choudary seemed to accept the jab as penance for his helplessness because there was no pithy remark in self-defense per usual. Typically, Jamal didn't enjoy watching people squirm, but this time he let Choudary do so as he transferred the needed marker codes from his map to his cohort's. He handed his dry map over with all but the tenth station to find.

"You will have to get the last one on your own. Follow the stream for another five hundred meters then come out of the water on this side. The final station will be up the next ridgeline. Don't get caught!"

"What about you?" asked Choudary, the obligatory nature of the comment written all over his face. His arms were crossed to keep his bare, skinny torso from shivering.

"I will pull them off your trail and turn in your map as mine."

"Thank you."

"Just go. There is no more time," said Jamal. He assumed the dogs were halfway down the ridge by now. Choudary took off downstream before he halted and turned around.

"Jamal."

"What now?"

"Igor is up there."

"How do you know?"

"I led them in a big circle, so I could double back and mix my tracks in with theirs. I saw a clean boot print that had to be his. Nobody else in the camp has feet that big."

Jamal's mind flashed to one of the many kicks those boots had delivered to every inch of his body throughout the summer. Instinct caused him to touch a healing bruise on his cheekbone from the latest. He offered his one and only smile during his encounter with Choudary.

"It is good to see you learned something useful from the Cherokee other than how to gamble and drink whiskey."

"Peace be with you," said Choudary as he stomped off upstream.

"And upon you be peace."

Jamal hopped across the stream on the largest rocks. He tied Choudary's blood spotted tee shirt to his ankle and bound up the embankment.

Ready to run Igor? Better hope your vodka-soaked heart is.

CHAPTER 4

The ten of them walked in a single file along the narrow wooded trail. Only their booted footfalls and the occasional snap of a twig interrupted the wind as it pushed through the trees. Jamal was toward the back when they emerged from the forest and approached the great stone near the center of the glade. The boulder's jagged edges were animated by the light of several torches placed around the ancient ritual site, no doubt prepared by their Native American hosts. Gusts of wind whipped at the flames, and the knee-high grass outside their radiance shimmered under a cloudless moon. Once the men circled the boulder, an eerie calm built a bridge to the task at hand.

Jamal shook his head, still stinging from the deceptive way in which they'd been led into this morbid test. Less than two hours ago, after completing the land navigation course, they'd all erupted in spontaneous laughter when Choudary came in soaking wet and shirtless—including the cadre, which all of a sudden seemed to lighten up toward them. They were all transported back to the camp, supposedly to grab personal effects for the long-awaited leave. The joy they'd all shared on that bumpy ride in the back of an Army five-ton truck provided the most fraternal moment of their training.

When they arrived, the recruits were locked in a room and told by Igor that before their leave would commence, they must prove their loyalty to the program and sacrifice one of their own, chosen by a secret ballot taken from each recruit. Before the men could recover from their stunned silence, they were each separated for ten minutes to consider quitting once and for all, no questions asked. At least that was what they were told. But no one had taken the offer.

Each man now fingered a folded piece of paper as they stood in silence around the stone. All wore grave faces that told the story of their displeasure. Jamal opened his paper and looked one last time at the name he'd forced himself to write and quickly stole a glance toward Choudary on the other side of the circle. Jamal pitied him for his physical weakness and haughty overtures but chose him because he knew those qualities would make him a questionable agent. Still, he didn't think the Pakistani would get all the votes. Khalid al-Douri, the Iraqi Shiite, had rubbed several of the others the wrong way with his coarse manner. None of them deserved this.

Jamal scanned the circle of faces, which represented several races from just as many continents. Each showed resignation for the task ahead. He saw the Russian, Victor Katseyev, shake his head in silent protest. Jamal wondered whom he'd selected because the two of them had quarreled more than once. Everyone had chosen someone standing here.

Farouk al-Hakim, the Bedouin, spoke as the chosen leader. "It is time." He looked around as if to forestall the inevitable and nervously asked the men to pass their papers around. He read each one to himself. When he looked up, his gaze settled on the Pakistani.

"Choudary."

Jamal heard the doomed man gasp. Choudary hadn't expected this outcome. His eyes darted around the circle seeking a friendly face, but all that waited for him were downward stares. He began to edge backward, but the men on either side of him moved to cut off any attempt at escape.

The rest of the recruits moved around the boulder. Some hung back, nervous. It seemed to Jamal the moment was frozen in time.

Anger welled up toward the major for forcing this bullshit test on them, even though the hesitation he sensed around him seemed to justify it. During their missions, the agents would have to sink to the lowest levels of human depravity to be in league with the likes of *al Qaeda*. Each of them might have to look a Westerner in the eye and kill him with their new bosses watching. They wouldn't even be able to flinch in doing so, or they'd be out, maybe even dead. Everything they'd endured would be for naught, the potential of the program put to the match.

This is nothing compared to all that.

It was something to murder someone, though. To murder someone for symbolic reasons was even worse. Yet this obstacle to the sanctioned vengeance he sought was before him, one he had to clear in order to advance, and he did want to advance, to get over there and dive into the mission. He was prepared for what lay ahead, no doubt. He needed a reminder, though, of what drove him to be here in the first place. So, instead of Choudary trembling before him, backlit by flickering torches, he imagined the mounted raider rising in the foreground of his burning village, just before the worst moment of his life. He relived the torturous memory of how radical Islamists had ruined everything one more time. While he rekindled his rage, he hoped the others could supplant their reasons for being here and follow his actions, as unforgivable as they were. He pulled the knife out of the jacket and took his first step toward Choudary.

On the edge of the glade, just inside the tree line, Major Winters was close enough to smell the kerosene burning in the torches. He stared wide-eyed at the screen of his hand-held camera while the Iraqi and the Afghan accosted Choudary and dragged him toward the boulder. The others moved around, pulling knives from their jackets. Choudary was thrown against the great stone and spun with his back to it; terror was etched across his face. He drew his knife as the men closed in around him, but there was no hope of escape. The major's pounding heart made it difficult to steady the camera. This was the moment he'd prepared them for since the day they had entered the program. He sensed hesitation—which concerned him—and zoomed in to study their facial expressions.

Suddenly, Jamal pushed through the group, deflected an attempt at defense, and plunged the knife deep into Choudary's torso. The scream that followed gave the major chills as it shot across the open glade. Moonlight flashed off multiple blades held overhead. They were darkened and dripping the next time they were raised as the hacking commenced. Several of the men turned away to vomit. Two men stayed near the body, and one of the Arabs went to his knees in a state of apparent distress. The major heard Farouk speak again in heavily accented English.

"We had no choice! It could have been any of us."

Another said, "It was always him. We all knew it!"

Several nodded in agreement, with heads hung low. There was mumbling among them as they came together again over the corpse. The major desperately wanted to hear their words, but realized he didn't need to—the deed was done. The men had passed through this crucible and would enter the final phase of training. Though he wondered if they could do it out in the world, where the real killing fields existed, with so much more on the line. He put the camera in a small pack and backed his way into the forest.

On the way back to his vehicle, the wind started to pick up, and he heard thunder in the distance. It made him think of the figurative storm that approached, and how it compared to the Cold War threat he'd faced as a junior spy.

This enemy is more dangerous, less predictable. At least with the Soviets, we didn't worry about suicide bombers on the loose or nasty bugs dropped into our water and mail.

As he trudged through the lush canopy, a mist fell; the drippy darkness was symbolic of his career in espionage, he reckoned.

Murky. Again forging my way alone on some desperate mission.

His lonely thoughts morphed into guilt over the carnal act he'd just witnessed, exacerbated by the fact that the so-called boulder test had been manufactured by his mind. But he believed what he hoped his men had at least accepted, albeit begrudgingly. The sacrifice had been for the good of the program and, therefore, the country. At his core, he knew he was a patriot.

How many Americans raise and lower the stars and stripes every single day of the year at their home?

Once he'd emerged from the woods and was inside the vehicle, he used a secure satellite phone to call the general. Thunder rumbled closer over the ringing as the major waited. Only after the general had answered did the major think to look at the time.

"This better be damned good, Steve."

"My bad, sir. I'm about to leave the Qualla Boundary. It's done. They all passed."

"Did they pick who we thought they would?"

"They picked the right man."

"Anyone stand out?"

The major queued up the video and watched the first few seconds of the killing again. He saw Jamal surge to the front of the group and make the first blow. The frail Pakistani might have died right there, he realized. The ensuing attack from the group looked to be overkill, literally.

"Yeah," answered the major. "Jamal Muhammad helped them get over the hump when the rest hesitated. Not a surprise. He's probably been the best in the group. He seems to understand what we need from them."

"Good. Just in time for Iraq—the invasion will be sometime next spring is what I'm hearing," said the general. "What did our man in Washington say about the timing?"

"He's ready for them to go operational ASAP. It's all he talks about."

The general said, "We're going to have our hands full."

"I know. I'm ready for it. I doubt the nation is."

Jamal entered the suite he'd paid for in Asheville once the major had finally released them for their precious leave. He went directly to the spacious bathroom and turned on the hot water all the way. Morbid guilt plagued him as he pulled a crumpled receipt and some change from his hip pocket. Usually, his ordered self would straighten the bills and stack the coins by type out of habit. Instead, he tossed everything on the granite bar top, one of the coins rolling in a circle until it plunged off the edge and settled on the carpet. Death was heavy on his mind as he poured himself a bourbon and entered the steam-filled room.

It had been a while since he'd killed anyone. There was the horseman first. Then as a conscripted boy-soldier, the internal consequences of his senseless violence had been pushed away by fear and his need to survive. Later, he'd been forced to kill a bandit to protect the gaggle of young boys he led across Ethiopia. That was a no brainer. But he was an adult now, and the taking of life would always be heavier on the soul. He couldn't even address God on the matter and denied that urgent calling for now.

What have I gotten myself into?

Later that night over an enormous meal, he wondered what his mother would think of his chosen path to greater justice.

Mostly he just missed her laugh—and her wisdom. His drunken nostalgia lasted until he'd sunken himself in a real bed for the first time in months. It wasn't the best night of sleep, with dark dreams that came and went, but it was better than a dirt floor and the overwhelming smell of human waste.

For the next six months, Jamal gained more specialized training under the major's demanding yoke. In the meantime, the Bush Administration's march to war with Saddam Hussein was held in check. Even though the American President had agreed to wait for the United Nations weapons inspectors' findings, everyone knew the invasion was as imminent as their findings would be inconclusive—or to the people that mattered, unconvincing. Not surprisingly, the inspectors came away empty-handed, and the American vanguard promptly entered southern Iraq in March 2003.

After a lightning thrust aimed toward the capital, the tip of the American spear was now poised to strike Baghdad. Jamal waited at Fort Bragg with anticipation as the Iraqi Army crumbled further with each passing day; the major had held off insertion until after the inevitable collapse of the Hussein regime. In its absence, a vacuum of power would exist, and cells resisting the occupying forces would emerge, with which the agents could establish initial contact. In other words, Hassan Barzan would go into hiding soon.

CHAPTER 5

Jamal sat on a bench in the hall alone. He watched Farouk al-Hakim enter the sterile interior of the briefing room for a final mission statement from the major. Khalid al-Douri had gone first; Jamal would be last. Of the nine agents, only the three of them would deploy to Iraq.

Once in Iraq, they were to infiltrate separate enemy factions that under normal circumstances would not combine forces, but on their own, represented a unique threat to American security. Jamal would attempt to join the nascent Baathist insurgency led by general Hassan Barzan and his former Republican Guardsmen. Khalid al-Douri, a Shiite Muslim, would target the Shiite militias in the south known to be in league with the Iranians (the major had predicted Iran would stop at nothing to initiate a proxy war against America across its border with Iraq). Farouk al-Hakim would use his knowledge of the Bedouin smuggling routes to infiltrate the supply lines of homegrown Iraqi Islamists. Jamal assumed the three-pronged approach offered the best chance for at least one of the agents to pan out in the war zone.

Farouk stepped into the hall. The meeting had been quick, like Khalid's. An M.P. stood guard near the entrance to another secure area, precluding any mission-oriented discussion.

"I guess this is it, brother," said Jamal.

"Maybe on the other side."

Farouk reached to clasp hands, and both men bumped chests. They said a few words of encouragement to each other, and

Farouk departed. Jamal watched him until he turned the corner and wondered if they would ever meet again. He hoped so.

Jamal entered the spartan briefing room. Inside, the major sat behind the only table. The plain white walls, the buzz of the fluorescent light, and the hum of a small electronic device beside him provided a clinical, seemingly inauspicious start to Jamal's mission.

"Have a seat, Jamal." The major reached for a fingertip monitor. Its cord was attached to the device next to him. "Put this on your index finger. I assume you haven't had any stimulants or depressants in the last eight hours as ordered."

"Negative, sir."

"Don't worry. This is just a formality. We need to get some baseline information on record before we throw you out there with the wolves," said the major. "So to speak."

"Not a problem."

"Answer yes or no to my questions … Is your name Jamal Muhammad?"

"Yes."

"Are you enlisted in the United States Army?"

"Yes."

"Do you believe the attacks on New York and Washington were justified?"

"No."

The major asked more questions about Jamal's stance on terrorism.

"Have you killed a man as an adult?"

The ensuing silence caused the major to lift his eyes from the list of questions. Jamal's glare waited for them, the one that exposed lingering resentment over the Choudary incident.

"You know I have."

"Yes or no, please."

"Yes."

The major reached into a carrying case by his feet, produced a laptop computer, and pulled up a video file for Jamal to watch. The screen was dark at first, and rustling sounds could be heard. An image centered, and the lens zoomed in on the torches. Jamal knew what it was.

He saw the ten of them standing inside the circle of flame and watched as they began to move around the great boulder. There was hesitation as they stood before Choudary. Jamal was surprised to see in reality it wasn't the eternity it had felt like at the moment. He saw himself push forward to strike first. His mind replaced the detached happenings on the screen with his seared image of Choudary close up, blood spurting from his mouth with the look of sudden betrayal painted across his face. It was a look Jamal knew he would have to get used to.

"What's the point, sir? You know we did it."

The major froze the video and pushed a button on the device next to him. He turned it around so Jamal could see the monitor on its face.

"This isn't a lie detector. All it does is monitor your pulse. I know you're still pissed at me for what happened last fall. But I just asked you about a time when you killed someone you didn't think deserved to die; I showed you the video of yourself doing it. Take a look. What do you see?"

Jamal glanced at the readout on the device. He understood. "Nothing."

"That's right—not even a blip. We used to call that a cool customer back where I came from. Some might call it something else. The point is, you can do this. I knew it the day I met you."

There hadn't been too many times since joining the program when Jamal felt any soldiers' kinship with the major, especially in the six months since Choudary's death. Too much breaking down. Too little building up. Being forced to kill in that manner had taken him down pretty far. Yet he completed the training despite it. He was at a crossroads now. Every tragic event in his life—and some good ones—had led him to this place and time where he was being offered autonomy in meting out the justice he'd sought. The images flashed in a cascade of experiences: the burning village, the blood running from his mother's mouth, the violence with the militia, and the first glimpse of the refugee camp on the horizon. He shot an arrow prayer to God for guidance even though he'd been up half the night in deep meditation. But he hadn't received a sign yet, and the words had to come from his mouth.

He stared at the major and felt a switch flip in his mind once and for all, the burden of the decision lifted.

"What now?"

"You already know the mission. Establish contact with Hassan Barzan and join his Saddam loyalists. In Iraq, they'll be known as the *Bathyoun*—mostly made up of ex-Republican Guardsmen."

"Do we have Hassan's current location?"

The major opened one of the manila folders and showed Jamal a recent photograph of Hassan. He was much larger, even obese now, but still carried the heavy jaw line and a thick mustache, with more salt than pepper these days.

"My sources have confirmed he's survived the war to date and will most likely go to ground in Ramadi. It and Fallujah will be hotbeds of Sunni loyalty for the former regime. Both are in the heart of Anbar province, but Ramadi holds more strategic value for any militant cells. It's double the size of Fallujah and straddles the region's main thoroughfares. It could be critical for resupply and reinforcements. You're going home, my friend."

"You said the day we met that Barzan would be the foot in the door. What about making *al Qaeda* contacts?"

"Our timing is good. Since the invasion, we've heard chatter about jihadists on the move to Iraq—Sunni fighters possibly aligned with *al Qaeda*. Their relationship with Hassan and the

Bathyoun will be important for you to track. You need to get in there and make those connections. And on that note."

The major opened another manila folder and showed Jamal a page of several photographs. It took him a second or two to realize they were of the same man, just at different stages of his life. Jamal recognized one of them from the news. It was Abu Musab al-Zarqawi, the supposed *al Qaeda* connection to 9/11 that had partially justified the invasion of Iraq. Many believed those concerns were nothing more than overhyped intelligence.

"This guy *is* there, and he is connected with *al Qaeda*, albeit loosely," said the major. "He helped run a camp in Afghanistan in the nineties. He was there when we invaded in 2001, then got seriously wounded fighting alongside the Taliban. Now he's hiding out in northern Iraq. But Zarqawi ain't one of bin Laden's boys yet. He's just starting to impress, wants to join the club. Son of a bitch is ruthless, though," said the major while shaking his head.

"My guess is he will join the fold, so he is someone to pursue. He could get killed tomorrow too. You'll have to call the ball as you go. As we've discussed, this mission is very open-ended. Point is, *al Qaeda* will have leadership in the country, and soon. Remember, you are hunting for big game. A contact like this could lead you to higher levels of infiltration."

Jamal asked, "What about this Coalition Authority the U.S. wants to form? I seem to recall you weren't too optimistic about the post-invasion plans."

"The Bushies do have a plan. But the inner workings of it—let's say they're based on a lot of ifs. We think it's downright naïve. The Coalition Authority will temporarily rule the country while elections can be organized. Democracy in Iraq will not be self-discovered. We're farmin' it in, and then we're stickin' around just long enough to see if it can catch on."

"We work alone, though," said Jamal more for confirmation than clarification.

"Damn right. Don't reach out to anyone on our side. Once undercover, you will rely on everything we've taught you. I know you have good instincts that will carry you through the mission. Trust them. They will save your life. I guarantee it."

"Roger, sir. What about actively helping the coalition? Even if they are unaware I am doing so."

The major hesitated. "I know your conscience is going to want to assist our side to balance out your negative actions. Just remember the long-term goals of the program. You are sleeper agents. We're talking about one of you—when the time is right— pulling off a game seven, pinch-hit, the bottom of the ninth, walk-off grand slam that topples a terrorist organization.

Jamal shrugged his shoulders and shook his head to let the major know he hadn't a clue what he meant.

"Sorry, it's a baseball reference. I like baseball—the only pure American sport. What I said means you get to be the hero that saves the game. Or, in our case, great numbers of American lives someday."

The major sat back in his chair and let the statement have its effect.

"But spending half your time trying to win this bullshit war by helping the home team as they bumble along ... You'll run out of steam, or you'll get yourself killed. Then who'll be there to stop the next 9/11?"

Jamal groused a little, but wouldn't rule out the possibility of doing things his way once he was on his own. He hadn't come on board to be just a wanton murderer.

"Just remember this," said the major. "Whenever you think you've delved deep into their networks, you can almost assuredly delve deeper. Stay under as long as your sanity can take it. Then push yourself further. You've proven you have the tools. It's time to put them to use over there."

CHAPTER 6

A week later, Jamal used several flights on different airlines, paid for in cash under a throwaway alias to reach Khartoum, Sudan. There he received fabricated Sudanese credentials from one of the major's operatives. With the new passport, he flew to Amman, Jordan, where he boarded a bus. After enduring a sweltering, bumpy ride across the Syrian Desert, he entered Iraq at a Jordanian-controlled border crossing near Tarbil. It was imperative that no one could trace Jamal back to the United States. His cover story had him remaining in Sudan after he'd returned from Iraq at the age of ten. In order to tie off that loose end, the major had ensured all existing documentation of Jamal's involvement in the U.N. refugee relocation program disappeared for good. If the enemy gained knowledge of that experience, it would be a game-ender for him.

The stopover in Khartoum was a quick one, but his curious nature led him to do some exploring. The thriving urban scene was a strange juxtaposition of forced modernity upon dusty streets, and haphazard dwellings were everywhere, a staple of the North African built environment; corrugated metal and chipped concrete seemed to be the only alternative to steel and glass—numerous yellow cabs of various makes and models patrolled non-stop in search of fares. The heat was overwhelming, so he walked under long arcades of Moorish style arches to take advantage of the shade. He knew Iraq would be the same.

Walking those dusty streets knowing it was where he'd been conceived made him think of his mother and the Iraqi father he'd never met. She hadn't elaborated on the man very much. All Jamal knew was that he'd impregnated her while in Sudan to finalize an oil contract and left without even knowing he'd done so. Or, he just didn't care. As a boy, the details hadn't been important to Jamal, but he was always glad she never seemed ashamed of it. Somehow it made being a bastard child less painful.

She'd given birth to Jamal out of wedlock—a taboo in conservative Sudanese culture—and was disowned by her Muslim parents. On her own with an infant, she cobbled together enough money to travel to Ramadi, Iraq, the hometown of Jamal's father. But upon arrival, she learned he'd been killed in a tribal dispute, and his extended family rejected her familial claims outright, turning them away. Crestfallen and destitute, they were forced to stay in Ramadi until they saved enough money to return. Jamal never understood why it had taken so long.

Ten long years.

Now he assumed it had something to do with Hassan Barzan. Apparently, there were secrets she'd kept from Jamal, probably out of necessity. He reached under the bus seat in front of him for the canvas satchel with a long shoulder strap he'd picked up at a second-hand store in Khartoum. Inside were fake banking statements, bogus discharge papers from the Sudanese Army—a key element to his cover story—and the new passport. He took it out and looked at the photo. He was officially undercover as himself. The thought made his heart flutter.

Would he be killed? In what manner? How many would he kill in Iraq? By what methods? How many would be Americans? One thing was for sure. Right after leaving Fort Bragg he had decided he would help the coalition as much as possible, which went against the major's mission statement.

My duty and my penance at the same time.

Knowing he could balance out the brutal side of his mission by helping the coalition, and thereby the civilian populous caused less anxiety about the outcome of his soul. He peered through the dirty windshield in the front of the bus, aware that beyond the horizon were the bountiful slopes of the Euphrates and Tigris river valleys, which had sustained man for thousands of years.

And then corruption found them. Now it's destroying them. They need new forms of governance. Only the West can provide the right conditions for the people. If I can remove even some of the cancer, maybe the body will survive.

The driver pulled the overloaded bus off the side of the road adjacent to an outdoor market in Ramadi, abandoned now that the day's business had concluded. Jamal experienced the relief associated with the end of a long journey, in more ways than one. He shuffled forward down the aisle with only a suitcase, and the canvas satchel slung on his shoulder. The local mosque's call to prayer echoed over the low buildings around the depot while passengers mingled with those awaiting their arrival. Some knelt to pray in a southwesterly direction toward Mecca. Jamal joined them once outside.

He'd been the only African on the bus and had sat right in the middle, noticeably larger than the Arabs around him. The women had not lifted their gazes, a nuance of Arab culture he hadn't forgotten. He'd ignored the stares of the men, but the narrowed eyes recalled memories of his boyhood in Iraq. Like his mother, he'd been saddened by the exclusion from the Arabs due to his mixed race. Now he felt empowered before them, charged by the immediacy of his mission and the solidity of his cover. Acting like he didn't give a damn was all for good show. He needed to be like a peacock strutting around until noticed by certain people.

Dark sunglasses shaded his eyes and, therefore, his shifting gaze. He was grateful for the breathability of the ankle-length *jallibiya* he wore. Around his head, the matching cloth wrapped in traditional Sudanese style, which kept the late afternoon sun from cooking his closely cropped scalp. An elderly Arab woman nearby had to be roasting in the traditional black *abaya* and *hijab*. Alone and struggling to move her worn leather suitcase after the stifling bus ride, Jamal wanted to help her, but portraying his new persona left the good deed undone.

Once new passengers had loaded the bus, the driver ground the gears into place. The engine protested, but Jamal watched the rickety vehicle sputter down the road toward eastern Ramadi. A few inquiries led him to a simple room for rent, which he paid for through the week. The young man who took his money showed him the one-room space with a basin, bed, refrigerator, and table and chairs. The place had a smell to it. Not offensive, just old. Once Jamal settled in, he washed up in the basin and prepared to leave the room for a couple of hours. He would begin his search for Hassan in the one place they shared a common experience, Ramadi's Great Mosque. Between the powerful technical tentacles the major possessed and one fairly risky pre-invasion incursion by another of his operatives, they'd been able to determine quite a bit about the general.

Hassan Barzan came from the powerful *Dulaim* tribe with strong ties to Anbar province. He was Arab by ethnicity, Sunni Muslim by faith, and wore his Baathist political stripes with the utmost pride. Early in his military career, Hassan's official records showed above-average performance as a junior infantry officer during the Iraq/Iran war. His tribal connections and performance during that brutal contest of attrition had skyrocketed him to field-grade rank within five years. By the end of the war in 1989, he carried the rank of colonel and joined the Republican Guard.

The dossier on Hassan proved he was cut from the cloth of ruthlessness, much like his mentor, Izzat Ibrahim, the fiery, redheaded Iraqi and head of the Revolutionary Council before the recent invasion. While it had been Ibrahim who relayed Saddam's order to eliminate thousands of Iraqi Kurds at the infamous Halabja chemical attack in 1988, Hassan had made it a real crime against humanity by releasing the gas. Jamal knew his entreaties toward these men needed to be of the same quality in order to gain their trust. But he wondered if the terrible experiences of fighting Saddam's wars had made Hassan forget about him and his mother completely.

CHAPTER 7

Hassan Barzan, a large enough man himself, sat wedged between his beefy bodyguards in the back seat of the stuffy sedan. Perspiration formed on his forehead, eliciting a flashback to when he was crammed into a T-72 tank while fighting the Iranians. He was leaner at that time, his world a sardine can surrounded by threats. It felt the same these days driving around on the crowded streets of Ramadi. The real possibility that an American satellite had a bead on him made his lower spine tingle. Or was that just sweat running down his crack? He took several deep breaths to calm his rising pulse.

Soon he would be at the most secure safe house in Anbar province, the western swath of Iraq where his cells enjoyed much support. He looked forward to seeing Izzat Ibrahim, who took his orders directly from Saddam. Having fled Baghdad weeks ago, Saddam and his sons now pulled strings from hidden bunkers. Communication was becoming difficult. Hassan couldn't speculate what even the next day would bring; the power structures could shift overnight if any of the major players were snuffed out, or worse, snatched up and made to talk. He envisioned the silly deck of cards the Americans manufactured to identify ranking Baathists still on the lam, felt a measure of pride that they'd made him one of the face cards at least.

When Saddam's *Bathyoun* had melted into the population after the disbanding of the military in May, Hassan quickly established several cells in Ramadi. It hadn't played a significant part in the invasion, but soon after was occupied by a contingent of the American Army. The relatively small amount of troops sent into the restive city encouraged violence against them. However, Hassan's attacks had amounted to little more than skirmishes with light weapons against the withering firepower the Americans were capable of producing. Scores of his men had died already, yet he surmised early losses were not the reason he'd been summoned by Ibrahim today.

The vehicle entered the neighborhood of low-slung villas with walled courtyards, much less appealing than Ibrahim's estate before the war. He wondered if his mentor hated living this new life as much as he did. It wasn't too long ago they'd operated as generals should, preparing for war behind a big desk, with people at their beck and call, the look of servitude and fear in their eyes.

Now I stay in a cellar all day only to come out at night like a rat. Is that the way of a soldier?

After he mulled the thought for a minute, he begrudgingly accepted this new way as that of the patriot, and the path to secure his country back from a foreign invasion. This was the only way for him now.

It will be different from the humiliation of the elder Bush's invasion. We will wage total war from the Iraqi streets this time, and throw them back into the Saudi wasteland from where they came.

His driver pulled up to a non-descript residential compound and stopped in the middle of the high, mud-brick wall surrounding it. In the dusk hour, a heavy steel door set deep inside a stone arch was shaded, appearing darker than the earth tones of the masonry around it. It swung inward, prompting Hassan and a guard to heave their bulk out of the car. Once inside the courtyard, he heard the clang of metal fitting into place as a guard closed the door again.

Izzat Ibrahim exited the low brick dwelling, his outreached hands and broad smile a welcome sight.

"Peace be upon you," said Hassan.

"And upon you be peace," answered Ibrahim.

While the two men touched cheeks, Hassan's security detail talked in low tones outside the compound. Inside, the sound of a trickling fountain echoed off the solid walls of the courtyard. The stillness provided a sense of security that Hassan welcomed.

"How was the road from Ramadi, my friend?" asked the older of the two with tired eyes, the stress of recent days upon him. His normally freckled, pale skin was even paler, and the wiry red hair tussled. Hassan suspected he'd been sleeping before his arrival.

"We took a slow way. No checkpoints."

The statement seemed to reassure Ibrahim, who turned and offered a wry smile with his next question. "Our world has certainly changed, hasn't it?"

"I was just thinking about that on the drive, sir," said Hassan with a newfound confidence. "I am prepared to live this way—like a rat if I have to—as long as it takes to run the Americans out."

The two entered the humble dwelling. No one was inside except a pair of bodyguards whom Ibrahim dismissed. He led Hassan into a room with a table and chairs. Hassan declined a seat. Ibrahim pulled the window shades back and opened the panes to let in cooler night breezes, typical in the arid expanse of Anbar. He moved over near the table, laden with tea and all the accouterments of a connoisseur, and prepared two glasses while Hassan waited.

The ensuing interlude intrigued Hassan. His host appeared lost in thought as he dropped two cubes of sugar in the narrow, tall glasses and reached for a small spoon. Hassan fixated on the rising steam, the slow patient stirring motion of his mentor's hand. The clinking of metal on glass was the only sound in the room, amplified by the lingering question of why he'd been called here.

In a tone reserved for a man who'd made a significant concession, Ibrahim said, "We need to ally ourselves with the *takfiri*."

Ibrahim hadn't looked up from stirring the tea while Hassan processed the surprising information. In Iraqi Arabic, the word was used to describe foreign radical Islamists who had come to wage against the Western occupying forces. But Muslim fighters of all creeds had poured across the borders for weeks now, so Hassan asked for clarification and received it.

"Yes, I do mean the Sunnis who are aligned with *al Qaeda* factions," said Ibrahim. "We now share common enemies in the Coalition Authority and the new Shiite government they have spawned. But Saddam managed to isolate us. Now we fight on an island. The *takfiri* are well funded, and we'll need their contacts outside Iraq to keep us armed."

"Sir, we have underground stockpiles of our war munitions that are vast."

Ibrahim handed him the saucer and sweetened tea before he asked, "And if they are discovered during the coalition's search for weapons of mass destruction, what then?"

Hassan took a slow sip while his downward stare remained on the Persian rug at his feet, aware that Ibrahim would accept it as his answer.

"Our conventional weapons are adequate, I will give you that," said Ibrahim. "But even if they are not discovered, they are limited in their ability to inflict real damage upon the coalition, especially the Americans. We require a pipeline to more modern weaponry such as better mines to place under their routes of travel, and armor-penetrating warheads for the RPG. We need the capability to destroy an Abrams tank when it rolls in the streets of our cities. If we cannot send that message …"

Hassan wanted to give his mentor the benefit of the doubt about his line of thinking, but it seemed he'd forgotten something. He leapt on the pause before Ibrahim's stare drifted.

"We still have our Russian contacts, sir."

"No," said Ibrahim with a shake of the head that seemed predetermined as well.

"They are being watched like hawks because of their objection to Bush's invasion. And I'm not so sure they will keep that position over the length of this conflict."

"And what of our Shiite cousins? Or the Kurds?" asked Hassan, his voice edging up. "Can we bend our pride and call for unity in the name of Iraq?"

Hassan didn't know why he'd even asked because he knew none of those possibilities would happen; the Baathists were on their own as far as most Iraqis were concerned. He wasn't worried about the reaction itself. He could be brash once in a while with the man before him when it was clear they were caught in a moment of commiseration. This seemed to be one of those moments. Ibrahim either let the comment slide completely or had slipped into his thoughts again. When he spoke, his tone was firm, and in the end, convincing for Hassan.

"No, my friend. We must reach out to the *takfiri* within the next week before they get acclimated to this war zone."

"It will be hard to trust them. Their agenda is-"

"Overarching," said Ibrahim, finishing the thought for him. "I know. Bigger than Iraq. For certain more popular outside this country than our cause, my friend. But the Islamists are committed to establishing a footprint here at this time. We will help them and benefit from the use of their supply lines."

"I will take the lead, sir. Who do we contact?" asked Hassan, consenting to this new directive.

"Tomorrow there will be a representative in Fallujah from a new organization, led by a Jordanian who fled Afghanistan with many fighters in tow. They will need outposts in the capital and here in Anbar province."

"I apologize for my insolence," said Hassan, displeased at his short-lived attempt to rise to the occasion. "I have to learn to accept this type of warfare better. It is the lot we have drawn after all."

Ibrahim nodded. He sat on one of the chairs, leaned forward, and reunited the glass of tea with its saucer on the table. "Speak to Rashid outside for the particulars of the meeting."

Hassan knew it was time to leave. "I will not let you down, sir." He snapped off a crisp salute. The older soldier returned it while seated. A bout of weakness seemingly came over him now that he'd given the orders. Hassan knew he required specific specialized medical treatment for diabetes that he was likely not receiving.

"Sir, if there is anything I can—"

"No," said Ibrahim, suddenly steeling himself. He rose and walked with Hassan down the hall. When they reached the door, Ibrahim turned to his protégé. "I have faith you will be a good host to the *takfiri* and see the bigger picture."

"I will do what is necessary," said Hassan. "Goodbye, sir."

He opened the door and peered into the empty courtyard. While he lit a cigarette, the steel door at the wall swung on its rusty hinges again, his cue.

Moments later, Izzat Ibrahim watched his obese general trod heavily across the courtyard. The big man dabbed a handkerchief on his broad forehead with one hand, flicked ash to the ground with the other. He wondered if Hassan would be able to manage this kind of war. He closed his eyes and remembered the revolution in 1958 when he and Saddam were at the bottom of the ladder of power. It was a bloodletting like he'd never imagined. How had they survived it? But they had somehow. Now the entire Baathist movement rested on their shoulders—his shoulders really—and men like Hassan.

CHAPTER 8

Jamal left the rented room and moved through the streets. He noticed they were not as rough-hewn as they used to be. Everything was different. Better now. Low buildings made of cheap materials had been replaced by larger ones made of steel and glass, while not impressing him with their aesthetics. It seemed Saddam had encouraged enterprise, at least. Billboards were more prevalent these days too, advertising a plethora of Western products.

As a boy, he and his mother had shared a tiny apartment in a diverse neighborhood where the one commonality was poverty. Jamal recalled the ever-present hunger. He was hungry now, in fact, and realized he hadn't eaten since boarding the bus in Jordan. Forgotten aromas catalyzed a wave of nostalgia as he walked along a row of food vendors. Packed into their stalls, they barked at passersby to taste their products. The smell of cooking lamb put him over the edge. He entered a hole-in-the-wall eatery with just two small tables and a countertop, behind which stood the proprietor. Nearby, a cook shaved meat off a rotisserie, but something sizzling alight in a skillet quickly grabbed the man's attention.

Jamal ordered *lahm b' ajeena*. After eating four of the small round pieces of flatbread with chopped meat and onions spread over the top, he'd barely put a dent in his hunger, so he returned to the counter. Over three kebabs and a plate of saffron rice, he planned his next move. Besides Hassan himself, his best option was to make contact with one of the quarter-million disbanded

Iraqi soldiers and their former paymasters who now sat home out of work.

What does a man like that do regardless of culture or creed? He congregates with men of his ilk — other pissed off soldiers.

He heard mention of a curfew imposed by the coalition. It meant barricades would go up, and many streets would close for the night. The mosque would be open, though.

He'd barely completed the thought when a boyhood memory flashed before his mind's eye—specifically, the one he'd recalled when he first met the major. Hassan walked just ahead of him, while the Great Mosque loomed in the foreground. This time the memory was extended, and Jamal saw Hassan greet several men who stood around tables near the street. An outdoor café, perhaps? They seemed subservient, suggesting he was their superior, and the setting indicated a gathering near the mosque. After attending evening prayers he would investigate with the understanding that this might take some time and effort. Hassan wasn't going to present himself and make it easy for him.

An hour later, after leaving the mosque with no leads, he searched the area near the massive compound for any cafes that seemed familiar. After passing several establishments that did not ring the bell of familiarity, he found a café which did strike a chord once he'd passed it, turned around, and approached it from the other direction. Finally, the dim outline of the mosque's high minaret matched his memory.

Plastic chairs were stacked and chained to the metal security gate protecting the storefront after hours. He planned to return the following day and see the kind of people who frequent it these days, more than fifteen years since he'd been there with Hassan. For now, he was content with his efforts but exhausted. He needed sleep.

Within the hour, he lay on the bed in the rented room, displeased that the mattress was too short and paper-thin, but his body relished the horizontal position, and he readied himself for his first night in Iraq. He wished he had his Bible to read, a bedtime habit of his. Despite risks to his cover, he knew he needed to stay grounded in The Word to face the evil with which he was about to sojourn. He decided he would keep one hidden upon the premises. Many verses were in his head, though. He'd prepared himself that way, and in the quiet of the room, he recited his favorite stanzas of the Eighteenth Psalm.

> *I will love you, O Lord, my strength.*
> *The Lord is my rock and my fortress and my deliverer;*
> *My God, my strength, in whom I will trust;*
> *My shield and the horn of my salvation, my stronghold.*
> *I will call upon the Lord, who is worthy to be praised;*
> *So shall I be saved from my enemies.*
>
> *I have pursued my enemies and overtaken them;*
> *Neither did I turn back again till they were destroyed.*
> *I have wounded them,*
> *So that they could not rise;*
> *They have fallen under my feet.*
> *For you have armed me with the strength for battle.*

Staring at the ceiling lasted a short while until his eyes grew heavy. Once the light was out, he was adrift in minutes.

The next morning at the café, Jamal chose one of the plastic tables near the noisy street and did some people watching. Only one pair of patrons drew his interest as they sat bent over a table in quiet discussion.

Something about the fleshy-faced one. The haircut looks military. Old habits, maybe.

The boots of the man's companion, who sat with his back turned toward Jamal, had new dirt on the soles that he'd tracked across the proprietor's floor. Jamal wondered if the man had been out digging holes for roadside bombs already today.

A teenage boy came over to take his order. After the customary salutations, Jamal learned some history of the place by being friendly with him. Jamal spoke the local dialect of Arabic with perfection, the first form of speech he'd ever known.

"So boy, do you work for the family, or is this a job you found on your own?"

"This is my father's place. I am grateful to help the family."

"Spoken like a good son."

The brief conversation drew the interest of his father as Jamal had hoped, a thin Arab with thick eyebrows who finished wiping a table down and came over to stand next to his son.

With a wary smile, he said, "Good morning. What can we do for you? Any tea you like here, hot or cold. Chai tea? Perhaps some sweet tea? Very sweet, very strong. It is the finest you will find in Ramadi."

Jamal nodded toward the man. "Then I will have some. Do you own this establishment?"

"Yes. Like my father before me. Hopefully, we will survive this war, and my son will brew the tea someday." With that, he mussed the kid's hair and sent him to prepare the order.

"Your father was the owner at the beginning of Saddam's reign?"

The café owner instinctually shrank in stature at the mere mention of the tyrant's name, a common reaction for the typical Iraqi citizen during the years when Hussein had his thumb on them.

"Yes," answered the proprietor with a furtive glance around. "He had the advantage of knowing influential people in the military. They looked out for him."

Jamal felt like he'd struck gold.

He made sure the two quiet men could hear his next words. "I only ask because I have been here before, long ago, when I was a boy. I lived in Ramadi for some years. It was through a military man named Barzan that I came to know this place and the Great Mosque."

He gestured toward the compound at his back. Jamal had spoken to the proprietor, but his peripheral vision indicated the fleshy-faced man had turned his head at the comment, just a twitch.

The proprietor asked, "Why have you come now? I fear we have not seen the worst of this war yet. And what I have seen has been enough."

Jamal held the gaze and set his jaw at once, a pose for effect if there ever was one. He felt like an actor on opening night, saddled with the vulnerable feeling of not knowing how believable he was to others. He looked around to appear cautious before dropping his only baited line for the day. This kind of fishing required patience.

"Let's just say I detest American troops patrolling the town in which I was raised." He leaned across the table and lowered his voice. "This city belongs to the *Bathyoun*."

The conversation continued until the son arrived with a tray, prompting the owner to nod approvingly at Jamal's comments. He shifted his attention to several new customers who'd come in off the street. The boy performed the tea service in silence while Jamal planned his next moves.

Drink this tea and then move out. See if any of these guys are curious.

He planned to replicate this very performance many times over the following days, in different settings and different neighborhoods, until he drew a reaction. He'd drop Hassan's name next in the Mulaab district, a Sunni bastion known for its strong support of the Hussein regime, and a likely location for insurgents to establish themselves.

After leaving the café, he blended into a gathering crowd near a row of vendors. Potential buyers crouched before a sea of hand-carved trinkets laid out on Persian rugs. Jamal nudged himself up to the front, knelt to disguise his height before gazing back through the crowd. He was just able to see the café owner summoned by the two questionable men.

The owner shuffled over quickly, and the fleshy-faced patron began a line of questioning that seemed amicable. There were no nods toward the table he'd occupied, or fingers pointed in the direction he'd headed. He decided he hadn't piqued their interest, and the café owner didn't seem like the militant type, so he resigned himself to work ahead. His training reminded him he should record some notes about the café in a ledger he'd carry at all times. He would use a form of encryption he'd learned from the Cherokee trackers, something no Arab could ever decipher.

Why would I think it would happen so fast, based on a boyhood memory? And a vague one at that.

Jamal smiled in self-admonishment and turned to face the turban-wearing, dentally-challenged vendor who waited to initiate the most cherished of Arab traditions; the art of haggling. The array of hand-carved objects made from wood, stone, or ivory offered many choices. A small talisman carved out of acacia wood caught his eye. It was the size of a large coin and only a little thicker, showing a scowling face. The eyes were punched holes that went through to the other side but appeared evil due to the expert carving around them.

Jamal picked it up and flipped it over. The face on the other side was a grimace, with the same holes for eyes. This time they exhibited mirth. He thought it might be a good symbol of his duplicitous life, so a short negotiation ensued with the jabbering vendor. Jamal paid in *dinar*, the Iraqi currency, which was becoming more and more worthless by the week. He pocketed the talisman and moved away from the gaggle of vendors and buyers. There was work to do studying the outposts set up by the Americans in the city.

Over the coming weeks, Jamal maintained the same routine. Every day he would eat a simple meal of bread, fruit, meat, and coffee (Sometimes he made eggs on a hot plate he'd purchased), go out and make himself visible in the city's neighborhoods, meet people, badmouth the coalition, talk up the former regime, drop Barzan's name when it seemed feasible without sounding forced, study American outposts from various vantage points, note the changes in personnel, establish duty shifts, watch their tendencies, pack up, eat dinner, go to the rented room, sleep, do it again. Jamal bought more clothes for different kinds of trolling. Sometimes he wore Western attire. Other times it was the linen *jallibiya* or a flowing Arab *dish-dash* with a headscarf called a *khafiyya* if he wanted to be more of an observer than the observed. When he was visible, he started to feel the stares penetrate more deeply. It didn't bother him. He wasn't a scared, out of place child anymore. The stares meant he was doing his job.

PART TWO

CHAPTER 9

Two Iraqi men stood before the open hood of a Volvo sedan. Next to them was a vacant, garbage-strewn lot. One man, taller, with the lean build of an athlete, bent over the engine with a wrench in hand. The smaller, skinnier one with a boyish face stood off to the side, holding a rag and a screwdriver. Every minute or so, the skinny one gazed across the lot toward a row of simple rooms for rent.

"So, what have you noticed about this foreigner?" asked the taller man.

"I've been following him for the last few days. He has a few routines, and he is mentioning Hassan's name around town."

"Could be a lure for coalition intelligence," said the taller man in a cautionary tone.

"It's possible, but why an African?"

Ahmed backed away from the engine and walked to the driver's seat. "Hassan has some connection with him from his past."

This surprised Fahim. He hadn't been told that when he was ordered to stake out the rented room. He watched Ahmed pretend to start the ignition to no avail and subsequently return to the front of the vehicle.

"How from his past?"

Ahmed shrugged. "I don't know. Since Hassan is my uncle, I have known him my whole life. I do not recall him mingling with non-Arabs."

"What if he slept with some *abed* (derogatory) whore after one of his victories in battle, and this is his bastard son?"

"Is that how you speak about your general, Fahim?"

Hassan was a known womanizer among the men who served with him, which explained the even tone of Ahmed's rebuke. Yet Fahim knew the rebuke had been more severe than not. Aside from Fahim's father, who was now dead, Ahmed was the most serious person he knew. Maybe that was why he had taken to Ahmed's leadership style and had begun to shadow him as much as possible during daily operations of the cell, itself part of the broader resistance under Hassan's command.

"I was only kidding," said Fahim with his trademark smirk and grin. "It's none of my business. I'm just supposed to follow him and report his doings. Here he goes now."

Fahim nodded toward the rented room, seventy-five yards away across the empty lot.

Ahmed tilted his head slightly and gazed in that direction. "That's one big African."

"That's what I thought when I saw him the other day. He's wearing traditional Arab clothing today. Probably means he's heading into one of the neighborhoods to ask more questions. The other day when he was around the 'Green Zone,' he wore Western style clothing. And he's not shy wherever he goes. What do you think he wants by using Hassan's name?" asked Fahim.

"It depends on how much truth there is to this shared history. He may want to help the cause. If it's true, Hassan will likely bring him in to hear him out, maybe even today. I'd be curious to sit in on that meeting, but he won't let it happen."

"Why?"

Ahmed chuckled. "In case what you suggested is true."

Fahim was relieved to be off the hook for his off-putting remark about Hassan. Still, he knew he needed to work on zipping his lip and cracking his jokes at more opportune times. He was a soldier now, and serious-minded men like Ahmed would not put up with his pedantic ways forever. Then again, forever wasn't part of his vocabulary anymore.

Since the death of his family at the onset of the war, he'd felt a deepening urge to join them. His sense of loss was so great that on some days, he could not get out of bed to face the war that had altered the course of his life. Unless he thought it might all end that day in a hail of bullets. He'd imagined it happening a dozen different ways. Each time he checked out of this world performing some act of bravery. How it happened was less important than the statement that would be attached to his death—one of defiance against a foreign invader.

He watched the African stride toward the broader avenue that led to the Mulaab district. He had developed a curiosity about his intentions. "And what if he's something else?"

"He'll be dead before the week is out."

"Come on," said Ahmed, pushing down the Volvo's hood with a bang before the two of them began to follow the big African on foot.

One evening a few weeks after his arrival in Ramadi, worn out from trolling days on end, Jamal fell asleep in his clothes on top of the mattress he'd come to loathe. He slept soundly until a noise outside his cracked and dirty window stirred him. Before he could react, the door was forced open and two men burst inside. It appeared his hard work had paid off.

Jamal had the hand-fighting skills and instincts to make his assailants regret the illegal entry, but there was nothing to prove yet. A piece of duct tape was slapped over his mouth before he could rise to the edge of the bed. Jamal mumbled some gibberish into the tape for effect and put up a token defense.

The second man through the door produced a black cloth hood and roughly covered Jamal's head while a pair of hands bound his wrists with plastic flex cuffs, which zipped and tightened. He suppressed a grunt of pain and resigned himself to go along for the ride. They manhandled him outside and into a waiting vehicle. Doors slammed, and tires pealed as the car roared down the lane along the row of rented rooms, skidded around the corner, and tore out onto the main road.

Jamal was between two men in the back seat. The barrel of a handgun compressed his right rib cage. Still, his captors, whose body odor was strong enough to penetrate the hood he wore, said nothing. The driver wheeled around a long curve in the road and accelerated through the turn. A lengthy straightaway confirmed what Jamal remembered seeing on a map. They headed toward the edge of town near an industrial core with many large buildings. If his memory served him correctly, it wasn't more than a ten-minute walk from the place he'd lived as a child.

Jamal mumbled some more and fidgeted in the seat, a show of distress he could afford putting on since he knew where he was at the moment. There was no response except a nudge of the gun's muzzle. Jamal was motionless again, using the stillness to cipher the ensuing turns and changes in speed. The drive was over soon, however. Sounds from outside suddenly came in from his front left, indicating the driver's window was being lowered.

A stern voice asked in Arabic, "Is this him?"

"Yes, we just grabbed him," said the driver.

"Take him around to the back. We need to get him ready first."

Jamal's pulse quickened at the words. The driver pulled away slowly and turned down a bumpier, gravelly sounding road, most likely an alley or drive. When the vehicle stopped, he was roughly handled out of the car and led inside a building where he smelled cooked food. Muffled voices indicated others were present but located in other rooms. He has shuffled along until someone in front of him spoke.

"You," said the voice to someone nearby. "Put him in here."

Jamal heard the mechanical sound of a heavy latch operating. He was pushed through what he guessed was another door and listened to a single pair of footsteps follow. The same door with the heavy latch was abruptly shut behind them.

"Turn around," ordered a voice in Arabic. Jamal felt the presence of the person close to him as the bonds loosened.

With his captive's hands free, the person pulled off the hood and quickly stepped back again. Jamal saw the fighter was armed with a version of the Kalashnikov assault rifle (AK); it was developed during the Second World War by its Russian namesake but had gone through numerous iterations of advancement since that time. Its many varieties remain the most common and battle-tested weapon worldwide outside of Western militaries. Not too many people still carried an original AK-47. This fighter's appeared to be the more recent AKM, and presently it was pointed at Jamal's chest.

The slightly built Iraqi possessed smooth olive skin that went with his boyish looks. The kid appeared to be less than twenty years old. Jamal got the sense he had grown up fast, displaying just a hint of adolescent fascination over the situation. A boy who was rushing toward manhood in a war zone, no doubt. He motioned for Jamal to remove the tape from his mouth.

Jamal did so and immediately yelled, "What is the meaning of this?"

"You will meet a man soon who will tell you," said the young fighter. "He will decide your fate, depending on your answers, which I advise to be truthful."

Regardless of his adolescence, the fighter did not exhibit fear of being in a room alone with an angry man who had nearly a hundred pounds on him, gun or no gun.

"I have nothing to hide. I've come to Iraq—to my birthplace—of my own free will. I have done nothing wrong!"

"Well, we will see about that."

After a knock on the door interrupted their brief conversation, the fighter left Jamal alone. For the first time, he stirred with uneasiness. Was this the beginning, or was it all going to end right here with a bullet to the head out in the alley? Looking around, he determined he was in a dry goods storage pantry, figured the building must be a residence.

A safe house. Or maybe a place for interrogations or torture.

Soon the locking mechanism worked again, and the door swung open. The same young fighter waved his rifle in a sweeping motion to one side, meaning Jamal was to exit the makeshift cell and lead the way. He complied once more, took it as a positive sign that they'd left him unbound with only one guard during transport. Perhaps this was a test.

They moved through a long hall, passing several rooms on either side along the way. Through the open doorways, he saw men who sorted ammunition, cleaned weapons, and packed equipment; soldiers' tasks done by individuals who were not soldiers anymore, who'd lost that status. This was the Baathist led insurgency, the *Bathyoun*, and he was about to meet his mark.

The end of the hall opened into a formal sitting room. Over by the window stood a large man who gazed into the night sky. He wore a rumpled dark blazer and dark suit pants. The guard stood behind Jamal while they waited for the man to acknowledge their presence. The interlude was agonizing. When Hassan Barzan did turn, Jamal saw a stony face and was crestfallen. He had the sinking feeling his concerns about whether Hassan would remember him were accurate. If so, Jamal knew he needed to play this well to survive the encounter.

"Have a seat," said Hassan curtly.

There was no inviting hand gesture toward either of the empty chairs in the center of the room, set on opposite sides of a small table. Jamal sat down and waited for Hassan to place his girth on the other one. After he did so, the big man reached into the inner breast pocket of his blazer, producing a thin yellowish cigarette and book of matches.

On a corner table behind Hassan, the dim glow of a single lamp partially lit the room and caused his face to appear mostly in shadow. The igniting of the sulfur showed paunchy eyes, and the stubble that grew high up on his cheeks resembled so many ants moving by the light of the flickering flame. Hassan's face was shrouded as he exhaled his first drag. When the wisps began to diminish, it was those eyes that penetrated the smoke before boring into Jamal.

With no inflection on any single word, he asked, "Why are you here?"

"I came to find you. When I left Iraq, you were a captain. The army has been good to you, it seems."

"I have been good for the army and the party. We have both suited each other well. Tell me, how did you know how to find me?"

"I thought you might regroup here after the capital fell. A photo of you with my mother in Ramadi was the only thread I had to go off. I have it with me if-"

Hassan waved off the offer. "I have some of my own. Your mother was very photogenic. But it has been a long time. Why, after all of these years? Why now in this time of war? You raise suspicion, you know."

"Because I am part Arab, part Iraqi. It's why I am here. I came to fight the occupiers. Surely you can help in that regard."

Hassan nodded. "And your mother?"

"She died years ago."

Hassan did not request any elaboration, catalyzing a sense of vulnerability that put Jamal on edge. After what appeared to be a moment of reflection, Hassan said, "She was a good woman. Strong."

"I'm glad you remember her."

Hassan gave a strange look and then sat back, dragging on his Gauloise, making Jamal question his next move. Maybe it was a sore subject.

Hassan said, "I remember you stuck out like a sore thumb. Because you are not, or do not look Arab. I felt sorry for you."

He turned away and exhaled a billow of cigarette smoke, remembrance seeming to pour in. When those eyes came back to Jamal, he said, "Your father died when she was pregnant. He probably never knew."

Jamal nodded at the possibility. "You met my mother after we had been on our own for a few years. I believe I was four years old. I barely remember. But I remember us being at the mosque."

It was Hassan's turn to nod in the affirmative before filling in some more details. "I took you to a few places, including the mosque. I tried to put some meat on your bones too. You were a reed of a kid. I'm glad to see you filled out over the years."

He hadn't said it with a level of warmth that indicated total acceptance, but Jamal was ecstatic the man before him remembered. The major had intended to provide a seamless and believable life story, which combined real memories Hassan would accept as accurate, and the fabricated cover life Jamal wanted him to take as accurate. This was supposed to create a psychological edge toward trusting Jamal enough to let him enter the ranks of the insurgency. Right now, that edge felt razor thin.

Jamal said, "After you left Ramadi to fight the Iranians, our lives fell into a downward spiral. We moved around for several years, before my mother and I left the country and returned to Sudan. It was better among our own people. But she died when I was still young. I was taken in by various organizations until old enough to join the Sudanese army."

This last bit of information seemed to pique Hassan's interest finally. Jamal sensed he was heading in the right direction.

"You are a soldier?"

"Was a soldier. I left the service to try some business endeavors."

"What were you trained in?"

"Small unit tactics and border security. I was a non-commissioned officer when I left last year. I gained experience fighting rebels within our borders."

As Jamal espoused his bogus qualifications for a few more minutes, he assessed the man before him. Although Jamal learned much about Hassan Barzan prior to Jamal's insertion, he'd always known that to understand the man himself—especially the one fighting a non-conventional war for the first time in his career—Jamal would need to eye Hassan up close; the internal levers of persuasion would need to be discerned on the job. For this reason, the major had taught all his agents how to accurately profile the numerous characters they would encounter along the way.

It was telling when Hassan made him and the guard wait upon entering the room earlier. The brief interlude created when he took his time lighting a cigarette built tension. It meant he enjoyed making people squirm under his authority. That tendency is the calling card of an insecure person, of someone who uses his stature as his psychological tool. Jamal sensed that Hassan was used to others stroking his ego and decided to bait his hook with fealty.

When the moment seemed right, he said, "General, it would be my honor to serve at your side …"

Afterward, he was led to a room that was a step up from the locked pantry. The small, windowless chamber with a cot and basin for washing was a welcome sight because it meant he was clearing hurdles. Their wanting to improve his comfort level was a promising sign. When the door was closed, he sat on the cot to clear his mind, adjusted to all the new variables. Five minutes passed before the door opened. A wash towel and bar of soap were placed on the floor, and he was told to prepare for a communal meal.

Jamal entered after Hassan. The room was long and narrow, crowded, and thick with the smell of cigarette smoke and cooked meat. A dozen or more hard-looking men turned to him. Many wore traditional robes with turbans; a few wore military clothing or the knock-off version of it. Jamal counted five who'd chosen not to reveal their identities to this newcomer and had tied a *khafiyya* around their faces below the eyes.

The men ceased their disparate conversations and began the ingrained, upward show of respect for the general; this time halted prematurely by a gesture from Hassan. They recoiled into the customary cross-legged style on their individual cushions. Each of these was placed around the long, linen-covered mat upon which the food dishes lay. Two empty cushions remained, one at each end of the spread. Hassan's bulk flattened the cushion nearest the door, and when Jamal was the only one left standing in the room, the stares were upon him, penetrating like never before. Their leader gave a simple nod, which prompted the men to make way for Jamal along one side.

He sat cross-legged like the others, making sure the soles of his feet did not touch the food mat, a grave insult. So many images flashed behind the blink of an eye. The major, the other agents, and the nightmarish training were all there at once. It was a needed affirmation of how he'd arrived at this place. He raised his head and received the stares with steely confidence.

"Good evening. Thank you for inviting me into your presence."

"Good evening to you as well," said a few men in the room.

Hassan said, "Please forgive our light meal. One of our supply stores was raided yesterday, and we are a little short on lamb."

Once an elder recited the pre-meal prayers, Jamal watched the men stab at meager portions of meat, chewing slowly, some of them in silence. He sensed the tension in the air from recent fighting. With this in mind, he knew even the idea of this interview was a distraction to some of them.

When the plate of meat reached him, he took the smallest piece remaining, made sure to use the right hand, another Arab custom. The small portion didn't go unnoticed by the man adjacent to him, prompting what seemed like a nod of respect. Jamal returned the gesture and passed the plate.

The man spoke to the group at large. "It seems our new friend either eats like a bird for his size or he is offended by the smell of our lamb."

The comment had not come American style, reassuring, with a wink, a smile, or a clap on the shoulder. It was delivered off-hand with only a touch of sarcasm. Few others found the humor, so Jamal felt awkward. Most likely just another little test, he figured.

"I am prepared to lose a few pounds in the fight against the Westerners. But for this meal, I am grateful. I have been eating off a hot plate for most of a month," he said.

The coyness among the others sparked a few grins and chuckles in return, and most of the men seemed to accept his statement. Traditional Arab males aren't the best at fending for themselves.

Jamal learned the others were Hassan's lieutenants—the leaders of the cells that made up the resistance in Anbar province.

Their collective goal was simple; stifle the tenacious heartbeat of democracy. Soon it became clear this gathering was indeed a second interview, this time led by the subordinates. Did it mean he'd cleared Hassan? He couldn't tell. Hassan sat unengaged from the happenings in the room, seemingly unaffected one way or the other by Jamal's answers. He continued to eat more than his hungry men—which Jamal found curious—while the lieutenants drilled Jamal on general military knowledge. The questions were barely a challenge, but he played it off well, not displaying his substantial knowledge base, which would make him overqualified as someone only looking to join the fight.

He was glad the mission called for entry-level at this point. Gunning for more responsibility initially would call for real-time credentials that the major would have a difficult time establishing within the cover story. Raw talent, however, needs no credentials. It just makes itself available, and the recipients eat it up.

After twenty minutes of questions, most of the lieutenants seemed impressed with Jamal's knowledge of small unit tactics. He gained the sense he'd passed the interview. One of the masked men even removed his facial covering and gave Jamal a nod of respect. Because of the near impossibility of training new men while under the watchful eye of Western intelligence services, Jamal guessed readymade soldiers would have a leg up in this vetting process over the months and years ahead. He learned that many men in the room had come to the meeting with a need for reinforcements already, in fact. Most of them shifted their attention to Hassan at the other end of the room once Jamal answered their questions.

Only a couple of the lieutenants—one young and eager, the other of middle age with a reticent look about him anyway—continued to press Jamal, expressing doubts about his usefulness to the cause. Born here, yes, they agreed. But for all intents and purposes, a foreigner who was not involved in the recent fighting. Nor did he have any Baathist loyalties.

The eager one was named Masoud. He sat two spots down from the man to whom Jamal had passed the lamb. He was handsome enough with a neatly trimmed goatee but wore a chip on his shoulder that grated on Jamal like a sharp stone to the forehead. He wouldn't let up with his insulting questions, which became more and more personal. Jamal tried not to show impatience, accepting there were still some doubters he needed to assuage. Before he could attempt to do so, Masoud stood up to speak before the group.

"General, if this mere foot soldier is to fill our ranks, why have we convened in this way? I have Marines patrolling in my sector as we speak. You have my approval, sir, if that is what you seek. But I will pass on his services if it will allow me to take my leave at this time. I am certain one of my peers could find a use for him," he said as he glared at Jamal. "We all have trash to take out."

Jamal knew a bigot when he saw one—and he'd bear ignorance and old stereotypes any day over unsettling thoughts about his cover being in jeopardy. He could tell Hassan was about to say something, perhaps stick up for him, because the big man seemed non-plussed at Masoud's outburst. Jamal decided a little feigned eagerness on his part would help in this situation. He dialed up a more passionate redux of what he'd said to Hassan earlier, glad the major had included acting lessons as part of the training.

"I can be useful!" he shouted over everyone. He stretched his frame, which put him a head above the rest, clenched his teeth and fists at once.

His brows were arched high above widened eyes. "I've come here to fight! … To drive the invaders out. This is Arab land, and I have Arab blood in me!"

He calmed himself visibly, took a moment to make eye contact with everyone because everyone certainly looked at him.

"I will be more than useful. Just give me a chance to show you."

A few of the men found humor in the passionate outburst from the newcomer, as evidenced by their low chuckles, but it seemed to Jamal that most had given credence to what he'd said. Masoud's sour expression told something entirely different.

"Then it is decided," said Hassan. "Jamal Muhammad will join Masoud's cell."

Masoud stared aghast at the general, who displayed the calm gaze of someone who would not be questioned. Snickering from the men at Masoud's expense lifted Jamal out of the moment. He glanced at his antagonist. The narrowing of Masoud's eyes meant this wasn't over.

The others became visibly antsy. The reason for the meeting was behind them, the sidebars with Hassan complete. Outside these walls waited numerous unpleasant possibilities for each of them as hunted men, and gathering in numbers was unsafe. Hassan was the first to stand, taking a position by the door to deliver a personal salutation to each man as he left.

They exchanged embraces as they waited for their turn before the general. There was a sullen tone in the small space, low talking among brothers in arms who feared never seeing each other again. Which ones will not make it back to this place of gathering? Always the question when soldiers depart from one another. Jamal saw one of them rib Masoud while another commented on the young leader's overplayed hand. The resulting laughter caused Jamal to feel awkward again as the catalyst.

Hassan noticed the situation and moved to end it. "Masoud, who better to send him with than the one who questions him the most. I am sure you will leave no stone unturned in finding out if he will be useful to our cause." More chiding laughter ensued, this time louder.

Being the last man in line, Jamal studied the general while he spoke personally to each of his men, inquiring as to the health and well-being of his family if he had one, perhaps a friendly sentiment about a lost man, among other gestures of good leadership. After the customary touching of the cheeks three times and a man's embrace, he would turn to the next lieutenant. Jamal was puzzled. Previously, the man had exhibited boorish leadership qualities in Jamal's mind. But by all accounts, Hassan had the unquestioned loyalty of the men below him. What Jamal witnessed now was the type of moxie that made subordinates do more than they ever thought they would or could for their leader.

Jamal stored the information regarding Hassan's complex character for later and approached him when it was only the two of them left in the room. Hassan moved to close the door partially.

"So you are anxious to fight with us," he said with a clap to Jamal's meaty shoulder as he leaned in. Jamal was surprised to smell alcohol on his breath, even though he did not seem affected.

"Yes, sir," he answered, using the formality because it appeared he'd just gained a new commander.

But Hassan surprised him, heading off the need for it with a raised hand before Jamal. "You will call me Hassan. Even though we are all civilians now, these men know me from our former lives as military men. They will never see me as anything but their general. I knew you as a child, knew your mother for a time. She helped me then. Now her son is a man. We will address each other as such, and we will fight together."

"Thank you, Hassan. You will not be disappointed."

Hassan stepped back and seemed to relax in his stance, almost slumping with sudden weariness. He reached into his breast pocket for the cigarettes and involuntarily offered one to Jamal, who declined. A flick of the wrist with the soft pack in his hand produced the filtered ends of several. He pinched one out and began the process of lighting it as Jamal waited.

"As far as Masoud, he is my most … energetic of the cell leaders," said Hassan through the thickest part of an exhale before the rest billowed forth from his wide nostrils. I need to keep a tight leash on him. He runs my operations out of the Askan neighborhood on the eastern side of town. I often summon him to coordinate, more so than the others. Maybe you should come sometime."

"It would be my honor." It seemed Hassan had warmed up to him, the weariness hiding any pretense.

Hard to fake exhaustion, tired eyes. He's been on the run a lot. It's beginning to show. Give him whatever he wants and trust the cover. But how the hell did my mother help out a captain in the Republican Guard, enough to buy me a ticket into the most dangerous club in Iraq? Dying to know, but it's not essential, not now. He's buying in.

"Do not worry about Masoud," said Hassan. "And do not worry about his icy stares. I saw them. He doesn't like the color of your skin. That is all." Hassan pinched Jamal's cheek. "It is good that you are here, I think." He pulled Jamal close to touch cheeks customarily.

Jamal endured the pungent cigarette smoke that Hassan breathed as much as air. Being this close to him brought back the memory of the big man pressing against his mother. He imagined she'd tolerated his odorous breath many times, for reasons he could only guess. Jamal would learn to endure it for his purposes.

After the ritual concluded, the two moved down the long hall past the rooms with fighters at work. Jamal felt like a mafia member who'd just been kissed by the don. But he knew he wasn't made yet. That test was yet to come.

CHAPTER 10

Jamal raised the binoculars toward the squad of U.S. Army National Guardsmen. The Americans had manned this hastily built checkpoint near Ramadi's city center since the beginning of June. Jamal had noted their shoulder patches on an earlier reconnaissance job and later Googled the unit designation. They were members of the Fourth Battalion/131st Infantry Regiment, nicknamed the Hurricane Battalion.

Just a bunch of kids from Florida.

He stood by a window on the third floor of an office building, abandoned this morning when Masoud made the workers leave to gain use of their space. The cell leader had pistol-whipped the lone protester, who quickly submitted while co-workers looked on in horror, none of them brave enough to resist the brazen Iraqi-on-Iraqi violence.

Jamal switched his focus to the video equipment next to him, checked unnecessarily a half-dozen times in the last minute. It was a long minute to be sure as he waited for Masoud's attack to commence. It was clear why the Americans had chosen these two intersecting roads for the checkpoint. The soldiers manning it could view both avenues at all times. Theoretically, this would minimize enemy attempts to lay improvised explosive devices along these routes, which were used to move fuel convoys through the city.

Jamal needed to hide his nervousness for the Americans' well being because he was not alone in the office space. Behind him were two others. The guard who'd paraded him around the safe house still shadowed his every move daily, a direct order from Masoud. The guard's name was Fahim. He was the youngest of the fighters in Hassan's network and had joined the ranks of the Republican Guard at seventeen, one year before the war's onset. Jamal had learned from another junior fighter that Fahim mourned for his parents and a younger sister, all of whom had been killed on the first day of the war by an errant coalition smart bomb. Despite Masoud's mandate to keep a watchful eye on Jamal at all times, with each passing day, Fahim's level of distrust had appeared to diminish as he got to know Jamal. This allowed his sense of humor to emerge, and Jamal had even begun to take a liking to the kid.

The other man in the room, Ahmed, was an Iraqi from Fallujah and a member of the same clan as Hassan, itself part of the larger *Dulaim* tribe of Anbar province. Nearly everyone comprising Hassan's inner circle was from the same clan, except Masoud. Ahmed frequently used his familial status as leverage against Masoud's authority within the cell, Jamal had noticed. The friction between the two men was palpable, and Jamal could tell Masoud felt threatened by Ahmed. He assumed it wasn't just the tribal ties, though. Ahmed had more of a presence about him; he was larger than most Arabs, standing over six feet tall, and possessing natural leadership skills. When the two of them walked into a room together, it was Ahmed people were drawn to, not Masoud.

During his short time in the cell, Jamal had learned much about the reasons these men were fighting. He'd begun to understand that this war was not just about regaining lost national political power for the Baathists; the Baathist movement was a relatively new development, representing a mere sliver of time in a long line of Arab power brokers. It was Anbar province for which the clans fought. This made sense to Jamal, considering he'd met fighters from Hassan's clan who could trace their roots ten generations back when the banks of the Euphrates were lusher and less cluttered by oil-driven industry.

Nervousness caused Jamal to look at his new cell phone. It was almost time. He checked the camera once again. He'd been given the lowly job, he assumed, because it ensured he stayed on the sidelines, shooting video rather than bullets. Masoud had kept him on the fringes during the planning as well. Jamal was made to run simple errands most days for the procurement of needed supplies. Trust would be let out slowly like a leash on a temperamental dog, almost a month now since Jamal had been snatched out of his bed in the rented room, which he continued to pay for and use when he wasn't with the cell. All of this allowed him to settle into his role in Hassan's network. For this, he was grateful.

Thank you, Lord, for getting me this far. Please grant me the wisdom to know how to lessen their attacks while still gaining their trust. Allow me to ascend their ranks so that I can inflict more significant damage on them. Lastly, Lord, forgive them and me for what we are about to do.

He heard it then. His muscles tensed, and his heart jumped as the cement mixer packed full of explosives barreled around a corner at the end of the street. He pressed the record button and looked out the window. For a few moments, he saw a terrified look on the driver's face through the windshield, clutching the wheel as he leaned into imminent death.

The truck accelerated past his building. It entered the camera's framed view and hurtled toward the Army checkpoint. There weren't many civilians around, most choosing to avoid the American presence in their city like the plague. But those who were sought cover quickly. The engine was loud enough to alert the squad of infantrymen, and they immediately waved hand and arm signals in its direction. They must have sensed imminent danger because they all opened fire at once. Within seconds the truck rolled to a stop more than seventy-five meters from the checkpoint and sat there benignly for a moment. Then it detonated.

The shock wave was a punch in the diaphragm to Jamal. He instinctually shielded his face with his forearm. Chunks of steel and rubber jettisoned in all directions from the instantaneous cauldron of the explosion. Ahmed and Fahim regained their balance from the shaking of the building and now gawked at the scene as black smoke roiled out of the twenty-foot crater in the road. Several of the American soldiers had been toppled by the blast as well, but they were outside the kill radius. Jamal was heartened to see them up again, reacting toward a defensive posture before the expanding smoke and dust temporarily obscured his view of the checkpoint.

Gunfire aimed at the Americans ensued, from fighters positioned around the intersection. Through the thinning smoke, he saw the soldiers return a volley of their own. The deadly Mark-19, a semi-automatic 30 millimeter grenade launcher mounted on top of a vehicle turret, arched high-explosive rounds into the concealed firing positions of the fighters. The explosions thumped in quick succession. An M2 Browning .50 caliber machine gun mounted on a second vehicle raked a shoulder-high masonry wall, from behind which a torrent of insurgent fire had erupted. The M2 rounds punched daylight across the crumbling edifice and killed several of the fighters. Next, Jamal saw something he couldn't believe. Fighters emerged from nearby buildings, advancing into the face of the determined American defenses.

They will be chewed up. The checkpoint was to have been in shambles from the bomb when this attack went in. Those grunts are at full strength and pissing vinegar.

Jamal thought his job would not be so hard if the *Bathyoun* were this tactically unsound. Ahmed dispelled hope through gritted teeth.

"Why is Masoud sending them in?"

Jamal made a note of the Iraqi's quick understanding, measured out a grain of professional respect, and stored the knowledge away in the growing mental database of profiles he'd been creating.

"Would the general approve?"

Ahmed was curt. "No, he would not."

Fahim chimed in, needing to raise his voice over the uptick in the soldiers' aggregate rate of fire. "The general does not waste men. But Masoud is too eager to please, too ambitious. He was going nowhere in the real army-"

"Shut up, Fahim. That's not important now," said Ahmed.

The conversation halted as several hand grenades exploded in quick succession; each one compressed the air around them. A dozen fighters made desperate rushes across fifty yards of open ground. They fell in all manner of contorted shapes, flailing and firing their weapons to the last gasp. The Army guns were silent. The Florida boys reloaded and waited; the threat nullified for the time being.

"What a waste," said Ahmed with a grunt of disgust. "It's time to go. Coalition reinforcements will be flooding the area."

Ahmed told Jamal and Fahim to gather up their weapons and equipment before the three of them left the deserted office building. On the way out, they passed a portrait of Saddam Hussein hanging askew on the wall. Jamal was in the lead and reached out to touch the fleshy-faced "Butcher of Baghdad." Fahim was right behind him and followed suit.

Back at the cell's base of operations—a public school commandeered with the same methods used at the office building—Masoud sent a desk flying on its end before it crashed into the wall. Young students' works of art scattered like dead leaves under an autumn maple. The innocence of their earnest production was out of place in this room; currently, it was a den of negativity, full of grown men after combat, their morale diminished from just hours before. So was the headcount. Masoud sat down on a chair, seemingly perplexed as to how the attack could have gone so wrong.

"What happened to the truck!" shouted one of the other fighters.

Jamal knew the answer but didn't speak. Even though Masoud hadn't let him near the truck, he'd caught a glimpse of the sketchy electrical rigging for the explosives. He'd also noted the lack of armor for the driver. He hoped one of the two would lead to failure. Fortunately, it happened. Jamal knew this was a situation where insurgents were learning on the job. These early months were a test of their ability to work under limited conditions. As squared away as the Republican Guard thought they were before the invasion, Jamal assumed they hadn't trained on how to convert a cement truck into a useful tool of war.

The men rushing across open fields of fire—cut down the way they were—was directly on Masoud. He had to learn on the job as well. Jamal would let the man fail, of course, sapping the cell's confidence in his leadership, creating a possible job opening for himself. It already seemed Masoud was on the ropes in the overall network, so Jamal figured turning some heads soon was in order. Especially if Ahmed had aspirations of being cell leader too.

"Why didn't he make it as far as we needed him to!" shouted Masoud.

A dozen men in the room shook their heads, none of them with an answer, or unwilling to confront Masoud. Many were distraught after suffering heavy losses. A few cried into their headscarves, a difficulty for the Arab soldier.

Masoud's cell phone rang. He left the room in a huff to take the call, no doubt a tongue lashing from Hassan. When Masoud slammed the door behind him on the way into the usurped principal's office, the mood of the room lightened immediately. Men visibly sank in their chairs. Some lay on the floor amid the cluttered equipment, thrown down when they came forlornly into the school a few minutes ago. The weepers were consoled. Jamal tried to help. Some of the men accepted his gestures, a simple way for him to endear himself to them.

"I have an idea," said Jamal over his meal a couple of hours later. The inhabitants of the room turned to him at once. The look on Masoud's face was priceless as he ate a piece of bread.

His eyebrows arched in disbelief when he said, "What, you have an idea to make your blurry video better?"

Jamal spoke to the cell at large, disregarding Masoud's comment. "I think we should try to snatch a couple of hostages from the checkpoint. We could offer demands, play up our cause in the Western media."

The statement seemed to draw interest. A senior member asked, "Wouldn't we have to attack it again to take hostages?"

"Not necessarily." He moved from the corner of the room to a spot where all could see him. "I have studied their tendencies. Because our attack failed, they will not alter their defenses, or their routines, both of which have weaknesses."

Jamal saw the ire rise again in Masoud. "What makes you think the general would approve of this?"

"I don't know if he will. If he does, you can take credit for the idea. But I think it will do more for us in the long run. If not, we can rig another truck bomb. Maybe it will work the next time." Jamal left the ball bouncing up around the rim and was pleased when Ahmed unwittingly tipped it in for him.

"We should have protected the driver with armor, Masoud. It's why he didn't make it to the barriers."

"And the tires too ... with steel plates attached to the frame," said Fahim.

"But more importantly, Masoud, why did you send the attack in?" asked Ahmed. "I lost a cousin and the man you chose to lead it was someone I've fought alongside for years. Someone we could use. Look at what we have left." His sweeping gesture took in the room of solemn men.

As the ad hoc second in command, Ahmed was using the opportunity to get his pound of flesh. Jamal sensed feistiness among the men after Ahmed's voicing of sentiments that were no doubt shared by the others. Now they felt emboldened enough to grouse in agreement, the least risky move in a mutinous situation, but the one that solidified where the embattled leader stands. The dynamics of the room were shifting like sand under Masoud's feet, and his tenuous grip of authority slipping by the minute.

"We will do whatever it takes to drive out the invaders!" shouted Masoud. "Do you think Saddam would balk at attacking an American checkpoint head-on? He would call us patriots and honor our fallen brothers in the way sons of Anbar should be."

"And where is our Supreme Leader to give us this honor?" asked a member of the cell.

Masoud said, "I cannot say. We are getting our commands from the general, and he is in contact with the highest levels of remaining leadership. We must continue to coordinate with our brothers in the neighborhoods, and we must hurt the coalition forces in our sector."

He turned to Jamal with a dismissive look. "What makes you think this will work?"

Jamal stepped forward, looked over the room, and espoused his plan.

"The squad has a sergeant in charge. The men seem to be disciplined and alert whenever he's the senior ranking man at the checkpoint. Second in charge is a corporal. He looks less prepared for things to go awry. Whenever an Iraqi civilian walks up to them with knowledge of our whereabouts or activities, they are taken in for an immediate debriefing, sometimes for a cash reward from what I've heard. The sergeant regularly escorts the civilian to the base, and when he does, the corporal is in charge. That is when we will have an opportunity to isolate two of the younger soldiers. We only need a diversionary attack."

"What will we do with them?" asked Fahim. He was young, but Jamal had come to understand he was probably the most intelligent person in the room besides himself.

Masoud—obviously wanting to take as much ownership of the idea as early as possible—spoke while keeping one eye on Jamal.

"We will show them to the media and make our demands known. If not-"

"We will kill them and horrify the American public," said Jamal, drawing his first nod of respect from Masoud, followed by a round of nods and grunts of agreement from the room. "An operation like this will cause more American hand-wringing than the death of soldiers from a simple truck bomb." It was a lie. Jamal knew a squad's worth of flag-draped coffins in one day was a punch in the gut for the American public.

Masoud showed ignorance by asking Jamal whom had been on duty at the time of the attack. Jamal knew the answer, but since no one else in the room had even considered it, he chose to say that which would benefit himself in the long run, even with the hit he was about to take.

"The sergeant."

There was an audible groan among the men, bitter at the notion that the attack could have gone off at a time when conditions were more optimal—another strike against Masoud.

"Why did you not say this?" asked Ahmed, using the only card he had to play. Others nodded in concurrence with the question.

Jamal knew he needed to feign hand wringing now. "I probably should have. I didn't think it was my place on this first operation to question my leader." He looked at Masoud. The men all knew how Jamal had been treated these first few weeks. "I thought it wouldn't matter anyway once I saw how many explosives were in that truck."

Jamal picked up on the tone of the room; he knew it was time to back off the agenda. The slumped shoulders and blank stares out the grimy classroom windows said it all. It was the acceptance of their overall failure, their poorly executed plan, their leader, their luck, all of it. Jamal could tell Masoud was ready to move off the uncomfortable subject of his failures. He wasn't out of the woods yet, though.

Ahmed spoke for the men. "Masoud, you have our loyalty, and the cause is still just. But you must be more judicious with the men who pledge their lives to that cause."

Masoud stirred visibly at the verbal censure. The cell had changed this day, probably for good, thought Jamal. Its leader was being challenged on two fronts. Masoud might understand it coming from Ahmed. He was ambitious and had Hassan's ear with the tribal bloodline and such.

But from me, an abed … That must really burn his ass.

Masoud was forced to listen while Ahmed continued validating Jamal's plan. "I think taking hostages could set us apart in the general's eyes. It will make up for the losses we have suffered today. But we have to pull it off. No mistakes, Masoud."

The fighters looked around for safety in numbers, and once a couple of respected men signaled their approval, the rest fell like dominoes in support of Ahmed's stance. Masoud paused only a moment before grasping some of the initiative he'd lost in the kangaroo court.

"We will try Jamal Muhammad's idea, but once we get them back here, we do what I want with them." He turned to Jamal. "So let us hear your plan. I assume you already have it worked out."

"Not exactly," answered Jamal with careful consideration painted across his face. "First we need to decide who will approach the Americans and fabricate some intel-"

"To lure the sergeant away!" said Fahim with a broad smile. Several men nodded in understanding.

"Exactly," said Jamal.

CHAPTER 11

Jamal watched the Hummer drive away from the checkpoint. Inside the vehicle was a local who'd agreed to pose as an informant. As suspected, the sergeant was with him, as well as his driver. The corporal was now in charge, and less than ten soldiers manned the Army position. Jamal tested the wind one last time by tossing a handful of dry scrub into the air. It flew off in the direction he wanted, so he nodded at the fighter next to him.

"Do it."

The fighter approached a pile of gasoline-soaked tires and tossed a lit match onto it before scurrying away. A whooshing sound accompanied the blast of radiant heat that singed Jamal's eyebrows. He backed up a few steps and raised the binoculars toward the Americans. Thick black smoke from the burning rubber was already advancing toward them.

He had chosen the location of the fire after he'd studied the soldiers' positioning and considered prevailing winds from the south that were typical during summer. They were brisk enough today for the smoke to remain low and concentrated as it drifted through the checkpoint one hundred yards ahead of him. It looked like the wall of smoke would bisect their perimeter just as he'd hoped. He raised the radio to his lips.

"Ahmed, it's time."

No response came across the airwaves, but the sudden outburst of machine-gun fire off to Jamal's right indicated the message was received. The corporal in charge started shifting soldiers in that direction, moving men from one side of the smoke barrier to face a threat on the other side. Perimeter integrity must be maintained, however, so the corporal left two soldiers in their original position. They were quickly isolated, with an opaque curtain of smoke between themselves and their cohorts. He should have left more.

Satisfied that the diversionary attack was doing its job, Jamal used the binoculars to watch the soldiers they would take as hostages. The two Americans hunkered down behind a stack of sandbags to his left. One of them vigilantly scanned his field of fire for more threats, while the other's head was on a swivel, repeatedly turning around to stare into the thick smoke. Jamal put down the binoculars and pulled out his compass. He took a quick reading and spoke into the radio again.

"Now, Fahim."

Several smoke grenades were tossed out of a building near the isolated soldiers. A yellow-colored haze began to mix in with the black smoke from the tires, and the whole area took on a hellish hue that enveloped the fighters and the soldiers alike.

"Let's go," said Jamal to the armed fighter with him.

They both donned gas masks and advanced into the thickening haze with weapons drawn. Jamal held the compass up close to his visor. The fighter stayed close behind, so as to not become lost in the cloud of smoke for its density. Jamal heard coughing ahead and cursing, in English. He checked the azimuth on his compass. It had to be them. He slowed to a walking crouch, reaching back to signal to the fighter behind him. Through the smoke, a waist-high wall of sandbags appeared.

Jamal and the fighter shouted in Arabic with weapons drawn on the two soldiers, who spun around, surprised. The larger of the two moved to aim his weapon, but the fighter jabbed the nose of his AK up close to his face and shouted another threat. The soldier backed down. Both Americans lowered their weapons and put their hands behind their Kevlar helmets. It was over. Jamal grabbed the big one by the collar of his fatigues, put the nose of the pistol against the soldier's spine, and hurried him off in a direction indicated on the compass. The other fighter shoved along the terrified soldier as wayward bullets from the diversionary attack skipped off the pavement around them. In the next moment, all four disappeared into the haze while the gunfight raged on.

Pedestrians scattered as the convoy of vehicles skidded to a stop in front of the school. In an instant, the scene was chaotic. Fighters ran off mingling locals, and orders were shouted to form a perimeter around the area. Jamal was in the back seat of the last car, taking a deep breath now that it was over. Through the windshield, he saw the hooded and bound hostages being roughly jerked out of the sedan in front of him. He got out the car himself and put the .45 caliber pistol he'd finally been issued inside the waist of his jeans. He had the urge to move toward the hostages and make sure nothing happened to them. On the heels of that desire was the knowledge that he could not intervene.

Let it ride for now. They're too valuable to be killed outright. You banked on them knowing that, on Masoud understanding it, Jamal. Look for the advantageous moment, manipulate only as necessary.

While worried about Masoud's unpredictability, he knew the *Bathyoun* needed to take ownership of the situation for a while. Hopefully, they would come to him with inclusion on their minds because his plan—in actuality, the plan he and Ahmed had fine-tuned together—just went off without a hitch. The fluid manner in which the two of them had cohorted didn't go unnoticed, and Jamal was beginning to understand how important it would be to foster that relationship.

This should get me in good standing with the cell. Ahmed will put in a good word for me with the higher leadership. Gotta keep in mind that he has eyes on Masoud's job as well.

Inside the school, the hostages were rushed into a windowless room in the center of the one-story building. Masoud, Ahmed, and some of the others entered the makeshift cell while Jamal watched from the dimly lit corridor. Incandescent lights swung close to the hooded heads of the two Americans as they stood with their backs against the wall.

The taller, more muscular soldier's nametag read 'Johanssen.' He was a Private First Class, as indicated by the rank on his collar. As the hoods were lifted, Jamal saw Johanssen's blond buzz cut and red face, the square Nordic jaw emphasized by clenched teeth. He decided the kid was more angry than scared at the moment. Not so for Rothchild. A little younger-looking, his teeth chattered from raw fear. Was that a whiff of urine Jamal had caught when Rothchild was hustled by him a moment ago?

Of course, the kid pissed his pants. They're finding heads out there in the streets every week.

Masoud approached with an interpreter close behind. He spoke in Arabic to the one he perceived as weaker. The interpreter relayed his question.

"He wants to know the purpose of the checkpoint?"

Rothchild was nearly incoherent from fear, however, so Masoud slapped him across the face. Jamal cringed.

"Jakey ... Jakey!" yelled Rothchild, losing all military bearing. "What's going to happen to us, man!"

"Calm down, Rothchild!" said Johanssen. "Cool it, all right. They're not going to kill us."

A glance from Masoud prompted translation of the exchange. Masoud spoke again, followed by the interpreter.

"He said it is up to you whether you live or die. I suggest you tell him why the Americans have set up the checkpoint where they did."

The statement negatively affected the kid, and he couldn't control himself. It looked like Masoud was about to slap him again when Johanssen spat in Masoud's face, shifting attention from his comrade with his defiance. Jamal considered it a noble and brave act. Masoud, however, recoiled as if hit by thrown acid, and Jamal's stomach turned when he saw the rage boil up. The beatings began with bare-knuckle punches to Johanssen's face. It opened up quickly, and after a minute or two, his uniform was covered in blood. Jamal took in the smells of blood and anxious sweat, pungent enough to escape the small room. He clenched his jaw as Rothchild sobbed in the corner.

Shut up. Just shut the hell up, you fool. It's only going to make it worse. These people feed on weakness.

He couldn't bear it any longer, ambled down the corridor, and tried not to appear disturbed. The look of relish on the faces he passed incited anger that he would have to become adept at hiding. For now, it was tempered with a reminder that his plans for the hostages weren't yet complete. The internal conflict produced feelings of success and failure at once. For the first time, he understood what the major had always told them. The nature of this work would pull on the agents in ways that are contrary to humane living. The constant emotional tugging in different directions. Stretching. Thinning. The major said you'd know when you were stretched too thin. A zero-sum feeling would pervade that all your work was for naught because of the sacrifices made. Jamal stiffened his resolve, knew he wasn't anywhere close to that yet.

And these two kids from Florida aren't as bad off as they think.

"This school may be already known to the coalition," said Ahmed, perturbed that he even needed to make the point. He and a senior fighter stood before Masoud in the principal's office, discussing their next actions. "We should move them to a more secluded location and keep moving them every day,"

Masoud stated rather than posed a question to Ahmed. "You think they are not safe here."

"I am simply saying we brought them straight here. If anyone opposed to us saw us arrive with the Americans, they will tell the coalition. Then their special forces will come, probably in the next few hours."

"Then, we will do the initial video within the hour and move them immediately afterward."

"What are your plans, Masoud? asked the fighter. In what ways shall we gain from this act?"

"Simple. We will demand the Army dismantle all checkpoints in Ramadi and leave the city, or we will kill them. What choice will they have?" He turned to Ahmed. "I need you to find our next location for them. I will call you when we are through with the video. Tell Jamal to get his camera ready in the interrogation room. We will do this quick. First, we need masks and a banner. I want to use the party flag."

Uncertainty crossed the elder's face before he asked, "Are you sure, Masoud? Maybe we should be more mysterious, more general, so they have to look in many places for us. A Baathist banner will make it somewhat easy for them."

Ahmed offered an alternative. "Maybe we should make them think we are *takfiri*."

Masoud was non-plussed at the idea, and Ahmed felt the friction between the two of them intensify by the second. He tried again, nonetheless. "How about the 'Iraqi Front' then?"

"No," said Masoud. "We fight for Anbar." Another grunt of agreement from the elder fighter shot Ahmed's idea down officially.

In that moment, Masoud seemed inspired. "Saddam built the giant crossed swords of *Qadisiyah* in Baghdad to symbolize Iraqi strength. That will be a part of our banner."

"The Anbar Brigade." said the elder fighter.

Masoud nodded and raised Ahmed's arms in two bent arcs mimicking the enormous monument in central Baghdad. Then he cupped one of his own hands over them as if envisioning words there. "Anbar Brigade ..."

"Then it is settled," said Ahmed, with a level of presumption that he knew full well would irk Masoud.

Masoud narrowed his eyes. "I will think about it. Have Jamal retrieve some supplies to make a banner. By the time you return, I will have made my decision."

The tension remained, but Ahmed quelled the desire to get the last word in. Serving under poor leadership was part of being a soldier, he reminded himself. He'd done it in the regular Iraqi Army before joining the Republican Guard a few years ago. He'd bite his tongue now too. But this was a desperate situation, and consistently killing off your precious supply of manpower would lead to disaster. He decided it was time to stop needling Masoud and start making entreaties toward his uncle for gaining control of the cell. He wanted to see how this hostage-taking business worked out first, though. It was possible Masoud would ruin the whole thing and pave the way for him. Time would tell over the next few days. Tonight they had to move quickly.

Jamal assumed the role of cinematographer. Masoud made him stay behind the camera while several of the others posed. The masked and heavily armed fighters stood abreast of one another, while the bound Americans knelt before them. Masoud placed himself in the middle and held a list of demands—actually a rather long manifesto he'd worked on since the day Jamal brought up the idea of a kidnapping. His other hand held a thirty-inch scimitar, used to style the depiction of two crossed swords on the banner, which was raised behind the motley crew of kidnappers.

As a masked Masoud brandished the weapon, vehemently espousing his manifesto, the weaker of the two hostages—Rothchild—was a wreck. He nearly passed out from his anxiety and had to be propped up due to his trembling knees. This only slowed down the production even more, as it was not ideal for the hostages to appear weak.

Because everyone feared a sudden intrusion by coalition forces, the whole production was rushed. The silver paint used for the swords was still wet against the red backdrop and green lettering when Jamal started recording. Still, it required several takes for Masoud to get through the manifesto without stumbling on his own words more than just a couple of times. This only increased the nervousness of the men, and Jamal was forced to suppress a grin when they started bickering like frustrated siblings.

Jamal squirmed to gain legroom in the back seat of the Volvo as it raced through the broken, uneven streets of Ramadi. Next to him sat Rothchild with a hood over his head and bound wrists, while Ahmed occupied the driver's seat. Masoud and two other fighters had taken a different route with Johanssen. Both vehicles were expected at a warehouse owned by a prominent tribal member and close associate of Hassan's.

Jamal hoped Masoud would play the hostage situation out as long as possible by using the media to garner attention. The whole endeavor would become the cell's main focus for a while if that were the case. He assumed the logistical and security needs would be significant in keeping the hostages out of the public eye. Attention would be diverted from more direct violence against more substantial numbers of American forces, a primary goal of Jamal's all along. Even if the major would not agree. Next, with time on his side, Jamal would devise a way to spring the hostages before any demands were met. It would all add up to a massive waste of time and energy, hopefully even manpower. But if Masoud suddenly announced plans to kill them, an escape plan would need to be devised quickly. And hasty plans are not always the best ones.

He forced himself to acknowledge a third scenario where the hostages did die in captivity, possibly by his hand. If Masoud felt the need to test Jamal by making him kill the Americans, he'd have to do it. He gave that scenario an outside chance of presenting itself, though, and would only cross that bridge if forced to walk it. More likely, Masoud would try to grab the spotlight by doing the deed himself on camera.

The disparate outcomes spun in his head, and he told himself to be patient and let the situation run its course. None of those things were happening presently. Tonight, Jamal had been given the simple job of guarding the hostages at the warehouse. It was a welcome step up after the successful kidnapping and an indication that Masoud at least recognized his role in it.

The Volvo stopped at the security gate of the expansive warehouse property. While Ahmed left the car to remove the chain and padlock from the fencing, Jamal studied the area from the back seat. The rectangular building looked new, with a dozen loading docks for trucks on the long side. The whitish hue of security lighting provided the only illumination in the area. Its location in the color spectrum indicated they were metal-halide lighting fixtures, which meant they required an eight-to ten-minute restart time if shut off suddenly, an odd bit of training information coming to fruition, but one he was grateful for. He stored the knowledge away for later use and continued to scan his surroundings.

Adjacent to the warehouse property on both sides were older, boarded-up buildings. The vacant structures provided a natural barrier to potential voyeurs who could report the hustling of hostages into the warehouse. After Masoud's vehicle arrived, he instructed the fighters to bring the Americans inside.

The interior was dim, lit by only a few of the metal-halide lights since it was after regular hours of operation. The open floor with a high ceiling was filled with storage containers of various sizes and shapes, but Jamal saw that a corner of the building's interior was partitioned off with what he assumed were offices. His hunch was confirmed when someone emerged from a door. Desks and computers were inside. The man, an older Arab in a business suit, motioned for the group to follow him down a carpeted hallway to another door.

"Here," the man said.

Jamal shoved Rothchild through the open door. The room was spartan but clean, with two steel cots on the floor. As soon as Johanssen was inside, Masoud moved toward both men, tightening their plastic flex cuffs. Rothchild complained, and Masoud cruelly gave one more tug to make it worse. Leaving the hostages in the room, he closed the door on the way out. In the hallway, he assigned the night's duties to Jamal and two other low-ranking fighters.

"It is now 2100 hours. I want six one-hour shifts until Ahmed brings the new guards at 0300 and takes you back to the school. One of you is to stay by this door at all times. No one goes in or out. The other two will patrol the warehouse inside, and the fenced perimeter outside. Rotate out with each other every hour, so you stay alert."

The three of them nodded in understanding.

Masoud turned to Ahmed. "Have the other place ready before morning, Ahmed. We move them once more, then I'm going to kill them for the world to see, and the Americans can keep their damned checkpoints."

Jamal felt the hairs stand up on the back of his neck.

Son of a...

CHAPTER 12

Jamal moved on foot with a duffle bag in hand, immersed in the shadows whenever possible. He wore a knitted black mask, long sleeves, and gloves to avoid recognition. Dogs barked nearby, but not at him. Welcome distractions. He found a vehicle to use once he was safely out of the cell's area of operations. From the duffle bag, he produced a homemade 'slim Jim' to pop the locked door. Fifteen seconds later, he was inside the minibus, tossing the bag on the passenger seat. Thanks to the major's training, he could hotwire an engine like this in his sleep, so it was only a moment before he was on his way. The time was 0400 hours. Ahmed had dropped him off at the rented room less than twenty minutes prior and said he would return at 0630 to pick him up. Jamal had just over two hours to make this happen.

He reflected on the night's developments. After Masoud's surprise announcement at the warehouse, Jamal's mind had raced from fear that he'd gambled with the hostages' lives and was about to lose. While on guard duty, he'd tried to come up with a hasty plan to free them but knew that after their shift ended, Ahmed was supposed to take him and the other guards to the school for some rest. The following few hours would have been the only opportunity to spring the hostages if Masoud planned to kill them later in the day. Leaving the school was nearly impossible, though, while under Masoud's watchful eye. But then it seemed divine intervention occurred on Jamal's behalf.

Ahmed surprised him by dropping the other two guards off at the school as planned but told Jamal in front of them that he needed his help with one final task of the long night. At first, Jamal was crestfallen, believing he'd lost his one chance to free the Americans. In truth, Ahmed intended to reward Jamal for his yet unrewarded contributions within the cell. He'd noticed how Masoud seemed to kick Jamal's cot every time he walked past it.

Thank you, Lord. Ahmed dropping me off at the room to get some real sleep changed everything.

Jamal swerved the minibus to avoid a bomb crater left over from the initial invasion, glimpsed a pair of mangy canines rooting through the windblown garbage at the bottom of it. Jerking on the loose suspension allowed him to find the center of the road again, and the vehicle sputtered past the mud-brick homes of the slum through which he sped.

Minutes later, he made the final turn before the gated entry to the warehouse property. On the way in with Ahmed and Rothchild earlier tonight, the headlights of the Volvo had shown an abandoned service drive for the unkempt adjacent property. Arriving there now, he parked the minibus in the shadows and pulled some clean clothes for later out of the duffle bag he'd brought, leaving them inside the vehicle. With the bag and its remaining contents in hand, he grabbed his weapon and a silencer, and slowly crept toward the warehouse.

Neither piece would have been his first choice. Masoud issued the .45 caliber from the bottom of the barrel that was the cell's makeshift armory. It had taken a keen eye to rid the tiniest crevices of fine desert sand; Jamal swore the thing had spent some time buried in the stuff. The silencer was a crude one he'd picked up off the black market and modified in his rented room for better efficiency.

Earlier, he'd drawn perimeter duty first. Starting his rounds at the locked gate, he'd begun to walk the entirety of the property inside the fence. The condition of the new barbed wire had diminished the hope of finding a gap to slip in and out.

Fortunately, he'd discovered the fence on one side of the property belonged to the abandoned building with the service drive. It was still heavily barbed along its rusty length, but he'd found a place where a clasp was missing on the vertical support; the bottom of the chain-link fencing could raise just enough to shimmy under. He approached the spot. His timing couldn't have been better.

The outside guard had turned the corner of the building and began walking away from Jamal, who slid under the chain links with the duffle. Now, he was up and moving, reaching the building just before the guard made his next turn and disappeared around the far side. Jamal had calculated the timing earlier. He moved silently along the wall, drew the pistol, and calmly raised it to arm's length. When the Iraqi emerged around the corner of the building again, the shape in the shadows startled him. His attempt to pull up his AK was too slow.

THWAT … THWAT.

Two silenced rounds entered the guard's chest, and he went down, causing the AK to whack against the metal siding of the building. The noise was more than Jamal wanted, but he secured the muzzle with his free hand before the weapon could crash to the pavement, possibly firing off a couple of rounds. He placed it in the duffle and performed his first act of choreography, which was to drag the guard to a nearby door and orient the body a certain way.

During his shift patrolling the inside of the warehouse, he'd studied the lock on this steel door. He was confident a simple pick tool and tension wrench, purchased the same day as the silencer, would get him inside. He was glad for all the major's classes on tradecraft, surprised at how many of them he'd used already in just the last month. As he pulled the tools out of the duffle, he pictured the little Jewish locksmith who was their instructor.

"It's the sound and the touch that will get you through any locked device, but it's better to rely on the sound than the touch I tell you" … *Confusing little bastard, but he knew his shit.*

He looked around one last time before attaching the tension wrench and inserting the picks, then listened more than felt his way through the locked latch. He heard the tumbler slide, and the pressure lessened until the door was unlocked. He put the tools away and turned the knob slowly before cracking the door. After listening for several seconds, he slipped through the opening.

Just inside was a panel of light switches, which controlled the interior lighting, the main reason he'd chosen this door as his breach point. He flipped all of them off, and instantly, the warehouse went dark. The unexpected occurrence prompted the interior guards to communicate with one another, giving away their location over by the office area, a good seventy-five yards from Jamal. It was time to acquire his next prop. Earlier, he'd seen a workbench near the door with a box cutter on it and had checked to make sure it had a sharp blade.

His eyes began to adjust on his way to the workbench, allowing him to spot the tool. He grabbed it and removed his boots, stowing them behind the bench. In his socks, he padded off to his predetermined ambush spot for the first interior guard. While he moved, the guards continued talking, at first wondering if the lights were on a timer. They quickly decided it was the outside guard playing a joke on them. Jamal heard the door to the offices shut, followed by the sound of one man walking in Jamal's direction. The guard must have flipped the switches at the other end of the building first, though. The electric buzz of the lights fell over the space suddenly, yet only a dim glow was emitted from the bulbs while they charged up as Jamal had expected. He hid inside an alcove created by several large crates. While he waited with the layman's tool at the ready, he thought about one of the remaining guards on duty, someone about which he gave a shit.

His name was Safwan. The two had taken to one another while performing menial tasks at the school.

Safwan was a simple man but wholly committed to the Baathist cause. He was senior to Jamal in years, and their relationship was that of teacher and student. Jamal was the student by default because Safwan had decided he lacked an understanding of the Baathist political movement. When they would talk, Safwan went into great detail regarding matters in the party over recent years, how the Baathists had transformed the Arab penchant for settling on a weak leader into a real peoples' movement. Jamal assured him time and again that he was less interested in the past and looked toward the future of Iraq once the war was over.

Safwan had said with a smile, "The future of Iraq is the party." And imminently, his life was about to end.

The sound of shuffling feet grew louder as a flashlight beam shot up the aisle. Jamal waited until the guard appeared and swung out his arm level and swift in a chop to the Adam's apple, the hand flat and stiff as a two-by-four. The disabling blow deprived the guard of wind and balance at once, causing him to drop the flashlight. It clattered on the floor, but before the man himself could land in a loud heap, Jamal swung around and grabbed his tunic to break the fall. He noted it wasn't Safwan and pulled another AK from the guard's loose grip.

With the guard flat on his back now, staring wide-eyed but dazed, Jamal used a hand to cover the man's nose and mouth while pulling out the box cutter. He pressed hard over the airways to suppress the scream as the razor-sharp blade severed the jugular artery. The eyes bulged even wider as the fighter struggled to receive oxygen in both brain and lungs. Blood flowed heavily for more than a minute. Somewhere in that awful time, Jamal dropped the box cutter in the rapidly expanding dark pool and closed his eyes.

A gruesome memory stamped upon his mind. He felt life leaving the quivering body. When it was still, Jamal wiped his hands on the dead man's clothing and opened his tunic. Inside was a concealed pistol, which he put in the duffle. He carried the second AK in his free hand.

As the guard bled out on the floor, Jamal left the grisly scene and ambled down the aisle between the crates, tried to let the rawness of what he'd just done move through him so he could focus on the final guard, knowing it was Safwan. Time was ticking. Outside the offices, he held his pistol overhead while he opened and shut the door quickly to raise the curiosity of Safwan, who should be outside the hostage's door as ordered by Masoud. On cue, he heard footsteps inside the office. Jamal's muscles tensed when the door opened, and Safwan's torso leaned out.

The weight of the pistol came down in a sharp blow to the skull. Safwan's body went limp, and he was out cold on the floor. Jamal searched him for a weapon, but there wasn't one. He stood astride Safwan once he'd dragged the beefy man all the way into the room. Hesitancy crept in. Two days ago they'd laughed together. But he'd been conditioned for this moment, and before he knew it, his hands were around Safwan's fleshy throat from behind, squeezing hard to leave visible marks. He pressed until the unconscious man's system shocked itself into convulsions. It lasted about as long as the bloodletting had—too long.

He dragged the corpse over near the room in which the hostages were held. Next, he went back down the hall with the duffle bag to retrieve files he'd discovered earlier while posted here in the office. He hadn't had the opportunity to discern what was out on the warehouse floor. He didn't need to. This place would be a pile of ash by the time Masoud or anyone from the cell could get here. But some of the files told of other locations in Ramadi where munitions were stored.

It was clear the wealthy Arab who'd met them here earlier was a major financier of Hassan's war, a vital cog in the machinery of the insurgency. His name was all over the papers Jamal grabbed. He placed them in the bottom of the bag under the weapons and the Arab street clothing he'd packed for the hostages—soon to be escapees. On a nearby desk was a blank pad of paper and marker. He put a single piece on the hard surface of the desk and wrote only three letters in English, followed by an exclamation point. On the back, he drew a simple map that would lead them to the nearest coalition outpost, only a few kilometers away. Jamal glanced at his watch, causing a stir of anxiety when he realized he had less than forty-five minutes before Ahmed would be at the rented room to pick him up. He had to move.

While jogging back down the hall, it was hard not to look at Safwan. At the door, he noted how quiet it was inside. Maybe the hostages were asleep? He flipped off the switch for the lights to shroud his face when he opened the door and tossed the duffle inside. The second AK was thrown behind it on the floor. He hoped the appearance of a weapon would instantly signal the situation had changed, prompting them to act quickly. He left the door ajar and moved back down the hall, flipping the switch at the other end to turn on the light again. Once he was through the office and out onto the warehouse floor again, he retrieved his boots and hid behind a large crate. Precious seconds ticked off while he waited for them to emerge, hopefully on the double-time.

Private Rothchild hadn't stopped shaking since the two of them were pushed into this room. The images of a gruesome death at the hands of these insurgents would not leave his head, the beheading of which was a central theme. He bemoaned having been assigned to this squad on this day as a fill-in medic. The bitterness was borne of the bad feeling he'd had when he arrived at the checkpoint. The exposed nature of it with wary eyes all around them had given him the creeps.

I knew it. Freakin' no man's land.

He stared at Johanssen, sleeping like a baby. Nothing ever seemed to bother him. Rothchild was thankful he was here. But he knew his fellow soldier was callous toward his constant whining and dismal outlook.

"Jakey, he might try something to free us," muttered Rothchild ... "Or maybe just himself if you don't stop with the negativity," he said more forcefully, suddenly angry with his weaker side.

Buck up, soldier!

He'd heard those words a lot in his stint so far. So for once, he imagined himself fighting his way out of this dire situation. But the quickening of the scared country boy lasted all of a minute before he heard a thud outside the door, startling him out of the intoxicating indulgence that is hero envy. In an instant, his reality was there again, and along with it, the fear. It spiked when he heard footsteps, followed by the door opening. Something was tossed into the dark room, sliding to a stop in the space between the two cots.

Rothchild sat up and shot a look at Johanssen, which turned to incredulity when he saw him still asleep. His head jerked back toward the open door when he heard the metallic sound of a weapon sliding on concrete, which *did* cause Johanssen to awaken. The relative darkness in the room and the hall made it impossible to see who was out there, but in a few seconds, the hall light came on and revealed a dead guard at the foot of the door.

"What the fuck, Jake!"

Johanssen's tone was hushed but firm. "Shh! ... Shut the hell up, Rothchild."

Johanssen hopped off the cot. He peered out the door in both directions before lunging for the AK. Back at the door, he ordered Rothchild to search the bag. The trembling medic was on the verge of paralyzing fear again, but this time the fear was trumped, and he felt the new feeling of raw courage spur him on. Plus, he reasoned, his previous visions of bravery hadn't even included inside help.

He pulled apart the unzipped top of the bag. The first thing he saw was a single piece of white paper on top of some clothing.

"It says run! And there's a map on the other side that shows where a hole in the fence outside is and how to get back to the base!"

"SHHH. Lower that effin' voice, dammit," said Johanssen. "What else is in the bag?"

Rothchild pulled out two pairs of clothing, each a rolled-up bundle of cloth held together with a piece of rough twine. He undid the knots and laid the outfits on his bunk. In a more even tone that did not draw another rebuke from Johanssen, he described them with a pained look on his face.

"It's one of them man dresses. And sandals. And one of them headdress thingies with the rope."

"The robe's a *dish-dash*, and the *khafiyya* goes on the head like a big dew rag. Just pick the sandals that fit your feet and get the other stuff on so you can watch the door, and I can change."

While he fumbled through the process of donning Arab attire for the first time in his life, Rothchild noticed what remained at the bottom of the bag. Lying there on top of some manila folders was another assault rifle and a loaded pistol. He grabbed both and placed them on the cot, leaving the folders as they were.

"Jesus. More guns. Plus, these papers. I can't tell what the hell they are. Bunch of invoices or receipts in Arabic. Maybe they were just in the bag when he filled it."

"It's probably intel, you idiot. Put it back in the bag and finish changing into those clothes. We're taking it all with us."

Rothchild was anxious to do what the note said. How was it possible? Earlier, he'd played out his demise endlessly, an inhumane scene he'd almost come to accept as inevitable until his moment of courage. Next came this bag. And hope. But he'd felt the change in him before the bag. That was real, pure. Now it was mixed with a surge of adrenaline.

"What should I do with my uniform?"

Johanssen had the answer as if he'd already considered it.

"Put it in the duffle. Whoever helped us won't want people thinking we had inside help. If we were able to overpower the guard ourselves, we'd leave in our unis as fast as possible. Yeah, we're leaving this place pronto and taking everything."

CHAPTER 13

Jamal watched the wary escapees peer out the office door. He hid amid stacked crates and large drums of flammable fluid out on the warehouse floor. His thoughts centered on the two soldiers from the Hurricane Battalion. Would they be able to follow the map? Could they even pass the eye test of a local once they started moving through the streets? He'd anticipated it would take them over an hour to get to the base. He glanced at his watch; it was just after 0600 hours.

Time. Always the wrench in the works, but consistent and unalterable.

Less than a minute later, Jamal watched the two soldiers emerge from the office door. Once they seemed confident the vast warehouse was unoccupied, they made for the nearest exit, cracked it, and looked out into the fading darkness. Jamal sensed uncertainty. They couldn't know the way was already paved for them, but still.

Come on. Make the most of it and run. Trust me.

As if the thought spurred him on, Johanssen pushed out the door with the assault rifle at the ready and Rothchild right on his tail, the duffle in one hand and the pistol in the other. Jamal was relieved. He was almost done. He rushed from his hiding spot, gathered wood by smashing some empty palettes nearby. A crate of Russian vodka had been cracked open earlier in the day for Hassan, providing the necessary lighter fluid. He doused the wood with alcohol and tossed a match onto the pyre. Somehow the half-full bottle found its way to his lips. During the long pulls, warped flames licked at him through the curved glass of the bottle's neck. He tossed the empty bottle into the high, dark volume of the warehouse. On his way to the door, he fired several rounds into the drums and watched flammable liquid spread underneath a dozen wooden crates.

By the time he crawled back under the fence on the edge of the property, the windows that faced him flickered with orange. Smoke billowed out of the eaves and ridge of the roof. Dawn approached, so he ran back to the minibus with the killings etched into his mind. He changed into the fresh clothes he'd brought and bundled the bloodstained, smoky ones in a sack, which he would toss halfway through his drive. He used a liter of water to wash the blood off of his hands and rinse the smoke out of his hair before he hopped in the minibus and sped out of the industrial complex. He drove the vehicle as far as he dared, scrapping his plan to ditch it far away from the rented room. The risk of being seen by locals became secondary to arriving before Ahmed. In the end, he left the minibus only three blocks away, well inside the cell's area of operations.

He jogged in the retreating shadows as the eastern sky paled further, turned onto the lane that ran along the length of his building. He stopped in his tracks as a hot flash exploded through every pore in his body and raised the hairs on the back of his neck. Ahmed's car was parked next to his room.

What is he doing here early?

Jamal crept up along the passenger side. Through the window, he saw Ahmed in the reclined driver's seat, head craned back, mouth agape in a deep sleep. Jamal exhaled a sigh of relief, but this was the quietest time of day in Iraq. The stillness amplified his every footfall as he moved past the car and up to his door. He dreaded the heavy action of the deadbolt lock he was about to open. One glance back at Ahmed was encouraging, but when he turned to face the door again, he felt the apprehension of being seen from behind. A trickle of salty sweat traveled down his cheek, onto his lip while an image of Ahmed opening his eyes popped into his head. He turned the key. CLICK.

One more glance, and he was inside. He gently closed the door and turned the smaller lock on the handle itself, which barely made a sound. With his index finger, he nudged the edge of the dirty linen curtain at the adjacent window and saw Ahmed slumbering one last time. He'd done it.

For the next ten minutes, he lay on his bed and stared at the ceiling. Physical weariness hit him now that his body had expended every last drop of adrenaline, but the high of freeing the Americans drove his racing mind. It didn't last long. The smile across his face faded when he thought of Safwan, the image of his hands around the man's throat so fresh in his mind.

No more making friends.

He rationalized his guilt was better than the Florida boys being blown to bits by a better truck bomb.

A whole squad. All the ruined families.

He prayed for the safe return of the escapees and for the timely use of the intelligence he'd given them. Somehow that had to be worth something in the balance of his soul.

If it saves even more American lives, right?

Finally, he prayed for more opportunities to drain the enemy's resources, morale, and overall success. He continued to meditate on his bed in the pale blue light of encroaching dawn until he drifted off, found himself among warriors on a battlefield watching young David slay Goliath with his sling. After some grisly work, the boy held the severed head of the giant. Then the head appeared at Jamal's feet, but it had become Hassan's puffy face. He looked around, and no one was there. The armies had gone.

A dog barked, jarring him from the dream. He realized he'd fallen asleep and opened one bloodshot eye to look at the bedside clock, 0626 hours. The enveloping grasp of sleep came again, aided by the softness of the new mattress he'd purchased for himself. Minutes passed. He was awakened by the pinging noise of Ahmed's car door opening and closing. The fact it hadn't slammed was comforting to Jamal in his weariness. He sat up in the bed and rubbed his eyes, which had that sandy feeling one gets when torn from sleep. He was nervous when he opened the door, but the exhausted visage of Ahmed told Jamal he'd been hard asleep for some time.

"You look like hell, boss."

"Let's go," said Ahmed. "I need the strongest coffee this town has to offer. I just got a call from Masoud. He needs us at the school. He sounded angry."

"And this is new?" asked Jamal rhetorically.

"He sounded different this time, almost frantic. The call only lasted long enough for him to tell me to get there. As you have seen by now, it could be anything," he said with resignation. "First, the coffee and a roll. I won't face him on an empty stomach. Not today."

Rothchild could see the concrete blast barriers on the block ahead, which surrounded Camp Eagle's Nest. It was good timing; dawn had come and gone. The last few minutes had seen them jogging in the open, drawing odd looks from early morning passersby. Even the dogs barked at the armed pair carrying the duffle bag. But they'd concealed their Caucasian faces enough that he doubted anyone could say for sure they were Americans on the run.

Fifty yards from the heavily-fortified gate to the base, Johanssen had him throw the weapons in a nearby pile of garbage and go over the daily passwords, which he said would have rolled overnight. Johanssen slung the duffle with the intelligence over his shoulder and was about to approach the Military Police guarding the gate when Rothchild grabbed his arm.

He pointed to a towering cloud of smoke behind them. "Look, Jake ... back toward the warehouse. Do you think-"

"Yeah," answered Johanssen. "I bet it was him, whoever he was. C'mon."

They pulled off their *khafiyyas* and walked into the open, arms held in the air to show they were unarmed, much to the surprise of the MP's on duty.

CHAPTER 14

Jamal relished the silence as they drove, an unspoken agreement between two men who'd worked long hours over recent days; there wasn't the need to converse this early in the morning. Ahmed was the first to speak eventually.

"We will pull over ahead for some espresso."

Jamal felt compelled to acknowledge Ahmed's earlier kind gesture. "Thank you for dropping me at my place for a few hours. I slept better than I would have at the school."

"I thought you could use the rest and a few moments of peace away from him ... I finished what I needed to do and arrived at your place an hour early. I was so tired I would have slept on your floor. Just as I was about to knock and wake you, I decided it would be a different kind of cruelty, so I slept in the car."

Jamal's heart skipped a beat at the news. He stared out the windshield at the typical crisscross of electrical wires overhead, a veritable web hemming him in after the comment. His peripheral vision told him Ahmed hadn't turned to face him in anticipation of his response, and he sensed more divine intervention had occurred.

"Well, I appreciate it. You could have come in and slept on the floor, though. At least let me buy our coffee."

"Technically, I am your superior. Even in this unofficial army, I will not have my men paying my way. But thank you."

Ahmed broached another topic. This time he did turn his eyes intermittently from the road to gain Jamal's reaction.

"Listen, we are getting close to the school, and I won't be able to say this to you there. You have been a good addition to the cause. I am speaking to Hassan later today. Would you like to go across town with me and meet him? Masoud does not need to know."

Jamal answered in the affirmative, of course. Inwardly he grinned like the Cheshire cat. Now he just needed to make it through the next few hours. When they approached the school, it was apparent something was wrong. Men scampered about in a state of emergency, and Masoud stood outside the main entrance with a cell phone to his ear. His animated gestures and a heightened state of anxiety caused Ahmed and Jamal to look at each other without a word. Today was going to be interesting.

The convoy of vehicles neared the warehouse and its gated entry, which sat wide open now. A pair of fire trucks turned onto the road and picked up speed toward them. Their crew, volunteers under a nonexistent government, had run themselves ragged lately extinguishing all the bombing fires. As they passed, Jamal caught the faces of the men who'd been called out of their beds to fight the blaze he'd set. They looked dirty and tired. He could relate.

The charred building materials and water from dousing the fire had created a moat of sludge that extended ten yards from the footprint of the building. It reeked of smoldering wet ash, and some of the men pulled their tee shirts over their noses as they approached. There was nothing left of the warehouse or its contents. Masoud met with two remaining fire officials who had waited for someone associated with the building to arrive. From the start of the conversation, Jamal perceived it to be combative. Masoud pointed to the gate, a clear sign he wanted them off the property. The Iraqi fireman in charge didn't appear to like

Masoud's temperament and moved chest to chest with him, raising his voice. Masoud backed away, drew his pistol, and shot the man twice.

The fireman slumped to the ground. His peer fell to his knees in shock beside the man. Everyone in the area froze. Jamal couldn't believe the audacity of Masoud, who now threatened the remaining fireman. The middle-aged man recognized the quick trigger finger of this *Bathyoun* and staggered away toward his vehicle, distraught.

Ahmed and some of the others ran off any civilians who arrived at the scene. But all had witnessed the shooting. Jamal watched Masoud enter the scorched office area alone, where only partial walls covered in soot remained. He realized the hostages had escaped, and his rage unleashed on a couple of unlucky fighters who happened to be standing nearby.

Jamal moved into what had been the vast storage space—now open to the sky above—and noticed Ahmed walking to a particular spot amid the charred remains of the warehouse floor. He cursed loud enough for half the men to turn their heads. When Jamal approached, it became clear what had sparked the anger. In the ash were the scorched carrying cases for a weapon system Jamal was very familiar with, the M82 Barrett .50 caliber sniper rifle, an American made product. It looked like there had been close to a dozen of them stacked here. Other lesser munitions were lying about, or what was left of them after the intense heat had re-forged the delicate working parts into useless metal.

Where in God's name did they get those Barretts?

Ahmed muttered, "These weapons ... they were supposed to get me out from under Masoud."

"I don't understand."

"I arranged for them through my contacts. They were supposed to be a surprise for the general today. Each of our cells would have received one. Think of the chaos we could have caused."

Jamal heard Masoud yell for them. The two shared a disdainful look before approaching the corpse of the guard with the slashed throat amidst the crates. Masoud knelt there in a crouch with his nose turned up at the charred husk of the Iraqi. Jamal noticed a large amount of blood remained despite the blaze, only boiled down and hardened into a sickening brown lacquer on the concrete. And that body sure did smell.

Masoud scowled and nodded toward the burnt office area.

"I was at the fool Safwan. He's not charred like this one. Marks on his neck show the hostages overpowered him outside the room. Strangled to death. This man had his throat cut with one of our shop tools." He stood and kicked the blackened box cutter, which still lay next to the remains. It clattered across the floor and disappeared into a pile of smoldering ash.

"They killed the only two guards inside," said Ahmed, pointing out the obvious flaw in Masoud's plan. "Then they had a couple of weapons, and the remaining guard was still outside."

Masoud shot an icy stare at him. "It looks like they exited over there. I am told the guard outside was shot twice in the chest right outside the door."

"Well aimed, up close," said Ahmed. "After killing the others, they must have set the fire to draw the third guard in, then surprised him."

Jamal was pleased with how the conversation was going. It was important to plant and nourish certain seeds of thought when one wanted to perpetuate a lie. In this instance, that the guards had died in the order Ahmed and Masoud were assuming, which was opposite reality but which indicated a spontaneous escape. Ahmed was unwittingly doing Jamal's work for him. One look at paranoid Masoud and Jamal's worries dissipated. The man was far too jealous and spent too much time looking over his shoulder to consider he'd been had on the hostage situation.

For Ahmed's part, Jamal was waiting for him to absolve himself somehow from the failure of the operation. Everyone in the cell knew Masoud had frequently sent Ahmed away from the cell before certain decisions were about to be made. Mistakes had occurred after the initial kidnapping. Jamal had said nothing for his reasons. Ahmed might have.

Masoud asked, "You think we should have had more guards?"

"A lot more. And radios on the ones patrolling," said Ahmed.

"I didn't trust the security of our radios."

"Demand better radios then."

The two antagonists stared each other down for a good five seconds, and Jamal felt obligated to break the ice, offering to organize a body removal detail. The practical consideration must have shaken Masoud from his mental downward spiral because he regained the semblance of a leader. He barked some orders from where he stood and immediately left without a word. Jamal and Ahmed stood alone above the reeking corpse. Ahmed shrugged dismissively, turning on his heel to attend to other matters. Jamal watched Masoud trudge off and shook his head a few times.

Look at him. He is no different than any other buck lieutenant in any man's war, any man's army. Every war starts with unproven leadership. The chaff gets themselves killed or thrown aside by superiors. Too many mistakes, not enough results.

He looked around at the wet soot. The smoldering heaps of destroyed production made him feel like an ant in an ashtray. There was his own layer of nappy filth, not to mention the pasty taste in his mouth from hunger and not having brushed his teeth in a day. His face felt oily, mixed with the first trickles of sweat from the heating of the day. His vodka buzz was gone. All of it layered over the ache of tired muscles. He squinted in the direction of the rising sun, raised his hand to shield his eyes. Only now would he allow himself to acknowledge that it was over. He'd passed go; the first planned solo operation was a success.

Time to recharge and regroup.

He found his way to a gathering of junior fighters near a large panel truck they'd filled with supplies before leaving the school. He looked at his peers. Not many were connected with Hassan and the upper ranks. But loyalty would be hard to come by in this looming street fight against the West. He could build off their loyalty when he rose above them. One way to garner it was to do the dirty work with them now. He retrieved some sheets of plastic from the truck, gathered up the men, and set about removing the bodies.

The sheets lay flat next to the dead Iraqis, who were rolled onto them. Two men per body lifted the corners and transported them to the truck. The Iraqi whose throat had been cut was the most burnt out of the three, nearly to a crisp when compared to the others. He came apart in the plastic after he was jostled. As desiccated as he appeared, fluid still ran out of the newly exposed openings in his flesh. It oozed onto the plastic and poured onto Fahim's legs, who turned his nose up and cursed loudly as the men around him laughed.

Just before the cell members left the warehouse, Ahmed pulled Jamal aside within earshot of Masoud and told him he was needed to help procure supplies. They departed from the group, and Ahmed dropped him off again at the rented room to get more unhindered rest. Ahmed said he would be back in three hours to pick him up for the meeting with Hassan. Jamal knew a shower was in order before the meeting, but his body ran on fumes. His mattress called his name.

He barely heard Ahmed's vehicle pull out of the gravelly lane and onto the main road before he was horizontal. Perspiration rolled across his temple as he entertained a dreamlike memory of sodden nights on the Cherokee reservation. That heat had been the muggy variety. This air was warm but not wet, more tolerable. Still, he told himself he needed to procure an air conditioner. Two men argued outside. Another sign of the heating of the day. It was his last thought before unburdened sleep.

On the way to Hassan's safe house, Jamal asked Ahmed, "What about the fireman? Does he have a family?"

Ahmed's jaw clenched, signaling his level of dissatisfaction with Masoud's killing earlier in the day. "Not sure. We'll find out and offer cash to make amends if he had one. It will come from Hassan, and maybe you can deliver it. The fool Masoud needs to learn a lesson for his actions. He's going to hurt the cause by murdering civilians in cold blood. You heard the men grumble earlier. Even they know that."

Ten minutes later, they were at the safe house. Several guards inconspicuously patrolled the exterior of the residence. One of them gave Ahmed the welcome nod when he idled by in the Volvo. After parking, they entered the rear door and passed the pantry Jamal had been locked in. Next, they moved into the hall, whose rooms were now empty. Jamal thought about the commonality he and Ahmed shared. They both had boyhood memories associated with Hassan and were almost of the same age. They could have been playmates had Hassan introduced his nephew to Jamal when they were kids. He looked at Ahmed, hoped he wouldn't have to kill him like he did Safwan. The look lingered enough to draw Ahmed's attention.

"What?"

Caught momentarily outside his duplicitous shell, Jamal played out a script. "Aren't you nervous?"

"Why should I be? Are you?"

"Of course. We just blew a big operation last night. He-"

"We did not blow the operation. It was Masoud's poor planning."

Jamal shook his head. "Maybe so, but we were a part of it."

"Hassan will not see it that way. You and I had worked for two days straight, making sure we got the hostages in the first place without killing half our cell. Remember Masoud's own words, 'Once we get them, we do it my way.' Jamal shrugged his shoulders to indicate uncertainty remained on his part.

"If I know the general," said Ahmed in a low voice, "he will make a change, possibly replacing Masoud with me. I am requesting that he make you my second in command."

"It would be my honor, brother."

Ahmed clapped him on the shoulder and nodded before heading down the hall to the sitting room where Hassan waited. Beyond the minaret shaped entry, smoke hovered in the upper regions of the space. When they entered, Hassan rose to greet them out of a bigger chair than had been there during Jamal's indoctrination. Two more similar leather armchairs were around a more contemporary table carved out of Acacia wood. Another addition to the room was a cabinet placed against the far wall. Through one of its upper glass doors, he saw the glisten of sunlight upon crystal. The idea of reigniting his alcohol buzz quickly turned into a craving.

"Sit, my able soldiers," said Hassan. "We will discuss our matters in short order but first a drink."

He turned toward the cabinet rather than taking his seat. Ahmed declined. Jamal was surprised to see Hassan pour three fingers of Johnnie Walker Black Label in a tumbler, neat. Jamal waited to partake until Hassan finished lighting another pale yellow Gauloise and took up his own glass of the top shelf, blended Scotch whisky. The electrifying burn of the liquor dulled any lingering edginess Jamal had felt coming into this meeting. He placed the near-empty glass on the table next to a couple of packs of Hassan's French cigarettes and a stack of loosely collated papers. Numbers and words in Arabic were scrawled across hand-drawn grids. The look of it seemed wholly unprofessional, and Jamal wondered how the general was getting by without the standard support staff to which someone of his stature was accustomed.

"Have you been waiting long, sir?" asked Ahmed. "If so, I apologize."

Hassan raised a dismissive hand; the cigarette was firmly pinched between his index and middle fingers.

"Don't worry. Even in this kind of war, I have logistical needs to attend to while I wait." He strained to bend his upper body forward and snatched up the stack of papers.

"Requisition forms, in chicken scratch no less," he said.

With disdain, he tossed them down again. The papers knocked the cigarettes on the floor. Retrieving them would be something Masoud would have done out of reflex, thought Jamal. Today was about setting himself apart from Masoud. And perhaps even Ahmed. The whisky had been poured into his growling stomach only a minute ago, but already it afforded him just enough aloofness to look at the pack on the floor and not care whether Hassan had to burn a few calories getting to them. On the heels of that thought was an urge. He reached for his glass and found himself walking over by the cabinet.

This elicited a look of concern from Ahmed, while Hassan seemed to find delight in the manner of his bold new subordinate. Hassan finished off his drink, Jamal was at his side, filling the tumbler for him before placing the bottle on the table. He'd taken more whisky for himself, and as he sat again, took the initiative of the conversation too—the one needed for his reasons and theirs.

"What is to be done about Masoud?"

Ahmed had the same look of discomfort at the pressing of a delicate matter with the general, especially by a newcomer. Jamal wondered if he regretted bringing him along all of a sudden. But Hassan's demeanor became serious. He didn't appear to be moved by the delivery of the statement or who had made it.

"He is a fool," said Hassan. "A fool playing dangerous games. Despite your excellent planning, this latest failure at the warehouse was the last straw."

"What are your thoughts, uncle?" asked Ahmed with a sideways glance. Jamal took it as an exhibition of his own level of closeness to the man who controlled both their destinies.

"Kill him. He cannot be demoted or put on the streets. He is the type of person who would seek revenge."

"He would talk to the coalition," said Jamal. "A liability."

Hassan looked him in the eye and said, "You will do it ... before you take his place."

Ahmed moved to the edge of his seat and was on the verge of an objection when Hassan gestured for him to stand down.

"Relax, my eager nephew. There is plenty of need for your leadership skills. In addition to the loss of the warehouse and hostages, the Mulaab cell is leaderless as of this morning. An airstrike found him in his bed while he slept. You are both leaving here with bars on your shoulders. So to speak."

Hassan raised himself out of the cushions, the leather crackling after the departure of his bulk. "Let me offer you some food and drink before you go. I can tell when my men are hungry. And I have some ammunition for the cells." He raised the bottle of Scotch in the air and flashed a glassy-eyed grin. "At least we received a resupply."

Ahmed did not partake, because he was the most devout Muslim Jamal had met in the Baathist cells, but Hassan and Jamal continued to drink and bond as soldiers. The buzz slowed the repeating images of the men Jamal had killed only hours before. Lingering remorse for Safwan stung as it had for Choudary when the deaths of three good men came up. Jamal was relieved when the topic changed to the situation with the fireman. A sum of *dinars* was retrieved from the lower cabinet drawers and put in an envelope for Jamal to deliver to the family. Immediately, Hassan broached a new topic.

"I have something else for you, Jamal."

"I am at your service, Hassan. Anything for the cause."

Ahmed shot yet another sideways look toward Jamal at his use of the general's first name.

"We have made an ally in this war already. Do you know of whom I speak?" asked Hassan.

"The *takfiri*?"

"Yes. Foreign Islamic fighters who have come for other reasons than why we fight."

As if to reinforce the notion that strict tenets of the Muslim faith were not a driving force behind his motivations, Hassan drained the tumbler and reached for the bottle again.

"I want you to be our liaison with a few of their couriers," he said. "I think they will find you trustworthy because you are not cut from the same cloth as my military associates, whom they are somewhat skeptical of. You will feed them only the information that I give you. And you will frequently receive cash from them. We cannot win a war without the funds to do it."

"Where are your contacts located?" asked Jamal.

"Here in Ramadi. Fallujah too. Their leadership is east toward the capital. And they all move a lot. You will need a reliable driver and the ability to leave on short notice. Any planned operations will need to be suspended in your absence."

Jamal nodded, and Hassan moved toward the door as the smell of food filled the room. The business part of the meeting was ending. In the few free moments of mental freedom, while the men gathered themselves to leave for dinner, Jamal realized two things. For one, it seemed Ahmed was not privy to the details of his previous relationship with Hassan, judging by his reactions to their candor. Second, Hassan was buying into his cover enough to trust him with this new role. Things were proceeding as planned.

Amazed and energized at the turn of events, bumped a little higher by the effects of the alcohol, he told Hassan what he wanted to hear. The arrogant tone raised Ahmed's eyebrow one last time.

"Hassan, you don't have to worry about your operations in Askan anymore. From now on, we're going to be the most effective cell in your sector."

CHAPTER 15

Jamal was on his way to the school after Ahmed had given him the keys to the Volvo for a few days. It felt strange driving in Iraq, not that he'd done a lot of driving in his life anyway. He just hoped he didn't wreck his friend's car or run over some kid along the way because his mind was more focused on what he was about to do. Masoud had shown an evil streak the world's moral majority would not condone. He was assured of that.

This is an execution for taking a civilian life. If he were a soldier in a real army, he'd receive a court-martial. Possibly hang for murder. He'll get a soldier's death. Quick and painless.

Jamal turned off the main road and headed toward the Askan neighborhood. When he approached the school, he saw something he did not expect on this day of death. A tall African woman emerged from the main entrance in Western clothing, but for the *hijab* about her face. She carried several boxes while being rudely escorted from the premises by several fighters. Fahim was among them.

An old hatchback was parked along the curb. Jamal eased to a stop behind it. His initial sense told him she was not cowed by the coarse jibing of the men, most likely provoked by Masoud inside. The boxes in her arms blocked her view of him as she emerged from the Volvo. While he approached, she attempted to open her trunk with one hand, and the top box tumbled from the stack. Jamal was there to break its fall.

Like him, she seemed surprised—pleasantly, he hoped—to see another African. But any tells that might have revealed feminine attraction were quickly shrouded by a harder countenance.

"Excuse me," she said. "But I think I can manage myself." Her comment was curt, in thickly accented Arabic. She'd used the most formal version of it, revealing it was a second language to her.

She placed the boxes in the hatchback. Their eyes met once more for just a second when she relieved him of his burden. The last box was shoved in next to the others as if she were mad at it. She slammed the trunk shut. Jamal watched her fumble with her keys on her way to the driver's side of the car.

She is brave, but she is scared. Those keys sound like a tambourine from her shaking. And that glance, was there something in it?

She got behind the wheel, glaring at the fighters in front of the school one last time. After she started the car, it peeled away from the gravelly curb. The men cringed at the sound of her grinding the gears twice as she accelerated down the road. Jamal turned toward them, still amid a cloud of dust she'd stirred up.

"What in hell was that about?"

Fahim answered for them. "She's a teacher who came to get the few computers the school owned. Masoud said they belonged to the cause now. All he let her have was a few calculators and a bunch of paper and school supplies."

Jamal tried to appear unaffected by her poor treatment as he moved past the men and into the school, but an instinctual protective urge welled up. The almost bodily reaction caught him off guard in his mission-oriented persona. Once inside, he found Masoud in the principal's office, going over an upcoming operation.

In as sarcastic a tone as he could muster, Jamal said, "So who was the African queen?"

Masoud barely looked up but replied, "A misplaced person with misplaced intentions."

"I do not under-"

"She is not from here, but she cares so much for the children of this country who aren't getting to play school daily. She is a waste of my time. I told her not to come back, that she should just go back to Africa."

Play school? You took over a real school, asshole.

Jamal couldn't help but wonder if Masoud wanted him to go back to Africa too.

"So, what do you want to do with the computers?" He expected the forthcoming answer, but felt like egging Masoud on, a cruel endeavor during the last hours of a man's life.

"What computers?"

"The ones she came for. How are you going to use them for the cause?"

Masoud appeared mystified and dismissive at once with a wave of his hand. "Who cares! I don't need computers. I need more men and some luck!"

"Another thing you need is a more secure base of operations. I want to show you a place I have been looking at for us. I feel like eyes are on us every minute of the day here, brother."

"You and Ahmed never liked my choice of this school for our base. Neither of you supported me on that issue."

"Well, it isn't the most defensible position in the neighborhood," answered Jamal more deferentially now. His embedded humanity finally felt pity for the walking dead man before him. "But the cell is yours nonetheless. It was always your decision to make. The men, myself, even Ahmed, will fight to defend it. I only want to show you the other place."

The concession seemed to mollify the flailing ego of Masoud, and it was enough to get him to concede to Jamal's request.

"In one hour then," said Jamal before leaving to join the men, soon to be his men.

It was done near an abandoned truck dock at one of the industrial park's weed-overgrown relics. Jamal led the three of them to the place. When Masoud moved in front of him and Ahmed to enter the door first, Jamal shot him in the back of the head. The echo bounced off the high concrete walls around them and died there in the lonely place along with Masoud. They dragged the body back to the Volvo and heaved it into the trunk onto some plastic Jamal had laid inside. Next, they finished reconnoitering the empty, cavernous industrial building as a new home for the Anbar Brigade.

On the way back to the school, they dumped Masoud's body on a garbage pile in a Shiite slum. The news that he was no longer part of the resistance was met with mixed reactions. But he'd betrayed the cause in the eyes of too many with his cold-blooded view of the populace. By the time the blistering sun plunged into the western desert, Jamal had ascended another rung of the ladder.

For most of the grueling summer—an eternity for the hard-fighting man—his cell and Ahmed's battled the American and Iraqi security forces stationed in Ramadi. Jamal still had not killed an American directly, getting by on the accepted notion that leaders of soldiers aren't expected to do the actual killing. Jamal fulfilled his promise to Hassan, however, and was burdened with remorse over the violence his cell perpetrated. Following a string of successful operations, his steadfast leadership was enough to burnish him with certain respect among his men, and among the other cells in Hassan's network. Because every day is about survival in war, a soldier who can persevere is highly valued, more so if they can lead others to do the same. Jamal's men learned to persevere with regularity. Hassan began to give them the most high profile operations.

Eventually, the memory of Masoud's ham-handed tenure as leader of the Anbar Brigade seemed an age ago, the men having forged all new experiences under Jamal's leadership. Replacements moved in and out quickly. Many died in their first or second attack from lack of training. This further cemented the pecking order of surviving veterans. Assured of his place in the resistance, Jamal began to sense his commitment to his mission would soon be tested to its utmost.

CHAPTER 16

Hadiya thanked her host in Arabic as the middle-aged woman placed the tea glass and sugar bowl near her. The tired woman slumped into a seat across the linen-covered table and sipped from her glass. It seemed to relax her instantly. Hadiya had anticipated this respite herself after the stressful morning of placing groups of students in various ad hoc places of learning. Ever since the war's booted feet had kicked them out of their school a few weeks ago, the more dedicated educators had struggled to find temporary locations from which to teach.

Small groups had been put up in an abandoned storefront, another home, and a mosque. The remaining students were coming here to the headmaster's villa. It was nice enough, and within a relatively safe neighborhood—at least so far—she thought, a hedge against being overly optimistic in a war-ravaged country. The middle-aged woman before her was the headmaster's spouse, and Hadiya wondered how much she dreaded bringing so many young children inside her well-appointed home.

"It is extremely kind of you even to consider doing this," said Hadiya while offering a gentle smile that preceded another sip of the strong, sweet tea.

"People of means should help out in times of war," said the woman.

Some children entered the house, and two boys immediately proceeded to chase each other through the first floor, eventually making their way into the kitchen. One of them nearly caused the woman to spill her tea. Her pursed-lip, if only for a moment,

Hadiya noted, betrayed the sincerity of her preceding statement. Enough to know the woman had not committed without reservation.

Maybe she's going to need some time. We all know the place will never look the same after today.

More children entered the home, followed by the headmaster and another teacher. An argument between two older boys broke out over the soccer ball they would need to share during breaks. One jerked the ball from the other's hand and lost his grip, causing it to soar into a row of framed pictures arranged on an end table. The troublemakers fled the scene just as a teacher entered the room to break up the altercation.

"We will do our best to keep things in order," said Hadiya to the woman, who surprised Hadiya with a nonchalant glance toward the mess.

"Boys will be boys. I suppose I will have to get used to that. You know I raised two daughters," said the woman, who seemed in a state of submission, which Hadiya was glad to see.

"My mother had two daughters as well," said Hadiya. "I am the oldest."

One of the teachers came into the room and asked the host which electrical outlets she could use. The woman turned and looked idly for a moment at Hadiya. She lightly slapped the tabletop and said, "Excuse me."

"Of course. I still have my tea to finish."

When Hadiya was alone, a relative term in a houseful of hyperactive children, she thought about what the woman had said.

Boys being boys seems to be the precursor to men misbehaving. Where does all that aggression come from?

The Iraqi men who had kicked them out of their school in rough fashion a few weeks back certainly qualified as men misbehaving. She saw the African man shortly thereafter when she returned to claim some supplies, albeit unsuccessfully. He showed kindness, at least. She hadn't learned the man's name, but since then, she'd found herself thinking about him occasionally. There was a physicality about him that would make any woman feel safe when in his company. But with a man like that, safety would be another relative term. His life as an insurgent meant he would always be associated with danger.

Hadiya was surprised at her attraction to such a man, despite the anger she still felt toward him and his band of militants, and the danger he represented. She'd only edged up to real danger a few times in her life. Coming to Iraq to teach mathematics and advance her Arabic speaking skills had danger associated with it even before the Americans began their war footing. When the invasion became imminent, her decision to stay—despite the urgent pleadings of family in her native Kenya—had told her that she was no longer the tentative daughter of wealthy parents, who had known security and predictability her whole life.

She was aware that her newfound willingness to flirt with danger coincided with the decision-making period about coming to Iraq when she felt the strongest connection to God in her life. How many nights had she gone to bed fretting over being a Christian in Muslim lands? Only when she had recited the 23rd Psalm over and over again would she be able to find sleep finally.

Religious conviction, the backbone of humanity.

She wondered what convictions the African man held. Just because he was an insurgent didn't necessarily mean he was a Muslim zealot, a member of what the Iraqis call the *takfiri*. On the day the teachers were summarily evicted from school, there hadn't been time or courage to ask about religious leanings. The day after they came though, she'd heard from some locals that it was the holdouts from Saddam's former military that were moving into the neighborhood.

She would never even consider bridging the gap with an Islamic jihadist.

My backbone isn't that strong, Lord. But a non-religious man, or even a lukewarm Muslim? I could have the courage to witness to someone like that, especially if there was a mutual attraction to strengthen the bond, the closeness to a man which has alluded me—love.

She felt her heart skip a beat at the possibility but felt guilty for indulging in its recklessness. The safer bet was to stick with anger. Something her mother would appreciate.

CHAPTER 17

The cell operated primarily out of the industrial complex over the summer due to the shifting dynamics of Ramadi's battle space. One day in late July, Jamal supervised the clearing out of the school once and for all. He noticed a half-dozen desktop computers, monitors, and keyboards stacked in the corner of a storage room. It stirred thoughts of the African teacher, whom he'd lost track of in his crowded mind. On a whim—or maybe it was a more primal urge—he decided to load the machines and all the accessories into a van for delivery. Fahim asked a local whether he knew where the students were taught and if an African was with them. The local was not sure about the African and could not produce the address, but knew the neighborhood where the headmaster's villa was. The tall, gaunt man with a hungry look about him seemed pleased to have helped Jamal, who had made a name for himself among the citizens of Ramadi's Askan district.

The man seemed too intimidated to initiate small talk, however, and Jamal was always looking to recruit new men, so he sized him up and asked, "What skills do you possess?"

"I worked for a builder with Jordanian roots. He left the country with everything he owned before the invasion. Now I do anything I can to feed my brood. We have no electricity, so food must be found and eaten daily."

"You have a family?"

"Yes. A wife and three children. They are frightened to leave home. I only leave to find work or food."

"And have you completed these tasks yet today?" A softening of the man's eyes accompanied his head, shaking in the negative. "You are good with your hands, no?" asked Jamal.

"I figure handling weapons is not much different than handling tools."

"Get some food for your family over there." Jamal nodded to a nearby fighter who had just returned from a grocer, indicating the local could partake of their supplies. "Spread the word in the neighborhood. Tell any man who wants to join the cause that this is not a military or Baathist cell anymore. This is an Iraqi cell."

"Allah has truly blessed the people of Ramadi. You have my word. Tomorrow I will bring the men you request."

Jamal and Fahim drove around in the suburban neighborhood, looking for the headmaster's villa. They knew of no cells that operated here. As such, this residential enclave enjoyed a minimum coalition presence and therefore exuded a feeling of normalcy. The dwellings here were well kept one-or two-story villas. Most had palm trees and colorful plantings in the front. The children played soccer in the streets with a real ball. For their pickup games, some of the boys even wore shoes made for the game and replica jerseys from the African or European leagues. Not a care in the world it seemed for these rich Arab kids. They had such a simple job in the war, thought Jamal.

Go on being normal. We need to see it as adults. They need to feel it to survive. Some of them live the nightmare, though.

The side of Jamal—of his past really—that would have wanted to jump out of the van and play with them was turned off; a switch was flipped consciously for practical reasons of maintaining his adopted persona. On a deeper level, however, he'd been dulled by the daily violence he experienced. He had no joy to share with frolicking children. Sure, among the men, there was ball-busting humor, chiding remarks to put another man in his place that drew genuine laughter from the cell members. And there always was the hilarious sarcasm of Fahim that had gotten them through Masoud's absurd directives. But their days were not punctuated by truly joyful experiences. How could they be?

Fahim took one hand from the steering wheel and pointed. "There she is."

Jamal's morbid thoughts evaporated when he saw her. She walked their way on the sidewalk about fifty yards in front of them. A black and white patterned *hijab* covered the top of her head, exposing only her perfectly proportioned facial features. Her skin was lighter than his ebony tone, but only barely. He found her beautiful, elegant, and surprisingly imposing; her African genealogy held her taller than most Arab women, around six feet, he estimated. Just then, she turned and opened a low iron gate to enter the yard of a large villa. Jamal told Fahim to pull to the side of the street.

From there, they watched her approach the arched, double doors at the front of the villa. One was opened from the inside, and a dozen children ran past her. Some girls formed playgroups in the yard, while the older boys passed a soccer ball around in the street. The teacher followed them to the gate and took up a watchful position. Jamal watched her and noticed the gentle ease of her smile. It relaxed him. She seemed relaxed as well, daresay joyful. He wanted to enter her world.

"Pull up along the curb and stop by the house. Go slowly and don't scare them, okay?"

"This should be interesting," said Fahim as he shifted the van into gear and lightly touched the accelerator.

The motion of the vehicle must have caught her peripheral vision because she turned to face them. She looked toward the driver with no reaction. Perhaps she didn't recognize Fahim. One glance at the passenger seat, however, elicited a head tilt and pursing of the lip as soon as their eyes met. She folded her arms across her chest and turned back toward the children, but her expression did not change. Fahim laughed. Once near the house, they parked the van, and Jamal hopped out. She maintained her position behind the gate and held her narrow-eyed gaze, which could not be equaled by half the bloodthirsty terrorists in Iraq for its animosity.

"I have come to give you something," he said as several of the children looked over.

In the same accented Arabic as before, she replied with a disingenuous smile.

"Wait here. I have something for you as well."

Her long legs stamped off toward the villa, and Jamal was left to feel awkward among the children. Someone inside opened the door to the house for her. On the second floor, a curtain was pulled toward the jamb of a window. Small faces peered out at him, and he squirmed a little more. A minute passed, and she approached him again. This time she carried a handful of papers and that same angry look from the first day at the school. When she was ten paces away, she held them up, receipts it turns out.

"Why don't you take care of these? These are the costs of running a school out of someone's home."

Before Jamal could respond, she thrust the receipts at him. He was intent on diffusing her ire, so he calmly received them and tucked them into his pocket.

"It is done. You will be repaid in Euros, which are worth more than dollars and certainly Iraqi *dinars* these days."

He stood wide-legged with his arms folded across his chest now. Her slender fingers fidgeted with one another at her waist while she thought of what to say.

"I suppose that will be adequate."

Jamal jumped on the momentary reprieve to reveal the reason he'd come. He made a gesture toward the van, which included a nod in Fahim's direction. The young fighter opened the sliding door on the curbside, and Jamal gauged her reaction. He thought he could surprise her again, but she only turned to him and stared. There was a wariness he'd seen before in a woman's eyes. It was skepticism on the heels of wanting to trust him, to believe in him. He knew her mind raced in an attempt to find the right words. He let her off easy.

Already moving to unload the computers, he said, "You will not have to deal with Masoud anymore. I am in charge now. From now on, things will be different."

"When can we have the school back?"

There was less ire in her voice now. Jamal was glad for it. At least she could be a reasonable person. He broke the ice and already had a reason to come back again with the reimbursements. He would come alone for that errand.

"I am working on that as we speak."

CHAPTER 18

After the first week of August, Hassan summoned Jamal. When he arrived at the new safe house a short while later, he parked the Volvo along a dense row of palm trees. It was one of the hottest days of the summer, the smell of superheated asphalt thick in the air as he emerged from the air-conditioned vehicle. Following the shade line of the palms, he escaped the sun's brilliance for a block before he neared the entrance to a small courtyard between buildings. Armed members of Hassan's security detail patrolled the scorched rooftops nearby, while those on the ground granted him passage.

The air was still; the enclosed nature of the courtyard stifled the already anemic breeze outside. Hassan stood near a small fountain in a blazer drenched with sweat. The trickling sound of water echoed off the stone walls while he dabbed a handkerchief in the pool and applied it to the nape of his neck. Jamal noticed a flask in his hand when they greeted each other. He declined the usual offer of a cigarette but reached for the flask.

"I need you to meet with the *takfiri* today," said Hassan. "They are prepared to hand you a large amount of cash."

"When and where and how much am I picking up?"

"Noon in Fallujah," said Hassan with an outstretched hand that waited for the return of his flask. "The market near the river. Should be a half-million Euros. You will find a barbershop in a row of storefronts just north of the vendors, in between a looted television repair shop and a burned-out music store."

"Who am I meeting?"

"A fighter and a cleric."

"Not just a courier this time?"

"No. Higher-ups. I want you to spend some time talking to them. Get an understanding of their strength level and report back to me."

"I understand."

Jamal walked past the last vendor's cart, an okra peddler whose wilted product had been picked over for the morning. A gust of wind off the desert might as well have come from a blowtorch as he moved down the middle of the crowded street. No cars traveled here because the market behind him blocked access on this end. He noted that locals who exited the storefronts moved about their business without much delay. Many companies were boarded up or emptied of their contents from looting. The market had been subdued as well, with less frivolous wares on display and only essential food items for sale. He knew it was because of the ultra-conservative *takfiri* presence. They owned this turf now.

He felt a sense of pride that he'd come this far in the mission. Infiltrating ambitious, radical Islamists who craved to see America burn was the reason he'd been sent to Iraq. Today's contact represented the next level of a working relationship between them and Hassan's network of Baathist insurgents. He remembered Hassan had stressed the financial aspect of it several times.

Tribute money. Rent. I am collecting the rent. I wonder if we ... Hassan ... is hurting for cash. Maybe the private money is harder to come by than everyone thinks.

Another shot of blistering heat swirled around him, this one kicking up loose sand. He pulled the hood of his *dish-dash* over his head and pressed on, squinted to keep it out of his eyes. This was the micro-grain type. Airborne dust that seems to find every crevice. The crowd thinned out quickly once he'd walked away from the market, but he soon heard a commotion around a bend in the street ahead. An Arab woman in a traditional full length, black *Abaya* shuffled by him in the opposite direction. Their eyes met for but a moment. Hers showed the reason for her hasty pace; fear lingered after leaving the place he was going.

Nervous women. Usually means dangerous men in this part of the world.

He moved around the curved, narrow street, saw men in long beards chastising the local, clean-shaven men around them. The massing of zealots in the narrow thoroughfare created a bottleneck that shoppers were forced to pass through after they left the market. The bearded leader singled out a particular male, and he became a magnet, attracting several henchmen, also bearded. They accosted the brazen local who'd dared to shave before leaving his home. Verbal abuse quickly gave way to shoving and kicking while the man huddled himself amid the bullies. Several men held a dusty sandal in their hands as a flogging tool, a degrading gesture in Arab culture.

Jamal put the poor man out of his mind and focused on the leader, the gatekeeper here, who stood outside the barbershop of which Hassan had spoken. The bearded man turned in his direction, and Jamal's height above the fray allowed their gazes to intercept. He offered a slight nod from inside his hood. The man said something to a nearby lackey and moved off the stoop toward a narrow gangway between the barbershop and the torched music store. Jamal was led to the rear of the storefronts, where the sounds of the street diminished. They entered a foyer where the smell of incense burning and conditioned air pushed into his face. It was a welcome respite from the heat and dust, and stillness about the place beguiled Jamal as if danger was not yet added to the mix.

But danger was here to be sure, he reminded himself. These were radical foreign jihadists who would flay his skin without blinking an eye if his cover were blown. Without a word, the bearded man and his robe glided along a stone corridor until they reached a door. He rapped lightly and opened it. A whisper secured Jamal entry into the room unescorted, and he proceeded to climb the next rung on the ladder.

The room was as dim as the corridor except for the light from a flat-screen television mounted on the far wall. It was tuned to *al-Jazeera* with the volume on a low setting. On the wall adjacent to the television hung a banner with lettering in Arabic, *Jama' at al-Tawhid wal-Jihad.* Jamal translated it as "The Group for Religious Unity and Struggle." Beneath the banner, two jihadists sat alone.

The younger of the two rose from a contemporary steel and leather chair, three of which sat around a low glass table with a tea set in the middle. He wore regular Western-style trousers and a button-down work shirt. A scarf was tied around his neck to obscure his face below the eyes. Unless a pistol resided in the small of his back, he did not appear to be armed. The other man, an old cleric, remained seated. He offered Jamal the empty chair as well as a glass and saucer. Jamal pegged his accent as Jordanian.

"Please excuse the chaos outside," said the cleric with the pace of the elderly as he pulled on the thinning gray beard beneath his chin.

The loose sleeve of his *dish-dash* covered his other hand, which sat upon his lap. Jamal kept the thought close. *Was he an armed religious man?*

The fighter sat again. He did not partake in the steaming tea before him. Instead, his eyes never left Jamal's and were like lances through a body without armor. It seemed the man before him knew everything, and Jamal was aware that his armor—as thin as paper really—was only his ability to fool others. If that layer of protection were melted away, it would expose him in an instant.

Hold on, man. Hang with this guy. Remove fear like the major said and move on to the topic at hand.

"The unfaithful need to be reminded," said Jamal. "This, I understand. But I hope the type of schoolyard bullying outside is just an appetizer to the main meal."

The two *takfiri* looked at each other before the masked fighter turned toward Jamal. "The meal you speak of is being prepared even as we sit here. But we do not need to make this the beginning of our conversation. Today we are developing our partnership—a necessary partnership."

Jamal nodded in affirmation. "This is what my superiors have deemed as well." He sipped the sweet blend and was grateful for the liquid, his mouth like cotton from the adrenaline rush he was experiencing. After a few more minutes of small talk, the *takfiri* seemed ready to get to business—this time, the fighter initiated.

"Our first act of collaboration will be to attack that den of thieves, the United Nations headquarters. We need the plans of the building, and have learned the military possesses the existing blueprints."

This was news to Jamal, but it made sense. In the years following the Persian Gulf War, Saddam had at least pretended to have a vested interest in the U.N. inspectors' safety while they scoured his country, searching for weapons of mass destruction. Part of this pretense would be upheld if the security forces assigned to protect them maintained sole possession of the building plans for the U.N. headquarters.

Jamal nodded. "I will see what I can obtain from General Barzan. He may exact a price for such information."

The look on the fighter's face reflected his distaste for the profiteering aspect of this conflict. Perhaps it was in that moment the vast gulf between the ideologies was most apparent, a harbinger of the inevitable power struggle between the two resistance groups should the invaders be driven out. The fighter reached forward to pour a glass of tea. Jamal knew he only did it to find the space to calm himself. It happened quickly, and the fighter raised his eyes from the cup.

"You know, Allah will frown upon you if you gain or keep wealth at the cost of blessed *jihad*."

"The money will go from your war chest to ours," Jamal replied. "I swear in the name of the prophet; our operational needs are earnest. As I am sure you have learned, it costs a lot to run a war out of basements and back rooms."

The fighter chafed visibly at the mention of battling a Western enemy while hamstrung with apparent limitations, then espoused his mantra anyway.

"Back rooms or not, this war will be won in the streets by the Sons of Allah. We will clear this land of the infidel!" he said with a rising voice and a glint in his eye.

Jamal nodded, attempting to seem caught up in the man's vitriol while guarding against the overplayed hand.

The cleric spoke. "In the coming days, the roar of the Lion of Iraq will be heard. Be prepared for strong reactions from the coalition."

Jamal's puzzled look drew a response from the fighter. "Do you know of whom he speaks?"

"This Lion. Is he a foreigner?" asked Jamal.

The fighter answered, "Yes. A veteran of *jihad* in Afghanistan during the Soviet invasion. And recently, he was wounded fighting American Special Forces there. He is a noble fighter who came here to lay the first stones of the new Caliphate … this land between the two rivers, ancient and proud. This is where it will start again."

The cleric bounced his chin a couple of times in acknowledgment. As he did so, the old man's wrinkled fingertips pulled on the end of his tousled beard, his eyes darkened, and Jamal sensed his mind had gone to another place.

The fighter continued. "The Westerners have done us a favor and disbanded your general's beloved Republican Guard. The infidel now has to train a new standing army and piece together a national police force. All from the ground up."

Jamal nodded and dipped his toe into the fray. "Now is the time to strike. We must increase the tempo of attacks on patrols that venture into the neighborhoods. We will have to force their hand, though, because their infantry is tentative to engage at times."

"We have noticed this as well," said the fighter.

"The Army units in our sector will typically come to a halt upon encountering anything suspicious, call their higher command for direction, then wait for artillery or air support. Only then will they proceed into a defended area one building at a time. But they will clear the neighborhood. Very deliberate is the commander of 4-131."

Jamal's calculated use of a specific unit designation drew a puzzled response from the fighter this time. The cleric still seemed lost in his thoughts as he prepared a second cup of tea.

"Why do you know that?" asked the fighter.

"I know a lot about my enemy. I need to."

"You misunderstand. I am interested in how you came to this knowledge."

"After a successful attack, I tore the shoulder patch off of a dead soldier. Later, I looked up the unit designation online and learned they were a National Guard unit from Florida, a southern state in America. They call themselves the Hurricane Battalion. This is knowledge we can use."

"How so?" asked the fighter, edging up on his seat a touch. The cleric finally tuned in and waited on Jamal's response as well.

"I did some further research and learned that this invasion force is unique from almost all other imperialist invaders of the past. This group of American combatants happens to weigh on the heavy side with their National Guard and Reserve soldiers. Volunteers yes, but part-time soldiers on a tour of duty only months long. A lot of them are just college kids. Most have never seen war and don't even understand why they are fighting. It affects their decision making and morale, which I take advantage of."

The *takfiri* seemed impressed, which meant that type of knowledge was above their purview, the fruit Jamal had hoped to pick from his line of discussion. Of course, Jamal had seen the image of the patch through a set of binoculars and did his research. As for the effectiveness of the 4th Battalion, 131st Infantry Regiment, they'd been doing just fine in Ramadi since their arrival in March. Their roadblocks and disciplined maneuvers on foot patrols had been a thorn in his side from an operations standpoint.

The fighter added his own experience to the conversation. "We are seeing more and more of their new Striker vehicles up north, in Mosul …"

The fighter prated on about an operation in northern Iraq, which had yielded the death of two American service members. Jamal filtered the learned information.

Mosul. That is good to know. Must be their entry point. Probably cross at the border with Syria. I wonder if Farouk is working his way up there?

The *takfiri* and *Bathyoun* compared notes for a while longer after the fighter finished his story. Jamal learned information during the meal that he could use to hinder the efforts of this self-proclaimed Lion. He knew as sure as the day was hot that he needed to come face to face with the man. Today though, only the seed needed to be planted, so he stayed the entirety of the afternoon in the cool enclave of the *takfiri*, forging the new relationship as Hassan—and Major Winters—had instructed him to do. He stroked the ego of the standard-issue extremist fighter, whose path to a new global Caliphate would be soaked in the blood of innocents if he had his way.

Al Qaeda was the big game he'd come here to hunt. If these men were true jihadists, and this mysterious Lion of Iraq had conducted *jihad* alongside the Taliban in Afghanistan, chances were he had plenty of connections to *al Qaeda*. He needed to confirm the identity of the man. After being told the man had been wounded in Afghanistan, Jamal considered the major's intel before he'd left the States.

Could be Abu Musab al-Zarqawi ... The man in the pictures, and one of the administration's big reasons for invading.

He left the market street later that evening with a suitcase full of Euros. It was the time of day when life under curfew caused locals to scurry about, satisfying domestic needs before nightfall. Jamal relished the moment as he walked among them, allowed his thoughts to move freely, like an actor between performances. This last one would have drawn rave reviews. The fact that he was breathing was confirmation.

His thoughts went back to the cleric. It turns out he hadn't been armed, only self-conscious of a wound sustained during a fire in his mosque. More than anything the cleric had said during the meeting today, Jamal had noticed how lost in thought he became at times.

When was it? After the mention of the Lion and the attack on the U.N., or was it the talk of being outmatched by the enemy? Religious men are less concerned with tactical issues, more interested in the behavior of other men. Perhaps this Lion of Iraq—if he is, in fact, Zarqawi—is overreaching, and the cleric senses it. Attacking the

United Nations is bold. The "Lion" is unafraid to bite the hand that feeds the population ... the one group he truly needs to be able to continue his precious jihad.

CHAPTER 19

Jamal was on his way to see the teacher, just a week after dropping off the computers. It was something he'd thought about every day since then, a form of escape from thinking about this possible attack on the U.N. headquarters. Because he would serve as a courier at most, he lamented not being able to thwart any planning. His foot in the door wasn't enough to affect anything yet.

Earlier, he trimmed his afro and shaved the thick stubble he'd worn since mingling with the *takfiri*. He approached the villa with the satchel of money slung on his shoulder, and inquisitive eyes once again appeared in a window on the ground floor. Before he could knock on the door, the teacher opened it and came out onto the front stoop in her bare feet. She wore no *hijab* this time, so her straight, jet-black hair fell to just below her shoulders. He heard giggling as she quickly closed the door behind her. It appeared she was not inviting him inside.

"Sorry," she said. "They're being a little silly about you being here."

"It's all right. I understand. I'm just glad they're not scared of me."

"Should they be?"

"They have no reason to. I can promise you that."

"Should I?" she asked with a certain amount of coyness.

"Maybe."

They both smiled. The awkward pause borne of mutual attraction ensued until she ended it by thanking him for delivering the computers.

"It seems I owe you an apology. You are not anything like your predecessor."

"Well, I hope having them made your efforts a little easier. But with all the rolling blackouts, you may have used them less than hoped."

"It is true. But even a few hours a day is helpful. We are grateful."

They formally introduced themselves to each other. Hadiya, she explained, was an ethnic name from her native Kenya. Jamal made her laugh for the first time by informing her that in Arabic, her name meant guide to righteousness, or simply gift. Her easy self-deprecation showed an even more congenial side to her, which he found alluring.

Although Jamal noted the wariness never left her completely, as they talked, he sensed a new level of comfort between them. He impressed her again by handing her more than enough Euros to cover any past or present expenses. It went well after that exchange, and he asked if he could check on them in another week. She was amenable to the idea, so on the drive back to the war zone, he thought about her the whole way. He also heard alarm bells going off inside his head.

A spy with a civilian girlfriend on the side. What would the major think?

Jamal arrived at Hassan's latest safe house, this one a cramped hovel in a densely packed neighborhood. The quality of his accommodations had deteriorated already, just months into the conflict. It had been a bad week, too; an entire cell had been wiped out by the coalition in rough fashion.

Hassan was in a desultory mood when Jamal found him. After discussing another recent meeting with the *takfiri*, Jamal asked for a tidy sum to cover expenses. Hassan did not question his needs, instead reaching for a shoebox full of tightly stacked bills and grabbing a handful. Jamal saw large denominations and figured it totaled more than double the requested amount. In the back of his mind, he already knew some of it would go to the teachers and other displaced residents of Ramadi's various war-torn neighborhoods.

"Take what you can now," said Hassan. "You never know if I'll be dead before we meet again, and this money goes into the coffers of the enemy."

"You won't be dead, Hassan. Don't talk like that," said Jamal. He downed a snifter of the general's imported brandy, surprising himself at the sincerity of the sentiment. Hassan reached to fill the glass again. Somehow the words just fell out of Jamal's mouth.

"Tell me something about my mother."

"What do you want to know?"

Hassan's facial expression remained neutral after the random question, so Jamal proceeded. "Something other than a child's memories."

Hassan sat back in the cushions of the second-hand couch with a drink in hand. There was a gulf of knowledge behind those eyes. But Jamal could also see reluctance.

After a long drag on his cigarette, Hassan asked him, "You are good with numbers, aren't you?"

"Mathematics has always come easy, I suppose. I don't seem to have much use for it these days."

"Where do you think you got your quick mind from?"

"Probably from her," said Jamal. "I know she taught me numbers early."

"The way we met is another story, but I will tell you that she was a wizard with numbers. When I learned this, she and I made an arrangement of sorts."

Jamal merely raised his eyebrows. "And ..."

"Your mother only cared about your well being. She did whatever she had to do along those lines. And she was a clever negotiator, that woman." Hassan grinned, his eyes becoming distant from some memory it seemed.

"What could she possibly have done for a man in your position?"

"She helped me, and a few associates cook the quartermaster's books for years."

"You stole from the military. What, weapons?"

"Sometimes. Other times it was just supplies. Western sanctions crippled this country. We took what we could sell on the black market."

"Did you ever get caught?"

Hassan shrugged his shoulders. "One time. But no part of Iraq is not corrupt."

Jamal held his gaze. He decided to ask the one thing he really wanted to know. "Just tell me, was everything on the table in this arrangement of yours?"

"Your mother was no whore if that is what you mean."

"It's what I mean."

Hassan looked away to light another cigarette, and Jamal got the sense the question and answer session was over. What did any of it matter anyway? It was years ago. He left the story of how Hassan met his mother for another day, if ever. Maybe that didn't matter either. It all had served its purpose in getting him here. As for the memory of Hassan, forcing himself on her, what's done is done.

Maybe it just happened the one time when he was drunk or something. Bet he doesn't even remember it. And if he does, he doesn't know that I know, so he's not going to bring it up. But if she was desperate ... and men are men despite how they would treat her in public. He said she didn't lower herself, but Hassan might have lied to save me the embarrassment of learning I was a bastard boy with a whore for a mother. If that's who I am, then so be it.

He poured himself another brandy and led the conversation in another direction. They drank some more before their internal clocks told them it was time to adjourn.

"Would you believe I have encountered him face to face?"

Jamal glanced at the screen of Hadiya's laptop and went back to perusing the bookshelves of the library, the most articulated room in the villa turned schoolhouse. He'd already seen the Internet image of Saddam's dead, bloated son, Uday, anyway. Killed recently alongside his brother, Qusay, less than five months into the war, details of their lifestyle as the maniacal princes of Iraq were now fodder for the international press.

Jamal didn't feel like thinking about the Hussein brothers. In this space that was trimmed out in teak wood with woven bamboo floors, he felt a certain distance from the gritty side of his life. The stillness of the neighborhood outside only increased the sense of escape. Being here was a guilty pleasure to offset the mind-numbing decisions he faced every day, sometimes on the hour it seemed. He knew it was only possible because he had no handlers.

He looked her way again now that she'd turned her attention back to the Internet report. She was slumped diagonally in an oversized chair with her long legs over an armrest. He was completely attracted to her. For that reason, he put the book he held back on the shelf and sat on the opposite armrest, touching her hair while she told her tale. More importantly, he shut down the competing thought patterns and became present for her.

"When?"

"He came to our school one day about a month before the invasion. I suppose it was a way for him to show his face among the nervous citizens, but his presence only made it worse. He tried to have me whisked away to one of his palaces."

"Lucky you."

"It gave me the chills," she said with a shiver. "He was an ogler that one, and his bodyguard told me I would be leaving with him, that the son of the Supreme Leader had invited me to dine with him at his home."

"What did you say?"

"I said no! The others at the school had warned me he was a rapist. I was not going to let it happen. But Uday never threatened me. His glare across the room told me he knew he would get what he wanted. I was terrified. When I had the chance, I just left school."

"What, out the back door?"

"Out a window!" she squealed. She cupped her hands over her broad, contagious smile in the universal feminine gesture for disbelief of one's actions.

"So, you weren't seduced by that bastard?"

"You are funny. But I was scared out of my mind. I ran straight to a friend's house and hid like a frightened *kombo*."

Jamal gave a puzzled look.

"I do not know the Arabic. Maybe they don't live here. They are part of Kenyan wildlife—little nighttime animals, very timid. Some people call them bush babies."

"You were smart. Did he look for you?"

"If he did, the hunt was cut short. Rumor had it someone tried to assassinate him later that day. I am sure he forgot about me."

"I bet he just realized you were out of his league."

"A soldier and a comedian? The surprises just keep coming with you, Jamal Muhammad." She said it in Arabic with a sardonic grin. Then she giggled and spoke in her native tongue of Swahili, the national language of Kenya.

"What is that you said?"

"I do not know how to say it in Arabic. It comes from the older Kenyans. You need not worry," she said as the smile dissipated into a more alluring gaze. "It means something to the effect that I am crazy for you."

Hadiya leaned into him, and they kissed. After a moment, he pulled back.

"What about the others?"

"Gone for a whole day ..."

The next morning they relaxed together in the garden. Enclosed on three sides by a high stone wall, and nestled up against the rear of the two-story villa, its intimacy matched her mood. She sat on soft, green grass wearing a loose gown and no shoes. Nearby grew a healthy poplar tree, carefully maintained like the planted sod around its trunk. A moist southerly breeze complimented the shade it provided from across Lake Habbaniyah. She took in the fresh odor of life in the mostly arid climate. It gave her joy.

The garden was at its peak of health in mid-summer, even if some plants like the Jericho Rose had not yet reached their blooming season. She'd been told little white flowers would appear months from now throughout the shrub-like plants, which occupied much of the raised beds. Vertical stalks of Red Yucca exhibited their grayish-green hues, and a climber plant the Iraqis called the "*leef*" tree with spongy flowers had claimed much of the interior face of the garden wall. Other planted bulbs were mixed in with wild Iris and Yellow Chamomile as natural backdrops.

Jamal sat over by the trickling fountain along the wall. He wore khaki cargo shorts and nothing else, his broad, bare chest drawing her attention. She felt guilty for allowing him in her bed last night. Premarital relations were something she'd been conditioned to avoid, yet she was surprised at how her passions had welled up. Her thoughts lingered on the intimacy they shared, causing her to look away, blushing but smiling. She'd come very close to giving in to Jamal last night.

She tried to think of something else. For some reason, the dead Hussein brothers popped into her head again, but she was suddenly more captivated by the ongoing hunt for their father. "How long before the coalition finds Saddam?"

Jamal shook his head from across the garden in a dismissive way. "He could be anywhere. Rumors change every day. Many believe he has left the country."

"If he is here, then they will find him. One cannot live on the run forever."

He placed a finger on the page of his notebook and turned to her. "I don't know. There are lots of places to hide from the coalition."

"I guess you would know," she said with a smirk.

He nodded absently, the response making her realize he wasn't paying attention. She got up from the grass. Moving behind him, she rubbed the knottiness in his shoulders. After a quiet moment passed, she whispered in an octave lower than her usual tone of speech.

"I know something too …"

Jamal was caught off guard by the conspiratorial tone, causing the hairs on his neck to rise.

"What do you know?" he queried with his head tilted back to study her face, the action disguised as a plea for a kiss.

She obliged him, held his head there with her palms on his temples, and studied him for what seemed like an eternity.

What could she know? Did I talk in my sleep?

"God chose you to be here, no?"

He felt a sense of relief that it wasn't mission-related. She'd mentioned in passing that she'd been raised a Christian. Jamal believed what she asked to be true, as long as she wasn't referring to Allah. Yet he'd hidden that side of him from everyone he'd met in Iraq, including Hadiya. He decided to come at the subject in an obtuse way to be certain.

"Well, you know the men I am aligned with ... their links are to the former regime. Baathists are not as religious minded as the *takfiri*."

"Yes," she answered. "I am aware of that. But you know what I mean. I am talking about God, the father of Jesus."

Jamal was cornered. Without the solace of fellowship among other Christians, he'd felt spiritual distance for periods of time. Had God put her here to be a kindred soul in a sea of non-believers?

He looked off before giving his answer. "I will not deny my Christian faith to you, but it is complicated. I will say I have confusing thoughts on the matter, especially lately ... the people I'm with every day. It's just ..."

He trailed off, looked away. He could tell she was disappointed with his answer. She looked at the time on her cell phone.

"We have an hour left before everyone returns. I would like to hear about it. I will not press, however. I won't pretend to know how difficult it is out there for you. The fighting ... seeing others killed up close, the civilian deaths. It must be awful, especially for a believer."

They talked about the faith they shared a little longer. Jamal told her the parts of his religious upbringing that were true—up until the jump-off-point of his cover story, at least. He fabricated a few anecdotes about being a Christian in the Sudanese Army, never mentioned living in the refugee camp. He couldn't risk letting her into his secrets. Not yet, at least.

"Just know it is what sets you apart from the others you fight with," she said. "The light of the Lord is in you. I can see it. You do not have the anger they do."

Jamal paced anxiously along the pebble walk that bisected the garden. He felt he was on the verge of entering a muddy quagmire if he didn't choose his words carefully.

"My relationship with God has a lot to do with why I am here fighting. It is true. But my men, those above me, they fight for other reasons. Many fight for their homeland, for Anbar. Many fight to protect their way of living, their families. Many for just the killing. The last kind are just sheep though, caught up in hate they don't understand themselves."

"Can hate ever be understood?" she asked. "I have seen it in enough places that it does not surprise me when it rears its ugly head. Yet I will never understand it."

She approached him. When her cheek found the nook between his pectoral muscles, Jamal felt the connection more than ever. "I have seen much of it too. It fuels this war."

"Do you hate the Americans for starting it?"

"I do not," he said. "Nor do I hate the Shiites, or the Kurds, or anyone else."

"Then why do you fight? Why are you here?"

"As I said, it's complicated. And I come here to forget about all of it."

She must have accepted his answer for now by her silence. He offered to take her on a walk before he left to rejoin the cell. She shared some excellent memories of Africa, of a more regular upbringing. It was his pleasure to listen to her stories because he felt bereft of his own. He was beginning to learn that she was a unique soul, a light in this world, and the warmth of her glow spread to others. Therefore, it was a thing to cherish, whether God had brought them together or not.

He understood now that protecting her was a new priority to him, on par with the mission in his mind, as wrong as it might be to people like the major. When it was all said and done, the judge of all things would surely—despite the deplorable aspects of his time here—be pleased with his decision to see her in that way.

Surely He would. And I'll be a better person for it.

CHAPTER 20

One day in late September, Jamal awoke in a cold sweat. The dirty curtains in the rented room were closed, and the pale blue of dawn shone through. He lay there trying to remember the dream, but it was already gone. He had no doubt it centered on the violence that was part of his daily life.

The compressor kicked on for the window unit he'd picked up on the black market, fending off the late summer heat that was starting to wear everyone down. Moments later, chilled air jettisoned from the vent and met the beads on his face. It found the damp nape of his neck and caused him to shiver. He pulled the covers up over his face and wondered in his sleepy state, which would last the year, him, or this precious machine. He had good reasons not to bet on himself.

The previous day, he'd almost died when a clutch of bullets from a Marine machine gun slammed into the facade of the building he stood beside. One of his men had been hit; his head exploded not a foot away from Jamal. The week before that, he'd been late for a meeting with another cell leader. When he approached the designated location, coalition security personnel were starting to form a cordon around the area. In the middle of the block ahead, his destination had just been pulverized by dropped ordinance.

In addition to morbid thoughts about his mortality, he dreaded the coming operation he was to lead. A couple of weeks ago, Hassan had given a clear directive to increase attacks on soft targets and government infrastructure and lessen direct actions against the occupiers. This was the key to eventually turning the stomach of the American public.

Classic guerilla warfare doctrine.

Hassan had called for a devastating attack on one of the neighborhoods where the residents weren't as supportive. It was to coincide with the beginning of Ramadan, the Muslim month of fasting that would start in late October, less than a month away. Strategically, the operation was intended to draw the coalition out of certain key areas on Jamal's side of the city, to keep their patrols away from Hassan's bomb-making cells.

His phone rang. It was Hassan.

"What time? ... Where in Fallujah?"

Jamal hung up and sat on the edge of the bed, rubbed his grainy eyes. A meeting of the lieutenants had been called.

Time to go to work.

CHAPTER 21

Jamal took in the crowded room. Less than a dozen robed men awaited Hassan's arrival. The low buzz of conversation filled the space in anticipation of his speech. Missing were many of the lieutenants from Jamal's indoctrination dinner, killed or captured over recent months along with their cell members. Other fighters who had risen through the gutted ranks now sat in their places, eagerly waiting for recognition. They would have to wait a little longer. Jamal was being handed the operation; a guard had overheard a phone conversation between Hassan and Izzat Ibrahim earlier in the day that prompted the summons.

This safe house was not on Jamal's list of favorites. The single-family dwelling was cramped, with not much natural light. He knew Hassan's largesse required certain levels of spatial consideration so this place couldn't be high on his boss's list either. But Hassan would always choose security over comfort, and here the residents still were considered sympathetic to the cause. Moreover, a significant road was nearby for a quick getaway if necessary. Jamal didn't think any of it made Hassan feel safe.

Over the last week, Hassan's stance against targeting civilians had changed. A couple of his cell members had been wounded in a gunfight with locals from Ramadi's Ta'mim neighborhood. A weapons cache was discovered there, which belonged to fed-up residents arming themselves to fight the *Bathyoun*. Hassan had known the possibility of local resistance was there, but so soon? For him, it was one thing to kill thousands of ethnic Kurds in the north of Iraq, as he'd done under Saddam. But they weren't Arabs, so he never thought of them as his countrymen. In their private discussions, Jamal had learned the notion of slaughtering everyday Iraqis was very distressing to Hassan.

Hassan entered the room and Jamal could see the concern on his beefy face even now. After this day, it would seem bizarre that he once had Masoud executed for shooting a defenseless Iraqi firefighter.

The big man stood at the front until it became quiet. The tight quarters were already generating sweat lines on his face and neck, and his hands shook with rage.

"The two-faced people of Ta'mim have gathered against us!" he huffed. "We will make them regret choosing the path they are on."

Jamal reached into his pocket and felt both faces on the talisman he'd bought his first day in Ramadi, and which he always carried on him.

If he only knew.

The thought made him shudder as Hassan's angry stare traveled from face to face before settling on Jamal.

"Jamal Muhammad will lead this operation."

Jamal had gained enough respect and had advanced the cause enough that the looks were no longer jaded with bigotry or uncertainty as he stood to address the room full of angry men.

"There is only one target which will be appropriate," said Jamal. "We will destroy their beloved market."

As the group mulled over his last statement, Jamal reflected on the heavy losses incurred by the network over recent weeks. Much of it was due to him. He'd seen the advent of the roadside bomb, or Improvised Explosive Device as the U.S. military had dubbed it, dramatically increase coalition casualties from the beginning of the war.

Initially, the bombs were crudely buried along the rutted roads and travel routes used by the coalition. Unused artillery shells typically powered them and they were triggered by a detonation cord. The triggerman needed to be nearby for this type of explosion to occur. Sometimes anti-tank mines were buried in the center of a road for detonation by a pressure plate. Both tactics became less effective following adjustments by the coalition forces; soldiers and Marines became adept at spotting the burial sites or the wires leading from them. They used mine-clearing vehicles to pave the way for ordinary traffic.

As always though in war, each side had continually changed tactics to maintain or seize momentum. He began to see IED's detonate with increasingly clever technology. More powerful forms of explosives like imported Royal Demolition Explosives (a pure and versatile base material in many plastic explosives) were used. Jamal decided the bomb-makers needed to experience a setback when Hassan ordered a tunnel dug under an asphalt road, and filled with enough ordinance to completely overturn a sixty-ton Abrams tank.

Throughout the night, he made solo incursions into several of the ad hoc explosives factories. At 0400 hours, the silenced .45 caliber and a satchel of hand grenades had indeed set them back months. He became a veritable wrecking ball when he killed over twenty fighters as they slept and leveled the buildings that housed the surplus of explosive ordinance.

The fog of war, that anxiety-riddled feeling where one cannot discern the enemy's intention or capabilities, had kept Jamal in the clear. Hassan and his lieutenants attributed the losses to U.S. Special Forces and their penchant for surprise night raids. This only increased their belief that locals were informing against them—and Hassan's desire to strike back.

Despite all the hand wringing on his part, Jamal believed this one attack could legitimize his cover to the utmost and get him out of the trenches daily, perhaps vaulting him from lowly lieutenant to more of a powerbroker role in the overall resistance.

Lately, Hassan had touted Jamal's liaisons with the *takfiri* as beneficial to the cause, requiring more and more of his time for meetings in Fallujah and Baghdad. The feedback from the foreigners had been positive as well. He saw an opening to make the leap from the diminishing network of the *Bathyoun* to the burgeoning ranks of the *takfiri*.

All that hand wringing over one dreadful day in the course of his years-long mission reminded Jamal of Victor Katseyev, the Russian agent who had fretted the most over the mission's daunting mandate. The major had certainly earned his pay trying to sell the idea to him.

"It sounds crazy!" exclaimed Katseyev in his thick accent one day while they were waiting for an instructor. "How will we do it? I don't think I can be that much in the killing of regular people. If I go back to infiltrate Chechen warlord's camp, I do it knowing I will be helping the people of Grozny, not aiding in their slaughter. How do you expect me or any of us to do this?"

The major was undaunted.

"Victor, let me ask you this. Do you want to be a simple agent who gets inside a mid-level cell that builds car bombs, or maybe they're into kidnapping Russian soldiers and holding them hostage or whatever? Let's say you learn they're going to have an arms shipment delivered at a certain time and place. You set up a rendezvous with the Russian Security forces. A bunch of evil guys get packed up. Moscow sends them off to some hole in Siberia. And that's the biggest bust that comes from your work. You broke up a cell and probably disrupted the overall network for a while, but that would be it. We'd have to pull you because your cover would be blown the minute you didn't show up in that prison. You'd get a medal and a new assignment, which is great. But you'd be starting all over. That's standard undercover work. We're thinking bigger here. In a post-911 world, more risks need to be taken for bigger rewards."

A nod followed from Victor before the major went on.

"Or would you rather be the guy who guts it out for a year, enough to pull you out of the trenches and into the larger world of international terrorism? What if you become integral in linking your organization up with some Arab counterparts? Then you find yourself working with top *al Qaeda* operatives. What if you could one day bring waves and waves of security forces crashing down on them all at once all over the globe."

The other leaders at the meeting interrupted Jamal's thoughts. He accepted their congratulatory remarks on being handed the operation by Hassan. Soon the gathering started to break up, and the fighters jostled for face time with their general before departing. It wasn't something Jamal needed, so he gave a departing nod to Ahmed from across the room, gathered up his personal belongings, and left. On his way outside, he thought of the old Jordanian cleric and his upcoming meeting with him. If he was indeed about to be presented with an opening, he had some reading of the Koran to do. He needed to familiarize himself with the verses that supposedly justified all the killings, the maiming, and ultimately the support for men like Abu Musab al-Zarqawi. The next time he met with the cleric Jamal wanted him to believe he was beginning to embrace the ideology as a potential loyalist.

Once in the Volvo, he headed toward Hadiya's neighborhood. In her enclave, he would find a bottle and her embrace and forget about the war for a night. But by the end of the week, he would conduct an attack on the Ta'mim market so galling and malevolent, that he would more than endear himself to both the *Bathyoun* and the *takfiri*. From that day on, he would considered one of the most feared insurgents in Iraq and be granted higher status among them with a *nom de guerre*. After that, he would be known among the overall resistance as Muhammad al Sudani.

CHAPTER 22

Fatima strode through Ta'mim's busy *as-Siddiq* market, empty basket in hand. This early in the day, the coolness remained after the passage of night in the desert. A bit of rain had even fallen along the Euphrates River valley yesterday, settling the dust off the arid plain surrounding Ramadi.

As usual, the market was abuzz with customers eager to stake their claim on the freshest produce. Attendants stood by well-stocked carts ready to receive their daily beating from the hagglers so common in an Arab bazaar. Or was it the other way around? One could never really tell. An outsider would describe the scene as a chaotic free-for-all. As a native, however, she was aware of the pecking order between the vendors here, and the particular rules of business regularly maintained. Her mother used to proudly tell her that Arab traders had inspired the double-entry bookkeeping that spread across the globe over a thousand years ago.

Fatima had her own style of bookkeeping, which began the day her husband had beaten her for the tenth time. Determined to seek passage to Europe and a new life with her young daughter, she had calculated her moves in the most prudent ways for over four years. The arrangements were nearly complete, paid for with money scraped off the top of the weekly food budget.

Today, however, Fatima troubled herself to show two fingers instead of one to the merchant selling her husband's favorite type of bread. She'd have to find another way to pinch a few *dinars*. His staples had not changed a bit in the six years of their arranged marriage, so he'd noticed when they ran out two weeks in a row.

Consequently, he berated her for twenty minutes in front of their daughter on his way out the door. He preferred this bread because it was salty and rough.

Just like him.

She smiled at her next thought.

You are what you eat.

She'd heard the American phrase on a Richard Simmons exercise show late one night while her husband slumbered. His satellite television pulled in dozens of media channels from the West, introducing her to a constant parade of fascinating concepts. Some shows were even translated for Arabic viewers. She'd become envious of Western lifestyle and dreamed of having a life outside the home without her husband present or a male relative serving as his proxy. This was contrary to the customs of her family, which governed every aspect of her daily life. Her escort today was her brother-in-law, her husband's younger sibling—a man seventeen years older than her. Just now, he noticed her lingering smile, his larger than normal nose a proboscis seeking information as he tilted it up in her direction.

"What?"

"Nothing. I was thinking about how happy my daughter will be that I am preparing *Masguf* tonight. It is her favorite."

"What's so funny about that?" he said with his usual smugness.

"Nothing, I suppose. Especially for you after we go to the three places that carry the ingredients we need."

"Three here at the market?" he asked without a lot of confidence.

"No, three other places after the market."

Truthfully, all the ingredients could be purchased more efficiently, but several stops just made it easier to shuffle the money and achieve her goal. She enjoyed watching his smugness change to annoyance upon hearing the news, though, because while it was true that *she* needed an escort, *he* needed to eschew personal time to be an escort.

She passed a vendor who momentarily held off aggressive dealings with a local woman to bark at a grubby child who'd lightened his cart by a few oranges. She watched the kid dash off into the throng of people with his breakfast in hand. To her right was a vegetable stand with no canopy to protect the produce from the sun's strengthening rays. It struck her as odd. Already the leafy vegetables stacked in the cart looked wilted. Her glance at the vendor gave her the sense he was not ashamed of his stock, but rather, he displayed something else. What was it, she wondered?

Resignation perhaps. Resigned to being a hardscrabble farmer. What am I resigned to if I stay here? If my daughter must become a woman here?

The savory smell of spices came upon her as she approached the next vendor. In large open baskets to be scooped out and sold by weight were the ingredients of a good *baharat*, the typical Iraqi mixture of cinnamon, cardamom, cloves, coriander, cumin, nutmeg, and paprika. She and the Arab minding the spices, with whom she was regular, exchanged a warm smile.

An instant later, a horrendous explosion ruptured the calm morning, the force of the nearby blast propelling her and her brother-in-law into the side of a parked van. Her petite frame was momentarily sandwiched between his body and the forgiving aluminum skin of the vehicle before they both hit the pavement in a heap. Disorientation changed to panic as she found it difficult to breathe with his weight bearing down on her chest. His limp body told her he was either unconscious or dead. The ringing in her ears was more than she'd ever known, and while she had her vision, everything was clouded by smoke and debris dust around her. Worst of all was the inability to move her arms or legs. A shot of adrenaline surged.

Need to breathe.

She was able to wriggle her torso out from under him enough to expose her diaphragm. A deep breath led to violent spasms that produced a copious amount of blood. It continued until the wracking of her belly and chest caused her brother-in-law to roll off. When he landed on the ground, his bloodied face was close to hers. Wide eyes glared at her. She turned away, aghast, coughed again until her burning lungs eased. After a minute, she was coherent enough to look around, but because she was on her back, everything appeared upside down or sideways.

All around her, she heard heavy moaning and the crackling of small fires. Oddly, the smell of burnt produce stuck out in her mind, mixed with other more visceral odors. Some of the bewildered citizens stood around the area in shock. But they were counted among those lucky enough to be on the fringe of the blast radius. Everything within twenty-five meters of the detonation had been obliterated. She suspected she'd only survived because her brother-in-law absorbed most of the shrapnel. The ringing in her ears lessened enough that she thought she heard sirens, like muffled kittens crying out.

Praise be to Allah. Help.

Minutes passed as she thought of her poor daughter if she died today, growing up without her guidance. This gave her anguish above the destruction around her, killing more than just her bodily form. The sirens were closer now, though. Hope sprung that she might survive this, even if she were a paraplegic. She felt tingling in her lower extremities. Maybe she'd even walk out of here. The sudden hope turned into newfound energy, and she cried out hoarsely in Arabic.

"Help! Help!"

Four ambulances pulled up to the edge of the destroyed market. Dazed but able-bodied survivors moved past the emergency responders. Iraqi police arrived on the scene and attempted—if only halfheartedly, it appeared—to restore order because fear and shock ruled this chaotic moment. Those with the stomach for it waded into the sea of anguish. Soon the wounded were being helped to locations beyond the dreadful kill zone.

Fatima was close to receiving help when several dull thumps could be heard from multiple directions around the market. Some knew the tell tale warning of a mortar attack and shouted for those around them to find a piece of ground where they stood. There was no time to run.

Multiple explosions rocked the large market space. Fatima heard more thumps even before the echo of the first explosions had faded. She rolled herself onto her stomach and tried to crawl under the crumpled body of the van. Screams could be heard between the interruptive blasts, which sounded like the vicious bark of some giant mechanical canine. The compressive wave following each dented her chest as she struggled to reach safety.

Just when she managed to slide her gravely wounded body beneath the chassis of the van, a mortar exploded nearby. It was the last thing she remembered before losing consciousness.

The horror below appalled Jamal. From the third floor of an abandoned building, he watched what he'd done and it nauseated him. If others weren't present, he was certain he'd vomit, could taste the open spigot of saliva running even now. And this was only the beginning. The mortar attack would cause more casualties to be heaped upon the scene of destruction and he knew the delay for help would be longer this time. It might even come in the form of coalition troops. He'd have the option to end the attack then if it looked like his fighters might inflict heavy losses on them. He did not want American lives to be lost. Not today. On the other hand, if the coalition response were heavy-handed, maybe he would let his men engage them, a token sacrifice of *Bathyoun* to balance the scales a little.

Jamal took in the scene of destruction. Shaped charges had been placed beneath the vegetable cart, which sent the blast in horizontal directions only, creating the most lethality. It worked with devastating effect. The bomb, manually detonated by one of his men, killed dozens of Iraqis and wounded at least fifty more. Of the wounded, he figured more than half would perish before aid could reach them from burns, shrapnel wounds, vicious amputations, brain damage, blood loss, or internal bleeding. Later, suicide would claim even more after the hell of night sweats and excruciating rehabilitation finally exacted its toll. He even guessed that years later, some would die from the substance addictions resulting from efforts to forget the tragedy of this day. And then there was the aggregate grief felt by each of their extended families. Grief he had caused.

One day. One bomb.

Fatima awoke to a cold darkness. Her closed eyelids felt thick and heavy.

So tired. So very tired.

There was stillness all around. Her thoughts returned to her daughter. Next year they would leave Iraq, already having saved enough for passage to North Africa. Here there was nothing for them. Hubris-laden Western ideas of rights and democracy had turned out to be a hoax. The native power mongers would never let it flourish with all their backstabbing and marginalizing. She experienced the familiar feeling of doom associated with the Americans' experiment in "nation building." But something wasn't right.

Why do I feel so awful?

The first rip in the fabric of the surreal occurred when she wished to rub those heavy, sleep-swollen eyes. But she couldn't lift her arm to do it. At that moment, reality hit, shaking her into lucidity. Tears flowed again as the pain jumped to life. She felt their lubricating aspect working on her blood-caked eye sockets, partially dissolving the crusty layer, so her left eyelid opened halfway. Her dead brother-in-law was there. She felt nothing this time.

She saw an Iraqi soldier. Two more now—no—four of them approached the crumpled van in a crouch, weapons at the ready. A medic carried a satchel with a crescent moon emblazoned upon it. He knelt next to a wounded person nearby and the others stood behind the van looking around nervously. One of them shouted in Arabic to someone out of her limited line of sight. More booted footsteps rushed close by, men with equipment taking control of the area. Again, she thought she might survive.

A shot rang out. She saw a pink mist fly off the Iraqi medic's back, whom she could see in profile only five meters away. His head sank to his chest, and he fell limply to the ground. A small orange dot appeared at the limits of her vision and rapidly increased in size. Seconds later, it slammed into a concrete barrier set up on the side of the market road, exploding in a thunderous clap—a rocket-propelled grenade. More gunfire erupted, this time from automatic weapons and from multiple locations. She saw more Iraqi soldiers go down shooting, but their return fire was panicked, wild sprays of unaimed bullets. Another RPG exploded nearby.

A helicopter suddenly engulfed the sky above her and its rotors cast flickering shadows on the vertical surfaces within her view. The engine's roar was muted as the rotary guns opened fire, the rapid burping noise ripping the air as spent brass rained down. The pungent smell of gunpowder hit her. The realization that it had become an all-out battle increased her anxiety, already redlined from the traumas suffered. She saw the life she'd hoped for vanishing. She cursed the Americans for their foolish jaunt into the Arab world, cursed Western Society itself, now that it was unattainable to her. Her side seared when the bullets ripped into her and the blood ran. She started to enter that confused state again.

Maybe we'll go after all my darling. I was mad at something, what was it? No matter. We'll go together soon.

CHAPTER 23

Jamal shook his head in amazement when he saw a video of a frazzled Saddam Hussein in coalition custody, pulled from a hole in the ground in Northern Iraq by American troops. The sight of the unkempt Supreme Leader was painful for the *Bathyoun* to see and caused panic in some cells. Jamal remained surprised at the loyalty his fighters still felt toward Saddam. But when coordinated attacks lessened for a time while reorganization occurred, he was glad for the hiatus.

He celebrated his first Christmas in Iraq with Hadiya for part of the day and spent the remainder alone in his rented room. He read his Bible to remind himself of the gift of salvation, without which his mission was unthinkable. He pleaded to be forgiven for the violence he created and for better guidance on how to befuddle the enemy because the Ta'mim market bombing weighed so heavily on him.

In February 2004, members of Hassan's network infiltrated the police and security forces of Anbar. Moles were able to ascertain the local travel itinerary of the U.S. general heading the entire Middle Eastern Command. He was scheduled to ride alongside the commander of the 82nd Airborne, the sector commander, on a tour of Fallujah. When Jamal heard this, he knew Hassan would not miss his opportunity to cut off the head of the snake.

Jamal wasn't involved in the planning of the operation, however. His meetings with the *takfiri* had begun to occupy more of his time after the first of the year. As such, Ahmed would lead the fighters during the ambush of the generals, and Jamal would command a sniper team. He chafed at this lesser assignment because it meant he'd have less control over the outcome. The idea of two top commanders out for a drive in Fallujah made him very nervous. There was one saving grace with the assignment, however.

Jamal's advanced sniper training was unknown to Hassan or anyone else in the network. As for the men he led, higher knowledge of professional marksmanship was lost upon them. Trajectory, sun angle, mathematical calculations, and other aspects that Jamal had mastered did not enter the mind of even his best shooters. They were all raised on the AK, not known for accuracy beyond the length of a football field. He assumed when the ambush occurred, he'd be in some perch with one of his fighters operating a shitty rifle. He planned to use the aforementioned factors to lessen the effectiveness of his shooter.

On the day of the ambush, Jamal watched tentatively from his sniper's perch, a mosque's minaret tower along the generals' convoy route. He would perform the role of spotter while the shooter in the prone position next to him fired the weapon. The situation hadn't developed as he'd planned. He wasn't able to bring one of his men up here. Instead, the *takfiri* had offered one of their ace Chechen snipers, a loaner in the name of solidarity against a common enemy. How was he to refuse? Unlike his men, the Chechen wouldn't rely on Kentucky windage—a colloquial term he'd learned from his drill sergeants—to narrow in on his target. Consequently, most of the manipulations Jamal had in mind to preserve American life would not work, because this trained killer knew better.

To make matters worse, the Chechen had brought a Russian SV-98 sniper rifle with a high-powered scope, a far superior weapon than Jamal would have pulled out of the cell's depleted armory. Presently, the sniper prepared it for use while the convoy approached Ahmed's kill zone several blocks away. Once the ambush began, the running battle would move toward Jamal's location. The convoy would be exposed to plunging enfilade fire from the minaret tower.

Ahmed crouched behind the thick masonry parapet wall on the rooftop. He looked across the street at the fighters occupying other rooftops. Everyone appeared to be ready, so he shifted his gaze in the direction of the approaching convoy. Anticipation elevated his heart rate, and he could feel the bloodlust rise within him. It was just one of the stages he'd come to recognize after over twenty combat actions. Nervousness is replaced by anticipation, itself supplanted by the rawness and shock of action. Then comes the high of success if the operation goes as planned, which morphs into the sublime satisfaction of having done the will of Allah. Underlying all of it was the fear of getting hit. Not necessarily fear of death itself, but rather the bullet that slams into one's skull, or the piece of shrapnel that rips into one's gut.

At no point along Ahmed's spectrum of emotion did empathy for the enemy exist. They were the ones who would continue inflicting mortal wounds upon so many Iraqis. They had every kind of weapon or piece of equipment they wanted. They had hot food, body armor, tanks, and planes at their disposal. When a unit took casualties, they received replacements the next day. To Ahmed, the enemy was a monolithic, regenerative entity, a life force of its own whose members maintained a certain amount of naive belligerence. It incensed him that the Americans had the gall to come bumbling into his country and enforce self-governance on everyone.

Ahmed knew it would never take hold. The people of Mesopotamia had always craved influential leaders, like Saddam. But Saddam had only been interested in secular rule. And while Ahmed had used his family connections to infuse himself into the Baathist power structure, deep down, he pined for an Islamist-cled government. The Americans would never allow that either, but it was something worth fighting for to Ahmed.

His thoughts were interrupted when the convoy's lead vehicle, an armored Hummer, sped through the intersection and entered the city block designated as the kill zone. Now the second and third were across. The last two, a blacked-out sport-utility vehicle and a five-ton truck with a squad of infantry inside, crossed into the kill zone. Ahmed broke squelch on his radio twice—the signal.

The WHOOSH of an RPG preceded a thunderous explosion further down the block. The force of the blast completely overturned the Hummer. It landed on its top and spun once before becoming engulfed in flames, blocking the path of the convoy. Ahmed ran over to the door, which led to the stairs. As he bound down the three flights, he heard the second RPG explode, presumably aimed at the rear vehicle as planned. By the time he reached the ground floor, the whole convoy should be trapped, and his men on the rooftops could begin cutting the arrogant generals and their entourage to pieces with automatic weapons and grenades.

But instead of hearing the blessed sound of a well-executed ambush, Ahmed heard the roar of several engines accelerating. He raced to the building's front entry. Through a window, he saw vehicles rush by one after another as bullets punched their skins and kicked up dust around them.

"No!" shouted Ahmed over the gunfire, his face contorting into an angry sneer.

When he emerged from the building, he saw the convoy had pushed the lead vehicle out of the way, allowing them to escape the kill zone. The sound of engines was already fading, and Ahmed was left to stare at the burning, upside down Hummer. He heard a moan not far from where he stood; nearby was a man in civilian clothes crawling to reach cover. He must have been thrown from the Hummer when it flipped, but the convoy leaders presumed everyone inside had died instantly, so they left him behind. The wounded American appeared to be one of the contracted security personnel by his singed attire. Either that or he was a government staffer for the coalition. Both were worthy of summary execution. Ahmed approached, pistol drawn. He waited until the man rolled over and looked him in the eye. Then he shot him five times.

Through his binoculars in the minaret tower, Jamal watched the convoy push beyond the kill zone and stop to get their bearings, an odd bit of training information coming to fruition, but one he was grateful for. Soldiers established a perimeter around the armored Hummer in which the generals rode. An officer knocked on the bulletproof rear door window of the vehicle, waited for it to open, and asked a question of the nearest man inside. The opportunity was suddenly there. Portions of both generals were visible in the rear seats.

Each one wore a vest of plated, ceramic body armor. The roof of the vehicle blocked a full-body view of the general seated furthest away from the open window. He was only visible from the shoulders down but could be killed with a shot to the side of the torso, where only an elastic band held the front and back armored plates tight up against the body. The bullet would pass through the lungs or heart, killing the man within minutes, if not instantly.

The other general sat adjacent to the open window in the same type of vest, with his ribs protected by the armored door panel itself. However, his neck and shoulders were exposed from above. It was a definite kill shot where the bullet would dive into the upper body, wrecking crucial arteries and organs along its destructive path. Jamal watched the sniper move the index finger inside the trigger housing. If a shot like this had not presented itself, the Chechen would have probably survived this day. Instead, as he was about to squeeze off his first round, Jamal calmly fired a silenced pistol into the base of his skull.

Only gusting wind disrupted the stillness high in the minaret. Jamal reached over and picked up the rifle. He fired off two shots into the blue sky outside and tossed the weapon on the cobblestone floor next to the sniper's body. Next, he retreated to the narrow, winding stair. The decisive act was done, and he had prepared his fabricated reason for the Chechen's death. Tired, thirsty, and with time to kill, he sat on the top step and pulled out a bottle of water from his pack.

He looked at the corpse, thought about the death occurring out on the streets, and in the country overall. While the casualties mounted steadily—almost two per day for the Americans nationwide according to the news—death was starting to come quicker for the insurgents. Mostly it was due to the coalition's ability to put much more massive firepower on any fixed position of the enemy. Equally lethal were pinpoint airstrikes from thirty thousand feet. No sound precluded instant incineration. This created a measurable amount of unease for would-be leaders in the resistance.

For the coalition's efforts, they'd begun to form the semblance of a professionally trained, nationally recruited Iraqi Army since the invasion almost eleven months ago. Even if the rag-tag national police force had been corrupt from the start, a round of house cleaning had thinned their ranks of infiltrators. Baghdad and its environs were a daily mixed bag of success and tragic circumstance for all sides. Southern Iraq—presumably agent

Khalid al-Douri's area of operation—was a hotbed of Shiite militias just waiting to explode. However, the British had established a level of control over Basra and Iraq's only port city, Umm Qasr. Up north, success and failure were trending differently, seemingly going well for the Army troops under the commander of the 101st Airborne, some general named Petraeus.

In Jamal's estimation, Anbar province was the big question. He guessed the American war planners saw Ramadi and Fallujah as perpetual thorns in their sides. Soon they would ask the question. How heavy should we go when we do go into those cities? The political conundrum of establishing all the right approvals for such an overarching operation had to be immense and fraught with tribal and sectarian landmines. He knew the Americans and their allies would be unprepared. Of course, all of it was out of Jamal's control. All he could do when it happened was nudge the kill ratio in favor of the coalition.

He finished off the water bottle and moved five steps down the winder. It was far enough to escape the lethality of a hand grenade but close enough to receive a sufficient amount of cuts from the debris. He pulled the pin on one, leaned toward the top again, and rolled it around the curved inner wall of the stair. He covered his ears tightly.

Two. One.

CRUMP

The detonation compressed his chest like a punch to the diaphragm. Jamal removed his hands from the side of his head and covered his mouth and nose, kept his eyes squinted tightly for all the dust that flew for a few seconds more. He felt the sting of manageable lacerations on his face, neck, and arms, the metallic taste of his blood as it trickled over his upper lip and onto his tongue. There was also a chunk of flesh from the Chechen, which had ricocheted off the outer wall of the minaret and landed on

Jamal's boot. He picked it up and wiped some wetness on his clothing.

Straight from the special effects department. Ouch!

He felt tenderness in his leg, saw his trousers were ripped midway up his thigh. A small piece of shrapnel peeked out of the flesh. The wounds would verify his proximity to the Chechen at the time of death, fomenting the notion that he was lucky to have survived the explosion. He limped back up to the smoke-filled cupola, noticed looseness in the stone structure that had not been there before. He worked quickly to dig the bullet out of the Chechen's skull with his knife. Next, he rubbed mortar dust into the hole, blending it in with the surrounding tissue. Before he descended into the winder again, he grabbed the ruined sniper rifle. Only the corpse remained, and someone else could retrieve it for proper burial rituals, strictly adhered to by the *takfiri*.

He planned to say the Chechen had fired a couple of shots from the minaret position—killing a serviceman (why not credit the supposed martyr with a kill on his dying day, thought Jamal)—but the Americans must have seen the muzzle-flash and were able to return fire immediately. Just as the two of them retreated down the winding stairs, an American trooper hit the tower with a grenade launcher.

Jamal knew his men would razz him over the facial bandages and a semi-exaggerated limp he would maintain for the next few days, the apparent consequences of choosing such an unprotected spot. He'd play the whole thing off as a learning experience. It was worth it when he considered he'd spared many, from the President on down, a lot of hand-wringing had two top generals been killed on the same day. And there was one more killer of American troops off the board.

CHAPTER 24

Jamal sat down in the cell's declared operations room, an office in the abandoned industrial building they'd been using as a base. He was anxious to dive into the bowl of stew handed to him by a fighter's spouse. The smell of curry made his stomach growl. While he gorged to satiate it, his thoughts centered on the four contracted security personnel from Blackwater USA who'd been ambushed, killed, and burned in the streets of Fallujah during the last week of March. The incident had been a catalyst for greater violence against the coalition. Within days the wheels were set in motion toward the pacification of the restive city, as Jamal had predicted. When word got out—as it always did before a big coalition operation—Hassan had called Jamal and Ahmed for a meeting.

The two of them had just left his latest safe house with a new directive; leave Ramadi with bolstered cells to aid in the immediate defense of Fallujah. Since it was not Hassan's usual area of operations, they were to fold into the force structure of the *takfiri*. This meant they would be under the direct control of Abu Musab al-Zarqawi, the self-styled Lion of Iraq. After this meal, Jamal was supposed to gather the best armaments in Hassan's network and handpick forty men to round out a new cell. Ahmed was to do the same. They let Fahim decide which cell he would work with, and he chose Jamal's. Time had suddenly evaporated for Jamal. But if he could, he would see Hadiya on his way out of town.

Or I might never see her again.

Two days later, Jamal exited the abandoned commercial storefront, turned into a construction office, and used for that purpose while hastily building the defenses of Fallujah. Nearby was a gaggle of his lower-ranking fighters who all should be working instead of smoking and joking. He busted up the gathering by assigning several to fill sandbags until relieved. The others sulked away without a word. The unlucky ones groaned at the difficult task ahead but were moving toward the pile of empty bags and shovels as the utterances left their mouths. He'd been a private himself for a concise time, in both calendar days and mentality, but he understood their camaraderie born of commiseration. Grinning at the notion that privates are privates everywhere, he bent over to pick up one of the leaflets distributed throughout Fallujah by the coalition.

In Arabic, it requested the perpetrators of the Blackwater murders be turned in. It also notified civilians they would be granted an opportunity to leave the city in the coming days. No males of military age would be allowed back inside the cordon once they'd left. The operation was intended to "enhance the security of the citizens of Fallujah," as stated on the leaflet. Jamal was intrigued by this concept of the Americans laying siege to a city the size of Fallujah. He didn't see how it could work.

This is about Bush's so-called cowboy mentality, about exacting revenge. Top brass feels the embarrassment of having some civilian employees strung up by a band of militants. So they get a general to send a bunch of kids in here and show how big his dick is.

Considering the predicted size of the assault force and the type of defenses he'd been sent to prepare, Jamal figured hundreds of American lives would be lost in a fruitless endeavor. He'd do his best to swing the balance in their favor, but they were looking at house-to-house fighting in an urban environment, considered the meat grinder of all forms of modern combat.

The Iraqis agreeing to this is stupid. It's not the ground they need; it's the will of the people. This siege will only galvanize support for the resistance ... for the takfiri.

He crumpled up the leaflet and tossed it on the ground as he thought about how things would unfold here in the coming days. The insurgents' plan was based on protecting the core of *takfiri* strength in the city, the neighborhood of *Julan* in the northwest quarter. Jamal wondered how much mettle Zarqawi possessed and whether he would indeed die alongside the last foreign fighter as he'd been known to proclaim. Something told Jamal that was not going to happen. Strategically it didn't make sense.

Go out in a blaze of glory just when they're building strength? Even as the coalition struggles to gain momentum regarding their tall order of tasks?

He walked along a line of waist-high concrete barriers, which stretched the width of the road. A local contractor had forklifted them in place when pressed into service by Jamal's men. The cell's area of responsibility when the attack came was an approach to a bridge crossing the Euphrates River, which ran its winding course along the western edge of Fallujah. Across the river was Fallujah Hospital, a source of aid and comfort for the *takfiri* and ground they would defend dearly. Ahmed and his men were a few blocks away in the adjacent sector.

In a sense, he and Ahmed had been given the lesser job of guarding the neighborhood's back door. The main attack was expected to come from another direction, although no one could be sure until it began. Their defensive intent would merely be delay action. When it appeared the coalition would push through, they'd abandon this position for more hardened entrenchments deeper inside the neighborhood. In the space between, Zarqawi had ordered the placement of thousands of homemade bombs, mines, booby traps, and other effective means of hampering the enemy's progress. There would also be two more Chechen snipers lurking. Jamal considered thwarting their efforts one of his more significant difficulties.

He still carried the worn canvas satchel most places. Inside was the notebook he kept, basically a log of his mission. He pulled it out now. In the Cherokee code, he jotted simple notations detailing each position along this line of defense. He'd use the information to find that golden balance, which was always sought by him, advance the goals of the insurgency while lessening the blow to the coalition. The former task must be done in a way that appears successful, making success in the latter task bittersweet. He had always tried to sway the balance as much as possible every time he went out with his men; all vengeful killers bent on destroying perceived American hegemony. He'd consistently volunteered for Hassan's most robust operations, as well. This helped him mask the real reasons for the heavy losses he'd incur. He'd even killed a couple of his men on the spot when they were isolated from the cell and about to hurt Americans.

While recognizing his next thought was a form of rationalization, he knew his own perpetuated violence was but a drop of water in a bucket. Killings, beheadings even, were happening in every major city across the country. The value of human life here had dipped like a plummeting stock that no one dared sell short because of the stubborn belief in its upside. But he was learning the commodity of blood is a soul stripper to the traders involved. His soul was feeling pretty bare lately, yet that determination was still there, almost hard-wired into him.

He had to assume it was the same for any players in Iraq who believed too much was at stake to quit, each for their own reasons. The Baathists fought for retention of lopsided power; the Shiites for never having power; the Kurds for their autonomy; the *takfiri* for a new Caliphate; the Americans for many reasons depending on who one listens to; the British for the Americans;

the humanitarian aid providers from Japan to Denmark for managing that aspect of the conflict that was pushed aside by the warfighters; the civilian mercenaries for money and a combat fix; the civilian contractors for the promise of nation-building; and of course, the normal Iraqi civilians who just wanted it all to end. Yes, he was a drop of water in a bucket.

He put the notebook away, looked at his watch, then toward a garbage-strewn lot where Fahim and a couple of his men were setting a machine gun mount. He waited until the beeping sound from a nearby front-end loader stopped, and shouted over its motor.

"Fahim!"

The young fighter looked up and around until he spotted Jamal. He dropped his shovel and covered the distance between them at a trot, stopping on the other side of the concrete barrier.

Jamal asked, "When should we expect him? I thought you said this was happening before noon. It's 1400 hours, and I have to go to meet Ahmed for another briefing."

"I told you what I was told," answered Fahim with a shrug of the shoulders.

Many leaders have their favorites, men they allow to relax their military bearing when not around others. Fahim was that person because he'd been there since that first day when Jamal entered Hassan's network. Jamal always kept a watchful eye over him, especially during combat. And he could never kill him.

Fahim possessed a morbid curiosity about the *takfiri* and used it to justify his ideological differences between them and him. It was evident when the kid asked, "Did you hear about what they did to the shopkeeper who sold pornography?"

Jamal had a leery look. "Yes. Something about piano wire and his face."

"It is unbelievable. I almost lost my breakfast when I heard how they did it. Do you want to know how they did it?"

"I think you will tell me anyway, so let's hear it."

"A deep cut was made above the brow like this," he said as he drew his index finger across his sweat and dirt-encrusted forehead. His eyes suddenly shifted around Jamal's muscular frame.

Jamal turned around and saw three sport-utility vehicles with tinted windows approach from the other side of the bridge. He assumed the middle one carried the Lion of Iraq, come to inspect their progress. Jamal sent Fahim away and walked toward the vehicles as they parked. He noted how his men in the area went about their business seemingly unaffected by the arrival of the *takfiri*. He knew them better, knew a certain level of apprehension existed when in the presence of the foreign fighters. Likely, his homegrown fighting force was star struck, but too prideful to show it.

The foreign fighters were considered—or at the very least considered themselves—elite among the overall resistance, because their smaller numbers were able to inflict more significant damage. Even though the members of Hassan's network had recently shown an increased propensity for brutality themselves, the *takfiri* had an even higher disregard for human life from the day they arrived. Jamal considered the man he was about to meet for the first time in person, the man who had done his best to bring the good-old-fashioned beheading back in fashion.

All twelve doors from the vehicles opened except for one as if an order had been given by radio to exit simultaneously. The front seat passenger of the lead vehicle emerged. He was an Arab of considerable size. Not in girth but rather overall proportions. His beard was as full as a man's can be. It was long, thick, jet-black, and trimmed simply, or not at all. He wore a military field uniform with bloused trousers and combat boots. One hand carried an AK, the other a two-way radio.

His presence made it known he was in charge of the security detail. Jamal watched him efficiently scan the area, directing his gaze past the *Bathyoun* as if they weren't there because people were not what he assessed. More pertinent information could be gained from the size of the nearby buildings, the density of their walls, other avenues of approach the enemy might use to bypass the barricaded intersection.

The big man went to the middle vehicle, where several of his men had already gathered. When the last door opened, their leader emerged. The Lion of Iraq, Abu Musab al-Zarqawi, was shorter and more rotund than Jamal had imagined. He wore a *dish-dash* and a *kufi* atop his head. His beard was patchier than his security chief's. He wore dark sunglasses, and Jamal could tell by the way his head darted about that something he'd heard about this Lion was perhaps true.

He's paranoid as hell.

Jamal approached the group of vehicles. He'd prepared himself for this moment, intent on leaving a first impression distinguishable from their ingrained image of the *Bathyoun*, whom the *takfiri* considered brain-washed nationalists, and perpetually dour about their fall from power. Jamal was reminded of the English phrase he'd taken a liking to after hearing it in basic training.

Ain't that the pot calling the kettle black.

Each member of the security team carried some version of the AK or bore a sidearm. Zarqawi, like Jamal, was not armed. Instead, he carried a laptop computer case slung under his shoulder. The two of them made eye contact when Jamal stopped ten paces before the group.

Jamal bowed at the waist. "Peace be upon you," he said.

"And upon you be peace," they all muttered in low tones.

"We have been anxious for your arrival. My men are finishing the first levels of preparation as we speak. By the hand of Allah, we will be ready to face the infidel in two days."

The group seemed non-plussed at Jamal's Koranic references, but then again, their supposed arrogance would not permit them to bestow approval anyway. The big man spoke in a Jordanian dialect of Arabic.

"You are Muhammad al-Sudani?"

"Yes, I am Jamal Muhammad. Half Iraqi ... Born in Sudan, raised here in Anbar."

The big man showed no reaction as Zarqawi stepped forward. Jamal bowed again and raised his chin to meet the eye of the stout man from Zarqa, Jordan, who spoke next.

"I have heard about some of your successes. Most notably, the blessed attack on the Ta'mim market."

"We have indeed claimed victories against the occupiers," said Jamal. "But then again, a crazed dog is most dangerous only if he is cornered. Right now, the coalition is the opposite. They are spread thin, making it easy to exploit vulnerabilities."

The men before him seemed to appreciate Jamal's lack of self-promotion. Another thing Jamal had learned was that the *takfiri* believed the former Iraqi military fighters—Hassan's men—were too ready to accept credit and were needy of praise for the slightest achievement. He also knew the *takfiri* mostly wanted to talk about when and where to attack *next*.

"Praise be to Allah for the coming opportunity to strike at the viper," said Jamal.

"Even as he coils to strike himself," added Zarqawi with his patented half-grin. "Come, let us review the defenses."

Jamal nodded. "We are nearly prepared except for an additional layer of anti-personnel mines just behind the inner wire."

Zarqawi seemed to appreciate Jamal's use of allegorical language, which for Jamal had been a studied offering. He'd listened to Zarqawi's recorded rants against the Western occupiers and mimicked his antiquated and colorful way of speaking, an apparent necessity for card-carrying jihadists these days. The Arabs now softened their gazes and lowered their guard a bit as Zarqawi moved away from the vehicles to come alongside Jamal. Together they walked toward the barriers, and the razor wire strung like a thicket of thorny hedge across the broad intersection.

"I have just come from a meeting with General Barzan," said Zarqawi with a distressed tone.

"The number of fighters I was told to expect do not seem to be here."

A nod and a smile preceded Jamal's remark. "I'm sure his fat ass was not counting our reserve strength? Do not worry. He never likes anyone to know our true troop capacity." Jamal noted the puzzled reaction on Zarqawi's fleshy face. "I can assure you we will have the men needed to hold this position. I have put the call out to the neighborhoods. Our ranks will swell by nightfall tomorrow."

"Men from the streets?" queried Zarqawi.

"No. Trained men. When the coalition disbanded the Iraqi military, they put the fourth largest army in the world out of work. Most of them are still sitting at home; a lot are here in Fallujah. Ramadi too. This pre-announced siege of a major Sunni stronghold will bring many out. Men who'd felt lucky to have survived the initial invasion and found their homes safe after the disbanding of the army. Now those homes are threatened after all."

"You can guarantee this?"

"Almost certainly."

Zarqawi studied Jamal for a moment and asked, "Tell me, do you Iraqis slander your leaders like you just did or do you not respect the general?"

"Neither. I mean, no, but the general *is* obese. He knows it. I give him trouble about it. I can because we have a unique relationship. I have known him since I was a boy. He took me to Ramadi's Great Mosque for the first time. Now, he appreciates that I am not like all his ass-kissing former subordinates. Plus, I do good work for him."

"Yes. I have heard. He holds you in high regard."

Jamal stopped short of mentioning their penchant for drinking together, thought it wouldn't be helpful because the *takfiri* were known abstainers from alcohol or drugs. But lately, Jamal had heard some rumors that made him question that.

Zarqawi asked, "Are you a religious man?"

"By the will of Allah, I am a warrior."

"These are bound together. Are they not?"

"The warrior and his faith, yes, I believe so," said Jamal, more truthfully than Zarqawi could know.

Zarqawi smiled and put his hand on Jamal's shoulder. "Come, let us look at the defenses you have so ably prepared. We shall hope they cause the dogs to lament their decision to move upon this city."

CHAPTER 25

Jamal was early. He found an empty table in the café's small seating area and hung his jacket on a chair. An order was placed with the hurried proprietor, who was enveloped in a cloud of steam from the machines and kettles he worked.

"What can I do for you?"

Jamal pointed to his table. "Sweet tea over there for two, please. I am in no hurry."

The man seemed appreciative with his quick bow and frazzled smile, but then he refocused on the task at hand, pouring from two hot kettles at once. Jamal was curious about the few patrons in the establishment. The radio broadcasts pleading for noncombatants to flee Fallujah hadn't convinced these citizens. Now they braced for the first significant incursion into their city since the war began a year ago.

After Saddam's Army had folded in the early going, Jamal second-guessed the coalition's decision to put an American-backed town council in charge of Fallujah's citizens. As Sunnis, whose power had shifted to the Shiite majority in the new Iraqi government, the populace here quickly disregarded the puppets and embraced the resistance. Moreover, Hassan's Baathist cause was continually diluted by the forceful stance of Zarqawi's foreign *takfiri*. Jamal did not doubt that when the American assault force entered the city in a few days, they'd be here to fight jihadists, not Baathists.

The coalition must have assumed there would be little opposition here. And they have spread themselves too thin already, so they wrote it off. Same as Ramadi. Dangerous gamble. Now they have to clean it up the hard way.

The tea was delivered. Ahmed arrived just in time to receive his from the proprietor, who lifted the steaming kettle high while pouring into the sugar-packed glass. He bowed and smiled graciously on his way to another table of customers. A comfortable silence ensued as Jamal enjoyed the combination of bitterness and sweetness in the same rush of flavor, the hallmark of quality tea for an Iraqi.

Ahmed initiated the conversation with a tired look on his face. "I see you already had a chance to bathe today."

Jamal smiled. "You should be appreciative," he said, nodding toward an old man's donkey-powered cart as it clanked down the road out of town. It was laden with the personal belongings of the family that walked behind it. Toward the front rode a goat, whose bleating drove his barnyard mate.

"Until about an hour ago, I smelled worse than the pair of them together."

"I know. Why do you think I noticed?"

Ahmed had deadpanned the answer and continued sipping tea as he looked over the dwindling patrons around him. He wore dark aviator-style sunglasses, making it hard for Jamal to tell if he was kidding, which would be atypical for him.

"Well, since Zarqawi has granted us a night off before the coalition establishes their cordon around the city, I intend to find a woman. Brother, it might be the last time I am granted that pleasure on this Earth."

Ahmed removed his sunglasses and placed them on the table. His face changed. Jamal knew his friend well enough to know he'd pushed a button with the statement somehow. Most likely, regarding the talk of sex. In addition to abstaining from alcohol, the unmarried man remained chaste throughout his young life and now curled his lip. But there was a narrowing of his eyes as well.

Jamal had studied enough facial recognition techniques under the major's yoke to know that the lip movement meant disapproval. The eyes meant something else.

Confusion? Or, perhaps distrust.

"This leave he has granted our cells bothers me," said Ahmed, shaking his head. "Mark my words, some men will not come back."

Jamal understood a little better now, his level of anxiousness decreasing, but decided to let Ahmed keep talking.

"And Hassan only sent two cells here in support of this defense. People are questioning our commitment. Have you not noticed? How do I explain this to my men?"

Jamal had his thoughts on the matter. Like Fahim, Ahmed was someone Jamal wanted to keep close. He would have Jamal's back and would vouch for him if needed. Jamal hoped to lure Ahmed away from Hassan permanently and join the *takfiri* together. Ahmed's presence during their first few meetings with Hassan had made it easier somehow, diffusing the glare of one of the most dangerous men in the resistance at the time. Even though Jamal had made his inroads with Zarqawi, he believed two men approaching the *takfiri* to join them in the fight—one devout enough to be a true believer and both of them bona fide leaders— would be less suspicious than Jamal alone. Because of Ahmed's loyalty to his uncle and his clan, though, more sowing of prescribed thought patterns was in order.

"You said it yourself, Ahmed. Look around you." He gestured to the street. "These are not supporters of your uncle's cause ... of our reason we fight each day. These people have forgotten about Saddam and his lunatic sons, the Baathist movement, all of it. The men who are preparing for this battle are foreigners, outsiders who have convinced many Iraqis to fight alongside them."

"Why did Hassan send us then? He could have easily said this was not his fight. The coalition assault is retaliation for the mutilation of the four American mercenaries last month. We had no hand in that."

Jamal tilted his head in consideration. "Maybe he did it to save face, while not risking his entire force strength defending an act of lawlessness."

"In speaking to him, he seemed to think the Americans would come heavy, in an attempt to pacify the entire city. We cannot have that kind of loss in Anbar, so close to home. Ramadi will be next. He may be trying to endear himself to the *takfiri*, so they will return the favor when the time comes."

Jamal agreed. "But remember what he said."

"I know. Disappear into the desert if the tide turns quickly. We will have to find a way through the cordon. I believe it can be done."

Jamal had his doubts about that as the two sat back in their seats, sipped a little more tea. Ahmed still seemed bothered, though. Jamal wondered if it could be something other than the general's strategic moves.

"What is it, Ahmed? We have known each other for a long time, and I can tell there is-"

Ahmed cut him off with a raise of the hand and subsequently studied Jamal for a long moment, the same narrowing of the eyes occurring.

"I know you are not going to find *a* woman tonight. It is this woman you are involved with. You are going to her. You are leaving for Ramadi as soon as we are done here, no?"

Jamal was blindsided, unaware that Ahmed knew of his growing relationship with Hadiya. Did Ahmed see the extent of time he'd spent with her? Or did he only know the relationship existed? Or was it about the money he'd siphoned off Hassan's war chest for her cause? The scattered thoughts prompted the most challenging performance of his mission.

"There is nothing to hide," he said, unable to hold eye contact. "She should not concern you … She knows nothing of our operations. Just recharges me for more fighting. That is all."

Jamal didn't feel very good about his choppy delivery, and Ahmed studied him again, less cautiously this time.

"The general is mistrustful of civilians outside the cause these days. She is a foreigner?"

"A Kenyan. We fit together—this war will end someday. Who knows?"

"She has become a person of importance to you?"

Jamal stared away again, felt foolish for even entertaining the question. "I believe so."

"Then make sure she stays on the outside."

Hadiya saw the sign for the military surplus store on the block ahead. She crossed to the other side of Sadoon Street, part of the downtown commercial district of Baghdad. Many vendors who catered to Westerners had established themselves here. Therefore it was under constant threat of attack by any number of insurgent groups. Nervousness increased as she mingled among the citizenry. Just before she entered the surplus store, her phone chirped. She read a text message from Jamal, which caused a flood of emotion.

Oh, he's coming tonight! A surprise visit. Perfect timing to give him his birthday present.

She had decided her gift would serve as an olive branch of sorts. The last time they were together, she'd taken out her frustration on him regarding the constant violence in Ramadi. While it was true her disdain for the *Bathyoun* had decreased once she'd come to know Jamal, more so when it became clear the Americans had no practical plan for replacing Saddam Hussein, Hadiya still believed the new government should be given a chance to succeed. Democratic self-rule should at least be attempted, where an unending line of despots had so often failed the people of Iraq. She'd questioned the reasoning behind attacking civilians who waited in line at a police or military recruitment center; all those innocent victims had wanted was to ensure that Iraq was headed for the rule of law instead of the rule of the gun.

At first, Jamal had sarcastically said that, in truth, those Iraqis were only there to either collect a paycheck or to infiltrate the ranks of the defense forces. She'd responded with sarcasm of her own, and the conversation devolved into a heated argument. Eventually, he'd resorted to the hands-in-the-air approach, choosing to play the lowly lieutenant card, which signaled he didn't want to bicker anymore. He'd already met her stubborn side and must have known better, she guessed. Since that night, however, she'd seen some of those reasons in more of a positive light, and had come to wish she'd been less impulsive, less eager to put him in his place. Overeagerness was not something she wanted to project early in a relationship with a man. A better option would be to display her practical, less impulsive side.

Her practicality extended to her gift giving. As a child, she'd always liked receiving gifts she could use until she broke them or lost them, the typical fate of her birthday presents. She wanted to get Jamal something practical but was relatively ignorant about the needs of soldiers.

She replied to his text with a smiley face emoji and a question of the time he'd arrive. While she waited for his response, she recalled something from the last time he'd come to the villa. He'd never brought a gun inside as far as she knew. That day from a second-floor window, she'd seen him pull up and park. He leaned forward in the driver's seat, lifted the back of his t-shirt, and removed a pistol from the waistband of his pants before stowing it in the car. At the time, she'd just been glad that he met that unspoken expectation of hers on his own.

But that can't be safe, keeping a loaded gun in the seat of your pants.

She decided she would buy her new man a holster for his pistol, chuckled outwardly at the scandalous nature of such a gift. Both her parents hated guns. What would her father think of her even associating with a man who needed a holster? She suppressed her smile and spoke to the store attendant, who led her to a display case containing fine leather holsters. He also pointed to a dozen used holsters hanging by their belts on the adjacent wall. Hadiya thanked the man and began perusing his stock. She decided on the type that strapped to the shoulder and hung beneath the arm, rather than one that secured around the waist.

More modern, less hokey. After all, it wouldn't be a practical gift if he didn't use it.

She approached the cashier with a black leather holster in hand, resisting the urge to haggle over the price, because it was a gift.

"Here you are." said the Arab clerk with her change and a bag for the holster.

"Thank you for your business."

"You're welcome. Peace be upon you."

"And upon you as well."

She left the surplus store and headed toward her last stop, a printer. She'd made a bookmark for Jamal's Bible with her favorite passages from the Book of Psalms—and ones she thought Jamal would need. The words had been committed to memory long ago. She said them under her breath now as she walked.

Have mercy upon me, O God,
According to your loving kindness;
According to the multitude of your tender mercies,
Blot out my transgressions.
Wash me thoroughly from my iniquity,
And cleanse me from my sin …

Deliver me from the guilt of bloodshed, O God,
The God of my salvation,
And my tongue shall sing aloud of your righteousness.

CHAPTER 26

It was just after dawn on the fifth of April. The crushing noise of the coalition artillery barrage had ceased less than an hour earlier, replaced by the proverbial calm before the storm. The transition didn't last long. From points outside the city, Jamal heard the report of automatic gunfire over the low-slung built environment. They were only probing salvos, preceding a wave of men and vehicles.

"They're coming from the north, you say?" asked Jamal after pressing the transmit button on his two-way radio.

Ahmed's reply was affirmative, and Jamal signed off. The new knowledge helped him decide how to position the two Chechen snipers, who awaited orders from Jamal in the shade of the mosque compound's outer wall. He waved them over to his location now. The swarthy one carried a Dragunov SVD slung over his shoulder with a worn leather strap. The rifle was an older Russian military model with a limited range compared to newer weapons, but highly effective in the compressed arena of urban combat. He wore fatigue trousers and a t-shirt under a nylon web vest. Atop his crop of dark hair was a short-brimmed cap pulled low on the brow.

The other man stood six inches taller than his cohort. He was blond with a buzz cut and a square jaw that bore a lengthy scar from some vicious fight. Dark lenses covered his eyes. He wore civilian clothing except for desert-issue military boots. His weapon, the upgraded German Mauser, was cradled in lanky arms across his chest. A powerful scope was mounted on the receiver, and Jamal dreaded the prospect of so many coalition troops appearing in those crosshairs this first day of the assault.

In the twenty yards of dusty gravel between Jamal and the approaching snipers, fighters from various contingents dashed back and forth as they prepared for the imminent battle. The Chechens halted to let a group of vehicles cross their path, giving Jamal just a few more seconds to get his plan straight.

He'd racked his brain poring over a map of the city in an attempt to find the best locations to place them during the battle. He needed perches that would limit them in some way, yet offer enough advantages that subversion wouldn't be apparent. A key element to any plan he came up with was the origin of the main coalition attack. Until a moment ago, he hadn't been privy to that information.

From what Ahmed had said, it looked like they were coming from the north. Jamal was relieved. God was looking out for him today. He reasoned if he placed the snipers in elevated perches facing the attacking forces to the north, he could utilize westerly wind gusts currently streaming into the urban battlefield. The wind would travel perpendicular to the path of any rounds fired, pushing them off course to the right of the target each time. The Chechens were skilled enough to make the adjustments, but any added difficulty helped. He shot an arrow prayer toward Heaven that those shifting crosswinds maintained throughout the day.

Distance was a factor that could be used to his advantage as well, compounding the effects of crosswind. He knew the Chechens would prefer to be closer to the main attack, negating the need to factor for wind. A plethora of easy targets would present themselves in that context; sure kills both of them would rack up into double digits by lunchtime without his influence. If, however, he were to convince them that the attack from the north might be a diversionary attack, perches closer to the geographic center of the city would provide better overall coverage of the urban battlefield. It was a conservative strategy many commanders might adopt, and one the snipers would have a hard time arguing against.

In the end, he knew there wasn't much that could stop them. The bottom line was reducing their effectiveness. In a street fight like this, if he could keep the pair of them under ten kills on the day, he'd sleep better tonight. And they couldn't balk about being shut out.

The Chechens arrived. They had picked up a little Arabic since arriving in Iraq, so Jamal spoke to them using simple words and hand signals as he spread the map on the ground. He pinpointed his desired location for them, the tallest building near the city's center, explaining his fear of the diversionary attack. The snipers bent over the map and initiated a quick discussion in their language. The blond one indicated they knew of the place, seemingly accepting Jamal's reasoning. He nodded at Jamal before launching into a conversation with the other sniper. The swarthy man had no objections, either.

Jamal was relieved again, glad to let the physics of the wind and distance factors take over now. He shrugged off his worries about their kill count and tried to remember there were still a dozen other ways he planned to influence the outcome of today's battle.

"Go now," he said, raising his radio in the air and pointing to the building on the map again.

"Use your radio when you get there to tell us your position."

They both responded affirmatively and turned to leave.

As they walked away, Jamal uttered under his breath—in English—a sentiment straight from the heart. "Shitty hunting, you bastards."

He focused on the things he needed to do. There were a couple of to-do lists. One was associated with his outward responsibilities, procuring ammunition, positioning fighters, coordinating with units abreast of his sector, satisfying other logistical needs. Additionally, there was his mental list of tasks related to sabotage. He'd just checked the box on one of them. The next one was related to the radio he held.

Several weeks ago, he'd been given a couple of them by Zarqawi's quirky communications chief, another Jordanian, to accommodate their coordination with the *takfiri*. They were manufactured by an Indonesian company and were highly secure when used correctly. But Jamal had spent several hours one night in the rented room, testing out ways to breach their security and found success.

For the radio to work correctly, the user needed to connect it to an encryption device and follow a prescribed sequence of input and selection data during the download. He discovered that if the data stream were interrupted at a certain point in the process and reconnected immediately, it would yield the correct indicator lights when finished, making the user believe they were speaking on a secure channel, while they were not—a glitch in the software, he guessed.

He knew at least a dozen of the radios were lined up on battery chargers right now in the communications hub, ready for someone to upload the encryption program. He'd already buttered up the communications chief by offering to help with the preparations in the weeks prior, so access to the equipment was not a problem. Now was the time to do it if there ever was one. The plan would only be valid for today's codes because new ones would be provided tomorrow, and who knew if he'd be around to take a second bite at the apple. But the coalition listening in on the enemy for the first day of a major assault could potentially save many soldiers' lives. If this worked, he'd have to switch "to do" lists for a while before people noticed his men were unprepared to fight. Time was running out.

After leaving the communications hub, he checked another task off his mental list and reentered the mosque compound through the thick outer wall. Men gathered around a masonry block building, acting as an armory. Inside he would pick up 7.62 millimeter ammunition for the AK's his men would carry into today's battle. Jamal anticipated the gloves for both sides would come off in this fight, even though U.S. Marines and the Infantry of the Army had not seen this type of combat since Vietnam.

This is the real deal for the Americans. And my guys aren't going to know what hit them when their shock troops come at them. This isn't laying in some ambush and having the element of surprise on your side or taking potshots at coalition outposts.

He assumed the coalition would slowly advance to a point where they could establish a sizable base of operations inside Fallujah. Next, they would hunker down and flood the city with troops until some political compromise was made. They'd lose a lot of good men in the process, though. Those defending the city would lose even more, maybe ten times over. One thing was for certain; the city would never look the same again. As if on cue, he heard a concussive WHUMP to the north, something other than an artillery shell or mortar. He could only assume a high-flying jet had dropped guided, heavy ordinance on a *takfiri* position.

He edged forward in a short line of men seeking to stock up on ammunition. When it was his turn to receive, he placed an empty crate on a sturdy table near the side door of the armory. A sweaty Arab dumped bandolier after bandolier inside. Jamal allowed him to pile it high and hoisted the load onto the meaty portion of his shoulders. He regretted not bringing a couple of fighters with him. It was a long walk to his position by the bridge.

Ruminations about the upcoming battle ceased for good as heavy gunfire erupted amid smaller explosions further north. The assault was underway. The thumping sound of a helicopter echoed off the larger buildings around the mosque. On top of a nearby three-story building was a *takfiri* machine gun emplacement. He saw the crew spin the gun around to target the airborne threat. Jamal wasn't worried about being in the open. It was doubtful a coalition pilot would commit to striking the mosque this early in the battle for fear of political fallout.

Rules of engagement.

The machine gun crew on the roof fired its first salvo at the helicopter, now visible after emerging from behind a large building. It was an American AH-64 Apache, and the incoming rounds had served to alert the pilot to the fighters' location. He reacted by banking toward the three-story building. Suddenly a rocket-propelled grenade zipped into the sky and nearly hit the tail of the aircraft, but a slight dive by the pilot averted disaster. The *takfiri* machine gunner unloosed a stream of hot lead that proved accurate when sparks danced around the helicopter's armored shell. All of a sudden, the unmistakable BUURRRP of the Apache's rotary guns filled the air, and a burst pockmarked the masonry front of the building. Several hundred rounds tore into the sandbagged position, followed by the WHOOSH sound of a rocket that screamed toward the building and exploded. Target eliminated.

But the doomed gun crew had made their last shots count; the preponderance of bullets had hit the Apache's engine housing. The manifold gushed dark fluids down the side of the bulletproof glass canopy and suddenly spewed black smoke so thick that only the outer edges of the rotor blades protruded from the thickening haze. Dense smoke expanded, filling the air with the smell of burning oil, even from Jamal's distance more than a block away. The sudden loss of power forced the pilot to bank away and begin a wide arc that would return him to a secure airfield. Small arms fire from the ground further wounded the bird of prey as it sputtered home. Jamal picked up the crate and moved as fast as his legs would carry him.

Gonna be one hell of a day.

CHAPTER 27

Shadows lengthened by the minute as the dim light of dusk enveloped Jamal's sector of the defense. He was halfway down the line, distributing information and ammunition to his exhausted men. En route to the next position, he dashed across a battle-pocked street seeking cover. At least one American drew a bead on him when he jumped over a small crater, as bullets from an M4 rifle ricocheted off upturned chunks of sidewalk and pavement. Once on the other side, he ducked into a shattered storefront. Another clutch of bullets slammed into the metal doorframe around him, and for maybe the tenth time in his life, he heard the zzzipp of a bullet as it flew only inches from his head. The three fighters inside hugged the ground behind sandbag barriers. When Jamal was in their midst, they sat up to receive his instructions, while one of them peered over the barrier on watch.

This stretch of Highway Ten was in one of the most embattled sections of the city, and right now, the broad avenue before them represented no man's land. Jamal knew an American vanguard would slam through any time, but expected a reconnaissance element beforehand. He looked at the fighters hunched up against the sandbags. Two were relatively young and new to the cell—friends of Fahim's. The other was a veteran.

Jamal asked him, "Any reports of movement?"

"No. These two would shit their trousers if they saw more than a handful of Americans at once." He whiffed the air in front of him a few times, then shook his head in the negative.

"I think we're safe for now."

One of the fighters rolled his eyes, the other snickered.

Jamal knew the veteran was only mimicking his leadership style, honed long ago by Jamal when he'd led the boys from his village across North Africa to the refugee camp. They'd been so young that he'd become accustomed to making light of everything to ease their dread.

"Good. I'm glad. I'd kind of like to eat before they come. You should, too," said Jamal with a grin that had a positive effect on the young fighters.

To the veteran, he said, "Take these magazines. You'll have to make do with the warheads you have for the RPG. Remember, only use them on vehicles and troops close to each other—of no less than how many?"

The question had been directed at the younger fighters, who spoke in unison. "Four soldiers."

"That's right. I'll be on the radio. Use the frequencies we talked about and stay awake when you're on duty."

The veteran nodded as Jamal got up and exited the rear of the building. The route to his next stop was safer, so naturally, his thoughts drifted back to the fighting as he walked. Already, the resistance had seen dramatic losses across the board. He wondered whether he and Ahmed would cut and run, or stick around until the end of the fight. That call had yet to be made by Hassan.

Jamal approached a two-story structure chosen by him as a fixed defensive position. Its height above adjacent buildings covered several lesser positions by providing a perch for snipers and a machine gun. Fahim was upstairs with three other fighters, and Jamal had put him in charge of the team for the first watch. With those thoughts of cutting and running still on his mind, he entered the narrow back stairs of the house that led to the upper room. A second more formal stair was located at the front of the building and led to the same room. Suddenly, there was hoarse shouting upstairs, before the voluminous bark of automatic gunfire erupted. He heard the thumping of his fighters' AK's, but also discerned the quicker firing rate of American M4's. Two grenades exploded in quick succession, shaking dust loose in the stairwell, which Jamal charged up three steps at a time.

He burst into the shadowy room, pistol at the ready. The smell of gunpowder and exploded ordinance was heavy in the air. But the exchange of gunfire had ceased after the Americans rushed the room. Hand to hand combat now took place, making the scene chaotic; in the partial darkness, it looked like a jumble of camouflage and earth-toned tunics with only a splash of moonlight for discernment. As Jamal rushed to join the melee, he scanned the rest of the room and saw two of his fighters dead on the floor. One was missing half a leg from the grenades that must have been tossed in by the Americans. Over by the second stair door, an American writhed in agony while clutching his bloody throat.

Jamal thought he saw Fahim and dashed across the large room toward him. The scrawny kid's combatant had fifty pounds and several inches on him, not to mention heavy body armor. But it occurred to Jamal that the heavy loads the Americans wore made them less agile, and the flash of thought was validated when he saw Fahim dodge a roundhouse swing of the soldier's rifle butt. Fahim fell unbalanced into the shadows just as Jamal slammed into the American, driving him into a wall. The soldier was sandwiched by massive plates of armor on his chest and back and groaned when the two men fell to the floor.

Jamal hopped to a knee and used the butt of his pistol to bludgeon the American, who was still dazed from the tackle. Two solid blows to the side of the head knocked him out cold. On his feet again, Jamal saw one of the two remaining Americans stab another fighter with a combat knife. As the fighter screamed, the other soldier on his feet attempted to reload his rifle quickly and efficiently. Jamal began to raise the pistol instinctually, but out of the darkness behind him, a ten-round burst from an AK erupted. Strobe-like muzzle flashes illuminated the American holding the weapon like stop motion photography as he tumbled backward, the last several rounds pinning him to the wall against his blood splatter. The gunfire inside the concrete shell of a room nearly split Jamal's eardrums.

But his hearing was not a concern at the moment. The two-hundred-fifty pounds of knife-wielding, armor-plated, vinegar-pissing infantryman that charged across the room toward him *was* a concern. Jamal assumed Fahim had fired off what was left of an AK's magazine and was either out or reloading.

The American with the knife bore down on Jamal like a savage, projecting a guttural roar that Jamal only partially made out as curses in English. At the moment, it was impossible to register his assailant as some kid from the States he had to sacrifice to advance his mission. He was the enemy, and he wanted Jamal and Fahim dead. It was kill or be killed. When the soldier was halfway across the room, Jamal aimed and fired two shots at center mass. The .45 caliber at this range would typically be a man-stopper, even against body armor, but it barely slowed the charging bull, no doubt redlined with adrenaline. The knife started to come down, the edge of the blade glinting as it passed through a beam of moonlight. Jamal dropped to a knee with a two-handed grip on the pistol and unloaded the rest of his magazine until the soldier fell to the floor at his feet.

He still couldn't hear a thing, even his voice, as he turned to Fahim. "Come on. We have to get out of here. They will be coming to their aid in a matter of minutes, if not seconds. Just grab your weapon."

Fahim was in a state of near shock but did as told. They both ran down the back stairs and out into the alley.

A day later, Jamal waited outside while Fahim and several fighters burst into an abandoned automotive repair shop. They moved quickly through the bays, clearing the vast space of potential threats until Fahim signaled to Jamal that it was safe to occupy the building. This contingent comprised Jamal's reduced group of fighters, Ahmed and the remaining members of his cell, and a handful of *takfiri* who'd been picked up from decimated units on the front line. Attrition had caused the two leaders to merge their fighters only hours earlier.

The methodical coalition advance over the first two days had successfully breached multiple lines of defense. Still early in the overall incursion, the cost was relatively low in terms of coalition casualties by all news reports, and they were inflicting a much heavier toll on the defenders than the *takfiri* would ever admit. From Jamal's perspective, however, both sides were spending political capital, an essential component of asymmetric warfare, as if they were drunken sailors on overdue shore leave. Many of Fallujah's civilians had perished from guided missiles and artillery, which rained upon holed-up fighters who refused to release their human shields. Jamal knew specific targets would not be denied if they posed an imminent threat to advancing soldiers or Marines. This disregard for civilian life by both sides fanned the flames of resentment that the Iraqi public and their newly elected politicians held toward the coalition. It didn't sit well with the cable news-watching American taxpayers either, from what he'd seen on a satellite feed in the communications hub.

Indeed, the whole world is watching.

As far as slipping out of Fallujah, Ahmed had used a secure satellite phone to call Hassan with a situation report. At the time, it appeared less than a quarter of the city was under coalition control, far below a level of supremacy needed for them to claim any victory. Ahmed boasted to Hassan about the fighting abilities of the men, mentioning how they'd held their positions until the *takfiri* themselves called for withdrawals across the entire first lines of defense. And the two leaders had only lost a handful of men between them, with just as many wounded. Hassan was pleased enough to hedge his bet, and he told them to stay for the remainder of the operation. That was yesterday.

Today had seen the tightening of the cordon around the city and even harder fighting. Subsequent probes to find a weak point for a hasty escape proved fruitless, although it was believed the Lion of Iraq had slipped out of the city wearing a woman's *burqua* as a disguise. Jamal and all the men—even some *takfiri*—found mocking humor in that bit of news. But then there was the simple matter of being at the wrong place at the wrong time. Ahmed's cell came under heavy sniper fire and was further harassed by a mortar barrage. Just like that, fifteen fighters were dead and several more wounded.

Jamal had lost a half-dozen men earlier in the day when a roadside bomb set in place by his men exploded prematurely. And he'd incurred his losses to coalition sniper fire. Circumstances led both leaders to agree that consolidating their strength would help them bring the most men back to Ramadi, thereby mitigating the rage of Hassan.

Once together, they'd only been in their new defensive posture for a couple of hours when the lines shifted again. A mix of foreign and Iraqi jihadists defended the positions to their right and left. The fighting was fierce everywhere; the resistance appeared to repel the coalition vanguard. But when Jamal and Ahmed saw the profile of an Abrams tank two blocks to their left and retreating *takfiri* to their right, they ordered their fighters to fall back. Over the last thirty minutes, the cell members had run ten blocks with as much gear and ammunition as everyone could carry.

Once inside the automotive shop, most of the men were still winded from the exhausting retreat and several drank from a hose they found. They were now deep inside Julan, just outside the final line of defense. From here, Jamal and Ahmed would send patrols out to harass and hinder the coalition as they cleared the battle space they'd just won. Massive structures surrounded this garage, and out the back door was an alley, which led to the next route of escape. Jamal knew it was an eventuality. Until then, it could serve as a bunker. They needed to refit.

Jamal and Ahmed dropped their gear near two folding chairs. They seemed to both have the same idea and plopped down to give their tired legs a rest.

Still catching his breath, Ahmed said, "Been a while since I ran like that."

"We're going to need some real food after that shit!" Jamal rolled his head around on his shoulders in a tired way, searching for the fighter usually tasked with making meals in the field. When he found him, Jamal called the man over. The beefy fighter was, in fact, a butcher in his life outside the resistance, in addition to being a former Republican Guardsman himself.

"I temporarily relieve you from any duties requiring weaponry or the defense of this position!" said Jamal. "Take an armed fighter with you and go find some decent food for every man in this building to eat tonight. We will cook over an open fire right here on the floor if we have to."

The order seemed to energize the man. "I will find a way, Jamal."

Others had overheard, so men started acting like juveniles vying to be the one he selected. Anything was better than the mundane tasks of preparing for the next battle. There was also the notion of being present when a bounty of food was discovered. Whoever helped the cook could pocket certain items upfront and use them for barter when all the trading up and down commenced. Jamal smiled and looked at Ahmed, who reciprocated the gesture.

"That was a good call, brother."

"What do you mean?" muttered Jamal as he hunched over to loosen the laces on his boots.

"You know, making a production out of it here in the middle of the room. Letting him take someone because you knew it would liven them up."

Jamal shrugged. "Just hungry, my friend."

"Seriously, you know better how to endear the men to you. I can tell they would die for you if you asked them. My men ... I— "

Jamal waited a few seconds; he could tell Ahmed was struggling with the loss of so many fighters. His peer wasn't one to show emotion, but there was sadness in his eyes. After it appeared he'd drifted in his thoughts or was reluctant to express them, Jamal tried to move them past the moment.

"Well, let us hope it doesn't come to that. So far, I've lost too many men to accidents and unseen snipers. I asked for none of those men to die."

The statement failed to jar Ahmed from his dreadful place. "Right ..."

"Just like those damn mortars. Nothing you could have done."

Ahmed turned, an almost imperceptible shaking of the head accompanying his blank stare. "They had a bead on us. After the first ones came in, I moved us right away, but ..."

Jamal waited again; he put his hand on Ahmed's shoulder. "But they must have had a spotter with eyes on. Like I said, nothing you could have done."

Jamal sat back in the chair, felt the tension in his back drain away. He rubbed his messy beginnings of an afro and looked at himself, then Ahmed. Both men wore the signs of heavy fighting, just like all the men under their leadership. The entire contingent was dusty from head to toe, with scrapes and bruises on their elbows from firing on the hard urban ground, bloodshot eyes from lack of sleep for over two days.

In a minute, Ahmed seemed to emerge from his funk and called his senior fighters—the equivalent of sergeants in a normal army—and the backbone of any army. "Establish a perimeter outside," he said. "Place mines in the intersection we just crossed … and get some eyes on top of the taller building down the street. Do not make yourselves obvious. We have seen the enemy has highly capable snipers crawling all over this ruined town."

The ranking fighters spoke privately for a moment to come up with a plan before gathering with their subordinates, while Ahmed tended to a lightly wounded man who'd just limped in from the street. Jamal spotted a large workbench against the far wall. He used one long sweep of his arm to clear the entire surface of clutter. Auto parts, oil cans, and a handful of tools crashed to the concrete floor, turning heads. He spread a map of the city on the surface of the table and shouted for Fahim, who jogged over.

"The mortars are ready. Just tell me where you want us."

"Here," said Jamal.

He placed his index finger on the map by a large residential compound that offered high walls for protective cover from ground fire. It was between their present location and the next line of defense, right along the route the cell would use if they needed to fall back further.

"But would we not have a better chance of killing the enemy if we were up closer, maybe right here?" asked Fahim, pointing to a patch of open ground just two blocks away, nothing more than a lateral shift of their current position, not to mention exposed.

Jamal had known inquisitive Fahim would question him about the location he'd chosen because the kid knew better. Jamal had created that monster himself when it came to tactics. It was true; the mortars would be more effective against the coalition at Fahim's desired location, prompting Jamal's mission-oriented reason for denying it. But truth be told, it was more about protecting Fahim at this point. This battle would be over in a few days, and he'd be in the clear.

"It is a sacrifice we have to make," said Jamal firmly. "As nearby as your suggested position is, you still could be cut off from us. I cannot afford to lose those tubes. Hassan would have my balls on a platter if our best mortars got captured in this pissing contest."

Fahim reluctantly went along with Jamal's directive without further pestering and added a good reason of his own to set up further behind the lines.

"Besides, we will be able to protect this building fairly well from your residential compound."

Jamal clapped Fahim on the shoulder, "Good. I am glad you see it that way. You lead them there. Make sure you have a radio that is charged before leaving?"

"You got it, boss."

CHAPTER 28

"The American patrol approaches from the north!" exclaimed one member of the three-person reconnaissance team led by Fahim. Before he could respond, the third fighter bound down the stairs.

"A squad of Marines is clearing the south end of this block. We're about to be surrounded!"

"Damn," said Fahim. "Where the hell did they come from?"

The oldest of the three said, "I don't know, but it's time to move out."

"All right, gather your gear," said Fahim. "Rashid, prepare the grenade launcher."

After their meal the previous night, and once the mortars were in position, the cell had lain low in the automotive shop until dawn. Because the movements of coalition patrols were so hard to pin down, Jamal had dispatched Fahim's team an hour ago to clarify the enemy's strength in the neighborhood. Now they were caught between two converging patrols.

"We'll use the RPG to pin them down and then make a run for it across the street. There is good cover along the way with all the rubble," said Fahim. While he waited for a reaction, he drank to lessen his cottonmouth. He hoped they didn't see his hands shaking as he held the plastic water bottle to his lips. When finished, he tossed it on the floor.

"Then we bust ass to the plaza where the *takfiri* have a vehicle with a mounted gun."

"Why don't we just hide here until they've passed," said the younger of the two lower-ranking fighters.

"Because, you fool," retorted the older fighter, "you just said they are clearing the block. That means every building."

"Maybe they won't do this one."

Fahim endured the ensuing argument born of panic for only a few exchanges before he pulled rank—a rarity for him—and told them to shut up and get ready to move. Two minutes later, they were lined up at the door, and Fahim identified the target for the RPG, a sedan parked fifty yards down the street, adjacent to two kneeling Marines. One of them carried a radio on his back. That meant the other one speaking into the handset was a leader, maybe even an officer.

The young fighter's face was painted with nervousness.

"Hey, Rashid," said Fahim, "I'm scared too. We'll be back before you know it. Then we can get some food and rest."

Rashid looked down with his jaw clenched, and his eyes closed. Fahim was about to offer to fire the grenade when the fighter nodded his head and reached for the doorknob.

Fahim turned to the older fighter behind him. "As soon as the vehicle blows, we go."

The man nodded, his fear showing now.

Rashid moved outside with the grenade launcher balanced on his shoulder, shuffling out into the street for a clear shot at the sedan. He knelt on one knee and leveled the launcher, the cone-shaped, high-explosive warhead aimed toward the stationary vehicle. Fahim's internal clock started ticking when it appeared Rashid was having difficulty steadying the weapon.

Three ... Four ... Five.

"Fire, Rashid!" shouted both fighters in unison from the door opening.

As the words left their mouth, the WHOOSH of the rocket-propelled grenade drowned them out. An instant later, a burst of machine-gun fire found Rashid. Tracer rounds zipped across Fahim's line of vision with terrifying velocity; several hit Rashid while one ricocheted off the grenade launcher and tumbled away. The dead fighter slowly slumped to the pavement, but his aim had been true. The grenade hit its mark, and the resulting explosion halted the gunfire, if only momentarily—the diversion they needed. A secondary explosion of the vehicle's fuel tank engulfed the pair of wounded Marines, who crouched only a few paces away.

"Let's go, he's gone," said Fahim.

For the first couple of months, after he'd lost his family, Fahim would have been envious of Rashid's honorable death. He felt the underlying impulse to stop in the middle of the street and empty his magazine until the coalition guns found him too. But not today. He'd already lost one man and was determined to get the other one back safely, along with the intelligence he'd gathered.

The two exchanged one look of reassurance and quickly bolted from the building's front entry out into the war-torn street. The diversion only bought them a few seconds before the well-trained Marines opened fire again. Fahim knew he'd be cut down if he didn't find cover. He unleashed a long burst of suppressive fire from his hip, just enough to make it to a smoking wreck in the middle of the street. The older fighter fell in a heap on the pavement next to him, winded from the sprint under fire. Bullets slammed into the other side of the metal hulk, causing them to hunker down further.

"Give me one of the smoke grenades," shouted Fahim under the cacophony of gunfire.

"You can't be serious," said the fighter.

"If we stay here, they'll start dropping mortar rounds, or they'll flank us. We only have another thirty yards. You can do it."

Fahim swapped out his nearly empty banana-shaped magazine for a full one containing thirty rounds. The fighter did the same, and Fahim tossed the smoke grenade over the body of the sedan. The hissing noise accompanied the clattering of the metal canister bouncing on the pavement several times. Within seconds a yellowish cloud filled the air, as did the smell of sulfur. Because it was not windy, the smoke expanded throughout the general area, screening the side of the street to which they needed to get.

"Now," said Fahim.

They were up and running, with Fahim in the lead. The hairs on the back of his neck stood at attention for those first few steps, but then instinct took over, his legs propelling him toward the storefront directly in front of him, the finish line for this mad dash. He saw Marines moving through the haze, so he assumed they could see him as well. He knelt and fired two well-aimed bursts at a figure advancing into the smoke. The man went down.

Need to keep moving.

Incoming rounds skipped off the pavement around Fahim or zipped by, the laser-like flash of tracers traversing his path while he ran. Another figure appeared to his left. He shot from the hip as he ran this time, a spray of inaccurate rounds in the general direction. He thought he saw downward motion. Either he'd hit him or caused the Marine to dive for cover.

Ten more yards.

"Watch out!" shouted the older fighter from behind him. Fahim had almost run headlong into a mortar crater but managed to leap across it at the last moment. They each emptied their magazines in one final burst before making it to the deserted storefront.

"Come on," beckoned Fahim, catching his breath once they were inside. "On the other side of the block is the plaza. We'll be there in two minutes."

They exited the rear of the storefront and wound through back alleys. Soon they were on the edge of the open, rubble-strewn public square that had seen heavy fighting over the previous days. On the opposite end, Fahim saw the pickup truck with a recoilless rifle mounted in its bed. Several *takfiri* fighters operated it. Their body language told Fahim they'd been alerted to the advancing enemy. After Fahim signaled to cross the plaza, he and the fighter jogged toward the *takfiri*. Halfway across, they heard the booming sound of a Marine handheld rocket, which sent them to the pavement as the high-velocity ordinance tore across the plaza and impacted the truck. A fireball erupted, and two bodies flew in different directions. Several fighters managed to escape the blast, retreating into alleys behind them.

Once again, Fahim and the older fighter were up and running, desperate to reach the far end. They sprinted past the flaming pickup truck. The destroyed recoilless rifle lay across the dead gunner in its bed. Other bodies were in and around the vehicle, the sickening sweet smell emanating from those that burned.

Fahim and the fighter ducked into a narrow alley between two damaged buildings, just before the squad of Marines on their tail entered the opposite end of the plaza. The WHUP WHUP WHUP of a Blackhawk helicopter reverberated in his eardrums. It meant the Marines were attempting to use the ample open space as a landing zone for reinforcements, or they required medical evacuation. Fahim hoped it was the latter. If so, he was tempted to fire his remaining rounds into the gaggle of medics and flight crew that always formed around an aircraft right after it landed. He could almost taste the pain he would inflict. He thought better of it, though. For one, he was exhausted, famished, and nearly out of ammunition. So was the fighter with him.

Not a good time to pick a fight we can't finish.

He edged back toward the plaza anyway—against the verbal protest of his companion—to see if the Marines were still in pursuit. Gunfire erupted the moment he peered around the corner of the building. More bullets slammed into the already dimpled metal of the façade. He pulled back and heard shouts in what had to be English and the unmistakable sound of heavily laden men running in his direction. The predictable covering fire tore into the alley as the Marines advanced, but Fahim and the fighter had already disappeared into the twisting labyrinth of clustered buildings off the plaza.

A short while later, they approached a four-story tenement. The building was firmly entrenched in the ground owned by Zarqawi's men and would be used as a command center and field hospital throughout the remainder of the battle. The first three floors were occupied by the *takfiri*, who had crowded the remaining inhabitants into the top level. Groups of twenty were sent up to the roof in stints to discourage precision attacks by coalition warplanes. A raid by special operations forces was not out of the question, however, so the level of security surrounding the large, rectangular-shaped building was more than enough to ward off such an attack, or at least make the enemy pay dearly if they tried. All Fahim cared about was that it was a place to sleep.

The lower level had a spacious room, with stairwells leading to the floors above. Fighters who spoke in a half-dozen languages manned a communications hub. Vertical map boards and planning tables were being used in another part of the room; pockets of small groups worked intently, focused on their operations. Amid the chatter of all those people, Fahim told the fighter to find a bunk and some hot food, but to stay close while awaiting new orders.

Even though the loss of Rashid still stung, a sense of relief came over him the second the older fighter turned to walk away. He knew it was the weight of responsibility being lifted, sometimes wondered if people forgot how young he was. He'd invited this situation by enlisting at the earliest age he could get away with, but it was strange to him that less than two years ago, he was still getting in trouble for not cleaning up his room or not eating his vegetables. Both memories made him think of his mother. He felt a jolt of anguish that increased his weariness.

A pair of empty cots near the outer wall was more than acceptable, as far away as possible from the noise—and the body odor from so many unclean men. He claimed them both by tossing gear on them. One would be for Jamal if there weren't the time or the inclination to think about sleep. Fahim looked across the room occupied by dozens of fighters from all over the greater Arabic speaking world. He saw Jamal among them and marveled at the high energy level on display, realized he felt the complete opposite, and might be too tired to walk over and get food. Once again, he thought better of it. At least he would avoid the pangs that would no doubt awaken him after he drifted off to sleep.

He moved through the chow line and received a plate of bread and gravy, some carrots, and an orange. Disposable water bottles were available in abundance. Cold too. He drank two on the spot and grabbed two more for later. While he ate at his bunk, an artillery round exploded a block away from their building. He heard glass shatter outside, and the ground trembled underfoot. A generator powered the lights in the command center, which now flickered as the diesel engine cut a few times and finally went out, causing a torrent of curses in the room.

An order was shouted by one of the Jordanians. Someone shuffled off, and a minute later, the needed machine hiccupped through the startup process. The lights flickered for a second, and then they were on again. Fahim was glad someone had thought of the generator, even more so that they knew how to fix it when it gave trouble. It legitimized them in some way, he figured.

The idea of legitimacy was important to Fahim. When the Revolutionary Guard was disbanded, he had reservations about their ability to conduct modern guerilla warfare as insurgents. Even at his young age, he understood victory could not be won by a bunch of lightly armed rebels who went about the country haphazardly wreaking havoc on the coalition. It would take real leadership and a clear directive to achieve their binary goals of pushing out the occupying force and killing off a budding democratic government in Baghdad.

For a while, it seemed they had their men in Hassan, Izzat Ibrahim, all the former military leadership they needed, and of course, Saddam, the "Supreme Leader." And it seemed the coalition strategy had been off for the whole first year. Over that year, though, so many fighters had been captured or killed. But not Jamal Muhammad. By now, Fahim understood that if he were to survive this war, if there was hope for a life after the tragedy and ruin he'd experienced, his best bet was to stay close to Jamal and do his best to watch the big African's back in the process, a symbiotic relationship.

He used to believe Hassan was a great leader. But it seemed the general was becoming increasingly erratic in his decision-making. It had started with the growing strategy of killing Iraqis. Then came the relationship with the *takfiri*, who had not hesitated to kill man, woman, or child in the most brutal ways. There were the kidnappings, the videotaped beheadings like the one of the American in the orange jumpsuit. Zarqawi supposedly performed that one himself.

Fahim looked over at Jamal again. He knew that, like Hassan, his friend was drawn toward Zarqawi's group and their spectacular attacks. Fahim could never say this aloud, but in his eyes, their association with such extremists diminished both Hassan and Jamal. He knew there were other factors to be considered, matters of higher importance for both men to which Fahim was not privy. But on its surface, this alliance was with outsiders. Foreigners.

Just like the occupiers had designs on the nation's oil wealth, Fahim knew full well the designs the *takfiri* had for the people of Iraq. They didn't include him being an up and coming member of the powerful Baathist elite, something he'd set his sights on when he was but an adolescent. So what was the difference? Where had real Iraqis fit in either agenda? Were they just surrogates fighting for someone else's cause?

He understood his reasons for fighting were about revenge. Seeing so much red at the death of his family had made him reckless early on. Fortunately, Jamal had pulled him back several times—literally by the collar—from running headlong into a hail of bullets, denying him the death wish. They conferred in private on the matter away from the other men at first. Eventually, it became an inside joke between the two of them, because a man's shame is less of a burden when it can be shared in jest with someone he trusts. These many months later, he knew it all had been a rite of passage for him as a young soldier, a young man. People die. Others live. The concept hardened him and made him a better fighter for the cause.

Eventually, the death wish topic became a running joke within the cell at large, even to the point of Fahim adding it to his extensive repertoire of self-deprecating jokes. Despite the jokes, he noticed Jamal and the members of the cell who'd been around the longest kept a close eye on him.

He grew weary of thinking about the war and what it had done to him. Sleep beckoned, but he was leery of the passage of time until his next bout with reality. Lately, his dreams had been plagued with negativity, sometimes producing images worse than he'd seen during his hellish days. To ward them off, he closed his eyes and tried a trick from his childhood that even now he believed would work. He called it "setting his dreams."

Think about the bad things you've seen that day and tell yourself they're not allowed into your dreams. Next, think about one good thing and don't let any other thoughts in, good or bad. Carry the thought into sleep, and it will be the focus of your dreams. He chose to settle on a day in his tenth year. His family had come to Baghdad for one of Saddam's dedications to his glory.

It was the day Fahim decided he would be a soldier under the regime. His waking mind's eye still showed him the sharp uniforms and perfectly coordinated marching of the Republican Guardsmen. Fit and confident, they'd passed beneath the great arched swords of *Qadisiyah*, the sun glinting off the dark sunglasses the officers wore. He'd known he would be one of them someday.

But here he was, exhausted and battered and barely clinging to that dream. His life plan seemed as unrealistic and wistful as a real dream does when one awakens in the night to find oneself in bed. Fahim's thoughts slipped back to the war. He caught himself, tried again. This time he saw something that could never be corrupted. *A time long before the bad day.*

He indulged in a simpler memory, imagined himself before her. The smile on her face that was made only for him. The warmth he felt inside. It was his last lucid thought before joining his mother in her vegetable garden for a little while.

Jamal found Fahim drooling while sleeping, saw the personal effects on the empty cot, and appreciated his sidekick's thoughtfulness. He dropped the satchel there to indicate he'd been by, and grabbed a pair of binoculars on his way to the stairwell. When he reached the roof, and it's commanding four-story view, windblown smoke from some fire at street level assaulted his nostrils. He heard the staccato crackle of automatic gunfire and the deep thump of grenades and RPG's exploding in the distance. Aircraft roared overhead, just before their powerful bombs detonated among targets scattered throughout the city. This was the largest pitched battle of the war, and it raged all around him, the lines edging toward this contingent of *takfiri* and Iraqis. If a final stand were to happen, the battle would unfold here and in a couple of nearby mosques where so many munitions were stored.

Yet despite the chaos hemming him in, Jamal's understanding of the larger battle space led him to believe a decisive victory was not in store for the coalition. Too much ground to clear, too little time. The Iraqi Governing Council in Baghdad was already making pleas to the media for a cease-fire to the "illegal incursion" into Fallujah. He shook his head as he watched advancing Marines through his binoculars. Even now, Zarqawi and his top lieutenants were claiming their form of victory, albeit from some other locale.

The Americans talked it up too much. Anything short of complete pacification will be seen as a concession. And victory falls more firmly in Zarqawi's grip every time a guided bomb falls on a civilian, or one of our bullets kills another Marine. This will be over in days as the pressure increases exponentially on the generals out there.

Suddenly, he heard the unmistakable ripping sound of the most lethal tool of war on the battlefield. He jogged over to the far corner of the roof. Against the inky light of dusk, about a mile away, he saw a lumbering AC-130 bank in a continuous, circular flight path over its target. The four-prop, cargo-convert belched multiple beams of tracer light toward the ground from the inboard side of the fuselage. Even though tracers occur every fifth round in American belt-fed ammunition, the mesmerizing rate of fire gave the appearance of a continuous laser beam. The destructive power was nearly the same.

He knew each of the four rotary guns could send three thousand rounds per minute into the target area, fifty bullets per second times four. He lowered the binoculars and took in the chilling sight of the gunship raking the neighborhood below. Unfortunately, he also knew most of the insurgents were holed up in underground tunnels, protected from the deadly rain above. They would pop up somewhere else tomorrow and cause fits for the coalition patrols.

Americans and their reluctant allies could play whack-a-mole for weeks in this town.

Suddenly, the exhaustion from so much recent fighting took over his body, causing him to sit down along the inside face of the roof's waist-high parapet. He rubbed his temples, easing the throbbing between them. The flood of thoughts receded, and he drifted off with the thudding din of battle in the distance, sadly relegated to background noise in his war-weariness. But white noise becomes ineffective as a sleep inducer when punctuated by the odd, out of place sound.

In this case, Jamal, in his dozing state, heard the loudest bell he'd ever heard in Fallujah. It took a second to realize that truthfully, it was a bell he'd never heard in all of Iraq. It gonged again. And again. He had a flash of fear that brought him only halfway back to reality.

The end times. The bells … Ancient Babylon.

It was the guitar solo starting up that made him jump to his feet.

What's this?

He ran across the roof again, this time facing a portion of the city where the *takfiri* were especially dug in. The melody of the guitar began to roll even while the bell gonged. Next, a drum kicked in. Jamal thought he knew what it was, but he could not wrap his addled, sleep-deprived mind around why he heard it. He raised the binoculars, but couldn't discern specifically from where the music emanated. Instead, it was being projected throughout the whole neighborhood. Just as he heard Iraqis shouting from below, no doubt running from the planning room to see what this strange and offensive development was, he listened to the familiar lyrics,

> *I'm rolling thunder, pouring rain,*
> *I'm coming on like a hurricane.*
> *My lightning is flashing across the sky.*
> *You're only young, but you're gonna die.*

Jamal shook his head. His mind flashed to the time he'd first heard the song. They'd been cleaning in the barracks on a Sunday when only one drill sergeant was on duty. He allowed the privates to have music because it was the week before graduation. Jamal remembered this one by AC/DC had gotten the white kids going pretty good.

Hell's Bells, I think. Gotta be tactical Psy-Ops. Pretty clever. What will they try next?

He retreated to the stairwell after the stolen moment, where he reminded himself he was an American now. For once in his life, there was a home to go back to, and the thought rejuvenated him. By the time he'd reached the bottom of the stairs, his priorities had changed. His best ticket toward advancing the mission—and getting home—was bolstering his relationship with Zarqawi and his contacts outside of Iraq. Jamal needed to find out where Zarqawi had fled before the next round of fighting developed.

After stopping to check on a fast asleep Fahim, Jamal left the binoculars as evidence he'd been there and took the satchel and his weapon this time. While his men refitted, he had investigating to do. On his way out of the command center, he noted that AC/DC had been replaced by Metallica, another favorite of the guys in his basic training platoon. And truth be told, Jamal had taken to the pulsating sound of this band. The quick guitar and hammering cymbals right off the bat gave the song away for him.

Speaking of Zarqawi. "Master of Puppets." Nice.

CHAPTER 29

Hadiya turned to Jamal while he drove the Volvo. The fighting in Fallujah had taken a toll on him. He'd shed at least fifteen pounds while he was there. She could see it in his face, mostly. Already lean to begin with, his high cheekbones seemed more prominent with the weight loss. His hair, customarily cropped short, had grown into the beginnings of an afro. There was no shortage of cuts and bruises on him from head to toe either, giving him somewhat of a ruffian's appearance.

They'd ridden in silence for the most part; her awareness of his dark mood keen from the moment Jamal arrived at the villa to pick her up. His edginess was not new to her. She'd been there after hard days of fighting in the past. Sometimes he would talk to her about it, but she always sensed he held things back. How does one relate to others the sense of fear or the base knowledge learned from taking a life? One doesn't but instead keeps it inside.

"Nakupenda, Jamal."

She'd used the intimate Swahili word many times by now. His lack of reciprocation did not sting her. She felt it in his tenderness when they were close and saw it in the help he provided for her and the other teachers. She thought she understood why he wouldn't say it; some reluctance based on the likelihood he would be killed, thereby shattering any hope she maintained of a lasting relationship. Maybe he thought that would make her a bitter woman. Following his protective instincts is a sign of love as well, she reasoned. For her part, if there were even the slightest chance her own words could lead to him prioritizing self-preservation, she was willing to use them for that purpose.

Jamal fought to suppress his sullen mood as he left the gravelly road and parked at a designated overlook closer to Lake Habbianiyah. Across the shimmering body of water, even the more significant buildings resembled building blocks. Smoke rose above the cooking houses and puffs of steam emitted from the industrial sector. A yellowish haze of pollution hovered over Ramadi, a city containing a half-million inhabitants in normal times, and a place he was starting to hate. For someone who relied on control and order to keep his sanity intact, life in Anbar's capital had devolved into chaos. A handful of unexpected circumstances occurred every day, prompting decisions that he couldn't have imagined the previous day.

That smog might as well be a death shroud. The place is a powder keg waiting to explode. Since the coalition is tentative after the embarrassment of Fallujah, Hassan will strike hard against them in Ramadi. He'll want more from me. Maybe more than I can deliver.

Silence engulfed them when Jamal killed the engine. Awkwardness from his brooding was there, so he opened the driver's door to let in the sound of waves slapping the shore nearby. She opened her door, and the wind gusted through, tousling her long, straight hair that rarely came out from under the *hijab* when in town. His bloodshot eyes glistened as a single tear formed and ran down his cheek. She reached over and wiped it from his face.

He was embarrassed, but the gesture comforted him anyway. More tears flowed as steadily as the waves below them. She moved closer to him and rested her head on his chest, looking away until the trembling in him stopped, and he reached up to wipe both cheeks.

He was grateful for her presence, both here in the car and his life right now. As always, he'd been reluctant to tell her what bothered him during the drive. Instead of pressing, she focused on the man himself. In his experience, a woman with the capacity to do that was rare. She did it easily. He thought he should reward her for it.

Even if it's just me having a case of the ass.

He pulled away from her, ready to let her into his shitty world. Or at least a side of it.

"It's just this war. The ridiculous siege of Fallujah last month. So many died. Half the city gets destroyed, and they call a cease-fire, then hand over control to a bunch of ill-prepared lackeys, repeating the same mistake from last year."

"Maybe they will do a better job this time."

"No. The *takfiri* will run over them like they weren't even there. Then they'll be emboldened and grow in strength again. I tell you, I will be going back to Fallujah. And I am sure you have heard of the Abu Ghraib prison scandal. What were the Americans thinking to allow those prisoners to be treated that way? It's just going to perpetuate more violence."

"Abu Ghraib is ..." she said before stalling in translation.

Jamal finished the sentence with a choice selection of his own. "Reprehensible," he said in Arabic.

"I do not know that word."

"It means someone is worthy of punishment for their actions."

"It is a little stronger than what I was thinking of."

"Regrettable?" he offered.

"Regret. Thank you," she said. "I am sure for the Americans, Abu Ghraib is regrettable."

A morose aura still shrouded Jamal. "I am afraid these acts will instigate a blood feud. The word I chose is tied to some form of recourse for the Arabs, who are livid over this. *Fatwas* will be put forth against the occupiers."

"Hasn't that already been done? It is just words, no?"

Jamal cocked his head once in semi-agreement. "Fatwas serve the same purpose as signing bonuses offered by American recruiters. They are meant to lure in more people willing to fight for their cause. Those stupid guards just created more enemies for their peers."

She seemed to ponder his word usage a little longer and confirmed more than asked, "You think there was a deeper intent involved in their actions then. It is why you believe violence will come of it. But what if it was an isolated incident? I saw a picture of those guards who ran the prison. They seemed like simple-minded people. Perhaps they were ignorant enough to do it all on their own."

"Their leaders failed for not stopping them, and they should all be hung out to dry."

"But what they did was nothing compared to what the *takfiri* have done to everyday Iraqis. As far as I have heard, no one was murdered with a power drill. No word of beheadings has come out of Abu Ghraib, correct?"

Jamal responded to her sarcasm with a look of concession.

"I know. I just thought the Americans set a higher standard. Something like this will only make things worse. Like I said, reprisal attacks will be on the rise, vengeance will be sought … In other words, I will be asked to kill more. I have killed too much. And where has it gotten me?"

"Well, you're still alive."

"And for that I am grateful, believe me," he said.

"Is vengeance the only reason people are killing every day in this war? Aren't there more noble reasons you fight, Jamal?"

"We fight for many reasons. It is true." He gestured across the lake toward Ramadi. "But I find nobility to be very scarce over there. And there are too many competing interests with all the parties involved. The Americans will never be able to impose true democracy on the people of Iraq. So it will be in another form they say. Fine. But the self-minded fools here will never agree on what that will be. And once the Americans leave, the new Iraq will fall apart anyway."

"And what of your cause?" she asked in the second he'd taken a breath from his diatribe. He shot her a sideways look, unsure from her tone if she was facetious.

"The cause," he said, supplying his own facetiousness with a roll of the eyes. "It is a losing cause. Our leadership is wiped out. Saddam proved to be a gutless rat hiding in a hole in the ground. Anyone claiming to be a Baathist is shunned in the new government, or thrown in jail if they had any power before."

"Do you believe in the Baathist cause?"

"No, Hadiya! I never did. I came here to push the occupiers out of Iraq, period," retorted Jamal, feeling stranger than ever while putting on the standard performance for her. Oh, how he hated that feeling. Suddenly he was on the cusp of revealing everything to her, even entertaining the thought for the first time of just disappearing with her. Despite the urge, his training demanded the words that came out of his mouth were the usual dose of obfuscation.

"But this train I have hitched onto is a runaway wreck. I might as well start my own resistance cell. Hang my own damned banner. Why not? New ones are popping up every week."

"Then why fight at all? Why not leave this mess for others to work out?"

"Yes," he said, feeling as if she'd read his mind. He watched several American Blackhawk helicopters fly over the center of the lake in a tight formation.

"Why should I? Why should I at all?"

CHAPTER 30

Jamal and Ahmed walked along a shady street toward one of Ramadi's smaller mosques. They hadn't seen Hassan since leaving for the fight in Fallujah last month. Those who stayed behind in Ramadi joined the general uprising along the lower Euphrates, while the most massive pitched battle of the war raged further down the river. But without their two best leaders present, Hassan's cells had incurred higher than normal casualties. His once extensive network was now a gang of gunmen. Jamal sensed the recent fighting had been the death knell. Information was only passed via cell phone to Ahmed alone, so Jamal didn't know what to expect during this meeting with the big man.

It's fitting. Hassan using a mosque for the first time as a place to hide. A collision of circumstances and allegiances. Can I get Ahmed to shift away from his uncle, and the cause, to join the takfiri? Loosen the tribal ties and appeal to his practical sense to make him see the writing on the wall. The old guard ain't returning to glory.

Jamal glanced over at Ahmed, just long enough to draw a reaction.

"What?"

"Nothing," said Jamal shaking his head.

"You sure? Is it the same thing you started to say earlier before Fahim and the men interrupted us?"

"Yes. It is. I cannot have this discussion in their presence. Not yet, at least." Ahmed's curiosity seemed piqued. Jamal added, "Maybe I will wait until after we meet with the general. Who knows what may come of this meeting. My thoughts may change."

"Will you at least tell me what it regards?"

"I've been thinking about what you said that day at the café before the fighting started in Fallujah."

"About the girl?"

"No. You were right about her," said Jamal. "And I have taken your advice to heart on that matter, brother. It is your thoughts about our leader that have been occupying the forefront of my mind."

Once again, Jamal was using his green thumb of deception, planting scripted seeds of thought, which would blossom into the impression that Ahmed had been the catalyst of dissension.

"I have thought about what I said too. But I agree with you," said Ahmed. "Let's see how today goes. Remember, it was his decision to stay in Fallujah."

Jamal shook his head. "Still, I lost most of my men there. He will not let me go without a reprimand."

"We both lost more than he is willing to accept. I am certain to get an earful as well. But with you, it is different, Jamal."

"Why? Because we drink together?" scoffed Jamal. "Maybe you should accept it when he offers this time."

Ahmed seemed to take the ball busting as a cue. If there was a chip on his shoulder, he shrugged it off and returned to more congenial thoughts on Hassan.

"He does always offer, doesn't he? Even though he knows I abstain."

"Just like those awful French cigarettes he smokes. I have never once accepted, but he always asks."

"It's not because he is polite either," said Ahmed.

They walked in silence for a few paces as Jamal generated different images of Hassan and his peculiar traits. He assumed Ahmed was doing the same because he snickered under his breath once.

"Well," said Jamal, "one could say the politeness occurs in the offering itself, but it's the aloofness about me not being a smoker and you not being a drinker I find interesting."

"And telling."

Tension eased enough for them to enjoy a good laugh at the expense of Hassan while crossing the plaza in front of the mosque. Jamal was pleased he'd been able to set the stage for the more significant discussion. It wasn't easy for Ahmed to disparage Hassan, but at least the ball was in motion before the two of them entered the mosque.

Ahmed didn't know what to expect regarding the meeting with Hassan. He was nervous when their contact at the mosque told them his uncle waited in the least used portion of the building. When they found him, Hassan sat on a mattress with no sheets. The curtains were drawn, and the small room was musty with the smell of his Gauloises. Personal items were strewn about, and it appeared he'd been living there for weeks. He wore trousers and a rumpled, button-down shirt. He was in his socks, but one hung loosely off his toes. His hair was longer than normal, slightly tousled, and he was unshaven.

Clarity flooded in over Hassan's reclusiveness of late. Ahmed was instantly put off, but his self-discipline precluded an impulsive reaction. Instead, he used sarcasm to disguise his shock.

"Uncle, this is like being out in the field … At least there are no scorpions to roust you in the night."

"Ahh, but there are other things to worry about. Which reminds me, will one of you dispose of that when you leave?" He pointed to a dead rat in the corner of the room behind some stored folding chairs. Hassan had cornered the rodent and impaled it upon a metal rod. "I cannot even take out my trash for fear of getting snatched up."

Jamal walked over to a card table with some bottles arranged on it. "Is the bar open?"

Ahmed knew the question was rhetorical. Hassan held a flask in his hand already, and Jamal didn't seem to wait for an answer, filling a tumbler full of liquor for himself. Ahmed stared at Hassan, felt the disappointment wash over him. He was not at all as Ahmed had imagined. He was much worse.

Somber over the phone lately, yes. But he still had maintained his military bearing. Sometimes drunk, but mostly at night. Today he seems more hungover than high, yet the flask remains nearby early in the day, even in a place of worship.

Ahmed was embarrassed and more than a little bothered if the clerics knew he was drinking down here like this. Mostly, Ahmed's negativity was from the state of these living conditions.

No security detail, near squalor in this dank part of the mosque. Rats.

He pitied his uncle suddenly; realized Hassan was burned out as a frontline commander. He'd made it just over a year living on the run and was a surviving member of the coalition's infamous deck of cards. There weren't many others.

Hassan raised his girth upon a chair and set the flask on an adjacent table. After wiping the beading sweat from his brow, he laid out his concerns for his two trusted lieutenants.

"I am sorry you have to see me like this. I never wanted to live like a rat," he said with a roll of the eyes toward the carcass in the corner. "Or among them."

Both men nodded at the rare candor by him. Ahmed was fully aware of the difficulty an older, respected Arab man might have when he's seen humbled. For that reason alone, the embedded pride in his uncle was not fully diminished. But this was difficult for Ahmed to watch.

Hassan continued. "I have sent my security teams to join the cells because they are so depleted."

The statement had stung Ahmed. Hassan let it linger, taking the opportunity to light another cigarette while the two of them suffered his belligerence. No offer to share had been forthcoming this time. Ahmed didn't know how to respond. He felt the desert sands shifting under his feet, looked at Jamal, who showed no reaction one way or the other. Ahmed was used to that. Then it was upon them. Hassan wanted his pound of flesh for the losses in Fallujah. He began debriefing them. While graphic descriptions of the harsh urban combat seemed to give him a sense of the conditions under which they'd fought, he still bristled at the near decimation of two well-equipped cells he'd sent into another warlord's fight. He'd gambled and lost; now, he was bitter about it. Ahmed could see it in his face.

Hassan reached for the flask and took a triple swig before making his final pronouncement.

"I want you to go underground ... even more than we have needed to operate up until now."

The two younger men shared an uncertain look. Ahmed spoke first.

"I do not understand."

Once again, Jamal feigned disappointment while exuberance welled inside. Hassan's ship had run aground—with Jamal's help, of course. Now it was time to jump ship.

He leaned back in his chair, arms crossed. "He means we need to shut down for a while."

After more discussion, the real reason became apparent for why Hassan had sent them to Fallujah in the first place. He was short on cash. Coalition bean counters had ferreted out wire transfer routes used by the former regime, and their patrols had consistently uncovered one pile of hidden cash after another; Euros, *Dinars*, Dollars, other foreign currency left behind by panicked officials. Hassan told them they were temporary setbacks, but Jamal saw forlornness in his less than convincing reassurances.

Ahmed stared at the floor, he understood now; the cause was running out of steam. Hassan hadn't sent them to Fallujah to save face at all, let alone show solidarity against the coalition. Hassan had sent the two best cells with the best leaders because he could command a higher premium for their services, to fund his fight here in Ramadi. In the back of his military-trained mind, Ahmed knew it might be akin to a surgeon accepting the notion of cutting off a limb to save the body. But a decision like that would require a certain level of coldness. Both he and Jamal could have easily died in Fallujah. Ahmed decided he would apply the same coldness to future thoughts about his father's brother.

"Will you drive? I think you know why," said Jamal. He tossed the keys to Ahmed as he stumbled on a hole in the rutted pavement along the wall of the mosque, verifying his level of inebriation.

"Yes. I think I'll drive if we want to get where we're going without attracting too much attention. Where *are* we going? We have no cells to speak of."

"Let's just drive. We need to talk. We haven't eaten in a while either. And I'm getting hungry."

"Of course you are," said Ahmed with a smirk. "Okay. We drive first, though. My stomach is not doing so well from all the cigarette smoke in that tiny room of his."

"And the little bit of cognac you drank? How'd that feel on your empty stomach? I'm glad you indulged him this time."

"I think I needed some to get through that."

Ahmed stood outside the driver's side of the Volvo. The two made eye contact while Jamal held his hand on the passenger side handle, waiting for the lock to disengage. When Jamal realized his friend was going to say something serious, he let go and stood upright at mock attention. His drunken mannerisms provoked another smirk from Ahmed.

"It's just …" Ahmed trailed off before turning to the side, focusing on nothing in particular.

"I know, Ahmed."

A deflated look accompanied the statement, only half created for effect. But Jamal said no more because he wanted to hear Ahmed say the words. Jamal stood there, swaying in his stupor. Ahmed shook his head again, fighting disbelief through silent repetition of the motion.

"You saw him. He is done," said Ahmed. "Now what are we to do?"

They opened the doors, and Ahmed started the car. Jamal settled into the passenger seat and slid it back to gain more legroom. He was pleased. He could tell Ahmed was adamant by his tone.

"What do you mean done?" asked Jamal. "I would say he's had a bad week. But you think he's become ineffective?"

"You saw him. He says he sent the security attachment down to the cells to bolster their ranks. I say he pushed them away so he can drink all day. It is unfitting for an officer of his rank and caliber."

"He still leads us, though. We are experiencing some setbacks. I will give you that," said Jamal with a few drunken nods of the head. He belched before putting on a mock-serious face, raising a finger. "But the cause is still just!"

Ahmed would not have it, though, ignored the alcohol-driven sentiment.

"You saw the way the people of Fallujah responded to the *takfiri* defending the city. But how many pats on the back did you get? How many saw us as heroes? We were just there as rented property in Hassan's eyes and hired guns to the *takfiri*. Now we come back to our area of operations and find that the ranks are depleted, there is no money, our leader is cooked, and since we have nothing to fight with, we have to go underground and sit on our hands."

Maybe it was the alcohol, but Jamal decided to take Ahmed to the edge. "Well, you asked the question, brother. What *are* we to do? We have to fight the enemy."

"Because they are definitely not going away," added Ahmed. "Elections are coming to Ramadi. A transfer of power is set to happen any week now!"

Ahmed banged the steering wheel in frustration. He was pensive for a half-minute before he said the words Jamal wanted to hear. "There are other groups we can fight with."

"Do you mean the *takfiri*?"

"Yes."

"But Zarqawi is not crazy about the secular outlook of the *Bathyoun*," said Jamal, knowing, in fact, that Ahmed was closer to the religious motivations than most men fighting in Hassan's ranks.

"But we have experience and the same deep hatred for the occupiers as he does. That's our in."

Both men sought assurance from each other for the big step. They spoke a little more about Hassan. Not surprisingly, there was less sympathy for him now that he'd lost their confidence. After they finished talking, Jamal tilted the seat back a few notches and reclined with his eyes closed. He felt a certain peace, which he could only attribute to graciousness. He was grateful the Lord had laid the groundwork for this next phase of his mission, getting him that much closer to finishing. As for officially gaining entry to Zarqawi's network, he knew there was a lot of praying to be done to assume that identity. Their recent attacks had shown a level of malice and cunning that made the Ta'mim market bombing look like child's play.

CHAPTER 31

The major had received the disturbing call two days earlier at a Memorial Day cookout. After the general's directive, "I need you here ASAP," the major had hopped the first available military flight, endured the cargo netting seat inside the fuselage of the C-141 Starlifter, froze his ass off at 40,000 feet above the Atlantic, and all the while worried about the clusterfuck waiting for him in Iraq. All told, he'd traveled for thirty hours, and that was to get to Baghdad International Airport. Less than a minute after de-boarding, he dripped with sweat on the blazing tarmac as he waited for a shuttle to the terminal. An airfield worker handed him a water bottle, and he chugged its coldness right down.

Like any other stateside newbie to the war, his next order of business was to brave real danger by traveling on the infamous "Road of Death" to reach the protected Green Zone in central Baghdad. On most days, small arms and rocket-fire repeatedly targeted the seven-mile stretch. For that reason, when he entered the terminal for U.S. military personnel, two armed operators in civilian clothes waited for him. The general had arranged for the escorts, as well as body armor, a Glock pistol and ammunition, and an edible GPS tracker to be swallowed upon arrival.

Son of a bitch really wants me standing tall before him.

It had been a while since the major had carried a loaded weapon. The weight on his hip again felt good, especially on the bus trip into central Baghdad, which was uneventful until gunfire erupted nearby. The driver had been given a mission of his own, though—don't stop for anything.

Once inside the Green Zone, the major found his arranged accommodations with a view of the broad and slow Tigris River. He shaved and showered in the common latrine before changing into a fresh pair of desert fatigues. Once inside the mess hall for all soldiers, he overheard a corporal talking to a crewmate about their upcoming flight to Hillah, a central Iraqi city along the lower Euphrates, one hundred kilometers from Baghdad. Fire Base Stack was outside Hillah, where the general's detachment of Special Forces resided. He decided to make a stop at the command tent of the aviation unit. Once in country, the name of the general carried a lot of weight, and he figured he could finagle a ride.

Thirty minutes later, he sat in the spacious interior of a C-47 Chinook helicopter as it lifted its bulk from the tarmac. The major felt very insignificant compared to the immense organization of war around him. The busyness of the Green Zone had opened his eyes to the Coalition Authority's massive undertaking.

Bunch of glad handers playing games like kids with matches.

He'd been able to spot the CIA snobs from a mile away. The boots and khaki-wearing do-gooders from the State Department were even easier to pick out. He'd even spied an Iraqi civilian off in some corner, taking pictures of the main gate to the Green Zone with his phone, but concluded it was somebody else's problem. He assumed the fool was being recorded on video anyway with all the cameras installed throughout the place, guessed it was only a matter of time before deadly attacks could be successful inside its barriers.

Too many people with keys to the castle.

Thoughts of treachery were heavy on his mind, always a bitter pill for him to accept. There was no way around it, though. According to the general, Khalid al-Douri had turned toward the Islamists he infiltrated and then was caught by the coalition.

The major wondered if something akin to Stockholm Syndrome had occurred in the young agent's psyche. To be as deep inside as they'd been programmed to borough, as immersed in the ideology as they'd been trained to infuse themselves, it certainly had been a concern for any of the agents. Now it was a reality.

The dread he felt was for the other agents in country—Farouk al-Hakim and Jamal Muhammad. Khalid knew them in their duplicitous roles. Until the major obtained transcripts of the initial interrogation, he couldn't say how long ago the Shiite Iraqi had changed allegiances. Khalid could have divulged that there were undercover agents embedded in the resistance. The two agents could be hunted men as he stood here.

Hell, they could be dead. And we're 'oh for three in Iraq.

Ten minutes after landing in Hillah, the major found the command center. Near the entry doors stood a water buffalo containing potable water. He was dehydrated after the helicopter flight and slaked his thirst with a long pull from the spigot. The treated water's iodine aftertaste saturated his taste buds as he stood there, drinking and thinking for more than a minute. He tried to find some experience from his past that would help in his present situation. He was stalling, and he knew it, after busting ass to get here.

Upon entering the command hub, the major instantly removed his helmet, ran his fingers through sweat-matted hair, and looked around. Next, he asked someone for directions to the general's office. Soon he reached an open door with no markings on it. Peering in, he saw the general behind a desk. The overhead light gleamed off the top of his bald head, which tilted down toward a stack of papers. The major knocked on the open door as the general scribbled some notes.

"Be with you in a minute."

The major had been nervous since receiving the general's phone call. Instinctually, he shrouded his vulnerability with sarcasm, an element of their typical conversations. "Jeez, sir, this place feels like the trailer park version of what you got going back at Bragg."

The general stopped writing. The motionless pause that preceded the meeting of their eyes brought nervousness to the forefront, and the major's stomach knotted up once again.

"Steve ... why don't you close the door behind you."

The major did as ordered and plopped down in one of the two empty seats before the desk.

"Hope you won't be offended if I head back to Baghdad tonight and take advantage of the plusher digs."

It seemed the general wasn't buying the major's attempt at nonchalance, and no easy reply was forthcoming. But it wasn't anger the major saw in his eyes. Other than the expected weariness from war, he thought he saw fear, probably of the career-related kind for a man of his stature and pedigree. It put them on common ground and he no longer felt the impetus for pretense.

"Do what you want," said the general. "We have hot showers here and decent chow. Got an air-conditioned Conex for you if you want it."

"I'll think about it," answered the major in a normal tone now. Still, the awkward pause that ensued was torturous.

"I'll get a full report to you," said the general, "but the bottom line is your man Khalid al-Douri was rounded up with a highly active cell ... part of the Mahdi Army, Moqtada al-Sadr's gang of Shiite militants. He killed three Americans in the raid that caught him."

"You know the mission required-"

"I know the mission protocols," said the general, his facial expression belying any comfort with the notion. "It's not just that. It's what he's saying."

The major's stomach turned again, his mind offering images of al-Douri invoking his name under duress. But the general surprised him.

"Don't worry too much. He hasn't given you up yet. But he is talking about the program, Major," said the general, the use of the rank the equivalent of a stern mother invoking her son's full Christian name. "He's hard to read; I'll give him that. It's like he can't commit one way or the other, or decide whom he wants to betray … It's as if the lines have become more than blurred for him. Either that or he's bullshitting us."

"Is anyone buying what he's selling?"

"Of course," answered the general. "There's some regular Army intel colonel who's thinking he's got a career move on his hands if he can validate it all."

"Where is al-Douri now?"

"He was picked up during a night raid in Sadr City in Baghdad, then detained at Abu Ghraib until his claims popped up on my radar. That was a week ago. I had him transferred in the middle of the night, and now he's here on the base. But that fucking colonel is not giving up. I got another call from him while you were en route."

"I see," said the major before another round of silence filled the room.

"It's over, Steve," deadpanned the general.

The words struck the major at his core even though he'd rehearsed this moment a hundred times on the flights over. He just hoped he hadn't shown an adverse reaction that could cause wariness on the general's part, which would be well placed. The major had no intention of ending the program, at least not entirely. But he would play along today. Despite their close relationship, the general was not someone to openly challenge.

"Things are different than before the war," explained the general. "When we had the luxury of thinking ideally. This place is a mess. I've got more than enough to worry about right here. Not to mention the oversight staffers taking numbers in Washington to inquire about bad shootings, bad interrogations, and it all adds up to bad press. That's when I start getting calls from generals with more stars than me. I can't afford to roll the dice on this anymore."

So the major nodded and cringed his mouth as if he'd already accepted the inevitable. "You've spoken to our friend in Washington then."

"We talked at length. He needed some convincing, but he's on board."

"How clean do we need to make it?"

A narrowing of the eyes occurred before the general stood and reached into the pocket of his camouflage trousers. The only sound in the room was the muffled clinking of brass. Then he produced a handful of live bullets.

"You have three agents in Iraq, correct?"

The major knew the general was damned well aware of how many agents were here in Iraq, but he acknowledged in the affirmative anyway. The general stood one of the rounds upright on the desk between them and added two more until they looked like three soldiers standing at attention. The two stared each other down, clarity suddenly coming to the major.

Damn. He summoned me over here to do wet work.

"And this colonel who is barking up our tree?" asked the major.

Their eyes met again, and no words were spoken. The general placed the final round in line with but slightly apart from the others, a peculiar product of his highly-ordered mind, figured the major.

The major stood. As he turned to leave, the general clarified for him just how much cleaning up there was to do, "So where will you be heading after you leave this God-forsaken country?"

The major kept his back to the general. "I hear Chechnya is nice this time of year."

CHAPTER 32

A robed *takfiri* fighter led Jamal and Ahmed down a rutted alley in Baghdad. The narrow thoroughfare was filled with the cast-off debris from war; scorched bike frames, the twisted metal from blown-out storefronts, piles of broken concrete and bricks dumped here by a front-end loader. Half a charred Fiat lay on its side against the adjacent concrete structure. The melted tires had solidified in their gooey state after a fireman doused the vehicle.

One of Zarqawi's car bombs had killed over thirty Iraqis two weeks prior in this neighborhood, called Saydiyah, part of the Rashid district in southern Baghdad. Jamal was amazed at the bravery of normal Iraqis who lived under the oppressive hand of the *takfiri* in this conservative Sunni stronghold. No Shiites lived here any longer, or Christians, or Jews for that matter. All had been killed or run out within months of the militants moving in.

The bombing was a lesson learned for some of the more stubborn Sunni business owners. Before the invasion—and the *takfiri* presence—satellite dishes had sold like air conditioners in the summertime. The *takfiri* frowned on this practice of allowing Western television into Muslim homes, and when the storeowners said they would stop, but only shifted their business to the black market, Zarqawi made them pay dearly.

A dog barked on the other side of a cinder block wall. The robed man raised a radio to his mouth, communicating with a guard inside the commercial building where the secret *Shura* council meeting was being held tonight. The roar of a military jet drowned out the mumbling voice on the radio and the exhortations of the dog. Jamal felt the Pavlovian tingling from the reminder of coalition air superiority. But he knew if this building were a target, he'd already be blown apart. The hypersonic plane would be long gone—and its ordinance dropped—by the time the sound wave rolled over them.

When the rumbles faded, a mechanical lock buzzed. Access was granted. They were escorted through a frame-making workshop and past an opening, which led them down a hallway. At the end was a minaret-shaped passage to a large room with dim lighting.

"Are you ready for this, brother?" said Jamal to Ahmed.

"Our paths have led us here. These foreigners can help us drive the occupiers out and regain power from the Shiite dogs. I believe the Lion speaks crudely but justly because Allah has bestowed strength in him."

Jamal stopped and put his hand on Ahmed's arm. "Do you feel that strongly against the Shiites?"

"They are untrustworthy. I fear the new government in Baghdad will become proxies for the Shiites running Tehran. Where will Sunnis be then?"

Jamal nodded, displayed acceptance of his friend's opinions, yet he feared Ahmed would be enlisted to slay more and more fellow Iraqis. Shiites in droves. Maybe he would as well. He thought of the bombings in Karbala and Baghdad in March, where the *takfiri* had killed hundreds of Shiite pilgrims during the Holy Day of *Ashura*. He dreaded having to plan operations like that, prayed that he would never get one. Both men walked the last steps in silence. Jamal's soul suddenly ached for all of the killing, past, and future. The negative feeling morphed with the underlying fear of exposure. He felt the adrenaline surge.

Get it together! This is the moment they sent you here for. The next way station. Maybe the last.

When they entered, only a few pair of eyes and the smell of tobacco burning in a hookah met them. This meeting was apparently not underway yet, as evidenced by the many empty cushions on the floor and the unoccupied chairs placed around the room's perimeter. Jamal experienced a measure of relief. Men in fatigues, modern street clothes, or various forms of traditional Arab dress stood in small clusters, engaged in earnest conversation. Local tribal elders all, except for the foreigners, who were Saudi, Yemeni, and Jordanian, others representing the steppe nations of Central Asia.

The locals had come from the smaller towns, which dotted the Euphrates river valley in Anbar. Several banners were hung on the walls near the groups they represented. At the front of the room, another banner hung over a raised dais with three wooden chairs upon it. A white circle punctuated a field of black, around which lettering in Arabic read *Jama' at al-Tawhid wal-Jihad.*

Jamal noted the name was still the same—"The Group for Religious Unity and Struggle." There was no banner for the Anbar Brigade or any other cell in Hassan's network. There was no Hassan either, and the two weren't here as his representatives. Jamal and Ahmed had come on the invitation of Zarqawi himself after meeting several times privately to discuss recruiting more young, devoted Iraqis for their thinning ranks.

Reinforcements. Every fighting body needs them. Hassan ran out of bodies. And money. This group is flush with cash but suffered heavy losses this spring in Fallujah.

During one of their meetings, Jamal had learned that Zarqawi's bloodlust for the Western occupiers had been usurped by his hatred for the Shiite community in Iraq. It was confirmed when the boastful Jordanian had read a portion of his ongoing correspondences with top tier *al Qaeda* leadership—in which Zarqawi still pined to be included—that expressed his plans to strike at the Shiites. The reading also confirmed he and Ahmed were in the clear. This council meeting was but a formality. Tonight they would swear an oath of allegiance to Zarqawi before those who had joined him in league already. This group was now the core of the most effective and ruthless resistance in the whole of Iraq. Highly skilled and bent on destroying any burgeoning democracy, these men walked with a swagger Jamal had seen grow in recent months. He knew he was in the right place. But could he sink to their level to advance the mission? The thought raised a few hairs.

During their last meeting with Zarqawi, he'd said the two of them would be thrown right into the mix as proven fighters with unique skills. Just what type of work that was remained a mystery, but not for much longer. The room had reached near capacity and felt stuffy to Jamal. He fanned the lapel of the tunic he wore, removed the *kufi* atop his head, and rubbed a bead of sweat into his brow. The hum of low voices halted when Zarqawi entered, spiritual advisors in tow. One of them was the old cleric from Jamal's very first face to face with the *takfiri* leadership.

Zarqawi walked swiftly with a commanding presence to their side of the room, but the older men moved more delicately than the swarthy and portly Lion. Jamal and Ahmed nodded respectfully before the three men seated themselves. Jamal suppressed a grin, recalling a peculiar thing he'd previously noticed about Zarqawi.

During one of their recent meetings, Zarqawi had taken them out of his desert safe house to fire captured coalition weapons with his security personnel. A dozen men shot at targets and familiarized themselves with the light arms of their enemy. Zarqawi picked up an American M249 Squad Automatic Weapon, known as the SAW. After needing help to load the weapon, he stood wide-legged as he tore through a drum containing one hundred rounds. The stance caused his low hanging *dish-dash* to come above his ankles, revealing the American-made running shoes he wore.

The situation had become entertaining. The cyclic rate of fire on the SAW was quicker than Zarqawi was used to with the thudding action of an AK, causing the front of the barrel to rise out of control while his finger remained fixed on the trigger. Glowing tracer rounds arched high in the air, standing out against the dull evening sky of the western Anbar plain, potentially giving away their position. Zarqawi hopped around in those running shoes as he tried to manage the weapon. When it jammed, he couldn't figure out how to clear it until one of his men stepped in and serviced the weapon himself. Zarqawi acted as if nothing happened. He did, however, go inside to change into his patented black fatigues and promptly return to fire again, this time with a cameraman filming him. He still wore those damned sneakers, though. Jamal wondered if he was wearing them now under his ceremonial floor-length robe. Nikes if he remembered right.

What a hypocrite. Hates America but buys American. Probably made in China via the global market, another thing he despises.

"Brothers!" shouted Zarqawi from his chair, against which an AK leaned for show, empty as it was. To his left were Jamal and Ahmed. "Allah has blessed us with more fighters who are willing to die for the cause of *jihad* ..."

Once it began, they each followed his lead, as he delivered the oath with a certain level of fluidity. Zarqawi prayed aloud with his eyes closed, arms raised. Jamal bent his head.

He's done this many times. Like a pastor does weddings. So many have come here in the name of jihad. I have to become like them. God, how will I be believable? I cannot disown you to complete my mission. Please give me ways to hinder their efforts and disguise my true beliefs at the same time. God, forgive me for needing to ask that. Mostly Lord, please show me a way to do this without killing in the name of Allah. The men in this room will do enough of that.

Jamal lifted his head; he realized Zarqawi had stopped. The room was still again, and Zarqawi looked at him, expressionless while he rubbed his patchy beard. Slowly, he turned to the room.

"We all know of our father Muhammad-ibn-Abdal al-Wahab, who spoke about the state of ignorance the barbarians existed in before the coming of the prophet. We, brothers, also know it is the same today. The pig occupiers and now the Shiite dogs they are in alliance with have brought a state of ignorance to the land between the two rivers. They wish to introduce impure ways of living to the sons of your tribes ... rights for women, and the stain of homosexuality. They wish to disallow the *Sharia*, our very laws!"

Zarqawi offered a slight bow of the head to the cleric closest to him.

"The Sheikh has told us the words of the prophet. We know them as we know our wives, 'Whoever slaughters a non-Muslim sincerely for the sake of Allah, Allah will make hellfire prohibited upon him.' My brothers, we must know that only with duty performed come these rewards. Now, while we walk this earth, we must perform the duty of destroying the occupiers who are here to rape and murder your daughters, to force capitalism on the people of Iraq. This assault of Western ideas is ruinous! It cannot happen."

Zarqawi paused to drink water from a small cup on a table behind him and continued in a more relaxed state. "Our victory in Fallujah this spring showed our strength," he said in an assuring tone, even offering his crooked smile. Calculated or not, it was effective at drawing in the listener. Jamal began to understand the allure of this hard-minded man.

"And we showed we are just in our cause. The pigs were shamed. I tell you, nothing is more satisfying than seeing the face of a beaten Marine."

The group was aroused at the statement, eliciting from Zarqawi another upturned lip, the scowl that served as his ruffian's grin. His head nodded in agreement while others vocally asserted theirs. Jamal chose the former, Ahmed the latter, releasing a banshee howl that filled the room and drew a pleasing look from the leader. Jamal watched his comrade in arms next to him, glad for his vehemence. He would tap into that, assimilate the thought patterns mined from their future conversations regarding *jihad.*

Even now, he heard the major's trainers telling him he needed to become the enemy. He knew all he could do was try. If he didn't pass, he'd be killed. No adrenaline flowed at the frequent thought. No hairs prickled on the nape of his neck. Instant death from above was one thing, but he'd become used to thinking it would all end in an agonizing scene that took place in a *takfiri* torture chamber. Everything he'd done would be meaningless then. He'd begun to wonder if it were meaningless in death, perhaps it was meaningless in life. The major would say the answer to that question was tied to results.

"Save Washington D.C. or any other large American city from a nuke. Everything's worth it. One of our foreign bases from the same fate. Worth it. One of our European ally's cities or bases. Worth it. Stop a disastrous biological or nerve agent attack somewhere in the world. Worth it."

To make that much of a difference, Jamal knew he'd have to show the terrorists he was complicit in such plans. Now that it was an actual possibility, he wondered if he had the mettle to portray himself that way.

No one is asking me to do those things today. Take it one day at a time. He will guide me. If it becomes too much to bear, then screw the mission. You can still disappear with her.

Ahmed sat through the *Shura* council, which moved into a discussion of strategy, logistics, and the use of the media to advance their efforts. At this point, some of the attendees lit pipes and the hookah. Tobacco smoke, and after a while, the sweet smell of opiates filled the room, which bothered Ahmed. As a newcomer, though, he tried not to judge. The haze thickened, and the men began to socialize as the larger meeting morphed into small group discussions. Ahmed knew this would not last as the anxiety of so many leaders in one place precluded lengthy gatherings. Indicative of the sentiment, Zarqawi, now more jittery than before, moved to speak privately to him and Jamal.

"You have heard me say Allah has bestowed upon us a victory in Fallujah. But one does not need the foresight of a prophet to know their wicked desires will lead them back to the city. The next time they will come at us with full strength and a will to achieve victory where it was so feebly attempted before."

Ahmed was relieved to know his new leader was not blind to the nature of the victory they'd achieved in Fallujah, pyrrhic as it was in his mind due to the staggering losses the resistance had suffered. If Zarqawi knew they'd won control of the city because the coalition hadn't made it a harder fight with greater cost, then he must be aware the next battle would require stouter defensive positions and a greater number of fighters to maintain them. Once again, Zarqawi impressed him, almost taking the thoughts from his mind.

He looked at Ahmed. "Fallujah is your city of birth, no?"

"It is."

"It wasn't lost upon me that the positions you two held were the last to fall during the previous fight," said Zarqawi, cordially nodding in Jamal's direction.

Both men acknowledged the compliment.

He continued. "Because of this, I am assigning you both to Fallujah. Expect a tougher fight from our enemy next time. You will be given an ample fortune to establish an equivalent defense force. I will send as many men as possible to get the defenses going, but we must draw upon loyalties recently gained in the lower Euphrates. Locals must be engaged in this fight, even if I'm bringing in fifty to a hundred new fighters per week from Tal Afar, where our Sunni brothers are doing their part moving men and munitions across the Syrian border."

Ahmed was pleased, more so because Jamal had finally been persuaded to join Zarqawi's group with him. Both the discussions to convince him and the reluctance to do so had diminished over recent weeks. Abandoning the general to his drinking and newfound slovenliness had been difficult for both of them. But the fight must go on. Now it was guaranteed to do so.

Jamal logged away the intelligence. He'd like to know more specifics about the border operation but knew not to push the question. Instead, he furthered Zarqawi's thought.

"The loyalty of the people stems from the land for which we fight. For Anbar. It is our home. The people will support us!" he added with zeal.

While not quite as vocal as Ahmed had been earlier, it did the job. Zarqawi was satisfied, clasped both men on the shoulder, raising his arms to the taller men.

"Our men will fight alongside your homegrown force then. Together we will drive the dogs out of this province … Now, you must remember two things," he said before looking them both in the eye. "The banner of our group must fly in your area of operations. In the streets. On poles and buildings. Make the public believe it will always fly until the Great Destruction and the Day of Judgment."

They nodded in understanding. Once again, Zarqawi was regurgitating the indoctrination checklist.

"Also, as you have seen, and the world has seen, we have the will of a lion when it comes to our ability to mete out justice to the occupiers. A key component to that is our use of the human element to ensure successful operations. We cannot win this war using planted bombs and conducting ambushes with light arms. Vehicle-borne bombs must be driven into their targets. Explosive belts must be walked right up to a target."

Ahmed answered for both of them. "You have graciously given us a platform and the means to continue fighting the evil which has set up in Baghdad. We are in your debt and will fight using your methods under the only banner that matters now. Allahu Akbar!"

Marching orders were given. Jamal had proven himself in the first battle for Fallujah by making the building-to-building job for the Marines as difficult as possible. Primarily in his sector, there had been low-slung, mud-brick dwellings, but numerous modern buildings of two-or three-stories had sprung up in the urban fabric over the years. In the context of the urban battlefield, they were hard-fought high ground, key during the push through the city as places for observation and perches for snipers. The coalition desperately craved that same turf, however. Jamal and his men had learned to brick up main points of entry to taller buildings, funneling the surprised Marines into areas he wanted them, either a booby-trapped secondary entry or a prearranged field of fire.

If the coalition had gained entry, many times, they faced fighters hiding behind concrete barriers that had been forklifted into the building prior to the attack. These could withstand the blast of a hand grenade, typically tossed into a room by Americans before they rushed in, guns blazing. Once cleared of the enemy, the coalition members had found the stairs destroyed at the highest level, disallowing access to the roof. Or, some stairs had been left intact, but the roof joists of the building were cut. When men and equipment were placed on top, a collapse had occurred.

Zarqawi found this use of the urban landscape ingenious and wanted Jamal to reproduce such efforts on a larger scale within Fallujah. In essence, he wanted Jamal to put down his weapon and pick up his engineer's tools. Later that night, after arriving back in Ramadi to tell the handful of remaining men, including Fahim, what their options were, Jamal finally experienced peace and stillness. He could only attribute this gift of a sanctioned hiatus from killing to his God and Lord. A prayer answered.

What an awesome God You are.

He lay awake most of the night, devising ways to find that golden balance between maintaining his cover and mission success. His last thoughts were of the fighters during the first battle for Fallujah, who had hidden under the streets from the AC-130. *What if there were more tunnels, connecting buildings underground, connecting different parts of the city even? They would be highly useful if kept secret until the battle ... But very expensive, exhaustive, and, most of all, useless if somehow the coalition learned of the tunnels once they were complete.* His thoughts ended on that note around four in the morning, and he drifted off to the best sleep he'd had in months.

PART THREE

PART THREE

CHAPTER 33

Jamal and Ahmed spent the first part of June 2004 establishing their new command in and around Fallujah. They recruited and trained scores of young Iraqis, while at the same time constantly improving the defenses of Fallujah. Jamal's days were filled with planning and maintaining his duplicitous life. Sometimes he would escape to see Hadiya, but it was becoming a rare occurrence. He was drawn to her as always, but the need to keep her safe now trumped the impulse. Both of them knew they were biding time until the war ended.

But one day while in Baghdad, a new thread worked its way into his daily concerns; a development he immediately knew would alter the entire dynamic of his mission. Jamal caught the headline in bold print as he passed a newsstand.

" Hezbollah leader Anwahli killed ...   "

He paid for a copy and read the details of the story. It confirmed the major was bringing him in from the cold, using a mission protocol known only by the nine agents and the major. From what Jamal could tell, it happened the exact way the major had said it would. The name, explosives under a car, ball bearings added for maximum effect, a little known Sunni group claiming victory over their Shiite cousins, then retracting their statement the following day. Even the location in Beirut had been spot on.

The course of action had been devised to ensure the safety of the agents and any intelligence material they might bring across the lines. While the agents had been trained not to reach out to the major after insertion (or anyone else on the American side for that matter), he'd reserved the right to recall any of them should he fear for their imminent safety. He assured them it would only occur if necessary. Jamal hadn't objected in the least to the major standing by with a lifeline, nor had any of the other agents; they'd all agreed to heed the call if alive and able to meet the protocols.

The alert was to go out in the form of a newsworthy event within the agents' respective areas of operation, a story sure to be carried by regional and Western media outlets, and certainly important enough to show up on the Internet. The event itself was different for each agent and known only by themselves and the major. For Jamal, it had been the assassination of a prominent leader within the ranks of Lebanese Hezbollah, forty-one-year-old Ishmael Anwahli. The man was chosen because his stature allowed him to be insulated from the daily violence, so he wasn't likely to be killed by it. But if he were targeted for assassination, that same stature would mean his death made headlines throughout the Middle East. Upon arrival in Iraq, Jamal had made *al Jazeera's* online publication, and some Lebanese websites favorites on his new smartphone and checked it frequently.

If Jamal's safety was indeed the reason the major had reached out to him, the news hadn't jarred him like he'd always imagined it would. He guessed the lack of a reaction had to do with all his rotten deeds and the effectiveness with which they had solidified his cover. On the heels of the disturbing thought was piquing curiosity, though. Maybe the major wasn't intending to warn him of danger. Perhaps he was looking to cash in on Jamal's gains as an agent instead. The Americans were looking pretty desperate these days. His next thought jolted him.

And I get to cash out with her.

He smiled, closed his eyes, and lifted them to the brilliant midday sun, enjoyed its warmth on his skin. The desire for freedom remained for a few seconds longer than the hardwired, driven side of him wanted. The intelligence he could provide would certainly do a fair amount of damage to the cells operating in Anbar Province and Baghdad. Now that he was in with Zarqawi, though, he was poised to make the leap the program had intended. Either way, it looked like Jamal would be making a quick trip back to Ramadi and the Great Mosque. He'd have his answers soon enough. First, he needed to do a little shopping.

Jamal approached the mosque from across the large public space. Once again, it was the backdrop to another pivotal point in his mission, in his life. It was chosen as the meeting place because it was within his original intended area of operation and was assumed to be there for years to come if ever recall was needed.

For the initial meeting, a courier sent by the major might recognize an agent, but the agent would have no way to recognize the courier. A simple system of color coordination was used to make it work. At dusk, the day after their respective newsworthy event had broken, the agent in question was supposed to present himself wearing an outfit displaying two specific colors in the material itself. A third color was to be used somewhere upon a traditional piece of headgear, depending on the locale. The courier had his trio of colors to coordinate. Once either party spotted the other, they were to approach for recognition purposes only, then break contact until the next day. The following day the agent and the courier were to arrive at the same location, each wearing the other's colors from the initial meet to complete the protocol. Once contact was made a second time, the courier was to pass information giving the time and location of the real face to face with the major.

Jamal had memorized his color codes long ago; for him, brown and gold with red up top. The major's courier would be wearing blue and green, with yellow on the headgear. As Jamal entered the mosque, he adjusted the sash on his new *dish-dash*. Its cream-colored cloth had brown hems, the edges of which were stitched in gold embroidery. On his head, he wore a brown *kufi* with dark red stitching. The colors were subtle, as they had been during the major's training excursions. Usually, these consisted of hours upon hours spent at shopping malls near Fort Bragg. A couple of times, it had been on the busy quad of a college campus. Several agents would try to spot the major's man, woman, or child in the passersby. The name of the game had been quickening the process of elimination when assessing each person within their purview.

As he went about the routines of the mosque service and moved among the men in the room, he began taking those quick mental snapshots. The training paid off. Within twenty minutes, Jamal narrowed it down to one man who'd gathered for prayers that evening. But the man kept a certain distance and made no eye contact, even though the opportunity was there. He seemed to be just another Muslim at the mosque.

When the dusk prayer session ended, Jamal moved with a crowd toward the main doors that opened onto the square. Out of the corner of his eye, he watched the Arab in question move closer to him. Before he knew it, the man was right next to him but still did not attempt to engage. As soon as more space opened up, he and Jamal parted ways. Jamal couldn't even be sure if it was him, but the protocols had been there. Blue and green in the loose-fitting pantaloons, a light-colored shirt and dark wool tunic, which were considered neutral, and a pale yellow band in the turban he wore. The man had moved within his personal space, if only for a few seconds.

The guy was good if that was him.

Jamal left the mosque and moved to a central location in the crowded square, looked around in all directions for any sign of trouble. Seeing none, he drove to the rented room. He stopped and paid for a month's arrears and one month extra for the good hospitality, explaining that he was now a resident of Fallujah. The man was grateful and only asked that Jamal not leave anything behind.

When he was alone in the room, his items already loaded into the vehicle, he made sure the curtain was closed and pulled a loose panel off the wall to remove a Bible he'd purchased. Lying on the sheetless mattress, he opened the Old Testament to the book of Judges, where the feats of Samson had intrigued Jamal as a teenager growing into a man's body. During Bible study sessions in the U. N. refugee camp, Jamal had learned Samson was but one of twelve judges for the Israelites.

Under the leadership of Joshua, the Israelites had served God without rebellion. But the generation that followed Joshua did not know the Lord. So God appointed for the Israelites a succession of judges—almost superhuman military and political leaders who were given high power to keep the enemies of His people at bay. Even so, the Israelites remained in a cyclical pattern of sin, servitude, and salvation throughout the period of the judges. Jamal had always been amazed at the unrelenting mercy of God toward His chosen people.

Since joining the program, Jamal had again read the book of Judges several times. He wondered if God had any modern-day judges. Abraham Lincoln came to mind, he'd read Lincoln was convinced the Almighty had visited the atrocity of civil war upon the young nation—a nation founded in His name—because of its apathy toward abolishing slavery for so many years after its founding. Lincoln further believed in part that while the North held the moral upper hand during the conflict. God would not bless them with victory until they freed the slaves, hence his incredible drive to issue the Emancipation Proclamation.

Lincoln seemed to have a strong connection to God and understood that he was an instrument of His will. Just like a judge of old. Jamal reasoned that Lincoln's effort to preserve the Union was almost superhuman, exemplified by the colossal will he maintained to achieve victory. But he had succeeded, and freedom was a less hypocritical word after that in America, even though Jamal's brief experience in America told him black Americans still did not receive the respect they were due as part of the original fabric of the nation.

Jamal prayed for understanding of God's larger plan, wondered if America would be punished for this preemptive war in Iraq. For just as the judges had been sanctioned by God to perform great feats in His name, so had He turned away from them during the times they acted with impunity. The story of Gideon, another judge, showed how haughty a man could become with such power behind him.

Jamal thought about his own decisions, wondered if it had happened that way with him. He'd felt sanctioned early on, the goals of the program meant to be a deliverance from the scourge of Islamic-inspired terrorism, a declared enemy of the United States and Israel, and therefore, he believed, an enemy of God. He'd genuinely felt the guiding hand of God during some of his early successes in this country. But his decision to attack the Ta'mim market didn't feel the same way; the hell it unleashed burdened his soul. The gnawing guilt exposed it as an earthly, not divinely inspired decision.

He read for thirty minutes more about the unwise choices of Samson until his eyes became heavy. Weariness came over his body. He closed the Bible and laid it on his chest, felt a twinge of fear that God had more planned for him than he imagined. Officially moving into the world of the *takfiri* gave him the sense of being at a crossroads, the new direction leading toward a vast brooding sky across the horizon, propelling warm, charged air against his face. An average person would seek shelter from such a storm, but he was about to walk toward it. It was a lonesome feeling.

God won't give me more than I can handle, and He'll be with me the whole way.

The anxious feeling subsided, and weariness took over again.

Always tired. Always tired fighting two wars.

The next morning he left the rented room for good and filled the day in Ramadi by recruiting men for his new cell in Fallujah. He had an eye for anyone who could assist him with building tunnels for his defense plan and reached out to the locals who owned heavy equipment. Some gave them his ear and were motivated to help in defense of their sister city, not to mention being on the right side of the *takfiri*. Others needed to be convinced.

By dusk and the call to worship, he was in position at the mosque again. He'd changed into Western-Style blue jeans, a green shirt, and a cap with a yellow stripe through it. Once inside, he saw the man from the previous evening wearing the correct colors. Jamal made sure to sidle up to him when all the men moved to pray as a group. They faced in the direction of the *Ka'bah* in Mecca and placed mats next to each other on the floor. When the exhortations began, and men moved up and down from the kneeling position in prayer, the courier placed a folded piece of paper under the front corner of his mat. In the middle of another repetition, Jamal retrieved the note.

Once the session ended, he found his way to an alley off the square and read the note,

Tomorrow, Baghdad, Ibn Zanbour Kebab House, 1700.

He pulled a lighter out of his pocket, lit a corner of the flash paper, and watched it flutter to the ground into nothing.

CHAPTER 34

The major peered through binoculars from the driver's seat of the armored sport-utility vehicle. A hundred meters down the crowded street was the kebab house where he was supposed to meet Jamal, itself a short walk from the protected Green Zone in central Baghdad. It appeared many government workers, police, and coalition personnel frequented *Ibn Zanbour*, which translated as "Son of the Wasp." He scanned the patrons occupying the cluster of outdoor tables. It didn't look like Jamal had arrived yet, so the major lowered the binoculars and rubbed his tired eyes. He'd spent the previous two days alleviating the general's angst regarding the program.

In short order, the major had done away with the nosy intelligence officer with a heart-attack-inducing substance in his coffee, disappeared agent Khalid al Douri from the stockade, and reeled in Farouk al-Hakim using the recall protocols. It turned out Khalid had blown Farouk's cover, and he was already on the run from the groups he'd infiltrated. Since his gains as an agent turned into broken promises, he'd become the expendable liability the general viewed him as. Therefore, the major had done away with him too.

While the general's mandate had been clear—eliminate everyone associated with the program—the major was determined to salvage what he could from the remaining seven agents who were scattered across the globe. He planned to make contact with each one and surmise whether they were in a position to advance their respective mission. If so, he'd inform them that everyone—

including himself—was on their own, leave them a secure contact number and a few toys, and wish them luck. He'd also warn them to watch their backs. If they didn't pass muster, however, he'd abide by the general's directive.

The major raised the binoculars again toward the kebab house. A tall black man in cargo pants, a loose shirt, and sunglasses had just arrived and sat alone at a table.

It's been over a year for Christ's sake, but it's gotta be him. He's shed a lot of the muscle he came in with. Hair's a lot longer too.

The major exited the vehicle and approached the kebab house. He hoped Jamal was squared away because he, of all the agents, was the one for which he'd held the highest hope of success.

After placing an order for tea, Jamal chose a table outdoors at the popular eating establishment just outside the Green Zone. A quick look at his cell phone informed him it was 1655. Out in the street, passersby moved quickly through the busy area. They were brave enough to use the services of these businesses that catered to the influx of Westerners, smart enough to conduct their business quickly and get home. Down the street, Iraqi soldiers stood guard at street corners near the Green Zone perimeter, or staffed vehicle checkpoints near the entrance.

Here at the "Son of the Wasp," tables were filled with Westerners and their Arab cohorts who conversed in several different languages. He wondered how many of the patrons were aware they were sitting in the poster child for soft targets. For that matter, he wondered why the major had picked this place, became a little antsy himself. He felt the urge to get up and leave, but any fear was trumped by curiosity over the major and his reasons for reaching out.

The tea arrived. He sipped from the slender clear glass and placed it back on the saucer. When he looked up, the major approached from across the crowded street. He wore a suit and tie with sunglasses, providing the appearance of a foreign businessman. They made eye contact when Jamal rose halfway out of his seat and tipped his sunglasses. He sat again at recognition and filled the second glass of sweet tea, dark and rich, just like most of the major's entreaties. Jamal beckoned for him to take the empty seat, the politeness not just for show.

The major obliged, and after he was seated, bent to tie his shoe. Jamal noticed he leaned over a little more than he needed to and in the process, shot the subtlest of trained glances toward the underside of the table, no doubt inspecting it for listening devices. If there'd been a napkin holder on the table, he'd probably have inspected it as well. But there wasn't one. No handshake or man hug occurred during the greeting, but warmth existed in the major's expression that Jamal was glad to see.

"Thank God you're alive," said the major.

"I do. Believe me. But I have been praying to Allah more lately."

The major picked up on the improvised code, nodded. "Good. I'm glad to hear you are on the right path."

An awkward pause occurred before his forced change of subject.

"Thank you for the tea. I've missed good Iraqi tea."

Jamal wondered if he'd spoken out of turn, decided to let the major guide him through this. Maybe this was just an eye test. He figured it would help if he removed the sunglasses. He placed them on the table, leaned in, and followed the major's lead with small talk.

"How are you liking the heat? I seem to remember you were not too crazy about the desert."

"Beats the cold any day. Plus, it's a dry heat. Not like Bragg or Benning in August."

"Or the hills of North Carolina …" said Jamal, trailing off with a grin, referencing the most challenging portion of their training.

The major fanned the lapel of his suit. He sat upright at the table near the tea service. When he removed his aviator-style sunglasses, he revealed a worrisome visage.

"Jamal, Khalid turned on us."

"Oh, man."

"Kind of lost it if you ask me," said the major, looking out into the street. Irritated drivers honked while a delivery truck driver selfishly attempted an eight-or nine-point turn in the middle of traffic.

"What circumstances led to-"

"He was captured by coalition troops while fighting with a Shiite militia. Made the mistake of holding the wrong person hostage … some aid worker whose daddy has friends in Washington is what I heard. Anyway, they send in-"

"Who is they?"

The major shrugged. "The High Command," he said with widened eyes. "Hell, I don't know. Whoever takes calls from Congressmen over here. Point is, they sent in a team of operators to rescue the hostage. Woulda been all over the papers the next week. They even took embedded reporters along. Big opportunity for the media play on this crazy war … Anyway, our buddy Khalid wasted two SEALs from Dam Neck prior to the coalition seizing control of the building they were holed up in. Then he decides to go hand to hand with the SEAL team leader."

The major shook his head before looking off.

Jamal assumed the pregnant pause was some test for eagerness or desperation on Jamal's part, which the major might consider a tell regarding his status. The student was intent on winning the stalemate, though.

The major sipped some tea and finished the story. "So three dead American operators. Ten dead Iraqi Commandos. They nearly shot down a helicopter until they finally ran out of ammunition and surrendered. He and one other fighter walked out of there alive. Khalid gets under the lights and starts singing."

"To who?"

"To some colonel from intelligence who questioned him for a few days."

"This was recent?"

"Last week, I had no clue and was getting ready to start the next group back home."

"Really ..."

Only a single nod was forthcoming from the major. "Luckily, no one believed him at first, until this colonel up the chain of command took an interest. It's not a problem anymore."

Jamal took in the statement, full of gravitas. "And the reporters. The video. How'd that go away?"

"That's the one good thing. Brass were embarrassed. Squelched the tape and made a deal for more embedded time with the reporter. Khalid's role was not brought to light. The story is we just took a few casualties during the raid. Happens sometimes, you know. Congressman's happy, at least. It's a good thing the reporter didn't get wind of Khalid's claims, though." The major's smirk drew one from Jamal.

"Doesn't sound so bad. Why the meet?" he asked, sensing there was more to this than just a warning.

"I thought you needed to know. I've gone over all the transcripts of Khalid's interrogations. It's hard to tell what he told others inside or outside his organization, but I think you might be in the clear. Still, I'm telling you, I observed him. He blew a gasket. Plain and simple. Talking about stuff from training but mixed in with things he'd seen over here. He'd go off on the Army for making him some weapon, and yet he'd give no names. Then he'd start crying."

"You spoke to him?"

The major's eyes left Jamal's for a second. "Just once."

Jamal shifted in his seat, uncomfortable all of a sudden at certain possibilities, but used a steely gaze to let the major know he wasn't as naïve as when he'd sent him into this "crazy war."

"I understand."

The major gave a single dip of the chin, and he broached the other reason for meeting as Jamal had suspected.

"As I'm sure you know, so many things have gone wrong with the war effort … the post-invasion planning, the governance in the interim by a bunch of New Republicans playing Monopoly inside the Green Zone, shit like Abu Ghraib," he said. His level of contempt pleased Jamal, who once again followed the major's lead and added to the pile.

"How about showing up here in the first place with a conventional fighting force and a doctrine to go with it."

"It must seem like madness to you out there. Their plan, or lack thereof."

"I've scratched my head a few times," said Jamal. "The coalition doesn't have a handle on the populace. The trust is not there yet. It won't happen until they get out of their fortified bases and operate among the people."

"And what about them? How are they viewing all this?"

"With a healthy dose of normal Arab skepticism, of course, which doesn't help, but has been there from the start. They know the game. They've all played it before. Wait it out, and someone will emerge on top. Kind of hard to tell the score, though, so they hedge their bets. The way they act depends on who is standing before them."

The major only nodded in affirmation, so Jamal kept talking. "A patrol comes into some village for the afternoon, and the people let the kids receive the candy and smiles. The patrol leaves, the rats come out, and the people are in fear again. For days at a time."

"I know. But they are reworking the counterinsurgency doctrine as we speak. Guy named Petraeus. He was the divisional commander of the 101st up in Mosul from the start. Guess he had a good handle on things, so he's going to lead the charge on a new approach."

"I've heard of him. Kinda late, isn't it?"

"Not for a committed group of nation builders it isn't. If Bush holds onto the presidency this fall, you can bet on our military being here for the long haul. Haven't you heard?" said the major with a sardonic grin, "we're supposed to stay the course. This war cannot be lost outright."

"Plain and simple, right?"

The major received it the right way, smirked again. "It's never been my war. You've all known that. We didn't come in here working for the coalition."

The segue seemed to present itself, so Jamal pushed the question. "So, what else?"

"What else is they want us to shut the whole thing down."

Jamal shook his head. "Why? Because of one agent, or because the war is going bad?"

"Both. Protests are getting pretty bad at home. Abu Ghraib and Fallujah made us look bad. If any of you are exposed before you meet success ... Let's say it could have serious consequences beyond the war effort. We got lucky with Khalid."

The major had just said, "They want to shut it down." Jamal wondered if that meant he was against it.

"But you don't agree," said Jamal.

"It didn't come from me, so no."

"And."

The major looked around and studied Jamal for a long moment. "If you continue, you'd be on your own. And you would need to stay under the radar for the rest of this war, at least. I don't think you should enter the United States or any country we're friendly with under your true name. But I will leave a secure contact number for you to reach me at any time, good for a couple of years, at least."

Jamal began to understand. He looked off, shook his head so the major knew he was disappointed, which he was.

So much for going home.

Jamal said, "You're going against orders right now, aren't you?"

"You could say that."

"How will it work?"

The major reached into his pocket for a small case, which he tossed across the table to Jamal. It was black plastic and not much bigger than a smartphone. Jamal caught it and put it inside the pocket of his cargo pants.

"This is your "Q" moment, 007. Sorry I don't have any exploding pens for you."

"Huh?" said Jamal perplexed.

"Jesus. Sorry. I forget, sometimes. Anyway, there are a few micro GPS markers in there, and an infrared device to laze a target if needed. It is the latest thing. The secure number is in there too, along with some communication protocols. I've got loyal people who will take care of our needs."

"When should I contact you?"

"Rarely. I'm in the same boat as you. And only do it on a burner phone. But I'm committed to seeing this thing through. I'd like to think you are too."

Jamal shook his head in disgust. "Man, after all you've done, they're going to hang you out to dry."

"No. After what I've just done ... I'm trying to look at the big picture. We may be heroes if we succeed, but we'll never be recognized for it. I can live with that. What about you?"

Jamal looked at him. "I had my troubles for sure. But like you said one time, we would eventually get used to working alone. I have done a lot on my own. I guess it won't be any different. And I never cared about being some hero."

A silence fell over them, the agent processing this new tasking, the mentor's displeasure with the new direction evident. But Jamal was still curious.

"What of Farouk?"

"He is alive and well," said the major with no change in demeanor whatsoever. Jamal took his answer at face value. "He too has made inroads to contacts outside of Iraq."

"Where is he?"

The major hesitated, letting Jamal know it wouldn't happen.

"Fine." Jamal placed his Ray-Bans on his face. He poured the last of the tea from the kettle into his glass, yielding a couple of sips worth of the dark liquid. After he'd reduced it by half again, he said, "You know, I've already done a lot for them. They don't even know it. You ever hear of a couple of soldiers who escaped from some warehouse in Ramadi with a bunch of intel in hand?"

"Yeah, but no identifications were ever made for the guy that sprung 'em. That was you?"

"Popped my cherry on that one. Got that thrill you used to tell us about when you hinder their operations ... messed up their IED factories pretty bad too. And I was at Fallujah."

"You got them looking inside yet?"

"Not more than they already do. Wouldn't be sitting here with you if I were wrong. But now you've given me something to be mindful of."

The major seemed to get antsy now himself, looked around at the street, and its activity. Two kids on a dust-covered Vespa sputtered up the narrow strip of sidewalk between the edge of the café and the street. Pedestrians shouted at them as they bypassed the cluttered vehicular traffic, nearly knocking over a mother and her small child. The wide-eyed driver steered wobbly along the uneven surface while his laughing passenger's feet extended at the sides. He nearly kicked the major's seat, which had been pushed back a moment ago, the sign the meeting was concluding. Jamal mimicked the action as the two of them smiled at the certainty that boys will be boys everywhere, even in wartime.

CHAPTER 35

Fahim stood knee-deep in the silty water sloshing around him, its turbulence caused by the broken water main overhead. This vast underground complex in Fallujah created years ago by Saddam's engineers had stood the test of time, but recent artillery shells exploding above ground shattered a section of the cast iron pipe. The barrage over now, Fahim and two-dozen fighters managed the crisis on their own while Jamal inspected other tunnel projects around the city. He wasn't even aware of the main break.

Fortunately, the corridor ahead of Fahim was only partially submerged, because its surface sloped upward toward Saddam's underground storehouses. The dank walls were slimed with greenish stains from moisture over the years. Bundled pipes near the low ceiling were rusted through in places, and dim incandescent light bulbs strung beside them provided the only lighting along its length. Fahim hoped the gushing water would not interrupt their power.

We'll have even more problems down here.

He watched men clamor like insects in a downpour as they emerged from the new tunnel opening, currently a hand-hewn hole in the sandy earth whose sides fell into the water even as he stood here. Each man carried tools and material to dry ground, their upper torsos drenched with the gritty, brown mud. Fahim saw panic in their eyes when they came out of the darkness, felt his heart flutter at the mere thought of drowning in rising water.

One *takfiri* fighter fell, and was submerged under the heavy timber he struggled to carry alone. Two others handed off their loads and worked to free him. When he came up gasping in their arms, the *takfiri* leader nearby shouted an insult at the young fighter. The kid frantically hefted the piece of wood out of the water again and moved on. Fahim shook his head. It was chaos down here, but hopefully not for long.

I'll be out of here soon enough when Jamal arrives. He'll pull me off this and stick some takfiri fighter down here in the mud instead.

Jamal always looked out for him, kind of like a big brother. He still wondered though about this allegiance his big brother had exhibited toward the *takfiri* during the first half of 2004. Prior to that, when the cell had operated primarily as part of Hassan's network, Jamal's rallying speeches had to do with patriotism and reclaiming Anbar Province. Recently, he seemed to have become an expert at creating religious zeal among the jihadists. Last week, while driving around together, Jamal had said leadership was about knowing your audience. It was a phrase Fahim hadn't heard before.

Maybe he learned it from the takfiri. Hopefully, he's not adopting all their ways. I'm not sure I could cut off someone's head.

Jamal planned to branch off the Saddam-era tunnels and burrow into the adjacent residential neighborhood, where they could enter the basements of two separate buildings from below. Should another fight break out in Fallujah, this would allow the *takfiri* to shift forces and conduct resupply operations without being seen by the coalition above, even during daylight hours. They hoped to reach the first building by mid-August—just one week away—and the second one by the end of the following month. Fahim doubted they would make the initial deadline due to this water problem. But Jamal had surprised him with his dedication to the tunnel-building project throughout the summer, despite Fahim's questioning such an enormous undertaking. As Fahim thought about the complicating factors involved in the needed repairs, he hoped again that Jamal would not make him stay until the problem was fixed.

Despite his claustrophobia, he would do it if asked by the man who'd pulled him back from the brink of desperate self-immolation more than once. Over time though, during many private discussions, Jamal had instilled in him a will to survive this war despite his losses. Fahim noticed their talks had lessened of late, wondered if maybe his African friend thought there'd been enough coddling, and didn't want the *takfiri* seeing that side of his leadership style. They tended to look down upon those who showed fear, perceiving it as a weakness. Those asides weren't needed as much lately anyway. He hoped Jamal knew that.

One thing had been easy for Fahim to understand from the start. His troubles were not from fear of dying. It was the fear of living with the remorse of so much personal loss, and for having created loss for others. Comrades were killed in grotesque ways, and civilians too, their families set on a path of perpetual mourning for which he felt responsible. He knew veterans of war talked of the hollow feeling created when one kills and maims to survive, as if the soul knows better and turns its back on the reality of it while the body does the hard work to live just one more day, one more minute sometimes. He'd felt it after a time, the empty repository of empathy for others, especially the enemy. Even the awareness of the emotional vacuum itself failed to jar him from it. Jamal had said the nightmares and sadness would go away with time. But Fahim wondered if it was possible to see past it all.

He hadn't witnessed the destruction of his family the day they became collateral damage from an errant airstrike, but he'd seen enough carnage since then to replace many a gruesome victim with his sister's, or his mother's face. One day during the battle for Fallujah, he saw a severed forearm with twisted dark hairs like those of his father. The thick, meaty fingers caused him to recall the ones that had grabbed him by the ear when he misbehaved.

His waking eyes had imagined his father's mutilated body attached to the arm. That particular night, Jamal pulled him off the line because Fahim had screamed in his sleep. They'd talked until dawn. After that, Fahim had tried to adopt Jamal's cool detachment from the lethality of their daily business, as if the death around him were but a subtext to a higher end.

Maybe that's how all the great leaders think. Colonels and generals, leaders of ragtag armies. The killing itself is another tool of war. Impersonal.

Two young foreigners approached Fahim in a huff, stifling his morbid thoughts for the time being. The oldest one, a Jordanian, spoke in rapid Arabic. "Fahim, the water is rising up the tunnel. Twenty more yards, and it will reach the ammunition we have stored along the wall."

Fahim looked beyond them into the dimly lit space of the Saddam era tunnel. His mind's eye was aware of the stacked crates of 7.62 millimeter ammunition, and past them the boxes of explosives. At least those were up on pallets.

"We will be fine. They left to go shut off the main over an hour ago. It should stop flowing any minute now. That is unless they ran into resistance from the civilians running the water plant."

"It is a sin to resist the call of *jihad*," said the Jordanian.

"Allah will make them shut down the water," said the other fighter. "These tunnels are too important."

Fahim crimped the corner of his mouth. "It isn't Allah that will persuade them. It is whatever torture implement Karim decides to use that makes the decision for them."

Both their eyes widened. But since they were young and without influence, Fahim knew they wouldn't react strongly against their cell leader's sidekick.

Karim was a thirty-year-old Kuwaiti citizen who was absolutely committed to Zarqawi's cause. Jamal had given him authority over the fighters on-site, including Fahim, whenever he was around. He'd quickly become one of Jamal's more trusted men, leading a group of ten fighters during operations. His means of coercion were typically brutal, and Fahim didn't think Karim had that hollow feeling.

The younger of the two fighters was a nappy-haired Yemeni who'd traded a shepherd's life to tote an AK. He said, "Any resistance to the will of Allah is only temporary. When the new Caliphate rises, everyone will bow."

This part of their mantra—nothing more than Zarqawi's speeches regurgitated—was where Fahim usually tuned out. Forcing the most fundamental strains of Islam on the people of Iraq, forcing them to choose life under Sharia Law was not sitting well with him. He decided to pick at this bone a little with these two.

"And if the people reject it, what then? There are many Iraqis who wish for secular rule."

"The will of Allah is the only truth."

Fahim's non-answer and gaze past the Yemeni was as effective as any retort. He knew there was no point to this. The *takfiri* redefined the word stubborn. Unbending was better.

The awkwardness lingered for only a little longer until the water stopped pouring from above, eliciting shouts of relief from the frazzled workers throughout the complex. It had risen to Fahim's waist while the tongue in cheek discussion took place with the young fighters. In the interest of coaxing more work out of them despite his briskness, he offered an olive branch of sorts.

"Come on, brothers. It looks like Allah has blessed us after all. Let us hope we are doubly blessed with a good plumber and many working pumps before Jamal gets here."

On this, they were all in agreement, and the two foreigners showed it with a pair of hasty nods in the affirmative.

Two hours later, several pumps chugged away, and a city plumbing crew was on site when Jamal arrived. Because the situation appeared to be on the mend, the fighters and locals were in much better spirits than just after the artillery barrage had broken the main. Jamal seemed to be despondent, however, a rare showing of emotion among his men. He pulled Fahim aside to provide an update nonetheless.

"Progress overall is good. But the workers on number three ran into a stone foundation from antiquity. Rerouting could take weeks, so I abandoned it until a decision can be made with Zarqawi. The men I pulled off that job will help with the cleanup efforts here, and I'd like you to stay in charge until Karim gets back."

Fahim attempted to suppress a cringe at the news and failed.

Jamal continued anyway. "Lost four men on number six. Damn thing caved in partially. We could only recover two of the bodies. That one should be back on track soon. Maybe lost a week on it."

"And the men?"

"Regrettable, of course," said Jamal with a sideways look that indicated he was keen to Fahim's chippy mood. "What do you care? They were all foreigners. Uighurs. You told me they'd make good tunnel rats because they're short."

Fahim smirked this time and shook his head. "All the way from remote China to fight Americans and they die in a hole in the ground, shovel in hand."

"They may have been buried alive, but they died upholding their cause. They believed the tunnels would help us win the next battle."

In a conciliatory tone that also reflected his stated objections regarding the massive undertaking, Fahim said, "Many others believe that too."

"Hey, we could be chopping Shiite heads daily. I fear that Ahmed has turned down a darker path than us ... I've heard things. Be thankful for that shovel in your hands. At least it has no blood on it."

Fahim stood down, aware he'd sounded like a malcontent after all, to both the young *takfiri* and Jamal. It was true. He couldn't give two shits about the foreign fighters. It was Jamal he cared about; he cared about the cohesion and morale of the fighters because it was a reflection on his friend as a leader. He decided he'd better get out of his funk because he still had influence within the cell. He also decided he'd begin tagging along on some of these trips Jamal was taking around Fallujah. Coalition patrols had picked up, and random checkpoints were being set up all the time. An extra pair of eyes couldn't hurt. After all, riding coattails is only effective when someone is there to wear the coat.

CHAPTER 36

Jamal drove eastward out of the Euphrates River Valley toward Diyala province. His destination was a place near *Baquba*, the provincial capital, after a summons from Zarqawi. Jamal was expected to deliver a positive report on the tunnel project, and would not disappoint. He'd never been to this safe house, a new one for the man who diligently kept on the move. Lately, Zarqawi had become increasingly paranoid of capture and tended to hide out in rural locales. Baquba was a less active area for the resistance, so a lesser coalition presence existed to sniff them out. Jamal had heard this place was tucked away pretty well.

He thought of his tunnels. Fixing the water main a few weeks ago and pumping out all the excess water and sludge was but one of many setbacks encountered. Nonetheless, the projects were progressing well on the mission side of the balance, by way of increased expense and a doubling of Zarqawi's manpower. On the other side was steady progress toward completion and meeting Zarqawi's expectations. Jamal had become the general contractor hard-pressed to finish for a demanding owner, cracking the whip on all his fighters turned construction workers, most of whom had come from a wide array of experience and education levels unrelated to the building trades. Indeed, many of the hardcore *takfiri* fighters had come straight from their *Madrassa* headmasters.

Unlike a real contractor, he was not striving for an early finish to be paid a premium. His plan from inception had been to maximize the *takfiri* efforts right up until the days before the next battle for Fallujah, to divert their energies away from the necessary above ground preparations. He'd imagined himself overseeing the final list of tasks toward completion, even as exhausted men scurried about filling the tunnels with the implements of war. But ever since the major had taken away his mandate, he'd frequently imagined himself disappearing with Hadiya and forgetting the whole thing.

All the introspection forced him to ask why he was still bent on driving men like Zarqawi into dust. As evil as the man was, he hadn't led the attack on Jamal's village in Sudan. That raider died the next week in another battle. At the age of twelve, Jamal had taken it as immediate justice served by God Almighty. Later, when he signed up with the major, he saw the mission as a chance to exact even greater justice upon the larger threat of Islamic extremism, and confirmation of God's overarching plan for him, just like his mother had said.

But this war was in the gutter. His soul was in peril as a participant, and he knew it. Nothing felt righteous anymore. Still, if he were to get out, he wanted to hand the Americans something big on a platter, something that could pile weight on the good side of the balance and tip the scales once and for all. His tunnels could do that because they were such an integral part of Fallujah's defense plan.

Can't reveal it to anybody with the major until the fighting starts. They'd be sure to screw it up. No. Gotta be a complete shift in momentum during the battle. It could wipe out Zarqawi's network.

He adjusted the air conditioning on the Volvo's dashboard to reduce the flow of chilled air, now that the heat of the day had passed. A bend in the road led him eastward. Through his rearview mirror, he saw vapors over Anbar's arid terrain distort the sun's otherwise perfect disk as it neared the horizon. On each side of the road, the shadows lengthened in the citrus groves, pointing him toward a mosque's copper minaret that sparkled in the distance.

He skirted Baquba itself, taking a dusty road north as instructed by one of Zarqawi's men, then parked the Volvo and started walking. By now, the sun hovered tentatively before its final plunge that would leave the restive nation in darkness. He was aware this little corner of Iraq had been relatively quiet for some time but wondered what the locals would think about the most wanted insurgent in Iraq living in their midst. The war touches everywhere, and everyone eventually.

After another twenty minutes of walking, he reached his destination. The gravel lane at the front of the property was infringed upon by hip-high, dry grasses growing along its edge, bent inward, so the center was the only place to walk without picking up the prickly burrs that rubbed off this particular kind of desert scrub. Other weeds and untended shrubs could be seen around the property, even growing right up to the modest two-story villa. A small shed was around the side and toward the back of the property. The overgrown look was intentional, of course, aided by a grove of tall trees in which the villa was nestled, itself surrounded by sprawling orange groves. Consequently, it would be difficult for coalition aerial reconnaissance to spot it.

When he was fifty yards from the house, a guard noticed him. Jamal didn't recognize the man and sensed a new security detail was in place. Moments later, from the bushes lining the lane, emerged another guard, brandishing an AK and speaking Arabic in a Saudi accent.

"Peace be upon you," said the guard gruffly.

"And upon you be peace."

"Muhammad al Sudani?"

"Yes, I just walked out from the edge of town. No one followed me."

The Saudi lowered his weapon to a less threatening position and relaxed his posture. "Come. He is waiting."

The two walked to the front door of the villa. The other Saudi searched Jamal's person and took the .45 caliber before it disappeared into his tunic. Finding no concealed weapons, the guard stepped back and nodded once again.

Jamal lowered his arms from behind his head, chiding him in the process. "It bothers me that you *takfiri* still do not trust us over a year and a half into this war." The two Saudis exchanged glares but said nothing. Jamal wasn't finished, however. "Is that the way a guest treats their host in your country?"

After an awkward moment, the appearance of Zarqawi ended the stare down. He stood on the stoop before the front entry. Even with the extra step of elevation, his short stature put him just at Jamal's eye level.

"Welcome, my brother," said the *takfiri* chieftain.

He offered his sneer, gestured for Jamal to enter, and dismissed the guards. Jamal's glare followed them as they returned to sentry duty.

Zarqawi wore a loose-fitting white *Jalabiya* with blue and gold designs stitched into the fabric around the open neckline. The blue *kufi* atop his head concealed most of the wavy black hair that Jamal knew was there. Upon entering the home, they stood in a small entry foyer. Ahead was a low, arched corridor with several oil-burning wall sconces along the sides. The ceiling flickered with the warm hue of their light.

As the pair moved toward the corridor, his host explained, "I know you do not approve of the foreign guards I employ. But remember, I am a foreigner myself, Jamal. Many have come to aid you and your countrymen in this *jihad* against the infidels. You must see them as fulfilling the will of Allah, despite their ways that sometimes offend you. They are only a little nervous now because we had a flyover this morning," he said. He turned to look at Jamal, pausing in his already slow gait to clarify the statement.

"The pigs were moving troops in a couple of Chinooks. Nothing to worry about."

But Jamal could see the glimmer of worry in his eyes; he knew the man was just as skittish and paranoid as the guards outside. He decided to sharpen Zarqawi's edginess a little bit.

"You must have deeply feared betrayal by the local protection you were using because if it's peace of mind you are looking for, I'm not sure Saudis are who I would have gone with. Most of them seem nervous all the time ... makes the people around them nervous too. It's just something I've noticed," he said dismissively.

"Yes, but they know what they are doing, and that is all I give a shit about." The topic was getting under Zarqawi's skin. "Let us not be bothered by who is on the payroll this month. It could change next week, could change tomorrow. We do what we have to, don't we, my friend?"

"So we do."

They passed a set of stairs to the second floor and entered a rectangular-shaped room with a large, stained glass window high on the far wall. There was no other fenestration. Jamal assumed the lack of daylight did not do its beauty justice.

"Sit. We will talk."

In a sweeping motion, Zarqawi pointed to a large cushion on the floor. It matched one on the opposite side of a beautiful Persian rug, which could seat another ten cushions if needed.

Zarqawi took his place across from Jamal. He picked up a small audio recorder beside the pillow. Jamal knew how this would be used. The man liked to have multiple tapes on hand of himself ranting. The best ones were used in propaganda videos he made for followers of the otherwise peaceful religion he'd helped hijack. He'd been in the middle of making one when Jamal arrived, so he started the machine and picked up the diatribe where he had left off. After a minute, Jamal knew where it was going because he'd heard this one before. It was mostly verbiage from a letter Zarqawi had written to Osama bin Laden some months ago. As long-winded as the correspondence itself had been, it was, in the end, an entreaty for fealty. Jamal knew that even now, Zarqawi was waiting to hear the *al Qaeda* leader's decision on whether he could include himself as a figurehead within their network, which in many ways resembled an international conglomerate with many franchises.

He has gall. Right after he tells me he's here to help push out the Westerners, he goes into this stuff about re-establishing the Caliphate here in Iraq, in the name of al Qaeda Inc. no less.

He tuned Zarqawi out while engrossing himself in prayers of his own. Soon he could hear the level of the hateful man's voice begin to rise.

"Oh, American Crusader. Die a thousand deaths!"

Zarqawi's letter had told bin Laden the Americans were easy, mouth-watering targets for his fighters. It also declared Zarqawi's intention to foment civil war by drawing the people of Iraq into "the furnace of battle." The present rant went on, and soon, Zarqawi delved into what was becoming the focus of his ire these days.

"The Shiites are the looming danger with hideous rancor toward the Sunnis. They are the crafty snake, the malicious scorpion!"

Jamal endured the diatribe and the enthusiasm he'd predicted when Zarqawi learned of his recent progress on the system of tunnels throughout Fallujah. He was also given a satchel of cash to fuel the final preparations in Fallujah. After the departing salutations on the porch outside and one more stare down with the guards when Jamal received his gun, he walked down the dark, deserted road to his car. He wouldn't see Zarqawi again until they met on the battlefield in the coming weeks. Jamal had the odd sense he'd be protecting the murderous thug once the bullets started flying. After all, he thought, a meal ticket is worthless if the thing is burned.

CHAPTER 37

Weeks of hard work passed until Jamal craved the stillness of her villa. Whenever he would visit, she usually arranged for it to be empty for at least a few hours. She understood his need for space without conflict, without a reason to be the man he was outside her world. She did not know that man but knew it was part of him. It was their unspoken agreement that he would leave the war at the door. They would seclude themselves in the enclosed garden behind the villa day or night. A pair of hawks would sometimes circle high above the fray below, uncaring and free, or at least it seemed that way to him. He wanted the same for the two of them. *Far away. Untouchable.*

The early morning sun glared through the dirty windshield, a reminder he'd forgotten to clean it when he gassed up the Volvo earlier. His stomach growled, and his head throbbed as he reached over to the passenger seat and pawed at a large, flat piece of *khubz*. He chewed the bread slowly, his maw fickle after a night of drinking whiskey. The emptiness needed to be filled, so he bit off another portion and choked it down despite the cottonmouth. After a few more audible groans at the forced feeding, he reached for the large black coffee in the cup holder, further aiding that which ailed him. He breathed in its aroma, ate more bread. Soon the knottiness began to loosen, and he focused on extracting some of the mental malaise from which he suffered.

The first few weeks in October had been a grind, the defensive preparations of Fallujah taking a mental and physical toll on him and his men. The one consolation was that the extended summer heat had begun to wane and made for better labor conditions, on some days at least. Annually, the prevailing summer winds would shift from southerly temperate ones to gusts that streamed in from the north, bringing moisture with them.

The previous day, Zarqawi had ordered a final recruiting effort before the looming battle. A half-dozen handpicked leaders of the newly organized cells had left his Baquba safe house with suitcases full of cash. Their mandate was to cover all provinces with Sunni population centers. Jamal was glad he'd been selected. This excursion was much needed, the equivalent of leave granted. It included low-key travel throughout his home region of the lower Euphrates, and some of the northern towns along the Syrian border, in Nineva province. Finally, he'd been given a free pass to see the border operation up close. With any luck, he'd learn a way to disrupt it.

After stops in Al Qaim first, then Tal Afar, he would swing through Baghdad and report to one of Zarqawi's couriers with a list of recruits. Vetting them was not his problem. From there, he would return to Fallujah and resume final preparations for the second defense of the city, a fight Zarqawi was hoping to pick sometime in November. But before any of that, Jamal was going to Ramadi. This time he was going to surprise her.

Last month they'd spent an evening alone in the villa. When the occupants returned, he and Hadiya had stayed up talking with the owners. Neither were devout Muslims, so the alcohol flowed. After several drinks that night, tongues loosened. It was a rare treat for Jamal to pick bones about American hegemony with foreign intellectuals. Eye-opening as well, to the point he'd been thankful they didn't know his true identity. This produced a sullenness that could be interpreted as war-weariness fueled by alcohol. The civilians in the room knew better than to prod.

In truth, it was more of the same for Jamal, who lately had channeled frustration with fighting a war that more and more seemed to be a losing cause for all sides involved, as many as there were. By the end of the night, he'd drunk enough that his mood was entirely introspective, an indictment over his choice to keep Hadiya in the dark regarding his mission, shifting the loose moral sands beneath his feet even more. He hadn't prayed much in the weeks before or after that night, immersed in one of those periods where he felt the spiritual distance, and that night, he'd gone to bed without saying his prayers too.

The Volvo rounded a long, arching curve in the highway until the morning sun moved around enough for him to lift the windshield visor. He finished off the rest of the coffee and ate some more *kubhz*, his thoughts going back to that night at the villa. Letting his guard down with civilians had not been easy for Jamal. It made him realize just how on he had to be most of the time, how he needed to be ready to act whenever he turned a corner if he were engaged in mission-related activity. Usually, words had gotten him by if it seemed he'd been caught doing something suspicious, hinged to the respect he'd garnered within the insurgency. Two occasions stood out in his mind where he'd been exposed and was forced to kill a *takfiri* fighter on the spot.

One time he'd been found tinkering with fuses that belonged to one of Zarqawi's bomb makers. The man knew something was amiss after a couple of pointed questions, and Jamal realized the game was up. He took advantage of their being alone and put three silenced rounds into the man's back as he ran for the closest door. Another time a *takfiri* fighter had stumbled across him while he was dumping rat poison in the water supply of a neighboring cell. That fighter had been shot in the head from point-blank range. Both bodies were deposited in the Euphrates.

Carnal memories of those two killings made him weigh the differences in how Americans value their fighters compared to an Arab insurgency.

Some private gets separated from his patrol, and the whole American public gets wind of it by the nightly news, every media outlet clamoring for a piece of the story. A couple of takfiri don't show up for roll call, and they threaten their families if their sons don't return to fight the infidel.

Equally disparate was the popular, glorified image most people in the West—and even some on the typical Arab street—had of a suicide bomber, the committed *jihadist*, ready to destroy himself in the face of the enemy and receive his virgins. In truth, Zarqawi had lessened his standards for such a role. Fathers were kidnapped and made to wear a suicide vest, at the peril of their family, held hostage by the *takfiri*. Drug addicts were pumped full of high-octane heroin, of which the *takfiri* had readily available, strapped with explosives and sent numbly walking into a crowd. There were mentally handicapped victims made to were the vest. Bombs were even planted in dead bodies, or wounded ones, and detonated when aid arrived.

None of it made sense to Jamal. Winning this war was about gaining the support of the populace. Whichever corner they threw their weight into would come out the victor. But Zarqawi was increasingly turning his nose up at them, the greatest weapon on the battlefield, and his brutal tactics were starting to infuriate many locals. The Sunni tribal networks in Anbar were especially concerned about the wagon to which they'd hitched themselves.

They will only be pushed so far. The tribes will unite against him. Next, it's lights on, and watch the cockroaches scurry for cover.

If the *takfiri* were viciously biting the hand that could feed them the power they craved, the Americans equally unobservant of one of the paradoxes of counterinsurgency warfare. The more you protect your force, the less secure you may be. He believed the coalition would fare better with the Iraqi hearts and minds if their operations were not so intelligence-driven and instead centered around establishing a presence among the locals.

It's counterintuitive to their modern war fighting mentality, though. The bombers, the tanks, cruise missiles fired from offshore. The groupthink got outdated. They forgot their experiences against the Viet Cong, their very roots as rebels against the crown.

The major had made sure his recruits were well-read on the topics of American military history, and the forays of Western nations into the Middle East. One thing was sure to Jamal. The Americans were a long way off from heeding the advice of one of the few genuinely successful Western leaders of an Arab counterinsurgency.

Several generations ago, T.E. Lawrence, author of *Lawrence of Arabia*, said, "Do not try to do too much with your own hands. Better the Arabs do it tolerably than you do it perfectly. It is their war, and you are to help them, not win it for them."

Jamal had watched the handover of sovereignty back at the beginning of summer, knew it to be a symbolic gesture. The Iraqis weren't even close to being able to hold up on their own.

And God help them once the Americans pull out.

A road sign indicated he was getting close to the hotbed of violence that was Ramadi. When he approached her neighborhood, he sensed something was wrong. No people were outside. Then he saw why. Lawns were torn up. Bullet holes pocked the facades of several buildings. One whole villa had been leveled, the charred husk from the resulting fire all that remained of it. He recalled a memory of an innocent enough looking family sitting on plastic chairs out front on a hot evening.

What happened here?

His pulse quickened as he made a turn and drove down the road to her villa. His hand moved toward his cell phone to call her, even as his feet preempted the action and floored the accelerator. Chunks of upturned asphalt lay strewn about the street. He swerved to avoid a crater. Mortar rounds had exploded here.

"This is not good," he said in English.

He saw her villa. The metal gate was crushed down over a ten-foot section, and the yard was torn up. But it seemed to have suffered no more or less than the other residences on the street. As he approached the curb to park, a pair of American military vehicles turned a corner ahead and raced in his direction. He suddenly worried he'd entered a cleared area and would be searched. He started to reach behind his back for his gun. The move felt instinctual, surprised him though. Instead, he put both hands on top of the wheel again until the first driver and his passenger stared at him when they zoomed by. Jamal waited for the dust to settle before parking and exiting the Volvo.

Damn ghost town. For it to look like this means one thing. Insurgents must have moved into the neighborhood, drawing coalition patrols. There must have been a fight.

He moved through the gate and into the yard, saw a pile of spent 5.56 millimeter brass behind the stone bench from which he and Hadiya watched the children play.

American ammo.

Discarded wrappers from field rations were scattered under a tree. Its low branches usually supported a pair of bird feeders made by the children. One of them was now on the ground crushed to pieces; the birdseed was gone to scavengers. He surmised it had been a couple of days since events transpired here, but no longer than that, or he would have heard of it while in Baquba. The solid wood front door to the villa was ajar when he approached, causing him to tighten up his motions into the efficient glide of a trained hunter, pistol drawn. His mind raced, as understanding coalesced by the second.

The MRE's. American soldiers only eat when it's safe to do so. They held up here in a position of strength during their push through the neighborhood.

It was all he cared to take the thought as he nudged the door open and moved through. Inside it was musty, the stale, hot air of a house that had been closed up for days. There was evidence of troop presence inside. Empty bottles of booze lay around, and cigarette butts had been ground into the floor. Dirt had been trudged inside and pressed into the boot prints of many soldiers. Hope diminished that they'd been some command element and, therefore, more likely to treat inhabitants civilly.

He went upstairs where Hadiya kept a small room with just enough space for a chest of drawers, and the queen-sized bed both their feet dangled over when they shared it. When he reached the top of the curving stair with a metal banister, he lost another measure of hope as empty pints of alcohol lay on the floor outside her door. A length of Army-issue nylon cord snaked into the hall. Inside the room, he saw it was part of a long strand tied to one of the four corner posts of the bed frame. Another length was tied to the opposite side.

A plate-sized brown stain marred the white cotton sheet, and the consistent color of it told him it was dried blood. His knees buckled as he was overcome with grief. At the bedside, his hand clutched the sheets into his fist, while his relentless mind played a rape scene before his eyes. He squinted hard to force it out, but still imagined a grubby private stripped to the waist with a bottle in his hand.

Tears leaked out of the vises that were his eyelids. He found a bottle with some alcohol left in it and lay on the bed, taking in the cheap swill like it was water. In this state, he languished for hours alone in the house. The light changed from the bright white of midday to the orange hue of late afternoon. When it faded to the bluish tint of twilight, he put his face near the stain, with his palm resting on it.

While he dozed in and out of fitful, drunken sleep, he saw Choudary and Safwan, his most remorseful murders. He saw

Masoud's head explode against the concrete wall of the abandoned truck dock, the killing that bothered him the least. Others in between made their appearance in the dream. He saw himself in some rubble-filled street fighting the enemy. Hadiya was there. A clutch of bullets from an unseen machine gun tore into the brick façade adjacent to her. The rounds hit her, ripping her apart.

He shot up from the bed in a cold sweat with his gun in his hand. It was dark. Stillness surrounded him, and his pulse leveled out after he took a few deep breaths. He went to the communal bathroom in the hall and discovered the plumbing still worked, so he splashed cold water on his face. He looked at the small mirror on the wall with fear of seeing what a broken spirit looked like, but since there was no power, the light wouldn't work. In truth, the darkened shadow of himself was an adequate manifestation of the collective pain inside. He cared less about his mission than ever.

He felt the prevailing winds of his loyalty shifting. It was only a thought, something he'd been warned might happen sometime during his mission, likely amplified because the agents' mandate had gone away. Now, this tragedy had occurred. It felt strange though, like an individual who knows he's just been infected by a virus but doesn't yet feel the effects. And like a sailor on open water tacks when his winds shift, but still sails onward, he would continue disrupting the most dangerous terrorists in the world for his own reasons, but he'd be tacking to compensate for building anger toward the Americans and their hubris.

Only for those who can't stand up to the likes of Zarqawi and Bin Laden. Screw the coalition. Screw America.

Jamal forced himself to recruit enough fighters over the coming weeks to make his time away from Fallujah worthwhile in the eyes of Zarqawi. He'd gone straight to the source of Arab bitterness. The mosques in the poor neighborhoods and the funeral processions of those already martyred by the Westerners were ripe with anger. Most of those who joined didn't know what they were getting themselves into. He didn't give a damn. He just needed numbers. Zarqawi's cadre of brainwashers and military trainers would take care of fostering the urge to die in the name of *jihad.*

He focused on picking low-hanging fruit to meet his recruiting quota but spent even more time searching for answers to what had happened in the villa. All the while, he felt himself slipping, and it became increasingly difficult to function amidst the uncertainty of her fate.

He tried the hospitals in Ramadi. He paid a local who worked at the large American base outside the city to find out if she'd been transported there for medical care. Maybe it hadn't happened the way his tortured mind imagined. Perhaps it wasn't her who'd been raped in her bed. But he was only warding off what his instincts knew to be true. Nothing panned out, and by the time he was back in Fallujah, he'd nearly given up hope. For her and him. The constant loss and sorrow of the brutal war finally caught up to him. He lived that way for the weeks leading up to the second battle for Fallujah. Eventually, one day in early November, the grinding inside his head ceased.

He was overseeing the construction of fighting positions for what would again be the final line of defense, the Julan neighborhood of Fallujah. Jamal was in the process of bolting one of many steel plates to the inside wall of a building, which would serve as a command bunker. A fighter approached him.

"Jamal, there is a man from Ramadi who wishes to speak with you. He says he heard you were looking for fighters but was away on business. He says he has men to bring to Fallujah with their weapons."

"Send him to Ahmed's cell," said Jamal with a lack of interest. "They have suffered recent losses fighting the Shiite militias."

"He says your speech motivated his men at the Great Mosque. They want to fight for you."

Irritated, Jamal put down the pneumatic hammer he'd been using and disconnected the air hose that supplied its power. It let out a sharp hiss and caused the compressor to kick on outside the door.

"Bring him here then."

Jamal stopped what he was doing and sat on a concrete knee wall outside the building. He drank from a water bottle and let his thoughts drift while he waited. When he saw the fighter approach again, this time with a recognizable face in tow, he felt emotions stir inside him, and he was on his feet moving toward them. Behind the fighter walked the owner of the villa in which Hadiya had lived. Jamal wanted to cover the twenty yards that stood between them rapidly, but restraint won out. They met in the middle of the street, and Jamal sent the fighter away. It was all he could do to exhibit a consistency in demeanor that would not draw attention from the *takfiri* around him. The man before him had nearly healed bruises on his face and a scab over his eye.

In a low tone, the owner of the villa said, "She is alive."

"Where?"

"Up north. We had to take her away from Ramadi. She ..."

"I know. I went there. I saw what was done. Americans, right?"

"Yes. I tried to stop them, but they beat me until I passed out," he said while touching the badges of honor. "It went on for a day until they had to leave with their unit."

Jamal gritted his teeth and clenched his fists. "Thank you."

He touched the man's shoulder, then retracted it with a wary look around. Now it was the man's turn to steady his composure. He struggled in doing so.

"I am sorry. What kind of new recruit tears up on the street after meeting his commander for the first time? But I should have done more."

Jamal spared him anymore anguish. "You did what you could, I am certain. And coming here was very brave. They would kill you if they knew you were not here to fight. Tell me, how is she?"

"She is not well. Her wrists are scarred, and her ... Moving around is difficult. But she is safe. My wife's mother is a doctor and is caring for her ... She asks for you, Jamal. What should I tell her?"

"A doctor? Good. Tell her I will come soon."

The man handed him a prewritten note with directions to an address in Arbil province, which Jamal knew to be Kurdish territory. Jamal tucked it into his pocket and felt the relief settle in.

Alive. At least she's alive and getting care.

Just five minutes ago, he couldn't have cared if he survived the looming battle or not. Now he had a reason to soldier on.

"Ahmed!" shouted Jamal from across the dusty street where only fighters or those trusted by the *takfiri* roamed in this quarter of the city. Here, a morose blanket of foreboding hung over the place where everyone knew heavy fighting would soon occur. Ahmed turned in his direction and stepped off the curb. When they embraced for the first time in over a month, Jamal thought his peer had lost some weight.

"What's happened to you, brother? You appear to be wasting away." He noted the haggard look about Ahmed; his eyes were swollen with darkened bags beneath them.

"What do you mean?" asked Ahmed in a tired voice.

"Fighting the Shiites down south has taken a toll on you, no?" Ahmed's serious demeanor was on display as usual. But he seemed different to Jamal.

"I have been away on training."

"Training? What kind of training?"

Ahmed looked around and briefly made eye contact again. He drew a finger across his throat in slow motion, a wicked smile crossing his face. Jamal knew right then and there the man he'd once felt a soldier's kinship with was gone. The man before him was filled with hatred fomented by Zarqawi. Ahmed indicated that instead of fighting Shiites down south, he'd been sent to a little known camp in Jordan where they teach methods of torture and beheading to the most zealous of believers. Or the most craven.

"I see. And now?"

"Back to Fallujah for round two, what else?"

Jamal decided a change of subject was needed. "So, have you heard the news?"

"You mean our new allegiance to the Sheikh?"

Jamal nodded in the affirmative.

The Sheikh was Osama bin Laden, who had recently named Zarqawi "Emir of Iraq."

The preceding day, Jamal heard Zarqawi read a letter before sending it by courier to Waziristan, the tribal northwest of Pakistan, where the *al Qaeda* leadership was presumed to be hiding. In it, he'd pledged loyalty to the world's leading terrorist organization. Upon this sought after recognition, Zarqawi changed the name of his group. Now the *takfiri* referred to themselves as *Tanzin Qaidat al-Jihad fi Bilad al Rafidayn.*

Jamal translated it as "The Organization of *Jihad's* base in the land between the two rivers." The coalition would refer to them as *Al Qaeda* in Iraq or AQI. Jamal had officially ascended the ladder of terror.

CHAPTER 38

Through a narrow gangway that divided two buildings, Jamal saw the profile of an M1 Abrams tank. Committed as usual to the path of least resistance, the coalition vanguard was on the other side of the block where a broad avenue offered direct access to the city center. Alternatively, side alleys like the one he occupied meandered through clusters of squat mud-brick homes. Those routes through Fallujah's older urban fabric might as well be quicksand to the advancing ground troops.

Crouched behind a burnt car, he waited until the platoon-sized foot patrol behind the tank had moved out of the area. He looked around, as the rumble of the mechanical beast grew distant. This was no place to establish a new base of operations. He needed concrete buildings with adequate height to place lookouts or snipers. The only option he could think of was perhaps a quarter mile away in a more modernized sector of the city.

He set off in that direction and after ten minutes of careful maneuver, approached a large roundabout, the terminus for several major streets that fed into this part of the city. In the center of the roundabout was a fountain. A third of its round, stone wall, which in better times had contained a pool of water, was now in pieces from some impact. He thought it would be a good location to place a machine gun crew because they would have a commanding view down several approaches likely to be used by the enemy when they came. Another street off the roundabout had more obvious signs of fighting than the others and led to the buildings he planned to use as his next base of operations.

He could see them now, a few hundred yards down the war-torn block. One of them was partially destroyed; more than half of it had been reduced to rubble from powerful ordinance. The explosion had sheared off one whole corner of it's brick and mortar façade, exposing the interior of its upper floors. The other building was still suitable for a defensive posture, however. Its four-stories made it one of the taller intact structures around. It appeared to have been spared from artillery or aerial bombardment, but its bullet-riddled brick exterior had taken a beating, and half its windows had been shot out.

One last look around revealed no apparent threats, so he darted across the roundabout toward the buildings. The block between was filled with ruined storefronts, abandoned for days now. Many were covered with bullet holes or had imploded after a nearby explosion. Power line poles lay around like pixie sticks, but the heaps of tangled wire that came down with them had already been looted. The actual street was filled with craters from artillery and several charred vehicles that couldn't have died in better locations if he'd placed them himself as obstacles against the enemy advance. If the enemy did come calling, they would halt at that roundabout, based on Jamal's observations of their tactics during this fight. A street like this one could and would be filled with mines and IED's. And this time around, Jamal wouldn't be so worried about offsetting the damage they would cause to the coalition.

He covered the last twenty yards in the instinctual crouch before he entered the four-story structure. Inside were truck docks and what looked like an empty dispatcher's office. Crates, pallets, and forklifts had been left out on the open floor; no doubt abandoned mid-shift when the fighting erupted. A stairwell in one corner led to the upper floors and showed a handrail down to a basement. Like all buildings since the first day of the battle, power had been cut off. The place appeared deserted, so he raised his radio to his lips.

"Two, this is One."

Static ensued.

A few seconds passed, and he heard, "One, this is Two."

Jamal told Karim his location, and then a short list of orders followed. "Send Ahmed and the others. We're secure here. Send the heavy machine gun too. I have a position in mind which will cover any approaches ... Two, is Fahim back from patrol yet?"

"No. Not yet."

"Any reports over the radio?"

"No. Will let you know if anything changes, over."

"Affirmative. One out."

He put the radio inside the satchel and pulled out his map of the city. He made notes that reflected the coalition troop movements on the boulevard before he tucked everything back inside the satchel. At the stairwell, he listened for movement coming from the lower level. Hearing nothing, he bound up the steps with the assault rifle in hand. At each landing, he opened the door and glanced down the halls on the other side but bypassed entering the first three floors. At the top of the stair, he saw a ladder and hatch-style door to gain access to the roof. When he poked his head up through the opening, he was pleased to see a waist-high parapet wall around the perimeter of the roof. A barrier like that could save a man's life from most sniper and small arms fire once the men occupied this rooftop. As he made his way through the opening and to the edge of the roof, he reflected on the coalition's second attempt to take Fallujah.

The main attack three days ago had come from the north, just as in April, but with additional thrusts from the south and west this time. At dawn on the first day, the Marines had moved in, accompanied by a ferocious artillery barrage. The coalition had quickly captured and secured the bridge on the western approach to the city while Jamal's cell took casualties fighting near Fallujah's train station. After losing more ground, his AQI fighters had sparked running battles and ambushed coalition foot patrols in the Hay Naib al-Dubat and al-Naziza districts. By dusk on the second day, Marine elements had reached the city center and abruptly stopped their push at Highway Ten. Today began with another artillery barrage, this time aimed at the core of the resistance. Consequently, the fighters in Julan district were preparing for the coalition's final push.

From behind the safety of the parapet wall, Jamal fended off worrisome thoughts about Fahim, reminded himself that it was common for AQI patrols to be held up when shadowing coalition troop movements. The Americans had all kinds of reasons to hurry up and wait; sometimes, they stopped for hours if they encountered something suspicious alongside the road they traveled. Ordinance disposal was a hot job in Iraq.

Jamal heard an explosion in the distance, close enough to where his men were that he was concerned for them; the urge to call on the radio was overwhelming.

"Two, this is One, over."

No reply came for ten seconds, so he tried again. Nothing. Another ten seconds passed, and he tried a third time. Finally, someone answered, but it was not Karim. Rather, it was a young fighter with panic in his voice.

"Jamal! Karim is hit!"

Gunfire and explosions crossed the airwaves just before the actual noises reached him from over ten blocks away. It was intense fire from American heavy weaponry. Jamal moved back toward the hatch, hoped Ahmed and the rest of the men were hunkered down better than Karim had been. On the way down the stairs to the loading area, he thought about how they would be tonight while cleaning weapons. Jamal had always been a stickler for clean weapons, especially during heavy fighting.

He'd seen how the men reflected their morale during the routine of weapon maintenance. If a day had been light on dangerous duty or perhaps the danger had passed after a successful operation, they cleaned not as well, but with jovial gusto, not caring if Jamal sent them away two or three times for failing inspection. They would back slap and jaw late into the night until he released them unto their cognizance. However, if men had been lost, or if even one particularly popular fighter such as Karim had been struck down by the coalition, the mood was always more somber.

At those times, the only audible sounds were the low murmur of quiet conversation and the clanking noises associated with the assembly and disassembly of weapons. The men seemed more focused on detail and found solace in peering with squinted eyes into the nooks and crannies of their weapon, in search of tiny carbon particles to sweep away with a bent Q-tip. Usually, the weapons were cleaned and put away in about half the time on nights like those.

Jamal knew the feeling that permeated a room of fighters like that was survivor's guilt, a burden frequently experienced by combat veterans with any conscience left in them. There was the nagging sense one could have done something different to prevent loss of life. Often, men lashed out at the dead man himself to cover up the shame of letting him die.

"Why did he expose himself to the lethal American gunfire the way he had?"

Deep down, one knew there was no fault, but cleaning one's weapon to perfection ensured that a malfunction wouldn't be the reason the man beside him fell in the next combat action.

Jamal reached the ground floor and waited for the cell to arrive, anxious to find out what Ahmed had heard and seen. When they pulled up in several vehicles, they unloaded equipment into the building per Jamal's instructions. He learned Karim had been killed in action, along with two other fighters. The men he'd led were already affected, so Jamal didn't waste time putting a new man in charge. He gave them marching orders while Ahmed spoke on the radio with someone about the procurement of needed ammunition.

Jamal milled around until the discussion was over. He assumed his friend with the newly gaunt cheeks hadn't eaten in a while, so he suggested they share a meal and discuss the night's activities. Because food was in short supply, it was only a few minutes later when the two exhausted leaders fell into silence as they put away what constituted a mess kit, nothing more than a knife and cloth on which to place food. Ahmed always carried a small tin of salt.

The quiet moment was filled by sporadic automatic weapons fire in the distance. It mitigated a new awkwardness between them. They had been through enough together that it shouldn't be there, lamented Jamal. He knew why but couldn't further the thought for being a hypocrite, couldn't judge the man, and his moral descent into torture and beheadings. He was digging his own hole that seemed to get deeper each passing week. Ahmed eventually spoke, though his tired gaze never left some inanimate object down the street.

"You picked a good place to set up. Feels like it could be defensible. For a time."

Jamal shrugged at the forced small talk and bounced his head a few times to validate the offering.

With a confident slap on Jamal's shoulder, Ahmed got to his feet unsteadily. "Fahim will be back, you watch."

Jamal noticed the gimpy leg, tried to act normal, and move past the moment like men do. "I know. You all right, brother?"

"Just a little sore. Landed on a brick while diving for cover in this mess," said Ahmed while waving the barrel of his assault rifle around the rubble-filled area, a good sampling of the city after several days of hard fighting.

Jamal rubbed his left shoulder. "I was thrown into a wall by an RPG explosion yesterday myself. Still bothering me."

"Do you need me to get a medic?"

"No. Do you need one for your leg?"

Both men smiled. The sardonic retorts elicited a snicker from Ahmed but no verbal response.

As he limped away, he said, "If they're not back in thirty minutes, I say we send someone to look for them. Then you need to get sleep. My men covered for me last night. I cover for you tonight. At least four hours straight, Jamal. We need to be at full strength tomorrow."

"What is tomorrow besides another day in this hell?"

"Maybe the day we die."

"What's wrong with dying tired?"

Ahmed shook his head again before turning and walking away.

Jamal shouted after him. "How about one hour. Then we go looking."

Ahmed peered over his shoulder. "One hour, it is."

Jamal was on the roof again, binoculars raised as he scanned the area for signs of Fahim and his tardy patrol. Nervous waiting was a standard activity for any leader with men in harm's way. Two hours had passed since he and Ahmed spoke. It was getting dark. He'd have to wait it out because truth be told, there weren't enough men to spare for a search. And what if they found trouble on their own while looking?

For ten minutes, he hadn't heard any gunfire or seen any movement in the streets below. The call to worship ended the eerie lull, which steadfastly echoed over the urban battlefield. He knelt to portray the evening prayer ritual like the others around him. When finished, he took up the binoculars again, but the stillness caused his mind to wander.

If he'd been granted a normal childhood with an intact family, maybe he would have had siblings. Perhaps a little brother. Fahim was like the little brother he'd never had, and one who'd been forced to grow up too fast under his watchful eye. For this reason, Jamal had hoped Fahim would put down arms before the cell settled in for the second defense of Fallujah, which they both knew would turn into the largest set battle of the war to date. He'd done his best to convince Fahim to leave the fray and lie low for a while, repeatedly downplaying the young Iraqi's concerns over abandoning the cell or quitting the fight against the Americans.

The Americans, Jamal had reassured him, were too busy shooting themselves in the foot to secure a decisive victory in the city, or the country at large for that matter. As for leaving the cell, he told Fahim he'd done his share by now, for Hassan, and more recently for Zarqawi. In essence, he told him he wasn't needed. The words had stung Fahim by the look on his face. Jamal did feel like a big brother, pushing a younger sibling away against his will, to protect him. Fahim had dug his heels in, though, declaring his intention to stay and fight the Americans, whether Jamal needed him or not. Even if he was a kid brother, the kid was a man now. The man still felt obligated to resist the occupiers until they left or died in place. Jamal had let it go after their third discussion on the matter. By then, the city was surrounded anyway, and attempting to leave was more dangerous than standing pat. But could he have said more to convince him?

Maybe that's what a real brother would have done.

He knew heaping guilt upon himself was not going to get Fahim safely inside the lines, so he shelved the worrisome thoughts and pondered the difference between the first fight for Fallujah six months prior, and the current one. This time around, Zarqawi's forces were stronger in numbers, weaponry, and defensive posture than before. But just as the defenders had upped the ante, so had the coalition. There was an obvious commitment to finish the job, as evidenced by the hundreds of fighters killed in the first couple of days, unable to match the firepower of the Americans. Jamal's cell of fifty fighters had been reduced by half. Ahmed had fared a little better.

For Jamal's part, the most significant difference between the two battles was his attitude because of what had happened to Hadiya, and because the major had cut him loose. Even the major's threat that he could be exposed provided little angst. His apathetic mental state meant he was a simple observer of the death around him. No emotional chord was struck if a coalition trooper went down across the battlefield, a foreign *al Qaeda* fighter detonated an explosive vest, or a homegrown Iraqi patriot was shot in the fighting position next to him.

He didn't end up turning over the intelligence on the tunnels either, yet the coalition seemed to be on the verge of discovering some of them on their own. His thoughts were mainly about protecting Fahim and when he would see Hadiya next. Because of this, his impatience with the Americans and their delay in ending the siege grew by the hour.

Through the binoculars, he watched the activity on the street below. Inside the abandoned storefronts were fighters who guarded the approach to the four-story building. He saw them carry ammunition and sandbags inside, preparing for the next action. Further down the street was the roundabout for cars with the damaged fountain in the middle. Jamal had instructed four fighters to occupy its circular base, stack sandbags on top of the remaining stone perimeter wall, and place a heavy machine gun in the center.

Most likely, the gun team would see the incoming patrol before anyone else. He focused the binoculars on them. The fountain was a few hundred yards away, and at that level of magnification, he needed to steady his hands to keep the image from bouncing around. Resting his elbows on the parapet wall helped, and he could now discern the fighters' body language. It appeared they had taken advantage of the lull in fighting to institute an eating plan; two fighters ate while the other two manned the weapon and ammunition. Jamal was about to look off in another direction when he saw the machine gunner turn and say something to the senior fighter on hand. The fighter put down his food and raised his binoculars toward some point out of Jamal's line of vision. He reached for radio as Jamal waited anxiously.

"One, this is Three."

"This is One," replied Jamal.

"Patrol is inbound, One. They just passed signal and are moving up to cross our field of fire."

"Praise be to Allah. Is everyone accounted for?"

Jamal watched the man strain to count the fighters who no doubt crept between points of cover to reach the friendly lines.

The senior fighter raised the radio again. "Four fighters inbound, One."

"Good. Let's guide them in safely now."

"Like stray lambs, One. Three out."

Jamal turned around and slid down the parapet wall until he sat on the rooftop. He rubbed his temples and breathed deep to calm his nerves. Soon Fahim would get what a younger brother deserved who'd made him sweat like that, an ass kicking. For now, he welcomed the relief from worry, the one emotional blip on the radar of his mind, and began to rub some tension out of his eye sockets.

A shot rang out of the stillness, high-caliber, and from a distance. The echo faded even as he hopped up and peered over the top of the parapet with the naked eye. The machine gun crew was scrambling. One of them had been hit. Jamal saw movement to their left. The patrol running for cover. Another shot was fired. From Jamal's rooftop position, he saw a muzzle flash nearly a kilometer away, set off against the dull evening sky. One of the fighters from the patrol went down. Jamal refocused the binoculars on him. The man lying in the street was a young Saudi. He saw Fahim crouched behind a crumpled vehicle, safe for now.

Jamal scanned the building where the flash had originated. It was three-stories tall with punched windows in a precast concrete structural frame and housed numerous antennae on its rooftop. Settling on the part of the façade with several open windows for thirty seconds yielded movement behind one of them; the blur of cloth had looked like camouflage. Another shot was fired. Another muzzle flash. Yes, that was it. He looked at the fountain and saw three men still breathing. The sniper must have missed that time.

He talked into the radio again, foregoing any protocols.

"Three. This is Jamal."

"Boss, we are under fire."

"I know. I think he is in the building down the road with all the antennae. Put some rounds on it so our guys can get behind some real cover."

The Marine sniper felt a bead of sweat trickle down his forehead after his last shot. He wiped it off with his Nomex glove. Within seconds the machine gun in the roundabout fired several bursts, hitting the broad side of the building in which he'd set up. They were on to him, he realized. It was time to go after his next shot.

The insurgents taking cover in the street seemingly readied themselves to make a run for a nearby storefront. From there, the sniper figured they could remain indoors to the four-story building they were using as a base of operations. He knew he needed to make this one count.

One shot, one kill.

Covering fire from the machine gun continued to pepper the facade, shattering glass up and down it. But it was all bark and no bite. The sniper remained in his prone firing position, ten feet inside the room on a long table, which supported the rifle's bipod. All the while, the crosshairs hovered around the one hiding behind the vehicle. Then the fighter ran. CRACK.

Jamal watched Fahim's body shudder from the impact of the round, the front of his t-shirt exploding before him in a pink mist. His head snapped back as he fell to the pavement, his grip lost on the AK, which tumbled away.

No!

Jamal stared through the binoculars. Nothing was steady between the high level of magnification and his shaking. Fahim seemed dead on impact when he hit the street in a heap. He couldn't be sure, though. Jamal had taught all his men to lie as still as possible if stranded in the open after getting hit.

Trained snipers know a single, high-velocity round such as .308 caliber can shred the insides of a human. Mortal wounds are created that claim the victim on the operating table or remove them from the battlefield for good, even if they live. A disciplined shooter will resist the message-sending second shot on a wounded man because it's a salacious indulgence that can pinpoint his location for the enemy. Jamal hoped Fahim was alive and heeding his instructions right now. He also hoped the sniper was the disciplined type. Jamal replayed the horrific image again, an act he would perform in perpetuity, and doubt shrouded hope that his little brother was still alive.

He reached for the radio. His hands no longer shook as he focused on the building where he believed the sniper was. He was no longer ambivalent about being a dealer of death.

In a calm voice, he said, "Three, this is One, over."

"This is Three," answered the fighter in the middle of a machine gun burst.

"Hold your position. I am coming up with an assault team."

"Yes, One … Jamal. It is Fahim."

"I know. I've seen everything. It's not your fault. The sniper is good, so stay behind cover. We will flush him out."

"I understand. Three out."

Minutes later, it was all over. Jamal had sent in a squad-sized element, and the sound of grenades and several AK's thumped and rattled. Shortly after, it was quiet, except for the exhortations of the fighters overcome with bloodlust, heard by those on the ground through the broken windows of the upper floors.

"Allahu Akbar! Allahu Akbar! Allahu Akbar!"

CHAPTER 39

Jamal could not watch for the shame of it while they dragged the coalition sniper team out into the street. Both were dead. He went straight to Fahim and knelt. When he rolled him over onto his back, there was no life in him. His eyes were still open, and their opaque gaze paralyzed Jamal. The zealotry of the fighters nearby disgusted him. Right now, he hated the wild men who were doing unspeakable things to the bodies. Men he also hated. Men he'd ordered killed. The negativity swirled inside him. He closed Fahim's eyes and lifted him off the ground. As he did so, several fighters peeled off the fray and came to express sorrow. They touched the limp corpse, which Jamal easily bore.

Fahim had been well liked, especially among the younger fighters, despite his coldness to the daily zealotry. It was a testament to his character that the least of the believers was most responsible for maintaining their morale, a part of war fighting as necessary as beans and bullets. No one understood the complexities of his loyalties, but they knew he'd made them laugh because all soldiers of all time need the release of laughter in their camp. Jamal felt the wave of guilt come over him. Maybe it hadn't been the Americans Fahim had stayed for after all.

And I told him I didn't need him. I never deserved to have a little brother.

Usually, Jamal would pray immediately upon the death of a close comrade. His numbness went to the core of his being, however, and he had no urge to speak to God. He held Fahim and walked down the street, the husk of a believing soul. When he reached the four-story building, he went straight to the basement. He found an empty room and lay him on the concrete. Without power and thus air conditioning, he knew it to be the coolest place to store the body until there were proper burial arrangements. Although there was no immediate family to call upon, Jamal was determined that Fahim wouldn't end up in the Euphrates River, or some unmarked grave in Abu Ghraib cemetery.

He found a tablecloth in a supply closet. When he carefully spread it over Fahim, blood soaked through the plain white linen. Jamal made sure the eyes stayed closed and touched his hair one more time before covering his face. He knelt, wallowed in the hollowness about which Fahim had spoken. Anger. Regret. Pain. All three formed the shell around that lonely place but were not inside it.

After a few minutes, he left the room and saw Ahmed bound down the steps to the basement. He must have just returned from somewhere, and someone surprised him with the news. Jamal stopped and waited for him to say something. His own words would not come.

"Jamal! Is it true? What happened? Tell me he's not dead."

Jamal didn't move. His lack of expression was all Ahmed needed to see.

"Where is he?"

Jamal motioned over his shoulder. Ahmed approached and was about to walk past him when he stopped and put his hand on Jamal's shoulder.

"You need to rest, my friend. Forget about tomorrow. I can handle the men, and you don't want to go through this completely exhausted. Take this room here," he said as he directed Jamal toward a room with a Persian rug on the floor. He cleared away some clutter and took Jamal's satchel and weapon. "Look, a place to lie down. Just take a couple of hours to gather yourself."

Jamal nodded obediently. He sloughed into the room and closed the door behind Ahmed without a word. He turned the light off and wept. Exhaustion was a rising tide, and after a while, he fell into a deep slumber for nearly three hours.

When he awoke, he rejoined his AQI comrades. In the days and weeks ahead, he moved and breathed and fought, but his mind was elsewhere. His self-styled mission became a tremendous grind. At times he was just an insurgent fighting the occupiers, and there was zero impetus to directly help the Americans who were letting Iraq fall into the cauldron of civil war unless his actions helped innocent Iraqis in the process, some form of penance for him. After months of living out that existence, he understood how difficult it would have been to run the mission as the major had always intended.

He kept his ties to Zarqawi, always with an eye to impress the local leadership, perhaps establish inroads with the *al Qaeda* shot callers outside Iraq. But his effectiveness had only proved his value to those in Iraq, so they would use him there until he was dead, and he knew it. On the days when he felt a connection to God, he prayed for the war to end. Guilt and shame prevented prayers for himself.

The only thing that made him feel alive for all of 2005 and even into 2006 were his trips up north, where he would stay for days at a time with Hadiya as she healed, mentally and physically. Her weakened state was the justification he needed to withhold from her the truth about him, although that burden became heavier each time he returned to fight for Zarqawi's increasingly violent campaign.

CHAPTER 40

Hadiya finished putting her clothes back on, folded the linen gown, and set it neatly on the countertop. She sat in the only chair in the small, sterile room beside the one that belonged to the doctor. Once again, the faraway stare settled in, this time aimed at nothing more than the painted cinder block wall three feet in front of her. Something deep inside demanded she not cry when the doctor returned this time, whether she bore good news or bad news. For once of late, she thought she could heed the internal voice she recognized as her previous self, the strong, independent voice of a woman who did not know rape. Yes, thought Hadiya, it was time to close off the spigot of tears.

It had been weeks since she'd awoken in a panic with the image of the three sweaty Americans stamped upon her vision, the musky male scent lingering, and the disgusting sexual sounds filling her head. In the months after that awful day, she'd existed in a strange state of ignorance about those details, which were not part of her conscious memory. They seemed so fresh in her recent nightmares, though. She understood now that the out of body experience she'd maintained during thirty hours of violent rape had served to spare her the agony of the ordeal. But the mind records everything, and it can only stay in the subconscious for so long.

Hadiya sat up in the chair, nervousness coming to the forefront as the doctor entered.

"Well, the venereal disease is gone," she said without lifting her eyes from the clipboard she held. The doctor took her seat and lifted the front page to scan the second. "There is no more bruising in and around the vagina, but I'm afraid there will be scars. They may affect your ability to bear children."

Hadiya heard the words, but they didn't register at first for the cold delivery. She'd become accustomed to the brisk bedside manner of the woman before her, who was also the mother of the villa owner's wife, and she was her host. But was it too much to ask for eye contact before such a bombshell?

"Do you mean getting pregnant at all? Or would the scarring only affect delivery?"

"Beyond the psychological affects, which may hinder your ability to be intimate, you may experience pain during intercourse. If you have the determination and can move past those obstacles, you may become pregnant without difficulty. But because of the severe traumas you have suffered, Hadiya, there is a good chance you will experience significant pre-term bleeding. Your predicament is something you would need to tell your future obstetrician."

"I understand," said Hadiya. "Thank you, doctor. For everything."

The doctor offered a rare smile and reached over to squeeze Hadiya's hand. She grabbed her clipboard and left the room. As she gathered her things, Hadiya thought about Jamal. She was disappointed he hadn't called in over a week. She'd seen those gaps in time increase ever since he was at Fallujah, where Fahim had died. In addition to the geographical distance that separated them, she sensed a growing emotional distance, but she believed their relationship would last. Even so, their dream of being together after the war had more obstacles than just the distance to overcome. It seemed there was ever-present danger associated with him. He could die on any given day. But she couldn't help herself. She saw him as the epitome of masculinity, and he had conviction for even the bad things he did in the war. She wondered if those around her believed she was only with him so she could change him.

Untrue.

She accepted him because she knew him well, knew there was good embedded in him that would define him after this terrible war. She reasoned that countless men had gone off to war, done awful things, and proceeded to live productive lives among loved ones and were able to give love too. She believed Jamal would heal in his own right, without her fixing him. If not, she'd take him with the nightmares and the distance.

Praying in her native Swahili for his safety and spiritual wellbeing had been a daily habit of hers for over two years. She did it now.

"Mungu, Praise be to you for sparing this man. Continue to use him in ways you see fit. Allow him to be your servant and allow me to serve him. Let us rejoin, so we both grow whole together again, as one. In the name of Jesus I pray, Amen."

PART FOUR

CHAPTER 41

Jamal and Ahmed stood a block away from the line of vehicles at the checkpoint. Civilians waited there for access to Ramadi's embattled government center, the latest target on Zarqawi's wish list. Today was a calm day, one in a string of eerily calm days. The lull in fighting was welcome after three years of war, but Jamal knew it wouldn't last as he took notes on the Marines guarding the compound. This enclave was one of a few that offered relative safety within the city for Western troops, Iraqi Army soldiers, or the piecemeal police force.

Jamal turned to Ahmed. "I say we use this rear gate for the initial breach point."

"I agree. It's a better option than the main one ... Fewer Marines here. We can fill the buildings down the street with fighters and overwhelm the guards once the vehicle explodes."

"We should use two in succession," said Jamal. "One will destroy the concrete barriers in front of the gate, so the other can penetrate closer to the walls before detonating. I'm considering using a tunnel to get some of us inside the perimeter as the attack commences. We'll surprise them from behind while they're focused on repelling the main body of the assault."

"You and your tunnels ... Sounds like a lot of work."

"I'll make it happen. You just focus on the vehicles and the assault team."

Ahmed responded with a simple nod, his thoughts seemingly drifting away from the discussion of tactics. Jamal guessed his distance had to do with Zarqawi's horrific bloodletting against the

Shiites, which Ahmed had been a key part of during the first half of 2006. Many long silences had occurred of late, yet Jamal hadn't offered Ahmed the proverbial penny for his thoughts. Who was he to offer any advice? At this point, they'd both seen and done terrible acts of violence in the war, and the end was nowhere in sight.

Jamal took his eyes off the checkpoint, rubbed out their graininess as he thought about all that violence. Ramadi, the southwestern point in the infamous Sunni Triangle, was now the most dangerous city in Iraq. The worst stories of brutality came from Ramadi and were spread around the country by those who fought there. The urban battle space was becoming more and more kinetic, with typically up to a dozen scattered firefights per week. Coalition patrols sent out from the large base outside the city entered whole neighborhoods under domination by AQI. Zarqawi's cells also controlled the Ramadi hospital where wounded insurgents were treated, and where the locals were afraid to go for needed care. Jamal had an inkling that the tension between the two demographics might change in the near future, however. He'd spoken to a member of the prominent *Alba Soda* tribe. They told him that the elders had become weary of living under the thumb of Zarqawi's foreign fighters.

Jamal had seen this before and hoped the locals would be stouter this time. Six months prior, at the end of 2005, a collection of local Sunni Sheikhs and their armed tribal members had organized a group called the Anbar People's Council. They'd planned to push back against the coalition and AQI in Anbar province. The movement never got off the ground, though, as internal disagreement preceded a brutal response by Zarqawi and his assassins. Over a half-dozen influential tribal leaders were killed in quick succession, ending the threat to his control. With younger leadership in place now, Jamal wondered if they would try again, and vocalized his question to Ahmed.

"No. They are uncertain if the Americans will fully support them. The tribes are not united. And there is no strength without numbers."

"I'm not so sure," said Jamal. "I heard more than a handful of Sheikhs met the other day to discuss forming a militia."

Once again, Ahmed shrugged away any further import on the matter, and both men continued to watch the checkpoint.

Jamal entered a residential compound through a gate at the rear of the property. He crept toward the villa, pistol drawn. Two bodies lay motionless in a death grip near the door. Another was shot to death, slumped over an outdoor table with the remains of some recent repast scattered across it. Jamal stepped around the fresh corpses and entered warily.

Inside it was a blood bath. The smell of spent gunpowder lingered. A gunfight between the AQI inhabitants of the safe house and members of the *Alba Soda* tribe had turned into a vicious, close-in struggle with knives and bare hands. The assault followed a tip Jamal had used a third and fourth party to convey to the more militant tribal elders. He approved of the dirty work they'd unwittingly done for him, pondered the implications of what had happened here today.

Finally. It looks like the tribes are starting to wake up and see what rotten partners they've gotten into bed with.

His reasons for instigating the fight had been twofold. He shifted his focus to the more selfish one, knew he had to move quickly before any number of people showed up to investigate—coalition troops, Iraqi police, tribal members, or cell members who had not been present when the fighting broke out. Stepping over more bodies, he entered another part of the house and heard movement. An AQI fighter on the floor was wounded but lucid.

He recognized Jamal and asked for help. Jamal saw the standard look of surprise that always turned to spite right before he put the fighter out of his misery with a silenced double-tap to the head.

The dead AQI fighters around him were members of another local cell. Their last successful operation had been the robbery of a coalition cash transfer by vehicle. After ambushing the convoy's Army escort, the cell made off with the armored car, and its members were shocked to find it nearly stuffed full of euros and dollars when they cut the doors open with a blowtorch. The bulk of the money had gone to AQI coffers for laundering, but not before the cell's leader skimmed a substantial amount of the loot. Jamal had learned most of their money was stashed here when he overheard a low-ranking fighter brag about the heist through the thin walls of another safe house. Jamal even knew where the cash was hidden.

He found the closet on the second floor of the villa where the duffle bag was. He opened the top zipper, and inside were stacks of crisp Euros and Dollars of denominations no less than one hundred. He grabbed the bag and bound down the stairs just as he heard voices in Arabic approaching the front door. The rear of the villa offered the only escape, so Jamal quietly made his way to the back gate and the shadows beyond.

A couple of weeks later, Jamal took another drink from his bottle and entered the empty warehouse. The tunnel work had been initiated here under his direction. Situated a block away from Ramadi's government center, the spacious building was outside the perimeter controlled by the Marines. The planned excavation would allow his assault team to emerge above ground at a location inside the compound, and within proximity to the gate breach point.

His night had started with the bottle. Swirling negativity had settled in before long, and he decided to come here because it was almost midnight, and he knew everyone would be gone. He took a swig of whiskey and lowered himself into the hole that had been dug under the busted up concrete floor of the warehouse. The opening of the tunnel was wide enough for two men to stand alongside one another, tall enough for Jamal's unkempt afro to clear the first of many ceiling timbers.

He slumped against the dirt wall and took a big pull from the bottle; he knew that without his interference, men would pour through here like a swarm of locusts. Then they would come out with a vengeance inside the Marines' perimeter. He'd come here to find a place to hide an explosive charge that would collapse the tunnel at his command—burying his men as they moved through it—thereby limiting the assault wave to Ahmed's fighters positioned above ground. It would most likely mean the difference between the government center and Marines being overrun, with dozens of civilian staffers brutally murdered or taken hostage, and the Marines repelling the attack if Ahmed's team had to try alone. He couldn't give a shit about the Marines. Saving those civilians was his only motivation.

Jamal could easily invent a reason to not be in here when the bomb detonated. It would be more challenging to feign the shock and disappointment of losing so many fighters. Then again, some of the performances he'd put on over the last three years must have been Oscar worthy, because he was still alive.

Three years. My God, has it been that long?

He drank some more whiskey and looked up at the ceiling for places to hide explosives. There weren't many due to the improved methods of construction his tunnel building teams had achieved. He decided the best place to plant a bomb was in the dirt floor, maybe somewhere closer to the warehouse.

He walked back in that direction and stopped where several crates of ammunition were set inside a hand-hewn niche in the side wall, so as not to impede the foot traffic of the narrow passage. He unstacked three of them and exposed the dirt floor inside the niche. He dug a hole the size of a shoebox using a nearby shovel, just large enough to hold several pieces of plastic explosive and a detonator controlled by a cell phone. He would wait until the day of the assault to place the actual explosives. For now, he scraped out the edges with his hand, removed the last bits of loose dirt, and set the crates over the top of the hole as they'd been before. He put the shovel precisely as it had been on the wall and used his shoe to scatter the loose dirt he'd excavated.

Satisfied, he stumbled back toward the warehouse, bottle in hand. Once above ground again, he filled his gullet with the last of the whiskey and tossed the bottle into a pile of packing crates. Even though he felt alcohol-fueled drowsiness coming on, he didn't want to go to sleep because of the fitful nights he'd had of late, whether he'd been drinking or not. His dreams had taken a darker tone, and most nights, he tossed and turned while racked with so much guilt over his choices. He hadn't spoken to God much and was regularly giving excuses not to go up north to see Hadiya.

He knew it had been a grave mistake not to tell her his real identity. After all this time, he understood how he could have trusted her with the secret. Instead, he'd kept a lie between them and figured she had every right to cast him off if the truth ever came out.

Why not? She deserves more than a murderer of one's people anyway.

He suddenly felt the urge to add a purple hue to his thickening haze. But he needed to go somewhere else to do that. He ambled toward the door of the warehouse and went out into the chilly, arid night.

On his way to the torture house, Jamal finally looked at his cell phone after he'd disregarded several calls throughout the drunken night. A few were from junior fighters in his cell, no doubt looking for instruction on a menial task he'd assigned them.

They can wait.

Another call had been from an AQI financier who wanted to meet in the coming days. Jamal knew he'd get the benefit of the doubt with the Saudi from Mecca if they didn't speak until tomorrow. Plus, the true believer would frown upon his use of alcohol, and Jamal was past the point of slurring his words.

Not urgent.

One call was from Ahmed, Jamal logged it away in the same category. The last call was from Hadiya. They hadn't spoken in over ten days, and she was probably starting to worry. He hated that he repeatedly put her through that, but dreaded the prospect of being in her presence with the lie still between them, even on the phone. His one solace was that her life on the rural property in Arbil province had become a safe living arrangement for her and over a dozen people. Most of them were displaced relatives of the villa owner from Ramadi. An hour's drive from Mosul, the forty acres of pastureland for grazing sheep was about as peaceful as it gets in Iraq; the trampling feet of the war and the misery left in its wake had little reason to go there. When Jamal forced himself to go, he usually kept his thoughts to himself and focused on Hadiya until he left.

He turned off his phone when he neared the latest building being used for interrogation, told himself he would call her tomorrow. He was too far gone and needed to sink even deeper into his self-inflicted morass. Coming to these awful dens of suffering was something he'd done on occasion to remind himself why he still pursued his mission, as nauseating as the place could be. On two occasions, he'd been so repulsed by the torture that he'd killed all the fighters on duty and set free all the captives. He waited for the blame to be assigned to the coalition, or more recently, a brazen assault by armed members of the tribes who were becoming increasingly restless under the thumb of AQI. As always, though, he couldn't do it every time, or Zarqawi would start looking inside for a traitor.

He approached the front door. He hadn't freed anyone from this place yet, so it was still being used. Jamal knew the guard outside had seen him come and go in the past, so he was quickly granted entry and moved down a hallway. To the left and right were rooms where prisoners were interrogated. He was relieved to see they were empty tonight. He passed the stairs that led to the basement, where fewer questions were asked. Upstairs was the room Jamal knew contained the hashish, raw opium, or heroin used to effect prisoners in various ways by their tormenters.

He heard a woman sobbing inside the last room before the stairs. He'd become accustomed to the bothersome feeling regarding AQI's treatment of women. Jamal knew there were wife beaters everywhere on the planet, but Zarqawi's interrogators— and quite a few run-of-the-mill fighters for that matter—had made all his previous points of reference to violent chauvinism pale in comparison.

Weak, pathetic men.

Upstairs in the opium den, several fighters were using the product that had made its way here from Afghanistan; the procurement and export of opium-based illicit drugs was now the cash cow of the globally syndicated *al Qaeda* organization. It was known to be effective in coaxing innocent civilians to perform suicide work—once they'd been force-fed enough of it to turn them into pleading addicts. For this reason, regular shipments arrived in Ramadi. As for the fighters getting high on their supply, Jamal had learned that the outwardly pious ways of jihadists who'd come to fight the infidel were many times a charade. He simply used it to forget.

He walked over to a table that contained anything he needed. Next to a nearly burned out candle was a tray with chunks of hashish on it. He picked up a glass bowl and lighter and put the pea-sized ball of the sticky brown stuff inside. He sat in a chair in the corner and lit up, taking in the thick smoke. He could feel it expand in his lungs as he closed his eyes and held it in for a few more seconds. Exhaling, he watched the purplish smoke fill the room, put his head back, and sank into the chair. His pulse quickened as he felt the heavy buzz layer over his drunkenness. He was aware that mixing whiskey and hashish might make for a bad ending to his night, but he didn't care.

Just need to check out.

His mind filled itself with a hashish dream, the violence he'd seen and done a central theme. But nearby was the notion that the other men in the room did the same without a hint of the guilt he bore like an anvil on his shoulders. He sensed the others were watching him, so he opened his eyes. Only one man stared, an older fighter with a gray, tousled beard. His eyes were slits from the opium he'd smoked.

"Why do you come here?"

Jamal did not answer. Instead, he smoked again and left the room. He felt the spins coming on as he descended the stairs and stumbled down the hall. He needed the fresh air of the night, but he had to remind himself of the hatred and insanity he'd fought against for all this time, the answer to the old fighter's question. He went into the basement and saw two Iraqis chained to the wall with shackles around their bloody wrists. It looked like they'd suffered for quite some time, through beatings, use of an electric cattle prod, as well as cigarette burns. One of the men was nearly naked and had been sodomized, showing dark streaks along the inside of his bare thighs. On a nearby table sat a soiled broom handle, more implements of torture, and a pitcher of water with a metal cup next to it.

No one minded these two right now, so Jamal gave them water and offered encouraging words. Inside another basement room, a man was bound and gagged and strapped to a wooden chair. Upon entering, the acrid odor of burnt skin was like smelling salts to a punch drunk boxer, and Jamal's buzz lessened. He became angry. The torturer was just about to pour more acid onto the already molten skin of the shuddering man in the chair when Jamal told him to stop.

"What is the point of this? The man can't tell you what you want to know, or he would have already."

The man recognized Jamal's authority and set down the canister of highly acidic industrial cleanser. He occupied himself by cleaning a tray full of bladed implements. Jamal got the impression the man had seen how drunk he was, had obliged Jamal's pulling of rank, and would wait until he went on his way to begin his sadistic practices again. Jamal decided to wait him out and sat on a chair in the corner, almost falling over as he picked up a manual for torture off the blood-stained floor. He'd seen the ridiculous publication here on other occasions. Distributed by the AQI leadership, its appearance was such that it could have been a sixth-grade school project titled "Torture Methods of Terrorists." It featured cartoonish images of power drills being inserted into the skulls and bones of captives, electric shock setups, the proper way to administer an acid drip, and many other ways to inflict great pain upon a suspected enemy.

Jamal was disgusted, felt that urge to lay some waste again, but knew this place was being watched, so he stumbled back upstairs. He took in the fresh air he needed to settle the spinning and decided he'd walk around all night because his sleep had been so highly overrated anyway lately.

CHAPTER 42

Jamal just finished addressing his men, over twenty committed fighters anxious to attack the government center. He grabbed the pistol and slung the satchel on his way to the tunnel entrance. The fighters went back to their final preparations for battle. Nearby were stacks of crated munitions— 7.62 millimeter rounds for the AK's, grenades, RPG warheads, and satchel charges. Among them were Jamal's cached explosives and a detonator. He grabbed the crate he'd discreetly marked and moved to enter the hole, guarded by a couple of fighters.

"Help me with this," he said to one of them. The guard who was new to the cell showed nervousness around Jamal and awkwardly hopped into the hole to assist.

Once they'd laid the crate in the tunnel entrance, Jamal asked, "Anyone else inside?"

"No. Two guards were posted beneath the building at the other end, as you ordered. No one else has gone in or out."

"Very good."

A clap on the shoulder seemed to bolster the young fighter's confidence. "May I carry that for you, Jamal?"

"No. Maintain your post. I have this." Jamal lifted the rope handles on either end of the wooden crate and moved into the tunnel.

He walked to the niche in the wall where the rest of the ammunition was stored, thirty yards inside the entrance, beyond the first turn and therefore out of the guards' line of sight. The hole he'd previously dug appeared undisturbed when he moved the stacked crates. Placing the explosives and setting the cell phone-triggered detonator to receive mode took less than a minute. After moving all the crates back into position, he looked at the arrangement one last time. It appeared normal enough to pull the burner cell phone out of his pocket and turn the power on, the final step. The charge would detonate simply by pressing a speed dial digit. He was about to turn and go back to the warehouse when he heard a noise from further down the tunnel. It sounded like movement, but he couldn't see around the next bend ahead of him. Warily, he drew his pistol and advanced.

Ahmed watched Jamal dutifully hoist the crate down to the tunnel entrance with the help of a guard. He regretted barking at Jamal for not having enough ammunition in there when they'd made the final walk-through together. Ahmed had made the comment in front of the men, something he would not have appreciated himself. It's probably why Jamal insisted they do the logistical math right then and there to prove him right. Uncharacteristically, Jamal's count had been off this time by one crate, so he'd offered to add another. He even said he'd carry the crate himself. For Ahmed's part, he wondered why he couldn't have been more light-hearted about it as Jamal would have been had the roles been reversed. That was Jamal's way, and one of the reasons his friend was so well respected among not only the Arab fighters but also the cadre of foreign leaders that led them.

No. My way is to be gruff and prideful. Even to the man who has kept me alive on more occasions than I can count.

He saw Jamal enter the tunnel alone with the crate and turned his attention to inserting rounds into the banana-shaped magazine for his AK. He thought about the first time he'd met Jamal at one of Hassan's early safe houses in Ramadi, not more than an hour after Jamal was yanked out of his bed at the rented room and whisked away to an unknown fate. Ahmed was one of the men around the communal dinner when Jamal—with not a hint of intimidation in his eyes—made his case for fighting alongside the *Bathyoun*. Once Hassan put them together, it hadn't taken long to realize the two of them worked well as a team. Divide and conquer always seemed to be the theme. Similar roles with equal rewards, which is why he regretted his condescending comment earlier, despite their having grown apart over the last year.

Ahmed put it out of his mind. He stood to assemble the men he was responsible for leading above ground during the assault. He barely registered the thought that Jamal was taking a while to drop off the crate when a loud explosion was heard in the direction of the tunnel. An instant later, a second, even louder explosion shook the floor of the warehouse as dust and smoke shot out of the tunnel entrance. The shock wave tossed the two guards near the entrance against the rubble as if they were rag dolls.

Ahmed and the fighters around him were stunned. Gasps and shouting filled the warehouse, replacing the rumbling echo of the explosions. All sounds were drowned out then by the cacophony that was the tunnel entrance collapsing, sealing off the underground route of attack. But Ahmed could only think of Jamal and how he was nowhere to be seen. Uncertainty flooded the warehouse interior as men grabbed their weapons and looked to their leaders for direction. Ahmed stood there in shock himself, even as men rushed toward the hole, frantically removing the rubble in the tunnel entrance.

"Jamal! Jamal!" they shouted while chunks of concrete and shovels-full of dirt flew out of the hole and onto the warehouse floor. But there was no answer from inside.

Suddenly, incoming rounds imploded the high windows on the side of the warehouse that faced the government center—and the Marines guarding it. The explosion inside the building had given away their position, and a heavily armed platoon now fired on them before they were ready, less one of their most effective leaders.

Ahmed snapped out of his daze and realized he needed to begin the assault without Jamal, or he could lose every one of their men right here inside the building. They'd become prime targets for an airstrike or an artillery barrage from the batteries outside the city. He rallied his leaders and told them they would attack in force from above ground. Jamal's twenty men would have to roll into the main body.

The senior fighters dispersed and quickly gathered their men as the tempo of incoming rounds increased. Fighters moved about in a rush to complete the final preparations for battle, while others occupied window openings and returned fire on the Marines. Ahmed used his radio to call the drivers of the explosive-laden vehicles, informing them to begin their runs from secure locations nearly a kilometer away.

He noticed Jamal's men were out of sorts, wide-eyed in disbelief as a matter of fact. But he knew they were disciplined enough to carry on, so he gathered those who lingered by the hole. They jogged off to the front of the building where the attack would spring from, while Ahmed looked back at the smoking tunnel entrance in disbelief.

The men will be significantly affected by the loss of Jamal. My friend, my brother. Allah, how did this tragedy happen?

CHAPTER 43

A loud clap awakened Jamal. It was pitch dark. He smelled loose soil, felt around the dirt floor he lay on, the room at the major's camp. Soreness existed in all parts of his body. The booming noise again rolled down the foothills of the Smoky Mountains northwest of the reservation. It meant Igor was going to have some fun with them in the mud this morning.

Just need a little more sleep.

Another loud rumble occurred, which shook the ground beneath him. Acute pain surged. His mind only maintained the surrealistic state a second longer before the dreadful reality was upon him. Her. Fahim. His soul. But what had happened in the tunnel?

The noise above ground meant the assault had begun, and those were artillery rounds exploding, not thunder. Right now, Ahmed and the men were chest-deep in a fight they'd expected him to help lead. With his ears still ringing and his head concussed, he tried to understand. He remembered being close to the middle of the tunnel after hearing the noise when two—yes, two—nearly simultaneous explosions had occurred. But he was sure the first one had come from the far end of the tunnel, launching his body back toward the warehouse. An instant later, his own bomb had detonated behind him and ping-ponged him into the wall. That was the last thing he remembered.

His left side seared with pain, so he assessed his bodily damage. It appeared significant. Heavy debris from the tunnel must have impacted his rib cage and torn its way into his chest cavity. He felt the sting of sweat mixing into cuts and scrapes on his face. The one on his chin gushed blood. He pressed a dirty finger on it to stem the flow, causing his hand to gain a sticky coating.

The artillery barrage still rained from above. He had to believe it was mighty 155 millimeter howitzers from outside the city, reducing the whole city block to rubble, salvo by salvo. The noise from each explosion seemed to get louder, however, and Jamal realized the high-explosive rounds were moving closer to the warehouse, and him. Now they were directly above. The shaking was horrific. So much dirt and debris fell from the tunnel ceiling that he was sure this dark hole would be his grave. He covered his face and screamed as it intensified. Through the panic, anger welled up toward everyone, everything to do with this war. Here in the dark, he'd finally reached his abyss. God had forsaken him, and no miracles were waiting to happen.

Why should I expect anything less? It's what I deserve.

The next thought was comforting.

Just let it happen.

A flash of honest self-assessment told him the light had always been in him, but he had neglected it to the point that it was but an ember in a storm, with little hope of burning bright again. Even amidst the chaos of the barrage, he experienced Godly sorrow over that knowledge. Tears flowed, but none of rage or fear. All he could do was beg for forgiveness, so he talked to God one last time while the earth shook around him. At least he would live out the last few minutes of his life with a clean slate. There was comfort in that.

After those harrowing minutes, the barrage ended, however. He was surprised the tunnel had not collapsed. His pulse lessened when it became quiet again, and he lingered in the peace of sanctification. Some time passed where no fighting was heard above ground. Maybe the battle was over, he thought. The peaceful feeling morphed into the semblance of hope that he wouldn't be buried alive. His thoughts became more practical. He crawled over by the wall to gain a sitting position, unslung the satchel, and laid it next to him. Inside was the case of GPS markers the major had given him so long ago, along with his notepads full of intelligence on AQI. Moments ago, it appeared neither would end up being used, but now he found himself checking them for damage. They weren't. He put them back and laid the .45 caliber on top of the satchel.

He touched his side again; he was aware this type of injury could easily lead to complications, namely infection, if not treated soon. Tearing a piece of cloth from the t-shirt he wore yielded a temporary bandage for direct pressure on his chin while he gathered his thoughts.

In that space of time, he decided this would not be the end of him. He wasn't sure how, but he needed to escape from this underground deathtrap. The tunnel supports could have become unsettled enough during the barrage to collapse on their own anytime. After he rested briefly, he crawled forward again through the utter blackness. Disappointment flooded in when his hands touched a barricade of fallen timbers and rocky soil in the tunnel. Crawling back toward the warehouse yielded the same results. Out of desperation, he clawed at the impasse, but it was hopeless. He was stuck.

He crawled back through the tunnel to where he'd been and rested there. He could hear the faintest sounds of human activity; only the sharpest and loudest vocalizations filtered down through the debris at the tunnel entrance, hoarse commands in Arabic no doubt directing survivors to uncover buried fighters in the rubble of the warehouse. Shouting for help would be fruitless, but he did it anyway. Several weakened utterances caused his side to sear, so he rested until the sharp pain had dulled to a throb, inducing a state of diminished lucidity.

After some time, he sat up straight to avoid drifting off with a concussion, took a deep breath to test the strength of his diaphragm. The pain forced him to cough, the absolute worst thing for his condition. Fully lucid again, he trembled in the dark from the dread of the next excruciating spasm. Consistent shallow breaths prevented it from happening, but he knew a telltale wheeze would develop if he had indeed pierced his left lung.

The stillness enveloped him for another unknown length of time. A sound caused him to open his eyes even though there was nothing to see for the pitch-blackness around him. He was sure it had come from nearby, possessing none of the muffled qualities of the human activity outside this potential tomb. He assumed a rat had found its way down here and now roamed in the dark nearby.

He pulled his legs into him and reached for the pistol, figuring to use it as a hammer against the rodent. His hand reached for the strap of the satchel and felt its way up to where the pistol was—no—where he was certain it had been! He was entirely unprepared for the voice that next filled the void.

"Do not be afraid, lad," said the voice in English, with a Scottish accent no less.

CHAPTER 44

There had been firmness to the words, an authoritative tone Jamal found completely believable, but it was likely this stranger had taken the pistol while he crawled around. Unsure of the presence in the dark, he spoke in Arabic to test the man.

"*Min Hunak?*" asked Jamal. Who is there?

Once again, the voice spoke in his brogue. "From what I can tell, we're both trapped down here. We may need to help each other, so don't you do something rash. Do you understand?"

Jamal's addled mind raced. It was dangerous for him to converse in fluent English with anyone, ever. He would stick to that script for now.

"*Shu haditht weeah islahty*?! What happened to my weapon?!"

The uptick in tone was matched by the voice. "Hey, there's no need to get all upset, lad!"

Myriad conflicting thoughts competed for primacy in Jamal's mind, yet through it, there was the thread of understanding that he was in no danger. It seemed like this man did not understand Arabic and was equally apprehensive, causing Jamal to take a leap of faith.

In English, he said, "Well, as you know, I can't shoot you because you have my weapon."

"A precaution for now … You speak English. Are you American?"

"Not really."

Jamal would remain vague about his identity but was gracious for the non-aggression if this man was armed with his weapon.

The voice asked, "Do you need water? I have some."

The loss of blood and internal injuries he'd suffered caused the bodily reaction of thirst. Jamal accepted the offer, and both men cautiously edged forward to make the exchange. In the pitch dark, his hand found the bottom of the bottle, but no physical contact was made with the stranger. He took a swallow and passed it back.

"You must be a British soldier," said Jamal through gritted teeth as the pain jumped in his side.

"Aye, a demolitions expert in the Black Watch Regiment, Scotland's pride and joy. I've been assigned to the Marines guarding the government center."

After a few seconds, the voice said, "Since you haven't tried to kill me, even without a gun in your hand, I'm wonderin' if you are something other than a run of the mill insurgent. Most of the fighters in this burg would be at my throat."

Jamal would not answer directly, but said, "Let's just say I'm working a couple of different angles in this shitty war."

A short silence preceded a grunt of acknowledgment from the Scotsman. Next, he said, "Lad, I can't think of a more dangerous job. I feel for you. But I can tell you we need someone working both sides."

"You all need a lot from what I've seen." Jamal didn't want to begin discussing the war, so he offered a question instead. "So, what are you doing stuck down in this rat trap?"

The Scotsman grumbled. "My bloody plan didn't work. We've known about this tunnel for a week. Your miners are not the quietest bunch of lads by the way."

"Thanks for the tip."

"We suspected which building you would come up under, and I was sent to blow the opening and either trap your fighters down here or make it useless for an attack."

Jamal offered dark humor to the voice out there. "You did a damn good job. I will give you that."

The Scotsman said, "Apparently those of us who work in the shadows sometimes get caught in them."

With Jamal's cat out of the bag, the tension eased somewhat. "So, what happened?"

"Don't know," answered the Scotsman. "Me and a couple of lads neutralized your guards under the building on our side of the wall; then I went down in the tunnel to set the charges. I had them rigged to go on a five-minute timer. I was all set, and then I got bloody curious."

"What do you mean?"

"I walked a little bit further into the tunnel when I heard movement."

"Uh-huh," said Jamal, "I was in here, setting a charge to blow the thing myself."

"That explains the second explosion. You used regular blasting caps, did you now?"

"Yeah."

"When my detonator went off prematurely, I'm bettin' the shock wave inside the tunnel set yours off. Finicky little bastards those caps are when it comes to heat or pressure. It's a good thing we both were between them when they blew. But now we're stuck."

"You don't seem to be injured. I wasn't so lucky."

"Aye. I can hear your breathin'."

"My left side took a beating," said Jamal with a grimace.

"You rest then, while I do some investigating. I'm going to leave this pistol here. I trust that's a move that won't kill me, eh?"

"It won't kill you. You may be the only way I get out of here."

"Is that supposed to be reassuring?"

"It's supposed to let you know how bad a shape I'm in."

The Scotsman put the pistol on the satchel next to Jamal and moved down the tunnel while Jamal repositioned himself to ease the soreness. His head throbbed, so he rubbed his temples and waited. Soon the lull was enough to cause Jamal to drift again. Time passed. The pain kept him semi-lucid for what seemed like hours. Being in that state caused him to prefer the waking reality of it all. He sat up, felt the stickiness of cottonmouth. The Scotsman was ready and waiting.

"Need a hoist, lad?"

"Huh, a lift, you mean?" Jamal was somewhat confused following his emergence.

"Nay, lad. A hoist like a drink. First, take some more water."

The liter-sized water bottle seemed as full as it had been before. He was glad they were not sparse yet, took a deep pull, and immediately felt guilty for doing it. He was so thirsty, though.

When Jamal passed the bottle back, the Scotsman said, "From the sounds you were making, you need a little relief. Here, take some of this. I'm sorry for having held out on you."

He handed over a flask. Jamal smelled inside the cap. Scotch whisky, of course.

"Thank you," said Jamal after several gulps. The burn of the liquor masked his chest pain. He rested the flask on his thigh and savored the fleeting feeling.

After another interlude of silence, Jamal decided this shrewd and reasonable foreigner, completely unrelated to either of his lives, would be his sounding board. Just once he wanted to seek genuine counsel.

"Everything okay over there?" asked Jamal in a hoarse voice.

"I'm fine. You sound worse, though, lad."

Jamal did feel a new tightness in his chest and heaviness in his breathing as if the lungs were cheated of some air each breath. And the wheezing was there now. When it became a gurgling sound, he would be moving to the next stage of trauma. Shallow breaths allowed him to ward off the coughing spasms, but he knew consistent short breaths would hinder the damaged lung further as his body lost the ability to exhale vapor. The fluid inside the lung would mix with blood from the wound. Next, it would fester. He started to get the fear. This was the most he'd ever been injured, and he was without medical aid.

"I'm guessing broken ribs from the blast."

"Think one of them punctured a lung? If so, we have to get you out of here."

"I'm all ears," said Jamal weakly.

"While you drifted off, I found a broken shovel."

"We can't dig a new tunnel with a broken shovel to the surface. We're fifteen feet below ground."

"Aye, but part of the tunnel closer to your end has collapsed in on itself. I know there's a path to the surface; I found a spot in the debris where the air is pushing down. It won't be easy, but we should be able to make it out of here."

Jamal wasn't as hopeful, the negativity still lingering.

"I'm not giving up on us yet, lad."

They agreed Jamal would rest while the Scotsman removed rubble and dirt. The Scotsman helped him down the tunnel to where they could converse while he worked, keeping Jamal awake for as long as possible. After a few minutes, Jamal opened up while his companion in the dark worked and listened.

"I watched one of the only Iraqis I gave a damn for die, killed by a coalition sniper team. I should have convinced him to give up the fight. I cannot forgive myself for that."

The Scotsman said, "There is one who will take all your burdens from you."

"I know of whom you speak."

"You know of Jesus?"

"Yes, my whole life I've known him. So, during the barrage earlier, I prayed to be forgiven for the awful things I've done," said Jamal. "But do desperate pleas count? It had been a while before that since I went to Him."

"Anytime you speak with the Lord, it counts. As long as you mean it. I can imagine the positions you've been put in have tested your faith."

"I won't lie. I may have lost my way. Good people have been hurt. Lives ruined."

"And I'm sure lives have been saved as well," said the Scotsman with believable authority.

Jamal looked in the direction of the voice, remembered all the reasons he'd come here. Too many seemed foolish now.

"I used to think I was doing right by God in undermining Islamic terrorists because these are people who will slit the throat of a Christian or Jew on a whim, and enjoy doing it. I studied the book of Judges in the Old Testament for a while. I learned God used earthly warriors to fight the enemies of His chosen people. The United States is a nation under God in its own right and the main ally of Israel. In my arrogance, I fashioned myself a modern-day judge for America, even though God had not spoken to me, and no angel had ever appeared to validate the idea. All I had were some crazy dreams and some strong convictions as validation. But when the war started going badly for the Americans last year, and for me personally, I didn't care anymore, didn't care about delivering them from their hubris. I was a fool for thinking any of it."

"I assume you were born a Muslim."

"Correct."

"So a Muslim boy ends up becoming a believer and defends his adopted nation from outright evil. The story has a nice ring to it, lad."

"And he encounters trouble along the way, enough to be written off by all parties. Maybe even the Lord."

The voice in the dark brushed off the comment with a snort and quick retort. "You think you're the first bloke to seek God's validation for the rotten things we do while fighting our wars?"

"Is it not right?"

"You serve under a nation, and the nation goes to war. We have our duties to fulfill as soldiers, even if they go against our nature. The believing man will always have a hard time killing. You are not alone in that struggle. But we know how to go about the business of war with honor, even if the larger reasons for us being here are less than honorable. It's probably why my curiosity sent me further into the tunnel. Everyone knows your group likes to use children in dangerous work. I've seen bombs stuffed inside wounded kids, so it wasn't a stretch to think you might have them down here digging for you. If I had found young folk in your tunnel, I wouldn't have blown it."

"You would not complete your mission? What about your duty?"

"I know yours does not, but our duty involves protecting the citizenry."

Jamal thought of the carnage at the Ta'mim market. His chin sunk to his chest. It had been wrong to put those innocents in the line of fire, even if it was a diversion that saved American lives for a period.

The Scotsman continued. "That's the difference between me and some of the other men with whom I serve. It's a burden I bear as a Christian at war."

"Well, it may have saved you this time," said Jamal as he adjusted himself into a more comfortable seated position. "You worrying about kids down here, walking away from a detonator that was about to blow four minutes early."

"Yes. That was a blessing, lad. I'll be thanking the Lord for that one."

With sadness in his voice, Jamal asked, "So what do we do if our war fighting creates a callous on our heart, and we speak to Him less because of it?"

"If you still have the presence to ask that, then you must pick yourself up and run to the cross. The Lord is waiting."

"You think there is hope for my soul, whether or not I finish my mission?"

"Has He not provided you ways to further your mission when you've asked for His will to be done?"

Jamal thought about his prayer to be delivered from the vicious tactics of Zarqawi's group when he joined them. Building the defenses of Fallujah had been his first assignment, given from the mouth of Zarqawi himself. Jamal remembered the book of Exodus, how God had put words in the mouth of the wicked Pharaoh concerning Moses and the Hebrew slaves, words that benefitted them in their escape from Egypt.

"He has."

"Good. Then know it will be your faith that carries you through your mission, and puts you in a place where you will find peace regarding the awful things you've done. As far as the Old Testament, you know it is characterized by the ways God intervened with the Israelites. They are His chosen people, and it took the judges to keep them on the right path. The judges, angels, prophets, even the pre-incarnate form of Jesus, these are the ways in which God conveyed his directives to people like Moses back then."

"Like the Ten Commandments?"

"Not just those basic laws, but the whole system of atonement and the specific ways of living He required of the Israelites. As for the twelve judges, they were a manifestation of His mercy for His people, allowing them to see when idolatry and unclean living blinded their eyes. You mentioned the concept of a modern-day judge. This is a bloody slippery slope, lad. Whereas the Old Testament has God intervening in direct ways to manage transgressions, the New Testament offers the gift of salvation through Jesus Christ to all those who choose him as their savior.

The hope of Christ supersedes all that eye for an eye stuff and the violence sanctioned by God in the past."

"I know. Because he died on the cross."

"Yes. As far as your *nation under God* is concerned—and I know you can't see me, but I am making mock quotation marks with my fingers right now—let them be warned that a people who talk the talk, had better walk the walk. Wars initiated for ideological or economic reasons could draw the rebuke of the Lord. Look at the mess here in Iraq, does this feel righteous?"

"At this point, no. Too much grinding. Too little support from the Iraqis. It's hard to tell what will turn out worse, lawful self-rule imposed by the West, or the Sharia forced on the Iraqis by the Islamists."

"The Arabs will choose according to God's will."

Jamal thought of Farouk's questions during their training. "And what of those who think they are born into their faith, who are not encouraged to think freely when it comes to religious choice?"

"Do you like riddles?" asked the Scotsman.

"Sure."

The Scotsman put his broken shovel down, cleared his throat before his poetic offering. "It is intertwined with fate yet unchained like the wind. It can dethrone kings and crown them too. Evil transforms men into sheep by taking it away. But a spiritual reward is reserved for those who trust it in the search for knowledge."

Jamal thought for a while, but his mind was not up for the challenge. It felt like someone had driven a lance into his side, and his head throbbed.

"I am sorry. Having a hard time focusing. I appreciate what you are doing, though."

"The answer is free will."

"Ahh."

"Man is blessed to have been born with free will. God gave it to the angels, and one third chose to turn against Him. Face to face with the Creator, and they rebel nonetheless. Point is, because of free will, some choose wisely; some choose poorly. It's how God knows the truly faithful."

Jamal thought on the matter while the Scotsman went back to work, chipping out loose rock as he talked.

"Any individual may believe their religion is part of who they are. Remember, though, all religion for human beings is nothing more than a mental construct. It can be reworked. We all have a choice. Free will is the vehicle to make that happen, especially when God is there, coaxing the changes through His grace. We believers are here to remind people of that. It's our mission, our duty."

"Have you witnessed to any Muslims while you've been here?"

"They are typically surprised to learn the gift of salvation is one that is given freely. And the ones who accept it come to see loving their enemies as a higher spiritual state than hating them."

Jamal nodded to himself in the dark, remembered the same feeling of comfort in the knowledge of the gift when it was learned years ago. "And what about someone like me ... who believes but has gone astray?"

"You've been given a hard road, lad. God must have seen something in you that He could use. And you can be forgiven for the sins of the past, but you must galvanize your trust in the one Savior, accept the path God has put you on, and follow it to the end. Heaven is the reward. But while we are here, men like you and I have work to do spreading the word of God."

"I understand."

"Speaking of work. I've got some to do up in this hole I've made. Here," said the Scotsman, "put your hand up." Their grubby hands met and exchanged the flask. "Rest now, while I finish this. Let's hope it doesn't take all night."

For hours he worked, moving rubble and dirt from above, ever ascending into the dark, to the point where Jamal heard his voice in muffled tones when the Scotsman would start clearing new material in his path. When he would come down to pull out a clump of roots or a piece of petrified wood left from the ages, they would talk to keep Jamal lucid. But his condition was worsening, and Jamal wondered if time would run out on him.

Jamal woke up. It was quiet. His pain had receded, for which he was grateful, but he now felt the ache of fever. He touched his brow and felt the clamminess. His head felt cloudy.

Infection setting in. Not good.

Panic welled up, and he called out in a weak, gravelly voice. "Are you there?"

At first, there was no answer, and Jamal felt strange. Had he imagined it all? He reached for the pistol. It was there, lying on top of the satchel.

He raised his voice, but the effort made it crackle again when he spoke.

"Are you in here?"

Nothing. Had he totally lost it? The odd feeling of not knowing what is real and what isn't came over him. The darkness was overpowering, disorienting him further. Despite the wracking pain in his side whenever he moved, he lifted himself, decided as far as those conversations were concerned, it didn't really matter to him whether they'd been real or not. They had affected him either way. Jamal settled into his position and resigned himself to waiting a bit, hoping it was all real. In a few minutes, the flicker of a flashlight emitted cold LED light from further down the tunnel. Uncertainty was there, so he reached for the pistol and slid the receiver back to chamber a round. In a moment, the light shone brightly, and Jamal was blinded by it enough to cover his brow with his forearm.

"You're bloody awake. About time. Have yourself a good nap did you, lad?"

"How about turning that light away?"

"Sorry. There you go."

The beam of light bounced off the walls of the tunnel. Jamal noticed a medic's kit on the ground near him. He looked toward the Scotsman and finally had a face to put to the voice. As was tradition in the Black Watch for many, he'd grown a thick mustache that buried the end of his nose and extended onto his ruddy cheeks. Curly reddish hair was matted down on his larger than average head, and he grinned at Jamal.

"I'm Michael. Nice to meet you. Ready to get out of this place?"

"I couldn't be more ready."

"I got it all lined up for us. How are the ribs, lad?"

Jamal felt the pain had lessened. "Uh, good. How long have I been out?"

"Probably ten hours."

"Huh?"

"That's right, lad."

"But I thought I needed to stay awake. And if I slept for that long with a concussion, was it a miracle I even woke up?"

"Perhaps. By the time I dug to the surface, you were out cold. I couldn't wake you. You had a fever. But you had a strong pulse, so I waited to go out until it was the middle of the night, then got to my gear. I came back and gave you a couple IV's I had in my pack."

He pointed the flashlight at two intravenous bags on the tunnel floor that had been sucked dry.

"But that wheezing is getting worse. It's time for you to see a surgeon."

"My pain is less. Did you give me something?"

"Morphine."

"I feel it," said Jamal groggily. He was amazed at what this man, whom he'd never met before, had done for him, above and beyond the call of his duty.

"Thank you for sticking around. I wouldn't have made it if not for you. You could have called in medics and been done with me. Why didn't you?"

"I don't believe God is through with you," he said in his convincing tone. "C'mon, we got a tight crawl ahead of us. You got a bloody plan for medical aid when you exit this place? You need it ASAP. I'm heading in a direction. If I'm wrong and you're ready to come in, or you don't think the men you're in with can patch you up well, we could go together-"

"No," interrupted Jamal. "I have my direction. You have done enough. More than you know."

"I'd ask your name, but I'd understand if you declined to answer. When we leave this place, we'll be outside the established perimeter. I could be captured before I get back and-"

"My name is J."

"Good to know you, J. You stick to the right path, lad, and you'll get out of this bloody mess. Then maybe you'll have a peaceful life."

"Hey. You got any food in that pack?"

Jamal fought off nausea from the morphine and ate rations only for the sake of nourishment. He slung the satchel with his pistol around his neck and followed the Scotsman to the way out. Five minutes later, Jamal could see up through the debris toward the pale gray of dusk, a decent time to emerge with the hope of safe passage through the battle zone.

Jamal's mind switched to another gear when the reality of the world outside beckoned. He realized it was his training instinctively kicking in, but over the top of those mental machinations was the perspective he'd gained while trapped underground. He knew exactly what he was going to do. Nonetheless, there was trepidation about leaving this man who'd brought him back from the abyss physically, mentally, and spiritually. He tugged at his pant leg now and asked for him to stop short of the surface.

"What is it, lad. Still hungry or something?" he said in a low tone.

"No. It's just … There is more to talk about. I have questions. And I feel I owe you a debt of gratitude."

"For the love of Christ, lad. Don't get all sappy on me now. I don't think we'll be able to settle up anyway."

"What base are you at? And what is your last name? That is all I need to know."

"McHugh. But it won't do you any good. This was my last mission. I rotate out in two days, and then I'm going back to Edinburgh. I'll be tending the wife's rose bushes by this time next week. You know, she doesn't like to get pricked by the thorns. Hates the sight of her own blood."

"That sounds a lot easier on the soul than blowing up tunnels with people in them."

"Easier on people in tunnels too," he said as he turned around again and started moving toward the light. C'mon, lad, it's time to rejoin the war. When you get topside, don't expect it to look like it did before. While you slept for half a day, artillery prepped the place again, and then the coalition patrols came in and cleaned up any pockets of resistance. They rolled tanks through here. Not a fun moment. Probably better off being out cold then."

Jamal followed close behind, and momentarily, they emerged to a desolate landscape. Jamal stood up and was shocked to see how much devastation the battle had created. This indeed had been a heavyweight bout. Ahmed probably used every last rocket, every last round, every last man to defend the counterattack by the

Americans. In vain, apparently. He doubted he'd ever see him again.

"Let's go, lad. The building over there with the white and blue lettering on the side will be where we split off. Ready to stretch those legs?"

"Roger that. After you."

CHAPTER 45

When they parted, Jamal took one last look at the collapsed warehouse, thanked the Lord above for sparing him. He figured he had less than six hours remaining of pain relief and benefits from the fluids. The Scotsman had given him an extra morphine ampoule to administer himself, the last of his supply. If he obtained a vehicle, he could get to Baquba in a few hours, taking a direct route to Zarqawi's most secure safe house to end this thing. Nuking AQI as it existed right now was going to be his final act as an agent. Zarqawi had become one of the most wanted men on the planet. He was too big for Iraq, and now he had to be stopped.

But that's as far as I go. I'm dead to the world for a while after that. Gotta get patched up and straighten out my head, see her.

Ultimate success required help from the coalition. He knew there were units out there explicitly tasked with hunting down men like Zarqawi, highly trained operators who'd honed their skills on the killing fields of Iraq. After tonight they could begin mangling AQI from top to bottom. But it would start with the leader himself. Cut off the head of the snake, let the coalition chop the body into pieces before a new head grows.

Sadly, he knew it would not end the Islamist threat to stability in Iraq. If the coalition could destabilize AQI long enough for a viable government to form and a new mindset of intolerance to set in for men like Zarqawi, then maybe the people of this country would have a fighting chance.

He managed to avoid any remaining AQI fighters in Ramadi until he welcomed the anonymity of darkness and boosted a sedan.

The desert at night provided cold air to slap his face while he drove eastward, working in concert with his teeth-chattering fever to keep him alert. Raising the volume on the radio helped, tuned to a local FM channel that played Middle Eastern club music. The fast-paced rhythms of the canned synthesizer were irritating enough to do the job, then there was the pain, which crept up through the morphine by the hour. He pulled over to administer the extra ampoule and felt the rush of bodily warmth set in.

These last couple hours will be a gut check. Just don't pass out and crash.

Jamal skirted the western edge of Baghdad. The landscape began to change as he turned northeast toward Baquba. The sight of moonlit orange groves was starkly different from the arid scrub of Anbar. He smelled green life, the olfactory sensation contrasting his rapidly deteriorating condition. He prayed for bodily strength to hold out for just a few hours longer. After that, he would simply dial the digits the major had given him during their last meeting, and a medevac would be anywhere he chose within thirty minutes, hopefully.

He noticed the gurgling had begun. By now, he was getting by on one lung, and the other one was becoming a cesspool. Several times the vehicle swerved off the road when he blacked out momentarily. It happened again twenty kilometers later, and the car careened off a steel guardrail this time, producing a sizable gash along the passenger side. Jamal pulled over and collected himself. He rode that jolt as long as he could, driving faster while possessing the edge. Speed caused more wind to rush in until the shitty music was barely discernible. He lost track of time, able to cover a sizable amount of ground, and soon he was close enough that he sensed he would at least get to the safe house. As bad as he felt, he couldn't guarantee much beyond that moment.

A sign blurred past him indicating Baquba was near, releasing another store of adrenaline. He opened the windows all the way, chattering teeth and all. The wind whipped around the interior of the sedan, causing tears to form under his eyes. Their wetness ran down his cheeks unhindered by a brush from his hands, which white-knuckled the steering wheel. When he entered the populated area, the streetlights retained a hazy, morphine-induced halo to his eye. It burned to look at them. He had to concentrate on not hitting any of the few cars that drove around this time of night. What a menace he was.

CHAPTER 46

Jamal parked the vehicle in an orange grove roughly a kilometer from the safe house outside Baquba. He got out of the car and stretched from the long drive, then retrieved his pistol and its makeshift silencer. It had lived in the satchel for a long time with the major's toys, which he also pocketed. In the trunk of the stolen car, he found some cord and a couple pieces of bar stock metal to fashion a garrote.

He locked the vehicle and hid the keys under a rock ten feet from the dusty trail, and began to move off in the direction of the safe house. The groves were dense enough that he didn't worry about being seen until he was within fifty yards of the property. From there, he crept under cover of night to the thick vegetation around the villa, which had grown up to the edges of the surrounding orange groves. Concealed behind some bushes, he scanned the area around the square, two-story building, the outside of which was dimly lit by a single incandescent bulb on the corner nearest to him. So far, he hadn't seen any guards on patrol.

After another five minutes, during which he endured a wave of drowsiness induced by the morphine, he saw a shadow on the ground in front of the villa. A guard appeared from the front toting an AK. He wore a checkered turban and walked toward Jamal, disappearing from view momentarily as he passed between the small outbuilding on the property and the villa. Jamal used the opportunity to emerge from the thicket and circle around the shed to lasso the guard's neck from behind with the garrote. He yanked it closed by crossing his arms and jerked the man toward the ground, where the guard struggled a bit and fell silent. The body and weapon were dragged into a weedy patch behind the shed. He quietly pulled the AK's bolt back to check for a round in the chamber. There wasn't one. It meant the guards were either not on their toes or tonight was just business as usual. He took the man's radio and turned down the volume to a whisper.

Skulking around the front of the villa, he approached the main entry. With his free hand, he reached above the door and into the light fixture mounted overhead, unscrewing the bulb just until the light went out, but leaving it in place. He retreated to the nearest shadows and waited. His elevated heart rate caused his head to throb through the morphine and dehydration made his mouth pasty. He felt awful and every second he waited was torture.

At last, the sound of the switch flicking several times could be heard inside the door. An unarmed guard stepped halfway out and looked up at the bulb. Jamal leapt out and swung the garrote over the man's head, yanking him off the stoop in a lightning-quick snatch. The man went to the ground and desperately clawed at the thin cord buried in his fleshy neck, unable to make audible noise. Eyes bulged, and muscles twitched. It didn't last long. Jamal assumed he'd caught him on the exhale.

He dragged the body into another thicket and hid in some bushes a few yards from the front door this time. Another excruciating ten minutes passed. Finally, another guard stood in the open door with a radio and a pistol. He flicked the switch a couple of times, stepped outside on the dark stoop and looked warily up at the non-functioning fixture. Instead of reaching for it, he scanned the yard and raised a pistol. The guard broke squelch on his radio, and Jamal lifted the barely audible speaker to his ear.

"Kamal, come in." The guard waited and listened for an answer. "Kamal, answer your radio."

The guard warily stepped down onto the yard, weapon at the ready, and walked around the back of the villa. Jamal quietly raised the silenced pistol.

THWAT. THWAT.

The man went down in a heap; the radio was still gripped in his hand. His weapon dropped to the patchy yard. Jamal advanced in a crouch, kicked the pistol into the bushes, and rolled the body in as well. He crept up on the stoop by the door and reached inside to flick off the interior hall light, ushering in darkness everywhere around him. Then he entered the villa.

It was quiet and musty smelling inside. Moonlight, through the open front door, provided the only ambiance on the dark tiled floor. Zarqawi would not allow air conditioners or fans to run while he was there. It wasn't for minimalistic religious reasons he disallowed the modern technology; Jamal had once overheard the guards say that Zarqawi was simply paranoid of the white noise and the possibility of them not hearing potential captors approach during a raid.

Jamal crept down the hall toward the second-floor stair. Just when he was about to ascend the first step, a floorboard at the landing creaked, halting his motion. It was a fortunate occurrence. A guard emerged from a shadowy corner with a long, bladed weapon and grunted from exertion as he slashed downward toward Jamal's shoulder. Jamal was able to bow backward just enough and avoided the potentially lethal strike, which sliced into the wall and caused the blade to stick. Jamal's knee flew upward in an instinctual counter-movement.

The blow to the diaphragm was made more forceful by the guard's downward momentum, and he doubled over, bereft of wind. Jamal put him in a standing headlock with his free arm. The nose of the silencer found the center of the man's spine, and he pulled the trigger twice, the body becoming dead weight instantly. He pulled the guard a few yards down the hall and returned to the stair. The exertion had flooded his body with pain. He fought the urge to let a coughing spasm take over, instead rested with his hands on his shaky knees and focused on steady breathing for more than a minute in the quiet house.

Upstairs, he moved down another dark hall, passed a closed door where gargled snoring could be heard inside. Probably a cleric, he guessed. Jamal had stayed in that very room, during one of the visits here. The house was an opium den that weekend. Zarqawi received a massive shipment from his Afghan brothers to help fund their operations, and Jamal played the part to sidle up to him, accepting the drugs and a young woman Zarqawi had brought in. He purged his mind of the carnal memories when he was at Zarqawi's door.

Jamal turned the knob and pushed the door open, just enough to slip through. The spartan room had a mattress on the floor and in the corner, a desk with a laptop on it. Under a sheet was a single, slumbering shape, whose girth and heavy breathing made Jamal think it was his mark. He held the pistol before him and moved around to see the face. It was him. Zarqawi scowled even in his sleep, Jamal noticed. On the floor were pieces of tin foil with tiny balls of a gooey dark substance on them, matches, and an unlit candle on a brass tray, paraphernalia for smoking opium or hashish. The room retained a hint of the sweet odor from their use.

Good. He's self-medicated. It probably explains the guards' behavior.

A stack of papers full of handwriting lay adjacent to the mattress. His curiosity was piqued, so he bent down to pick them up, then went to the laptop on the desk. He touched the space bar on the machine, and the screen saver popped up. Jamal saw the black banner of AQI. He used the ambient light to look over the cream-colored papers, recognized Zarqawi's handwriting. By the heading, he discerned it was a reply to a letter received earlier from *al Qaeda* leadership, still presumed to be holed up in Waziristan— the badlands of Pakistan. He lifted all but the back sheet and rubbed the last stroke of Zarqawi's signature with his finger. The ink smudged.

Fresh. This letter is outbound soon. A beautiful piece of intel that will make good reading later.

He folded the papers and tucked them away in his pocket, felt the old rush again. The possibility of advancing the mission to its ultimate goal was before him, as he'd always believed it would be whenever this moment came. He was confident there would be the type of information on Zarqawi's hard drive that could lead him to higher *al Qaeda* leadership.

This stuff could be my ticket out of Iraq, passage aboard the mother ship. Some cave in Pakistan … Afghanistan. Wherever the hell they are.

At that moment, he had another thought; it was born out of that certain perspective he'd gained from the Scotsman. As bad as he felt physically, Jamal felt a smile cross his face for the first time in a long while. He was about to be done and had no desire to go to Waziristan to track down *al Qaeda's* warlords. But he knew somebody who did. He opened a drawer in the desk. Inside were a handful of stick drives, which he shoved in his pocket. He shut down the laptop and put it in a carrying case next to the desk. Next, he activated one of the major's tiny GPS markers and placed it at the foot of the "Emir of Iraq's" bedding.

Enjoy the express ride to hell, Emir.

He looked at his watch. Coincidentally, it was early morning on June 6, 2006, another D-Day of his own making. He hoped this one would help the current war effort as much as the original had helped the Allies in the Second World War. He took the thought further.

060606. Could it really be a coincidence, Lord? Or are you mocking the evil one with this one's dying day?

Jamal left the room, laptop in hand, and moved down the hall toward the stairs. The cleric's snoring stopped, and the tussle of sheets got louder. He crept past the door and took the stairs wide-legged to minimize creaking. Once outside, he made for the vehicle, the achiness of fever and the pain increasing with every footstep.

Jamal retrieved the keys from under the rock. He sat in the car and put Zarqawi's laptop on the passenger seat, set the stick drives next to it. The pre-paid cell phone lit up when he started punching in the number the major had provided. He'd said someone would be listening. But that was nearly two years ago. After three rings, a voice answered, only it wasn't the major's. It was calm and crystal clear, making him think he was patched into some satellite connection.

"This is the ranch."

"This is Alpha Whiskey Seven authenticating for interdiction," said Jamal, reading with anticipation from a laminated card the major had given him.

"Go ahead, Seven."

"I authenticate Echo Four Golf ... Kilo Six Yankee."

The operator repeated similar codes, which Jamal checked off from his card. A twenty-second pause ensued that seemed like another year tacked onto his mission.

"Ready for marker designation, Alpha Whiskey Seven."

Jamal read off a serial number associated with the GPS marker he'd placed and informed the operator of the intended target.

Then they signed off. Jamal guessed that somewhere on a monitor displaying satellite imagery for the Air Force, a red dot appeared and started blinking in the middle of Baquba's orange groves. He wondered how long it would take the major's loyal lackeys to claim their prize. In the meantime, he looked at what was on the stick drives he'd taken. Some were loaded with intelligence-oriented data. Some had pornography. One was empty, and he used it after he'd perused Zarqawi's hard drive to find some particularly eye-raising material, which would be his bargaining chip should his next steps work against him.

After the download, he deleted those particular files from the laptop's hard drive permanently with a technique the major's own IT geeks had taught the agents.

Forty minutes later, the guided smart bomb exploded in the direction of the safe house, illuminating the inside of the vehicle.

Just like that, he's gone.

It was time for the medevac. He was running on fumes and needed to get well. The major would see to that. During recovery, he would be in much better shape to initiate some exit strategy. Before making the call, though, he had to hide the stick drive and the letter for use as collateral down the road. The hit on Zarqawi and his laptop would be enough to buy the immediate care he desperately needed.

CHAPTER 47

Major Winters sat in a chair under the light of a lamp. It was late. Jamal slept amidst the tubes and cords attached to his face, arms, and torso, themselves tethered to several machines that monitored his vital signs and more. His body had gone septic from the internal wounds that festered without treatment. He was sedated now and on massive doses of antibiotics after the major's tight-lipped medical team had earned their stipend to get him stable. Now he rested at a secret location in Baghdad, unbeknownst to the general or anyone else.

The major contemplated the laptop Jamal had brought in, supposedly right out of the hands of Zarqawi before he'd been killed. It was loaded with critical intelligence that was already being used to maul his network of terrorist cells. The hounds had been released, which was all well and good, but it hadn't gone unnoticed that the computer's hard drive had been manipulated and seemed to be missing key files. The major felt a measure of pride that Jamal had been savvy enough to create an insurance policy for himself; the missing files were just enough leverage to keep the major waiting patiently until Jamal could speak for himself.

The ultimate sleeper agent. Built for longevity and survivability.

Only a few flashes of lucidity had occurred for Jamal over the last week. Undoubtedly, they were distorted and detached moments, ripe with the fever that permeated his body. The major guessed Jamal had no idea of the great gaps of time between those episodes. One day. Four days. Two days. During his fever-induced ramblings, they'd only pulled bits and pieces of information regarding his status, and the motivations behind his actions remained undetermined. As such, he was under constant guard, and a video monitor recorded those ramblings should they shed some light on his recent history.

The major thought about the piece of paper they'd found on his person with the address in Arbil province written on it. He wondered if Jamal had left it for a reason.

Maybe it was some sort of request.

A few days ago, one of the major's freelance surveillance teams had easily determined the inhabitants of the rural farm were all harmless civilians. There was even a real doctor living on the premises. The African woman's presence was a curious addition to the mix, as well. The major mulled over the idea of letting Jamal heal there for a while, a place even more off the grid than his current location. It was the major's call now, and there was plenty of time to decide. Jamal wasn't going anywhere until he reached a certain level of progress. At that point, some tender loving care might be more beneficial than what the major could provide.

Hell. He earned it, I suppose. Really want this one to make it out.

CHAPTER 48

Hadiya got up from the chair and went over to kiss Jamal on the forehead. The mysterious but amicable military man had said he would be coming out of the sedative in the next few hours. She and the American had talked quite a bit. Consequently, Jamal had a lot of explaining to do. Apparently, she hadn't known a shred of truth about the man with whom she'd put herself.

She'd only believed he was a soldier in the midst of war. That notion itself had caused her to shake her head sometimes, but she'd never felt so compelled to give someone the benefit of the doubt once they'd become close. The download of information from the American had driven a wedge into her emotional state. Yet she knew this was all part of the Lord's plan for her. Her relationship with Jamal had always had a spiritual aspect to it. With his arrival, was she to believe that all her prayers for him—and them—had been answered? Or, was this new knowledge God sent, a sign she should escape from something the Lord never wanted for her to begin with? One could never really know His intentions. All she could do was pray and follow her instincts.

Jamal awoke, groggy and achy with sickness. It hurt to swallow. His head still throbbed. The thin cloth gown he wore was damp with sweat as he rolled his stiff neck around and took in the room. Sunlight basked one wall through the open pane of a window, possessing the orange quality of morning.

Where am I?

After the Zarqawi hit and the call for the medevac, things became fuzzy. He remembered a wind-blown helicopter ride and being wheeled into surgery. The next thing he knew, he was sick as hell in a hospital bed for some time. But it hadn't been a military one, nor had the doctors and nurses been military. The major was in and out, but so were Jamal's mental faculties. When they eventually spoke, Jamal told him he was done. The major chewed hard on that for a while. But because of Jamal's success in crippling a violent *al-Qaeda* offshoot organization, he'd agreed, as long as the missing intelligence was turned over. Jamal gave him the location of the stick drive, the letter, and his logbook, not caring in the least what Zarqawi's ramblings said.

He took in his surroundings. This room had the feel of a bedroom in a home, but he lay on a proper hospital bed with side rails. It was tilted upward slightly in a reclining position. An intravenous drip was hooked up to the back of his left hand, and a pulse monitor clamped his index finger. The sterile odor of oxygen gently pushed into his nostrils through small plastic tubing.

He turned his head in the other direction. A monitor on a cart stood next to the bed. On a wall, there were framed pictures of a female who looked familiar, but younger looking than he remembered.

The villa owner's wife. I'm here. Arbil.

He smiled. The major had taken care of him. But what else had he done or said?

A wave of nausea overcame him, and he closed his eyes, grateful for the cool flowing air. He drew it in until he felt the tightness in his chest build, then backed off and gave himself over to the weariness of this tiny dose of reality.

CHAPTER 49

This time when his eyes opened, the first thing he saw was Hadiya looking out the window. She did not see that he was awake, so he studied her for a moment. She looked different. A change had occurred in her eyes. They seemed less bright, with bags of sleep deprivation under them. She had lost weight since he saw her last, even though she'd been tall and slender already.

She turned in his direction slowly, a casual movement non-expectant of his return to lucidity. Part of him wanted to close his eyes before theirs met to put off facing the truth. He ignored the thought, the desire to reconnect more powerful, so his own puffy, encrusted eyes waited for hers. She did not react but to lift the corners of her mouth in the most melancholy of smiles.

"Jamal," she said and came to him.

"How long have I been here?"

"Just since this morning."

He looked away, nervous about asking the question. "Who brought me?"

"The only American you can trust now."

Jamal turned back. He felt the burn of the lie singe the hairs on the back of his neck for the very last time. The look in her eye told him she knew but was still with him. Still, he noticed a hint of the old wariness from when they'd first met.

CHAPTER 50

Jamal recovered on the rural farm for another month before telling Hadiya he had to go back to Anbar one more time, to retrieve something important to both of them. During the agents' training, the major had instructed each of them how to create a "go bag" in case their missions, or the program itself should go up in smoke. The bag comprised all things necessary to evaporate and begin a new existence under a false identity. Accordingly, Jamal had learned the finer points of forgery and document procurement. Since his arrival in Iraq over three years ago, he'd manufactured four complete personas—passports, driver's licenses, birth certificates, and credit cards. He had one completed for Hadiya as well, of which she wasn't aware. Once it was all over, and they settled somewhere secluded, he would create another one in the event they had to run again.

In addition to the identifications, Jamal's bag contained a new handgun and ammunition, a first aid kit with a veritable pharmacy inside, a shaving kit, two changes of clothes, several disguises, a four-pack of pre-paid phones, a flashlight, a Bible, and a fifth of whiskey.

Another key component of the bag was the funds to finance life on the run, perhaps indefinitely. When Jamal had initially served as an intermediary between Hassan's organization and the tribute paying *takfiri*, he'd frequently found himself around a lot of money. At times it had been laughably easy to pilfer stacks of currency for his purposes. A lot of that money had gone to helping fund Hadiya's efforts with the school, and he'd also given plenty away to families of fighters who'd perished. Some of it he'd changed into other forms of liquidity like gold and silver coins in rolls of ten. A dozen of those were in the bag. He'd also stored up precious stones and diamonds, which were in two silk pouches. The most recent addition was the cash he'd stolen from the cell in Ramadi.

In a borrowed vehicle, he approached the small deserted village set in the arid expanses of Anbar. It had been abandoned after the Persian Gulf War when the whole place burned under coalition bombs; rusted tank hulks and scorched armored personnel carriers still sat on the single road passing through a cluster of squat mud-brick homes. He parked behind a T-54 tank, its gun turret separated from the main body like a tortoise without a shell. A couple of vultures circled overhead as a reminder that other than himself, death had been the last visitor to this lonely place.

Shovel in hand, he entered the building where he'd hidden the bag. Rubble was strewn over a buried box, which contained the duffle. It didn't look like anyone had disturbed it, so he went to work uncovering it. When the bag was in the trunk of the car, he went back to the empty hole. He reached in his pocket for the two-faced talisman he still carried and flipped it in the air. It spun until it landed in the hole, bouncing a couple of times before settling with the more menacing side staring up at him. He buried it in the sands of Anbar, and fifteen minutes later drove away after removing only one item from the bag. He took his eyes off the road for a second, held the diamond ring in his finger, and watched the blazing desert sun glimmer off its many facets.

EPILOGUE

Cape Town, South Africa
September 2006

Jamal entered the busy home wares and appliance store in the heart of the city. He was here to price furniture, rugs, and a few kitchen items Hadiya wanted to fill out their new home. He had not been authorized to purchase anything. As such, he was more looking forward to stopping by the school that the two of them were building, with some of the funds they possessed, as it was starting to look like a real building.

The television screens lined up on the sales rack were all tuned to the international CNN channel and showed sanitized news footage of the latest suicide bombing in Iraq. Jamal's mind flashed to the Ta'mim market, which it always did whenever he found himself in a crowd. Because the sound was muted, he couldn't hear the words associated with the video. The anchorman's mouth moved until he paused, and the image changed to a mug shot of Paris Hilton. After that, it changed to the latest home run hit in America's baseball pennant race. Jamal cringed the corner of his mouth and went to find silverware and cooking pots.

He heard a customer's laugh that reminded him of Fahim, whom he thought about every day. He'd never learned the fate of Ahmed but mourned for the souls of both. As far as his soul was concerned, he'd given it over to the Lord. He would never fight again, never take another life for any reason, unless he needed to defend his home or family, should they make one. God willing. He'd gotten his drinking under control as well, with some help. The words of the Scotsman had set him on the road to redemption, even more so after the revelation that had occurred in Edinburgh.

He and Hadiya had used some of their money—and their fake passports—to honeymoon in several European cities. Jamal requested they visit the man who'd saved his life in Iraq. She obliged, and they made the trip north through the English countryside, which reminded them both of the northern pasturelands of Iraq. Especially the roving sheep that dotted the green slopes.

When they approached the address in a working man's neighborhood of Edinburgh, Jamal saw a woman in the attached garden. He interrupted her pruning a rose bush. She cursed in her brogue as she pricked open a flow of blood that matched the crimson petals. Jamal explained in vague terms who he'd been to her husband and asked whether he would return soon.

Jamal replayed her words now as he had a hundred times since they moved onto the land he now owned in South Africa. He felt the sorrow as always, the gratefulness too.

"My Michael. If only I could say he'd be right home. I wouldn't be doing this for certain. I lost him, lad. Just two days shy of him leaving bloody Iraq. Didn't make it back from his last mission is what I was told."

Twenty minutes after leaving the store, Jamal sat on a park bench near one of the more popular mosques in Cape Town. He held a Bible in his hand, and the notes Hadiya had helped him prepare. Unlike the cool savvy he'd possessed as an agent, he felt nervous about this new mission.

His mother had said God had a plan for him before she was killed, the knowledge he'd carried through all his experiences, and used to justify his stance against radical Islam. Only now had he completed the circle of understanding, one that was much larger than he'd thought. The violence that was infused into his life at such a young age, and furthered by the major and himself as a man, was just a hard lesson learned before the change. He'd emerged from it all, the ultimate witness to God's mercy for others trapped in the soul-wrenching cycle of retaliatory violence. He was amazed that all he'd done was part of God's plan. Yet it had happened, a bell that couldn't be unrung. God had spared him from the killing fields of Africa and Iraq, so the rest of his days could be spent doing battle solely in the spiritual realm. He opened the Bible to his new favorite, the fortieth Psalm.

I waited patiently for the Lord;
He turned to me and heard my cry.
He lifted me out of the slimy pit, out of the mud and mire;
He set my feet on a rock and gave me a firm place to stand.
He put a new song in my mouth, a hymn of praise to our God ...

Jamal stood up from the park bench and crossed the street as the mosque service ended, and people mingled in front of the building. The sun glared off its shiny dome. Its copper was new like a freshly minted penny, so it had yet to gain its intended patina, a maturing process he equated to his path. He was wiser now, the shiny luster of the holy-warrior intellect just fading. Finally, he was ready to do the real work God intended for him.

JOHN MELTON

John Melton is a sustainability consultant with a Master's degree in Architecture from the University of Illinois-Chicago, currently residing in Illinois. John enjoys the creative crossover between the two disciplines of writing and design, and notes many similarities in the processes of each.

John is an Army veteran and has been published in several hard-print or online venues, mostly in the growing military and the Arts community. In 2018 he was credited as a technical advisor on, "The President is Missing," the bestselling novel by Bill Clinton and James Patterson. He has also advised for David Ellis, winner of the Edgar Allen Poe Award circa 2002.

Acknowledgements

I would like to thank all my family members and friends who read for me during the development of this novel, especially Rick Jones. Thank you for your pointed insight.

Thanks to David Ellis for being a friend and mentor. I learned a ton from you, brother.

I am grateful to have had a chance to work with Evelyn, Maggie, Mary, and Rita at Zimbell House Publishing for their professionalism.

Finally, thank you to all our veterans and anyone who provided them or their families aid and comfort during these war years. They were made to fight against a brutal enemy with one hand tied behind their back.

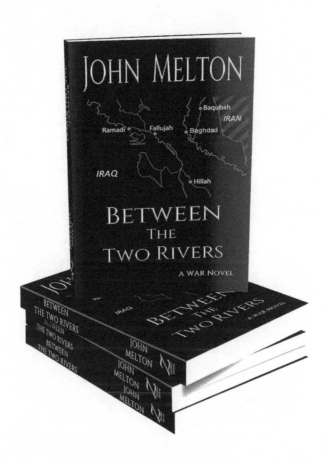

1. What was your initial impression of Jamal? How did it change throughout the book, especially after the Choudary incident?

2. Did you trust Jamal as a credible narrator?

3. What did you imagine Hadiya's and Jamal's future to look like?

4. How do you think the trajectory of Jamal's life would be had he not lost his mother?

5. What do you think about the progression of the relationship between Jamal and Major Winters?

6. Religion plays a big part in the novel. How do you think religion motivated, or prevented Jamal from taking certain actions?

7. What major themes did you recall throughout the novel?

8. Did you find yourself having more interest in foreign affairs after completing this book? What aspects would you like to learn more about?

9. What forms of racism did Jamal encounter, both in America, and once he began his mission?

10. At the end of the story, how did you feel toward Jamal?

11. If you could hear this story from a different narrator, who would you choose?

A NOTE FROM THE PUBLISHER

Dear Reader,

Thank you for reading John Melton's novel, *Between the Two Rivers*. We feel the best way to show appreciation for an author is by leaving a review. You may do so on any of the following sites:

www.ZimbellHousePublishing.com
Goodreads.com
or your favorite retailer

Join our mailing list to receive updates on new releases, discounts, bonus content, and other great books from John Melton and

Or visit us online to sign up at:
http://www.ZimbellHousePublishing.com

CPSIA information can be obtained
at www.ICGtesting.com
Printed in the USA
LVHW090543050820
662302LV00007B/155/J